M000309757

BEFORE THE FLOCK

A NOVEL
DAVID INGLISH

HORTON BAY BOOKS

Horton Bay Books
Copyright © 2014 by David Winston Inglish
All rights reserved.
ISBN: 061579081X
ISBN-13: 978-0615790817

DISCLAIMER

What follows is fiction. All persons and events are fictitious. None of this ever happened. None of these people ever lived, except the famous ones and their names and likenesses are used in a purely fictitious manner. Despite any and all reports to the contrary, over and against anything you may see on YouTube, notwithstanding any coincidental similarities to real life events, none of this story is real. This is fiction.

NOTHING

To the deceitful, the arrogant, the humorless, the peddlers of flesh and fancy.

EVERYTHING

To the dancers, the drinkers, the revelers, the people who carry gear, jam in basements, and play at parties. To waitresses who smile and sway to the music. To soundmen who give more vocal in monitors. To tributes, covers and originals. To the dirty folks who get clean. To my friends, and teachers at NYU. To my editors David Hough and Jay Schaefer. To my wonderful wife and family. To The Great Mystery and my friends who help me seek It.

TABLE OF CONTENTS

Table of Contents

Table of Contents

PROLOGUE:
ERIC THE LONGHAIR'S NOTE

I'm Eric Adams, nine. I pull the vinyl from the sleeve and put the KISS *Alive II* disc on my turntable. Before the first chunky power chord I can hear it all: the sound of electric air, anticipation, gunpowder, the sound of a gong as denim brushes against it. The hair on my arm stands up, saliva fills my cheeks, and I blush. This thought invades my head: *I'm gonna start a band, play in front of packed houses, be wanted by women and respected by men.* I get a drum set and pound away.

I'm ten, alone in the basement with the headphones on. I am ready, the kid the Stones are going to grab at the last minute to replace Charlie Watts when he's puking his guts out from food poisoning.

I'm sixteen. Jamming UFO tunes in a friend's basement seems insular. Plus, the dedicated drummers have already passed me. I need another angle, the rock life maybe. A nice car, a mayonnaise jar full of coke and one co-ed in particular are my goals.

I never make it. I snort half-vials, crash cars, lose my license months after I get it. The girl tells everyone I am a joke. Dangle in the wind for a while, then, I clean up.

I'm eighteen and the desire to rock rises up in me yet again. The '80s are happening, and bands like A Flock of Seagulls and the Psychedelic Furs make me think that the keyboards are the place to be. I buy a Korg and try to remember my piano lessons from childhood.

I'm twenty-three. I sit with my bros in a skyscraper inking a deal that is going to make us rock stars. I've figured it out: The trick to flying is don't look down.

PART ONE

"'Til there was rock, you only had God."
—David Bowie

FORTUNE FAVORS THE BOLD

When Kurt's father, Wayne, shows up in town from the desert for one night, Kurt is determined to share the miracle. Kurt calls the booker at the Spirit and says, "My band needs to play *tonight*."

"We're all booked up. How about a week from Tuesday."

"This is an emergency. It's gotta be tonight."

"Sorry. I got nothing."

Kurt phones EJ the drummer, Gary the bass player, and Dickey the guitar player and tells them all: "Be there. We're playing the Spirit. Tonight."

Dickey is of little faith. "C'mon, Kurt. Is this gig for real?"

"Just be there."

"Dad, we're playing tonight at the Spirit. I want you to come," Kurt says on the phone.

"Oh yeah?"

"Yeah, my band's getting good."

"You still play that rock and roll?"

"New Romantic. You should give it a chance."

"Why?"

"On this one song, during the solo, I flip from a major progression to the Mixolydian minor. It's heavy," Kurt says.

"Ooh, a key change. They've been doing that for, uh, what, three hundred years?"

"The whole show is different now. I'm different now. I'm off the drugs."

"We call them meds, Kurt. Those of us who still take them."

"I don't need them."

"We'll see."

"I was dead."

"You were stable."

"Just come to the show."

"I'll try."

The miracle happened a month ago. Kurt Franklin was alone. His wife, Priscilla, didn't have the heart to divorce him, didn't have any desire to live with him. She was at her mother's house in El Cajon. Pastor Ron had told Kurt the day that he married them on the beach, "The closer you get to God the harder the devil is going to fight to get into your life."

Kurt knew the devil, didn't like him, wished he'd quit talking shit in his ear, but this, breaking up his marriage, was too much. She just left. Then, she came back, with her mom, for her stuff but didn't say anything. Brown cardboard boxes were filled with plastic containers and Ziploc bags. Her mom did the talking. "Priscilla needs some time to think."

It was all a blur, the loneliness, the failure, the Mellaril. Other kids had gone to college. Kurt Franklin had gone on meds. Kurt should've never told that shrink at the high school that the devil tried to tell him what to do, as far as Kurt was concerned it wasn't a problem—he didn't listen. Nevertheless, he should've stuck with Pastor Ron. Pastor Ron understood.

The shrink wasn't all bad. She got Kurt on psychiatric disability, the "crazy checks" as Kurt called them. But that Mellaril, it was a thought suppressant, like earmuffs that you wore on the inside. Kurt felt like it partitioned his brain. When he was in the kitchen he couldn't hear the howling in the basement. On the good days he felt like Winnie the Pooh in a half-shirt. On the bad days he felt like Bela Lugosi in a bloodless world. Life was simple. He played his guitar, sang, and watched reruns of *CHiPs*. There was something soothing in the repetition. Ponch and John, they always got the bad guy the third time. Kurt could count on that.

He was well groomed, better than well groomed. He combed his hair for hours at a time. When he got hungry he walked down to the 7-Eleven for a microwave burrito and a pack of smokes. The clerk always shorted the change, but Kurt was too wracked with fear to say a word. Time to comb the hair.

The miracle began in the mirror. During an epic comb down session, Kurt noticed that there was another version of him in the mirror, the Malibu version. The other person shared Kurt's deep-set yet sensitive eyes, slightly turned up on the corners, but instead of the curly brown hair, the hair that was the bane of his existence, the hair that necessitated gel and comb for hours at a time, the other Kurt had long straight blonde hair and Buddy Holly style glasses.

"Hey!" the other Kurt said.

"James? Bro?" Kurt asked as the pieces drifted together. "Is that you? How did you get in my mirror?"

"I'm over here." James Franklin reached out and touched Kurt on the shoulder.

Kurt turned away from the mirror, in his brother's direction, and said, "Oh, that's how."

"How long?" James asked.

"What?"

"How long have you been here combing your hair? Staring at yourself in the mirror, how long?"

"I don't do that." Kurt put the comb on the counter, parallel to the toothbrush, to the left of the folded towel.

James's eyes became glossy behind his glasses. "Look, man, look at yourself."

"What do you think I'm doing in here?"

"No, man, look. You're a zombie."

"I'm a musician."

"No more pills."

"You don't understand. The State of California pays me to take those pills. I'll show you the check. That's what the doctor said. I'm doing my part for a better—"

"Kurt, look, God got me off blow and weed and window-pane, I won a contest in Laguna, everything's really good for me right now—and it's because I quit drugs."

Kurt refolded the towel and set it back next to the comb. "Me too. I'm stoked."

"What about Priscilla? Do you want your wife to come back?"

"Why do you have to bring that up?"

"If you quit drugs, maybe…"

Kurt turned to the mirror. He saw the hair, that one hair, sticking up. He reached for the comb.

James grabbed his hand. "No!"

Kurt started to cry. "Don't take that away from me."

James changed his tack. "Do you believe in God?"

"Fully," Kurt said.

"Then you know He can do anything."

"Yeah?"

James put the bottle in Kurt's hand and said, "Get on your knees and ask Him to get you off these drugs."

Kurt took the Mellaril, struggled with the safety cap, looked in at them all huddled together, held them above his head and poured them into the toilet. They bobbed in the water helplessly. He pushed the lever, and they began to spin around the edges. They gathered in the middle, screaming, and disappeared.

On his knees Kurt prayed: "Dear Lord, if You get me clean, everything I do will be for You. Every song I sing, every show I play."

For three weeks Kurt didn't sleep. By day he pounded nails. By night he sang in an empty parking garage. Love songs echoed underground.

He felt the ocean on his skin, saw his friends in the line-up, felt the power of a wave. In the evening the low sun illuminated the blue-green walls of water. He crouched in the face, front-side or switch-foot, surfing.

Kurt was alive.

Eighteen pounds disappeared. Everything white and pasty about Kurt sloughed away. Suddenly he was tan and muscular. The girls smiled at him. And on the inside, he wasn't afraid anymore, not even of the devil.

"You aren't playing here tonight" are the first words Kurt says to the lead singer of the other band when he shows up at the Spirit. The guy has long hair dyed black, pale skin, and a black leather jacket. Kurt knows it's a costume.

"There must be some kind of mistake," the singer says. "It's Friday, right?"

"No mistake. You can't play. Sorry."

"Do you work here?" he asks.

"No."

The poser longhair laughs. "Then who do you think you are?"

"Look. My band is playing here tonight. You can't play. I need your slot."

The singer isn't alone anymore. Two bandmates stand behind him. One twirls drumsticks.

"Hey, buddy, I don't know who you think you are. We made flyers. Do you get it?" the drummer says.

"Let's go," Kurt says, and puts up his fists.

"What are you doing, man?" asks the poser longhair.

"C'mon, you guys think you're gonna play here. There's the stage. I'm alone. Come and take it." Kurt stands with his heels against the painted particleboard.

"Are you fucking crazy?"

Kurt smiles. "Not anymore."

"Get out of my face…"

"C'mon!" Kurt lunges forward. "I'm ready to fight for my band! How 'bout you?"

The poser longhair looks at the stage. It is beaten and used, barely two feet above the dance floor. The whole place reeks of beer and urine.

"This is fucked man! You're a fucking…"

Kurt takes a quick step toward the guy. The poser takes two steps back. Kurt's eyes are unforgiving. The veins in his neck bulge.

"We're never playing this place. Ever again," the guy says.

"Yeah, this is bogus! X-Ray is out of here!" adds the drummer, and they take their things and leave.

When Dickey, Gary, and EJ show up, the bar is still empty. The soundman wears Carrera shades, a beret, and a baby-blue silk baseball jacket. He searches a clipboard in his hand. "What's your band called?"

"Thunderstick," Kurt answers in the mic from the stage.

"I don't have you on here. Oh well. This has got to be quick and dirty. We got three bands tonight. X-Ray never showed, so I guess you guys go last." The soundman notes four guys on the stage. "The usual? Two guitars, bass, and drums?"

"Yeah. I play the acoustic on some songs. Telecaster on others."

"Just one thing. Keep the stage volume low. Let me knock their socks off with the house speaks."

"No problem."

"Do what I say, and I'll make you sound like pros."

"Thanks, but we don't need *you* for *that*." Kurt looks slyly at Dickey.

"Oh really?"

"Yeah." Kurt picks his guitar, banjo style, *Deliverance*.

"If you guys are so great, what are you doing here?"

"I was gonna ask you the same thing."

"Hey fuck you, buddy."

Kurt continues picking his guitar. He smiles coolly.

"Can we just do the soundcheck?" EJ interjects. "We're pros. You're a pro. Let's just be professionals here and do our job." EJ is wearing a gray three-piece suit. He hasn't changed after work. His face is round with narrow dark eyes.

"Never fuck with the soundman. Have you ever heard that one before? If you guys think you're ever going to make it in *the biz*, you should remember that. I'm the rule around here. It's my way or the highway."

"Ten-four, good buddy," Kurt says in a trucker's CB voice, and smiles at Gary. Gary's expression is as stiff as his gelled hair.

By midnight, the Spirit is packed. The lights are low. The guys in the band change into their outfits. Gary wears a silver silk shirt with billowing sleeves. Dickey wears black jeans and a dynamite shirt. EJ has his black logger's boots, they make him taller, and his black T-shirt for the guns. Kurt wears his maroon dinner jacket with the rounded lapel, black slacks, and pointy, ankle-high Beatle boots.

When Kurt sees Wayne in the back in a brown cardigan sweater, he gives the signal to Dickey, who then picks the intro to "Sweetly She Talks So" with flawless rhythmic precision, the notes bouncing off one another and floating down from the rafters. EJ taps out a four-count and the band comes in together; blue light splashes the stage. Kurt feels the music like he hasn't felt it in years. Every part of his body is energized. He is barely on the stage. His right arm strums time, and the rest of him quivers. EJ is the backbone. His groove is a pocket in which the music rocks back and forth.

The song list is written in block letters down by Kurt's effects pedals. "Sweetly She Talks So." "Alone, Alone." "Kick It Clean." He wrote them all in the last few weeks. The dinner jacket comes off during "Alone, Alone." The Truth is on Kurt. He moves like a fish.

At the end of "Kick It Clean," he lights a smoke with his Zippo and speaks into the PA. "Can I get a little more vocal in the monitors?" Smoke rises from Kurt's mouth in the spotlight.

"Turn your guitar down, and I'll give you vocals," the sound-man speaks into a mic in his mixing board. His voice comes out of the stage monitors.

Kurt nods, walks back to his amp, and fingers the knobs, not really changing anything at all.

The next song, "I Wanted You," feels just right. It is salve for the soul. A pop love ballad with a secret: Kurt wrote it to God. *I wanted all of you.* The song has a break after the guitar solo. The band brings the dynamic down to a whisper. This is the moment. Kurt picks his acoustic and hums softly as if he were singing a southern spiritual. But then Kurt hears a "Fuck you!" It is a wicked voice. He is confused. Have they returned? The voices? Is it Wayne? No, Wayne is in the back with his arms folded. Is someone else on stage? "Fuck you. Hey, pal, it's me, fuck you." The voice continues. Does anyone else hear it? "Hey, fuck you. Turn your fucking guitar down."

Kurt steps back from the microphone still strumming. "Dickey, do you hear that?"

"It's the soundman, Kurt. He wants you to turn down your guitar," Dickey yells. "Turn it down."

Kurt looks behind the mixing board and the soundman is emphatically flipping him the bird.

"He's ruining our song," Kurt declares.

When the song ends, there is some applause. Then the soundman speaks and everyone can hear. "Hey, asshole!"

Kurt looks up from tuning his guitar.

"Yeah, you, you're blowing my mix. Would you turn your fucking guitar down?"

Someone in the audience laughs. Not Wayne, he nods his head and holds his thumb and forefinger close together. Kurt's brow creases. He puts down his acoustic. He shakes his head in dismay then an answer comes—"ROCK AND ROLL!" Kurt yells to Dickey, EJ, and Gary. "ROCK AND ROLL! NOW! LET'S GO!" Dickey takes the cue and plays the opening guitar riff of "Rock and Roll" by Lou Reed. Kurt pulls off his shirt, lights a smoke, slings the Tele over his shoulder, and sings: "Jenny said when she was just five years old . . ."

It's a song they know. Something starts to happen. Everything Kurt does, people on the dance floor do. He jumps. They jump. Kurt shakes. They shake.

Kurt lays into the lead and it sounds like all our expired summers, boiled down to one fleeting moment that matters.

Kurt sings the second verse into the mic but can't hear himself. There are no vocals in the PA. He keeps strumming and singing while emphatically signaling for some volume. The soundman returns a sarcastic wave then drags his finger across his throat. Incredulous, Kurt takes the microphone stand above his head and brings it straight down with a decisive slam. The audience shrieks with joy. The mic stand, now in two pieces, is at Kurt's feet.

The soundman screams into his mic, "You're gonna pay for that, asshole! You fucking asshole!"

The crowd cheers.

Kurt nods at EJ, walks back to his amp, runs his hand across the buttons from left to right. Everything now on ten, he hits the distortion pedal, bends the strings, and begins another solo.

The soundman has ears but cannot hear. He pushes a button below some rhythmic red lights and kills the power to the PA. It's just the amps and drums. Kurt goes from Gary's amp to Dickey's amp turning every knob to ten while still playing his own guitar. Gary turns his amp back to five. EJ brings more tempo and even more force to every strike. The audience doesn't miss the PA, girls are dancing, guys jump up and down, shake their heads. The band gains speed, playing faster and faster until the soundman darts behind the stage and in a sudden giant amplified groan, every electric instrument and every light on stage dies. Powerless. Nothing is left but the acoustic sound of EJ's drums and darkness. EJ does one final turnaround, crashes the cymbals, and says, "Let's get out of here."

"More! One more!" a drunk yells.

EJ reaches for a stand in a workmanlike manner and starts breaking it down. Gary and Dickey unplug, walk straight off the stage through the stage door, and put their guitars in Dickey's Toyota pickup.

Kurt follows Wayne through the club and out the front door. Kurt is shirtless and panting in the cool night air.

"Dad! What'd you think?"

"Kurt, I'm going back to the desert."

"Did you like it?"

"I don't know if that matters."

"That crowd. They were into it."

"Meds, Kurt, that's all I'm going to say. Goodnight."

Wayne gets into his diesel Rabbit, waits five seconds for the ignition light, starts the engine, and rattles down the street.

Kurt walks through the club. "Hey, asshole, come here!" the soundman yells.

"In a minute." Kurt walks out the stage door.

"Did you guys take my guitars and amp?" Kurt asks Dickey in the parking lot.

"Yeah, we got 'em."

"Right on. Heavy show."

"Kurt, that was pretty out of hand in there. Didn't have to go down like that."

"What do you mean? That was the best show we've ever played."

"Dickey's got a point," Gary adds.

"I'm just saying you could've turned your guitar down," Dickey says. "Then we wouldn't have to fight with that guy."

"What are you guys talking about? That wasn't a fight."

"C'mon, Kurt, you know what I mean," says Dickey.

"You guys were on stage. Couldn't you feel it?"

"I'm talking about the soundman."

"That guy had no respect. Every one of those guys is going to be sorry. We will get a record deal. We're gonna be the biggest band ever."

"Kurt, you've been saying that since I met you."

"It's true."

"It's been two years," Gary says.

"If this is what the gigs are gonna be like now, I'm just not into it," Dickey says. "The gigs were good before."

"What? I was dead. You can't put me back on…"

"It's just not working for me."

"What are you doing?"

"Me too," Gary says.

"What is this?" Kurt asks.

"We quit," they say.

"Sorry, Kurt," Gary adds.

"Don't quit. Give me a chance. Think about it. Just think about it."

Gary and Dickey leave Kurt standing in the parking lot. There is a concrete-block wall that has THE SPIRIT spray-painted graffiti style in orange and blue. Kurt lifts his hands to the sky, lights a cigarette, and walks back in the club.

"LISTEN, MAN! I DON'T OWE YOU A THING!" EJ is yelling at the soundman as he packs up the last of his things. "I DIDN'T BREAK IT!"

The soundman holds the pointy chrome mic stand in his hand. He tries to twirl it ninja style. "Hey, you're not leaving here until you pay me. Got that?"

"We're not paying you anything," Kurt says. "You tried to ruin our show."

"SECURITY! SECURITY!" the soundman screams.

By the door, on a stool, he turns and sits up on his hind legs and grows nearly to the rafters. He's a lot of leather and arm and beard and skull—a Hell's Angel maybe, a bouncer for certain.

"Are these guys giving you trouble? I like trouble."

"We're going to hold his drum set until they pay me," the soundman says. "Lock it in the utility closet."

The bouncer reaches for EJ's snare drum. EJ grabs the other end. "Don't take my things. I didn't break it!" EJ yells.

The bouncer pulls EJ into his armpit with ease, flexes, and starts squeezing his neck. EJ is turning red, flailing his arms wildly. The soundman laughs.

Like Moses giving orders to Pharaoh, Kurt yells, "LET MY DRUMMER GO!" Then he picks up a bar stool and aims the legs. "HEY, FAT ASS! DIDN'T YOU HEAR ME? LET MY DRUMMER GO!" The bouncer smirks and pushes EJ onto to the concrete dance floor. EJ lies in spilled beer, gasping for air.

"Kick his ass! Kick his fucking ass!" the soundman cheers from a safe distance, still holding the broken mic stand as if it were a weapon.

Kurt and the bouncer circle each other. A beer-bellied ogre and a tan, skinny surfer brandishing a bar stool.

"Here!" The soundman tosses the mic stand. The bouncer snatches it out of the air and holds it like a mace. He takes a broad swipe at Kurt but whacks the bar stool instead. This is it. The smoke in Kurt's mouth is down to a nub. EJ is floundering on the floor, wheezing. The bouncer attacks, aiming for Kurt's head in a giant chopping motion, but his makeshift ax catches on a hanging stage light and in that second of hesitation, EJ pounces for his legs. The bouncer stumbles. Kurt thrusts the bar stool forward. With a resounding crack, the falling leviathan's forehead hits the base of the bar stool. His knees buckle. His potbelly hits the ground. He lays face first and motionless on the floor, unconscious. Kurt smiles at EJ. EJ's eyes are uncharacteristically huge.

"I am calling the cops right now!" the soundman yells and runs away.

EJ bolts outside and throws the last two pieces of his drum set into his mom's station wagon. He slams the tailgate, starts the car, and spins the rear wheels as he takes off.

Kurt rolls the bouncer over. He has a perfect round welt on his forehead. He tries to open his eyes. He sees Kurt looking down.

"Who? You?" he asks, groggy.

"Thunderstick. Don't forget it."

The bouncer reaches for Kurt's neck with his heavy arms and grasps air. Kurt runs out the stage door. The cars are all gone.

The bouncer sits up, climbs to his feet, and stumbles after Kurt. At the door he sees a shirtless kid with Beatle boots sprinting down deserted Morena Boulevard in the lamplight.

In the far distance a station wagon slides around a corner and skids to a stop in front of Kurt. He dives head first through the open window on the passenger side. The station wagon sloshes from side to side on dead shocks, makes a little smoke, and turns right at the Jack in the Box. Kurt's feet dangle out the window. EJ drops him off at his apartment. He is alone. He rummages for some smokes. Finding none, he walks down La Jolla Boulevard to the 7-Eleven, a buck and a quarter in his hand.

BIG GIRLS (PART I)

They call them the Big Girls. The Big Girls make fourteen to twenty thousand a show, real money, Reagan money, Rambo money. Everybody has to have them. So if you are a Big Girl, you might do four shows a day during fashion week. Hair, makeup, strut, turn, sashay, Town Car. Hair, makeup, strut, turn, sashay, Town Car again. Yes, four times a day, imagine that, for a week. Hairdressers throw their hands above their heads and squeal something about child labor laws. Everyone laughs.

At some point the Big Girls will go out of style. It always changes. Then it will be girls with misshapen heads and goldfish eyes and no curves—grave and solemn and heroin chic. The Big Girls will end up doing a couple shows for the established designers, and then the cutting-edge types will replace them with their weary, ghoulish army. It is the art-school crowd's revenge on the cheer squad. But the Big Girls won't care. Care? They won't even notice. Nobody tells them. They do movies—one each. They marry rock stars, then billionaires. Rock stars first, but that never has legs, then billionaires because rock stars fade like mirrors. And billionaires wear hand-sewn leather loafers, designer jeans, and five-hundred-dollar dress shirts. Flying commercial is for salesmen and personal assistants. Billionaires pull the strings, open the restaurants, send the jet, buy the art, and make the artist.

Sophie Clark is a gangly eighth grader living in an American suburb, eating cafeteria sandwiches with ham pressed and saved like a rose in a book. She's a full head above the boys in gym class, but a little too awkward for volleyball. It is her mother who finds the ad in the *Poway Gazette*. Jean has always found the thin walls and aluminum awnings and dirt yard considerably below her, and now she finds herself in her Toyota Celica driving Sophie to Los Angeles to Aspire Model Management for an open casting call.

In the car, Sophie looks out the window as the avocado groves spin away into dry, rolling hills. "Why didn't we bring Audrey? She's pretty too," Sophie asks, and taps her long finger on the plastic sill.

Jean turns to look at her with a wry smile. "You think your sister's pretty? Isn't that sweet."

"She has pretty eyes."

"Audrey's got rings in her eyes, like her father, like a marmoset monkey."

"They're cute."

"Cute if you're swinging from branch to branch in the jungle, I guess. Cute to another marmoset."

Sophie laughs. "She doesn't look like a monkey."

"You look like me, but you're tall like Victor."

"I'm not going to get as tall as Dad am I? That would be totally wrong. I would be such a freak."

"God, no. You're five foot ten. That's the perfect height—I checked. And you got my eyes. Eyes like crystals. Nobody's ever gonna look in those eyes and think you did something wrong. Believe me, I've tried."

"No. What did I ever do?"

"Remember when you were just five, it was Thanksgiving, and the sink got all stopped up. I told you the plumber was coming to snake it?"

"Yeah. And I thought it was going to be a real snake, so I hid and fell asleep—"

"—under the dining-room table, beneath the white tablecloth. I had put it out for Victor's parents. When the plumber left, and I couldn't find you, calling your name over and over—I thought he had kidnapped you. I called the police. We had people looking. A policeman even stopped the plumber in his van and asked him questions. When I found you, I wanted to shake you and wring your little neck—you had embarrassed me so. And then you—"

"I know and then I looked up at you with my big bright eyes—"

"—and you were like a little doll with mussed-up hair, like a doll version of me, only better, a version of me that didn't have to make all the same mistakes, that didn't have to live hand to mouth." Jean squeezes the wheel, looks in the rearview mirror at her reflection, runs a finger under her left eye where the mascara has smudged. "A poor man will steal from his woman—and sometimes he doesn't even know he's doing it."

"Who steals from us?"

"Nobody. I've always wanted a better life for you. I just didn't know how to get it. Now I think I know."

Sophie leans her head out the window, and the breeze pushes her hair back. She imagines the feathered wing of a giant swan brushing against her cheek, a unicorn sprinting by the side of the car.

In Los Angeles they march them out in a queue, weighed and measured, fit to the task. Convention halls or shopping malls, it's all the same. Now and forever the name of the game is you— Sophie. It's the stage, and then it is over.

Giuseppe Cassavetes is the founder of Aspire Model Management, and for this decade he wears his customary white linen suit with a black shirt and white tie. On that Saturday he sits enthroned at the end of a long folding table with a vase of flowers in the middle. He casts a disparaging look at the arrangement. "Who did this? Who made up this table?"

Thick and young and business gray, Caitlin raises her hand.

"Come here. Look at this." Giuseppe extends his hand. "Did you arrange these flowers?"

"Yes, Mr. Cassavetes."

"This, this, this is *ugly!* This is not Aspire. Why do you do this to me?"

Caitlin opens her mouth and only a broken breath comes out.

"Don't give me none of this sad-girl bullshit. Let me tell you something, I am never going to stand in the way of your success— don't you ever fucking stand in the way of mine."

Caitlin's shoulder pads move in exaggerated trembles, and then she bursts into tears.

"Somebody make this room look like something other than shit. And bring me the girl. What is her name?"

"Sophie Clark. She's with her mother."

Giuseppe pauses and shakes his head. "What is this shit?"

"She's a minor. She needs her mother to sign the contract."

"You. Crying girl. Come here." Caitlin walks over slowly. When she is within reach, Giuseppe squeezes the back of her neck pulling her into his chest. He lets out a big, singular laugh. "We are all friends here. Go. Open the door."

On Monday there is an empty seat in Algebra, Spanish II, and English. Audrey is told that she's a big girl and the freezer is full. Feed the father. Her mother will be back in a week. Sophie is in the model's apartment with five other girls on the corner of Eightieth and Madison.

Jean is the guest of Mr. Cassavetes, and at thirty-eight she still has something about her. Giuseppe can't help but taste it. When it is done and she is naked and stroking his chest hairs, he tells her she can go back to wherever it is that she has come from, L.A., yes? Sophie will be fine. "I will make absolutely [sure] of it."

Back in Poway, Sophie's father, Victor, is ecstatic. He tells Jean as much when she walks in the door. "When you get your shot at the big leagues, you've got to take it to the hole and slam it down. When you see the other guy getting gassed, that's when you've got to give one hundred and ten percent, that's when you take it to the hoop, no mercy. Fuckin' A. This is just the break I need." He lifts his hands up and palms the acoustic tile on the ceiling. "Yes!"

The screen door slams, and Victor and Jean turn to find Audrey standing there with her backpack. "Where's Sophie?"

"Honey, she's in New York. Listen to this, I arranged for her to be the personal guest of Mr. Cassavetes!"

"So what?" Audrey drops her backpack in a chair.

"The founder of Aspire Model Management? Do you even know who I'm talking about?"

"Yeah. So?"

"Don't you get it? We're all going to be rich."

Audrey laughs and says, "Whatever."

It is New York in the eighties, and there are still places to be avoided. Sophie's been told and must try to remember, but she can't get over how nice everybody is. She tells Caitlin as much. "New Yorkers aren't rude. A man walked me all the way to the modeling agency—it was like so many blocks. Is this SoHo?"

Caitlin forces a smile. "We're sending you on tests."

Sophie is worried. "That's probably not a very good idea."

"Why?"

"I don't even know what they're on."

Caitlin looks at Sophie's lips and wonders if they are just a little bit too full, but then she decides it will be her distinguishing feature. "Sophie, it's not that kind of test."

Sophie is on her knees in front of a white backdrop wearing a neon orange T-shirt with the sleeves cut off at the shoulder. Her legs are in fishnet hose with a small pleated skirt and combat boots. Serge, the photographer, spins his finger above his head and looks through the camera's viewfinder. As if on command, she writhes from girlish position to girlish position, tossing her hair with each turn. "This is fun," she says.

"Yes. Yes. Good," Serge says. "Put your right hand flat on the ground, straighten your arm, push your right shoulder forward and look at me like you want to fuck my brains out."

Joy slides from Sophie's face. Suddenly she feels the crowd of busy people around her. She closes her mouth and lifts her lip at the camera.

"No. That's a sneer."

Sophie flips her hair forward into her face. She opens her eyes and everything is dark. She wonders if she can stay here. Then the brush of the white swan's feathers sweeps her forehead, pushing her hair, making her skin tingle, she opens her mouth and tilts her head back.

"Yes," Serge says. "Yes."

At the modeling agency, Caitlin hands Sophie an envelope and asks her if she has a passport.

"Like, no. What is this?"

"It's a passport application. Mr. Cassavetes wants you to be his guest at his compound in Jamaica. He's seen your tests. He's going to make you a star. You're very lucky. He doesn't do this for just anybody. He wants to talk to you. He's in there, in his office, go ahead, he's alone."

Sophie walks in hurried steps uptown, away from Aspire Model Management. She runs up to a payphone only to find a frayed cord where the handset should be. At a second phone, there is no dial tone. "Hey, that one works" a man in a suit says, and smiles at her. It starts to rain. Sophie huddles next to the phone. The man stands behind her. He shuffles from side to side in his suit, fumbles to open his umbrella, and holds it out over Sophie.

"Hey, actually, I'm fine. You don't have to." She shakes her head and clutches the phone at her neck and punches the keys—collect.

Audrey answers and accepts.

"Are you okay?" Audrey asks.

"No."

Jean puts the phone to her ear and asks, "What is it, sweetheart?"

"I want to come home."

"No, you don't sweetheart. No, you don't. You're just having a bad day. What's going on?"

Sophie looks around her. The businessman smiles and starts to say something; she turns back to the phone. "I'm standing on this street and it's called Prince Street. Isn't that Daddy's middle name?"

"Sophie, are you crying? What do we say about crying?"

"Shut. Up. I think he likes me."

"Who likes you?"

"Mr. Cassavetes."

"That's nothing to cry about. That's good. He's very important. He can help."

"Mom, not like that. Like in a weird way. I have to 'holiday' with him. None of the other girls are going. He's like fifty or something. It's kind of weird. If I don't go, like will he…"

"Sophie if you want to wreck everything that I've worked for, go ahead and come home. Don't go on this trip. Don't act polite. Don't be the woman I brought you up to be, just think of yourself and come home and go back to school. We'll manage somehow."

A black Lincoln Town Car pulls up in front of the models' apartment. Sophie hugs the other girls after the intercom buzzes. Caitlin is waiting in the car with a passport.

"You won't need that." Caitlin points to Sophie's bag. "Mr. Cassavetes has arranged for you to have all new clothing on this trip. All the top designers: Norma Kamali, Willi Smith, Stephen

Sprouse. He has chosen from their collections especially for you. Doesn't that make you happy?"

"I guess." Sophie rolls her eyes.

They drive to a private airport in New Jersey where a small jet waits.

As she ducks down and steps in, Sophie says, "There's like nobody else on the plane?"

"No, Sophie, there are two pilots."

"Shut. Up. You know what I mean. Why don't you come? There's lots of seats."

Caitlin laughs. "Sophie, I don't think that's what Mr. Cassavetes had in mind."

"Please, please, we would have so much fun. You and me. C'mon."

"I think you'll be just fine without me."

"No. Please. It would be really fun. It's supposed to be warm, and we can put on baby oil and read magazines."

"No."

Sophie reaches out and holds Caitlin's hand, her eyes welling up. Caitlin, looking up, notices something she has never noticed before; Sophie's right eye has a black inverted oval-shaped speck beneath the pupil. "You'll be fine."

Inside the plane, there are two black leather recliner chairs, one on either side of the aisle, and two thin leather banquettes behind them. Sophie sits in the seat on her left because it has a phone just beneath the large round window.

From the front of the cabin, Caitlin looks in at Sophie sitting in Giuseppe's seat and thinks to herself, *They all have that look, something like a colt, legs long and awkward—fragile, fleeting, ecstatic expressions, a skittish something in their eyes—they are all the same—and we find them wherever they are. We find them.* "Have fun," Caitlin says, with inauthentic levity.

The cabin door and stairs close, fold, and seal; and to Sophie it is like watching a spider that's been splashed with water. The cabin becomes dark except for the bright white light showing through the cockpit windows. Two silhouetted captains' hats turn toward Sophie. "Welcome aboard." Sophie's eyes adjust, and she can see the details of the tarmac, the other planes, the sky, the tree line. The jet turns on the runway. The engines fire, and Sophie is soon in the clouds.

When the plane door opens again, the air is moist and hot. A black man with a sweaty brow, close-cropped hair, and dazzling white teeth sticks his head in the cabin. "Welcome!"

In the limo Sophie rolls the window down so that the hot air can push her hair back. The car weaves through hand trucks and carts and colorful women then speeds through children and soccer balls and squat schools with murals. *The air feels like feathers,* she thinks to herself as she lets the warm rush of it float her hand outside the window.

A turn and then there are fields with tall green stalks, where dark black men hang on the sides of tall, grunting trucks. They leap to the ground, swing machetes, and eight-foot stalks are felled instantly. In the rearview mirror, the driver studies Sophie. "It's sugar. They're making sugar. I bet you never knew this is where your candy comes from!"

"I've never even been on this side of the road before!"

"Yes, of course!"

The roads are tight and circuitous. Plants reach out from every corner trying to touch the car on the curves, succeeding with whips and laughs.

"Some people think we drive crazy on the island."

With every turn, the road seems smaller and rougher. Now there is surely no way to get back to the airport, or back to New York, or back to Poway, or back to the school cafeteria. She tries to remember her locker combination and can't. There are books in there, and photos taped to the door, and other things that belonged to some silly little girl she doesn't really know anymore. The thought exhilarates her. She is going to be famous, and someday somebody will open that locker and say this once belonged to Sophie Clark. She holds her hands out and shakes her hair and says to herself, *Yes!*

They come onto a straightaway, and the jungle of cane fields and palms and banana trees falls away as two meadows rise up before them with a slim road in the middle that stretches beneath mature English oaks. "This is the old plantation." The driver smiles. And at the end of the road a large white colonial English manor sits in front of a circular driveway.

The sound of ice cubes, the feel of silk, each day the servants carry the living-room furniture to the veranda when the sun hits the large oak in the lawn, when the breeze turns around and blows softly off the hill, dry air bringing the intoxicating fragrance of orange blossoms. First, the Oriental rug, a Kerman, woven with silk threads by active hands, blood-colored reds, Roman purples, it rolls out toward the ocean, the center uniform and intricate as a bed of clover. Then the furniture, then the pillows, carried by black hands. Below the oak, on the Kerman, Sophie spreads her fingers, arches her back, and the breeze flows through her. She dreams that the jungle holds enchantment. If she can just turn her head when the spirits don't expect it. If she can surprise them, she can see them as they suck back behind the rocks and foliage, giggling. She can hear their high, thin laughter. And she smiles, knowing they are for her.

"What are you drinking?" His voice is deep. He stands in the frame of the French doors at the end of the Saltillo tiles.

"I'll have a Coke," Sophie says.

He laughs. "American Beaujolais, yes?"

Sophie shakes her head.

"It's a wine." He turns and calls orders into the house. "How do you like it here?"

"I like it."

"Yes." Giuseppe extends a crystal highball across the ocean and the hills. "This all belonged to a man my father worked for once. When I first saw it, I was much like you, young, tremendous potential. I had dreams, but I had no way to obtain them. I knew it would be mine, but I didn't know how."

"That's totally awesome."

A young man with sun-streaked hair holds a tray with a small bottle of Coca-Cola and a crystal tumbler filled with ice cubes. Sophie notices his bright blue eyes and the shell necklace that moves against his tan skin.

"Sophie, what are your dreams?"

She takes the drink and nods a thank-you. "I don't know."

"You can tell me." He laughs. "You never know, maybe I can help you with them. That will be all, Cyan." Giuseppe motions toward the house. Cyan and Sophie exchange one last glance. He is gone. A gust skips a broad leaf toward the ocean.

"I guess I want to be in…"

"Yes?"

"Don't you have a son?"

"Yes."

"Where is he?"

"Well, he is…I believe…He is…" Giuseppe forces a laugh. "You must know that he is, he is a pimply little boy. You are a woman."

"Am I?" Sophie laughs and tosses her head back.

The wind brings the sudden silence of white noise. The ocean churns white and blue and green.

When Sophie returns to her room after dinner, a servant girl with shy eyes has poured her a bath. The smell of lilac rises in little wispy clouds. As she sinks into the water, she feels a prickly tingle up her calf, through her thigh, in her lap, through her stomach, around her chest, stopping at the nape of her neck.

The girl picks up the pile of clothes on the tile floor. "Don't go," Sophie says. "Will you brush my hair?"

"Yes, miss, yes."

Each stroke tugs. Sophie grips the side of the claw-foot tub so she doesn't slide in.

Sophie dries herself, puts on a robe, and sits on the bed beneath the slow turn of the ceiling fan. She switches out the lights, but cannot sleep. She opens the window. Moist hot air surrounds her. She sees a light in the distance at the edge of the jungle and hears the faraway sound of laughter and music.

Days of sun, the white linen is blinding at lunch. The silver is cool to the touch. When Cyan bends over to pour Sophie's water, she reaches up to touch his shell necklace. The water glass overflows. She giggles.

"I am so sorry," he says.

"It's just water."

But Cyan is already heading toward the house. His rope belt looks high on his white pants.

"He is Creole. Looks French, but he's probably British. Very beautiful, yes?" Giuseppe remarks.

"He looks like the men who run from the bulls."

Giuseppe laughs. "Yes. You are right. I don't think you will find him running from any bulls. I usually find him chasing my chambermaids. The girls call him *mantell*. That's Jamaican for a male slut."

"Really?"

"Sissy." He waves his hand at one of the girls standing a few feet away with her hands behind her back. "Tell Sophie what you mean when you call Cyan a *mantell*."

"Dat mean 'im tan pon it long den mantell him fren." She smiles brightly, and Sophie and Giuseppe laugh.

REUNITED

The day after the Spirit gig, the day after Dickey and Gary quit, Kurt and EJ drive over to the Dugans' house. EJ has a real job. He trades bonds for Muckerman, makes thirty grand a year. He likes it, but it is someone else's life. A good second mate, EJ needs to master and be mastered. He grew up with a sadistic older brother who showed him the ropes, dragged him down the beach in a ball of seaweed, telling everybody that EJ was a Chinese egg roll. Ten years later, with those narrow eyes, EJ is still working it out in his head: He needs percussion.

Mrs. Dugan feeds them lasagna and says, "Bob's still asleep."

They find the Jovi on the sleeper sofa in the cabana by the pool. Crashed naked on the duvet, he has the vibe of an 18th century European aristocrat that has been left at his tropical outpost too long and gone native, a regal savage. He pushes down on the bed and looks up at the two of them. His hair is dark. It contrasts with his green eyes. "What's up?"

"Hey, bro," Kurt says, and pulls the shades.

The Jovi blinks like a mole. "Right on. Welcome, welcome." He stretches, yawns. "What time is it?"

"One."

"Fuck."

The Jovi rises, goes to the kitchenette, dumps some cigarette butts out of a cup, rinses it, pours in some coffee from the carafe, and scratches his balls. "You want some?"

EJ says, "Dude, c'mon, you're making me sick. Put some fucking clothes on."

Kurt shakes his head and laughs.

The Jovi gets back in bed, nurses the stale coffee and listens.

"We need you. Dickey and Gary quit."

"Whoa. Dude. I've got a paying gig. Do you know how insane that is? They cater our practice sessions."

"That music—it's not real," Kurt says.

"Paycheck's real," the Jovi says.

Kurt lights a cigarette. "We've been playing together for fifteen years. Nobody our age has that."

The Jovi motions for the smoke. Kurt hands it over.

"I know. But, dude, I can't quit my gig. I gotta move out— I'm twenty-two. I'm finally making some money."

"Since when do you care about money?"

"It's not that. It's a cool gig. These guys treat me alright. I want to play with you guys—like old times. I just don't want to let you down. If I got a paying gig with Belinda or Smithy, I can't be down here with you guys playing at the Pumphouse for nothing."

"Belinda Carlisle? From the Go-Go's?" Kurt lifts his hands in the air. "Brian Smith, wasn't he like a roadie for the Love Guns?"

"C'mon, Kurt. He played guitar. Smithy is a great guy!" The Jovi says.

"Face it. You're a backup in a couple solo projects. We're a band." EJ says, and stares intensely over the Jovi's shoulder. The

Jovi turns around to see what he is looking at, but there's nothing there. "Smithy and Belinda, both of them, their salad days were playing with their friends. Now they're just trying to cash in on faded glory. I never want to be that—the kind of guy who does projects. You're not a project guy either."

"I know. It's not like that. Dude."

"Look, if you can't be there all the time," Kurt says, "if that's all you can give us, that's fine with me. I can cover on guitar if I have to."

"I know you can, but is that fair to you guys? I don't want you flipping out over this, Kurt."

"I won't."

"Really?"

"I never start it—"

"That's what I'm talking—"

"Are you in?"

The Jovi sips some coffee, takes a last drag on Kurt's cigarette, drops the butt in the mug, and holds out his hand. "I'm in." Hands pop. "Yeah. I'm in."

BIG GIRLS (PART II)

Jamaican lazy afternoon, the sun seems to swirl with the wind, swirl and fill minds with everything warm and fluid and natural. It rubs her stomach until her navel is a tiny pool of sweat and oil. It pushes warmth through her, to the arch of her back that doesn't touch the towel, the arch where a single drop of moisture hangs from the trestle, hangs, then falls. Each time she opens her eyes, a blinding snapshot, silhouettes in white, figures in black, white before blue, black before green; arms are branches; hands are pools; and the sun swirls with the wind.

She rolls onto her front, tucks her face in the crook of her shoulder, watches her profile change in her shadow, and breathes in her own skin. It is something like home: She brought it with her. And the sun pushes down.

"Ms. Clark, is there anything I can bring you?"

The voice is different. Sophie rolls over, opens her eyes, and sits up. Cyan kneels before her, glowing in the afternoon sun.

"So sorry to wake you. Were you asleep?"

"No. Just dreaming."

He laughs. "You dream when you are awake?"

"Sometimes."

"That is good. You know what they say?"

"What?" She sweeps a blonde curl back.

"Those who dream in the day see more than those who dream at night."

Sophie smiles. "You think?"

"Yes. Tell me what you dream right now."

She looks at him, then at the rough blue surface of the ocean. "I dream that your eyes are frozen, and only I know how to make them melt." She wraps her fingers around his necklace, pulls him in, breathes him in, and turns away, shy and embarrassed.

"See, what I say is right. You see more than you know." He leans down and straightens her beach towel. "I should leave you to your dreams."

"No. Don't go."

"I will come for you tonight," he whispers, then quickly gets to his feet. "Yes, ma'am, one Coca-Cola, right away."

At dinner everything arrives on the left and departs on the right. There is a fork with three thick prongs, a knife with a straight edge and a swollen, rounded side but no sharp edge. Sophie holds the knife and remarks, "It's different here. Is this a Jamaican knife?"

"Yes, well, no, it's for fish." Giuseppe wipes his lips with a crisp white serviette.

"Why?"

"I don't know." He laughs. "We will be back in New York soon. You will be back at the models' apartment. I have so much work. This is our last night together. I want to make it last. Let me show you something." He walks behind Sophie, pulls out her chair, puts her sweater on her shoulders, and walks her onto the veranda. "Do you see that?"

The sea is black with streaks of silver. A sailboat is tethered to a mooring. Sophie watches as each tiny wave tosses the prow up and the rope jerks it back down. It is like a restless palomino staring out at the empty plains, an Indian's horse, captured by cowboys and saddled and bridled and longing for the grassy knolls of freedom.

"Have you ever sailed the Caribbean under a full moon? It's quite enchanting."

"I'm so sure it is."

"Shall we?" He extends his hand. "The captain is waiting."

She puts her hand in his. "I'm so tired right now. I think I'm just going to go to bed."

"But what about your dinner? We can bring it on the boat."

"You are so nice to me." She squeezes his hand and looks in his eyes. "I totally appreciate it, but I just can't go." Her lips brush the heavy stubble on his cheek, and she says goodnight near the black hairs that sprout from his ear.

Underneath the covers, Sophie has put on the Norma Kamali jacket and pleated skirt that Giuseppe gave her. She had contemplated a pair of fishnet pantyhose, but she looked at her tan legs and thought to herself, *They are fine.* In the mirror she painted her cheeks a rosy pink and put on eyeliner. She rolls onto her side and clicks out the light on the nightstand and waits in silent anticipation.

She is awoken by the touch of a hand on her thigh, and she gasps for air.

"*Shhhhh!*" Cyan places his other hand on her mouth. The covers are off the bed. "Come with me," he says, and takes her hand.

They cross the line of the hallway, and they are in the servants' side of the house. A staircase appears like a shrunken and sullied reflection. It is narrow with steep, dimly lit steps and many turns. There are bedrooms with small doors that muffle the sounds of snoring. The heavy musk of the servants' uniforms hangs in the hallway.

They are in the kitchen with its broad stove and deep sinks. There is a separate door and then the garden is revealed in moonlit lines. A path takes them under the broad-leafed banana trees that steal the silvery light. Sophie hears something, and suddenly it seems as if they are stalking a giant beast, following its heartbeat toward the edge of the jungle. As they walk hand in hand down the path, the heartbeat is stronger and more varied; it races then rests then races again with a shriek of human voices. A different kind of light comes from a shack, yellow with shadows that throw their hands above their heads then disappear. Now the heartbeat is under the music, under a man's mumbling, rhythmical voice. There's tremendous momentum and laughter in it all—then it stops suddenly in silent syncopation and, one, two—it begins again with more urgency.

"It's dancehall style," Cyan yells, and pulls her through the open door.

Nothing changes when Sophie and Cyan walk in; it's as if everyone is in a trance. The crowd is a momentous throng of faces and dreads and smiles and sweat. Cyan pulls a small bottle of golden water from his pocket. "Here. Drink this."

Sophie puts the bottle to her lips, and the rum is like mercury dripping from a broken thermometer, a metallic ball sprinting from corner to corner, running across a white sheet of paper, running yet staying intact. Sophie can feel it in her mouth, then her throat, then down to her heart, then in her veins, making everything gold and sunshine.

Cyan takes the bottle from her, tips it upside down in his mouth. She grabs it back and sucks, waiting for the glow again. It doesn't happen. She tries a larger gulp. It's just going to her head now. It's not the same. Cyan tries to pull the bottle from her hand; she smiles and swills more. He takes it, finishes it, pulls out another, and hands it to her, laughing.

Then they are dancing. Sophie is shaking her head and her hair, and now she knows exactly what the mumbling man is saying. She even knows just when the music is going to stop. It stops. She stops. It starts. She starts, seamlessly, as if she controls it. She grabs Cyan and starts kissing him, sloppy, and pushing her hips into his in time with the music, harder and faster, then stopping, pushing away, looking in his eyes, then the music starts again...

They are both covered in sweat. Her jacket and the second bottle are gone. She puts her hands on his chest and digs her nails into him, dropping her head back. He grabs the backs of her thighs and lifts her onto him. She can feel his hardness pressing between her legs. She digs her nails into his chest harder. Their teeth clank together. She turns her head to the side and sees the jungle. They are no longer inside, but the music seems just as loud. They are hidden from the moon beneath the overhang of the palapa, up against a white wall. He is pressing again, and she answers the pressure with quick and sudden thrusts of her own until she feels her panties being yanked hard into the corner of her thigh. *No*, she says silently. *No*. He slips below, and she feels a tearing inside her. The tearing scares her. She opens her mouth and yells *no*, but she can't hear it. He is taking it out. It was an accident. She softens. He thrusts it back in, dripping in moisture and sweat. She claws and pushes and opens her mouth again and thinks she yells *stop*. He does and she is relieved. Then he thrusts again harder and faster and again and again. And Sophie can feel it. She wills it to stop, and there is silence. In the moment of quiet, she screams "No!" and she can hear it this time, then the music starts again, and he is harder and faster, and she is torn and cold. He grunts, shudders, and falls away from her, spent and pitiful and drunk. She looks at him and doesn't understand, puts her hand down between her legs and lifts it up to find blood and cum. Watching her from a distant blankness, he stumbles backward and falls onto the ground, arms sprawled out, pants around his thighs, his penis curving and pulsing and shrinking.

"Why?" Sophie yells.

"What?" he says. And he runs his hand from his penis up to his chest, leaving a trail of blood on his white linen shirt. He looks at the blood on his hand and smiles a crooked smile.

The kitchen door is locked. Sophie bangs on the glass until Sissy opens it, startled, in a nightgown. Sissy reaches for Sophie, but Sophie pushes her away and moves quickly through the kitchen, through the pantry, and into the formal dining room, across the black-and-white marble floor to the window. The sailboat is still sitting there. It doesn't look like anything.

As she walks up each broad, carpeted step, she slides her hand along the thick, polished banister. Casablanca lilies sit in crystal vases on each landing.

The thick door shuts, she turns the key, and an eternal sounding click reverberates through her room. She flips on the faucet and steam rises from the tub. In the scalding hot water, she scrubs and scrubs at her skin.

In the morning Sophie looks for Giuseppe, but she finds the breakfast table unset and empty.

"Where is Mr. Cassavetes?" she asks a servant.

"New York," the servant responds. "Ms. Clark, the car is waiting for you."

Sophie turns toward the door and sees another servant holding her purse and the dresses that Giuseppe had bought for her.

"It is time for you to go."

The Kingston airport is a giant tin roof with no walls. She asks the driver, "Where's the plane?"

He laughs. "Mr. Cassavetes flew home this morning. Go to that counter right there—they have your ticket."

When she checks in, the clerk says, "We have you flying to San Diego, Ms. Clark."

Sophie reaches over the counter toward the ticket.

"Yes, we have you flying Kingston to Miami, Miami to Dallas, Dallas to San Diego."

"No. I'm supposed to go back to New York. Can you change it?"

"We have a flight at four o'clock." She types at her computer terminal. "That will be six hundred and fifty U.S. Cash or credit?" The clerk holds out her hand.

"I don't have any…"

"I am sorry, ma'am. Your ticket is for San Diego." The clerk puts the ticket on the counter and says, "Next."

On the plane, Sophie walks toward the back looking for 36E. It feels as if she were walking into the end of a dark sock. She finds her seat, a middle one between two sunburned, overweight tourists. The man has a baseball cap with flaps in the back that descend to his shoulders. The woman has her red hair done up in cornrows. The man and woman exchange suspicious glances; they seem to know each other.

Finally Sophie lands in San Diego just before sunset and inhales the moist ocean air. She calls Jean from a pay phone. An hour later they arrive in Victor's pickup. Audrey hops out and gets in the back. Sophie crawls over the tailgate and sits beside her. The sky is burnt orange in a crooked line above the hills. The tires vibrate and whir. Audrey notices Sophie's distant gaze, slides over to Sophie's lap, and holds her hand.

The din of lockers, people, and bells is foreign. Teachers hand her stacks of papers—two weeks' worth of work. The custodian opens her locker, and it is just as she left it, photos of puppies, a three-dimensional drawing of her name. In the cafeteria, planks of soggy dough masquerade as pizza.

The next morning Jean shakes her bed. "It's time to get up. Go to school."

Sophie opens her eyes, reluctant. "Again?"

Jean smiles. "It's not that bad."

After a week of days in this valley, car lots, strip malls, a lonely road that fills twice a day, she buys a pack of cigarettes and gives them to Audrey. Audrey takes off her headphones, nods her head, and tosses them on her stereo.

"Have you ever been with a boy?" Sophie asks quickly, before Audrey can put her headphones back on.

Audrey smiles. "Who is he?"

"No one. I just don't see what the difference is between a guy sticking his finger in you or sticking his thing in you. Except for it kind of hurts. Right? Isn't that what you said?"

"That goes away."

"Well, what's the difference then?"

"The guys like it more, mostly. I don't know… It's the closest two people can be."

"What if you thought you wanted to be close to someone, but you really didn't?"

"It's totally one of those things that after you do it with someone—you either become really close or it's over. I've seen it with my girlfriends. You'll know."

"Can you get pregnant? The first time?"

"You can. Just tell me who he is?"

"No one. Where do you get the pills?"

"Save it. Save it for someone you love."

"I just wanna know…"

The next day she walks with Audrey to school. When she gets within a block, Sophie says, "I forgot something. I'll see you later."

The day is bright and clear. She walks past the dry cleaners, past the resale boutique, past the McDonald's. There is a large cube of a building with tinted windows facing the street—the Salvation Army. She walks in and is overcome by the smell of old clothes. "Can you tell me where the clinic is?" she asks a woman whose apron strings are cutting her into three layers like a cake.

She finds the clinic, waits, and is soon sitting on the end of a table, naked. "I need the pill, and I think I have ingrown hairs," she says to the doctor when he walks in, an older man with a slight tremble and white hair.

The doctor bends down and stares through a rectangular magnifying glass with a bright pinpoint light. He stands up and says, "You can put your clothes on."

Sophie pulls her jeans up, puts on her T-shirt, and looks at the doctor anxiously.

"Miss, I… you have herpes," he says.

The gray light in the room seems to dip darker. Sophie feels drained and nauseous. "How? Can this…"

"Don't be alarmed. The social stigma is much worse than the disease. It's a virus that you will always have, the symptoms will come and go."

When she gets home, there is a letter addressed to Sophie Clark on the kitchen table. Sophie examines the typeface and green paper. She rips it open. It's a check for fifteen hundred dollars made out to her. She folds it several times and stuffs it in her jeans.

The next day after school, there's another one. This time it's for two thousand dollars. Two days later, there's a third, again for fifteen hundred. In her bedroom she spreads the three checks out on the bed and shows them to Audrey.

"What did you do?" Audrey asks.

"Nothing."

Sophie calls Caitlin and asks her about the checks. "They're yours, Sophie. You earned them."

"I want to come back."

"Sophie, this is a business for big girls. Mr. Cassavetes said he doesn't think you're ready."

"Send me a ticket."

KICK OUT THE JAMS

EJ is stout like a drummer should be. His small, fat hands are perfectly constructed to hold a drumstick. He can split melons with those hands. And he plays angry. EJ creates divots in his drumheads. He splits snares. He gives orders: "Alright, Spewing, stand over there and follow my lead. You take two steps from that spot and I'm going to slap you. You fall out of the pocket and I'll slap you. Come in nice and gentle…"

"Foreplay! I hear ya! Lick it before you stick it!" Spewing yells.

Kurt and EJ found Patrick Spewing under the rippling red and yellow streamers of a used-car lot in Pacific Beach. He was selling wheels to the wheeless. Spewing is spindly with spiky, frosted hair that jiggles when he talks.

"Dude," the Jovi tells him. "You're like a dildo left on and vibrating."

"Thanks, bro. Let's do this thing!"

Kurt fingerpicks the melody to "Alone, Alone," leaving open spaces between the chords for the Jovi. He dots them and brings them to life with harmonic notes and tones. Kurt sings above those notes in a falsetto that falls across the song like gray bolts of sunshine piercing cumulous clouds. Spewing uses every ounce of restraint he can muster, thumbing a muted bass string, letting the song build beneath him. It builds and builds until EJ snaps the snare drum and comes in with the heat, the dynamic jumps and the song is proud and serene, as if being alone is the only way. The song gains momentum until Kurt sings out his plea "I'm alone!"—holding on to the last word of the chorus as if it's all he's got left. The Jovi pulls in beneath with a guitar solo. The contemplative song ends in a rush and after the resonance slowly dies away, Kurt wheels around and yells: "GOD DAMN RIGHT! THAT'S WHAT FIFTEEN FUCKING YEARS SOUNDS LIKE! NOBODY HAS THAT! NOBODY! YOU AND ME HAVE BEEN PLAYING MUSIC TOGETHER SINCE WE WERE KIDS! WE'RE LIKE THE BEATLES WHEN THEY QUIT—AND WE'RE JUST GETTING STARTED! THIS IS THE BEST FUCKING BAND IN THE WORLD! PUT ANYBODY IN FRONT OF US AND WE'LL MAKE THEM CRY! WE'LL MAKE THEM WANT TO QUIT MUSIC!"

"Yeah, Kurt," the Jovi says. "It sounded good."

The door at the end of the studio swings open and a backlit figure about the height of a fireplug appears in a leather duster holding a scepter in one hand and a shrunken human skull in the other. The figure puts the stick in the base of the skull, makes a screwing motion, then the two pieces fall apart.

EJ asks, "What happened to your wand, Ivo?"

"What's with this fucking thing? Is not wand, is staff of authority. Supposed to make shitfuckers pay for practice. You going to fucking pay Ivo for practice this time? No more hickory dickory dock! You fucking pay Ivo!" Ivo shakes the headless staff of authority at the band. "What is with you guys? One day it's tits and ass, the next day it's balls on the chin!"

The Jovi looks at EJ and raises his eyebrows.

EJ says, "Ivo's a self-starter like me. He's Russian, but he taught himself the English language by watching Andrew Dice Clay videos. Hey, Ivo, I told you it's going to be tits and ass. Now put down the stick."

"Okay. You say tits and ass, but then you try to make me give you balls on the chin."

In an hour, it's balls on the chin. Kurt brought three dollars. His share is ten.

Kurt says, "Ivo, believe me, when we're the biggest band in the world, I'll make it worth your while."

"Fuck you. Pay me."

The Jovi covers for Kurt.

Five days later they play for the Windansea Surf Club at the Pumphouse. It's like the old days. They burn through all the Thunderstick songs and start playing old Full Nelson Mandela songs.

Then Doors covers: *Well, I woke up this morning and I got myself a beer.*

Then Lou Reed covers: *Thought of you as my mountaintop.*

Then Iggy Pop covers: *I'm bored. I'm the chairman of the bored.*
It's like being home.

ſHAKE YOUR LOVE

When Sophie arrives back in New York it's November 14, 1982. Some of the girls in the model's apartment have gone back to school. Some have gone to Paris or Milan. New girls have arrived from Topeka and Nashville and Toronto. Sophie wants to feel magical again. She wants to feel the swan feathers brush against her skin, she wants to see the unicorn and hear the voices, but instead she just sees the dirt and filth of the city. Standing on the street corner, she can't help but gaze into the big, open, iron drain at her feet. When she looks up she notices that men are staring at her and a cold shiver of terror runs through her body.

It starts again with go-sees, then castings, and then soon, within a matter of weeks, Caitlin tells her, "You're the fresh face, and they have to have you." She gets booked in town, for ads, for editorial. She spends a lot of time sitting in chairs, staring at a mirror, having a team of workers change her. After a while she starts to see the same faces, the same forearms, the same fingers. She can't figure out if the Sophie in the mirror is the bloom and she the plant or the other way around.

"Are we connected?" She asks one day sitting in the chair staring at the mirror.

"What's that, sweetheart?" the man with the small brush asks.

"Me and her." Sophie points to the mirror.

"Girlfriend? Are you on mushrooms?"

Sophie laughs. "No. It's just sometimes I wonder."

"She." The man points to the mirror. "Makes you all your money. She works for you."

Sophie smiles. "I like that. What's your name?"

"Randy George."

"Doesn't that mean something?"

"You don't miss a thing do you? Yes, you are right, I'm Randy and I'm George."

"Randy George will you be my friend?"

"I never say 'No' to a proposition."

Days come and days go. Home is nowhere. Work is Caitlin's office. Sophie enters. "Hi. I heard you wanted to talk me?"

"Sophie. I've got some good news. You're doing the shows. Two of them. But before I book it, I need to make sure you can walk."

"Are you kidding?" Sophie laughs and marches a little.

"Sophie, I mean a runway walk. It's not the same."

"Is this where I put a book on my head, like in those old movies. And we drink tea and wear button-down sweaters."

"That kind of walk doesn't work anymore. You need to learn to walk like a woman from a man."

Sophie rolls her eyes. "That is so stupid."

"Do you know any trannys?"

"What's a tranny?"

Sophie calls Randy George. Randy George sets the whole thing up. "Sophie, this is my good friend, the incomparable, the enigmatic, the elastic, the fantastic, Ava Wanda Wye." Ava spins around in some very high heels, blows a kiss, and bends gracefully at the waist until the back of her hand touches the floor.

"Wow!" Sophie says.

"Alright Ava, let's see the sashay."

From Ava Wanda Wye, Sophie learns to stomp. It's that little extra oomph in each step that makes all the jiggley parts tremble. It's fierce and feminine at the same time.

A week later, she turns the corner and the runway is below. The lights are blinding like a sneeze and the music moves her. When she gets to the end of the stage and rotates powerfully behind her jutted shoulder, she tosses her hair, her eyes flash, and glamour, glory, and girlishness spill off the stage. A whole section of men jump to their feet and their cameras explode.

ROUND AND ROUND

The day after the Pumphouse gig, Kurt wakes up, calls EJ at work, and says, "We need to play L.A. No one's going to sign us down here."

"We can drive up Friday night."

"My wife will come back to me when we get signed. Right?"

"She most certainly will."

EJ and Kurt load up the station wagon and head up to L.A. Kurt has a boombox in his lap and two tapes: Echo & the Bunnymen's *Porcupine* and Elvis's *Live at Madison Square Garden 1972*.

They crank it up and sing along, Kurt on lead vocals, EJ does the harmonies with his brassy tenor.

Up the 5 to the 101, get off on Highland, turn right on Sunset, and they're in a seedy area filled with strip malls and street walkers. The batteries in the boombox fade, and Elvis starts singing slower and lower until Kurt presses the stop key.

As they head west, Sunset Strip becomes Glam heaven. First is the Whisky a Go Go—Jim Morrison and the Doors played there. Now four community-college kids in matching pink spandex, half-shirts, and white Capezios unload Strat knockoffs from the back of a Honda hatchback. They've driven in from Van Nuys. Up the strip is Duke's Coffee Shop, where rock stars eat breakfast at three in the afternoon. Further west is the Roxy with its three-line, red-neon sign. Next is a little brick chateau that wears rock posters and billboards like a crackhead wears a sandwich board—it's the Rainbow Room. On the sidewalk in front, dudes with perms and bangs stare at cars.

"These poodle heads, what are they waiting for?" Kurt asks EJ.

"Ronnie James Dio or Lita Ford or someone else who sucks."

One poodle head in an acid-washed jumpsuit points his finger at EJ's mom's station wagon and laughs. Kurt leans out the window and yells, "Don't laugh at me, you poser! You don't even play music!" Kurt sits back in his seat and does his fake southern voice. "Alright. Look at me. I look like I'm in a band, but I don't even know how to play music! Alright! How mellow!"

They keep driving until they are in front of the façade at Gazzarri's. It has a giant airbrushed painting of a fat man in a fedora surrounded by sad, rubber-faced strippers. They pass Doheny and a Jag dealership, and suddenly the Strip ends in the uniform quiet of Beverly Hills.

"Well? What do you think?" EJ asks.

"Let's try the Roxy. It looks more modern."

Kurt and EJ walk into the blacklight world of the Roxy. A chick behind a plastic shield says, "Come back tomorrow. In the daytime. Nobody talks to the manager at night. You want to party? It's six bucks."

Kurt gets pissed. EJ gets him out onto the sidewalk. They meet a hippie chick. She's there to see Sally's Strung Out. She says they perform magic on stage—Santeria—and she thinks they're gonna get a deal with a major tonight. Arty Azimoff, Golden-Eared Arty, red-bearded Arty, Arty from Geffen Records is in there right now, and he's gonna sign Sally's Strung Out. Kurt, half horny, half looking for a record deal, gives the hippie chick his last copy of the demo. She's interested. She looks at him too long. He tries to kiss her, then says he's married, then says his wife left him. She gives him her number.

Kurt and EJ drive east on Sunset toward downtown. The signs change from English to Spanish. They pull the station wagon into the uneven parking lot of the downtown Tommy's Burgers. It's busy and buzzing at two in the morning. The mix of kids is one-third cholo, one-third ghetto, and one-third USC cracker. Everyone's drunk and happy, with dripping burgers in their hands.

"I used to frequent this establishment when I was at USC," EJ says to Kurt. "They serve a fine burger."

"When we get a record deal, you should buy this place."

EJ laughs. "I know, Kurt. I really should. What are you going to buy?"

"A house with a gate to keep the fans out. My wife wouldn't be too stoked on fans in our yard. You saw that chick tonight. Chicks like that won't leave me alone."

"Even with all those metal loops in her face—like fishing lures—she was kinda hot. Well, Kurt, I guess that's just one of your burdens. One I would gladly shoulder."

"It's like they know we're going to get a record deal."

"You may have something there, my good man."

"We need to make another demo and play up here, and people like that red-beard will sign us."

"Kurt, look, the rest of us can come up with two hundred dollars for a demo. You can't. We've got to figure something out."

"I know. I'll talk to Ivo."

As the night lingers on, there are a few less clouds, a little more haze, but the L.A. grid is lit in such a way that there is never a star in the sky, barely even a moon. EJ and Kurt drive slowly past several two-level Spanish apartment buildings in the Hollywood flats.

"I don't know, Kurt. Sven lives in one of these. I can't remember the number."

"I thought you never forget numbers."

"I never forget anything of a financial nature—house numbers are different."

Kurt throws his hands in the air and says sarcastically, "Alright! Panthers and Pathogens—what a cool band. Let's all wear felt hats, then we'll get a record deal."

"Kurt, cut that shit out. Sven is a good guy. It's not his fault his band belongs at a Renaissance Faire. He's a really good bass player." EJ shakes his head. "And Panthers and Pathogens is still really big in Japan."

They stop in front of a small apartment building.

"Well," Kurt says, "let's start ringing doorbells, I guess. It's that or sleep in the car. I don't care. It's the same to me."

"I'd like to see Sven."

They pick a house and knock. A lady screams "GO AWAY!" from behind the closed door.

They try a second building. Someone yells, "I'm calling the cops."

They try another. The lady says, "Those Robin Hood–looking boys live in the third one down on the left, downstairs. We call it Sherwood Forest, but young people nowadays don't even know what that means…Would you boys like to come in for some tea? I'm up anyway. Do you mind cats?"

Sven answers the door in a tunic with a rope belt. He is tall and thin, and blond roots show through his dyed black hair. "EJ. Kurt," he whispers. "What are…Dude, you guys can't stay here."

"That was quick," EJ responds.

"Look, man. Nicky's got a six A.M. call."

"Oh yeah? What's she in now?"

"It's a slasher film. She's getting disemboweled in the morning. She'll kill me if you wake her up."

"Hey, man, did you give our tape to your A&R guy?" EJ asks.

"Yeah, man. That's some Gothic-sounding shit you guys are into. Kind of like Echo & the B-men, huh?"

"It's New Romantic," EJ says.

"That demo is the best tape ever made," Kurt adds. "Tell that to your A&R guy."

"It's a tough sell. The A&R guys are still looking for Glam bands. They were pissed when our second album went from Glam to Wandering Minstrel. But, shit, you got to keep up with the times. In Silverlake it's Heroin Chic or Wandering Minstrel. Glam is dead."

"Tell that to the poodle heads in front of the Rainbow," Kurt says.

"Dokken dickheads," EJ adds.

"Fuck Warrant. Fuck Winger." Kurt bends his wrists and lifts his hands awkwardly above his head. "Fuck Cinderella too."

"Give the people what they want," Sven says, and cinches his rope belt.

"I'll fight all of those guys for my band," Kurt adds.

Sven pauses a moment and looks Kurt up and down, then stretches and yawns. "Hey, guys, it's been real, but I gotta go to bed. Call me tomorrow."

They leave the station wagon where it is. EJ crumples up a moldy towel, puts it under his head, and stretches out in the back. "I'm telling you Kurt. Someday we'll own this town."

Kurt props himself up between the front seat and the steering wheel. "Someday is coming soon."

Sunrise is cruel and soon when you sleep in a car. The only answer is to cram your head into a crevasse or cover it up with your jeans. That leaves your bare white legs splayed out for dog walkers and joggers. Finally you rise. AM/PM coffee is a yellowish brown like gasoline, one drop of creamer turns the whole cup opaque. It tastes like dishwater, but it works.

Kurt and EJ stand at the bar with the Roxy manager. Like every bar in the world, it smells like smoke, old beer, and urine in the daytime. The manager wipes the counter, tosses the rag in the sink, and looks Kurt in the eye. "So you want to play the Roxy? What makes you think you're ready?"

"Ever heard of Bad Bobby!?"

The manager shakes his head.

"That was my band. I played the Starlight Bowl when I was fifteen years old. I can handle the Roxy."

"You bring your demo?"

"Yeah." Kurt reaches in his pockets, looks at EJ, and says, "Shit. You bring one?"

EJ shakes his head. "You said you would bring it."

"I did, but I gave it to that chick."

The manager laughs. "You gave your only demo to a chick on Sunset Boulevard?"

"Dude, she knew that red-beard guy."

"Golden-Eared Arty? Is he coming to see you?" the manager asks.

"Yeah."

"Who else? What other labels?"

"All of 'em," Kurt says.

The manager likes lies. He smiles. "Right. So, you got a crowd? A crowd that drinks?"

EJ starts, "In San Diego we have a huge—"

Kurt cuts him off. "Look, people up here know us."

"What? You got some ad in the *Weekly?* How do people in L.A. know a San Diego band?"

"My guitar player. He plays with Brian Smith. You know him?"

"Yeah, I know Smithy. Everyone knows Smithy—from the Love Guns. I know that guitar player too—good-looking, hair, rides a louder than shit black chopper. What's that guitar player's name?"

"Bobby Dugan," Kurt says.

"No. That's not it."

"The Jovi."

"Yeah, his name is the Jovi. I know that guy. Comes in here with some hot chicks. That guy's in your band? Why didn't you say so? How's about a week from Friday at eleven?"

"That's cool."

The manager pulls out a bunch of tickets stuck together with a rubber band. "Okay. Forty tickets."

Kurt and EJ look at each other, excited.

"Five bucks a pop. That'll be two hundred bucks."

Kurt says, "That seems fair. When do we get it?"

The manager laughs. "You pay us. You sell the tickets to your friends—That's how you make the money back."

"Can we pay you that night?" Kurt asks.

"No, you gotta pay when we book it."

"We'll be back." Kurt turns for the door. "We need to go to the bank."

"You're gonna need an account," the manager says as they are walking for the door. "Or a gun."

CRUEL SUMMER

In May of 1983, Sophie is summoned. She appears. Caitlin says, "We're sending you to Paris then Milan. Pack your bags. You'll be gone for a while."

"No, I don't want to go."

"Look. Sophie, this is the next step for you. All the up and coming photographers are in Paris and Milan. We're building your career. This is part of the plan."

"Is he in there?" Sophie motions towards the door to Mr. Cassavetes's office.

"Sophie, pack your bags."

In his apartment, Sophie holds Randy George in a desperate embrace.

"Oh come on. Don't be so dramatic," He says.

"I can't help it." She answers into his neck. "You smell good."

"It's just Paris. You'll meet a boy. You'll meet lots of boys. I just know it. You'll have fun."

"That's the problem."

"Sweetie, fun is not the problem."

"Boys!"

"Boys aren't the problem either. What's wrong?"

"I like the bad ones. And I don't even know they're bad until…"

"That's half the fun."

"No, it isn't. The last time I did, something terrible happened."

"Oh… I'm sor— What?"

"I don't want to talk about it. Just trust me a bad person hurt me."

"Terrible things happen in life. Wonderful things happen in life." Randy George holds Sophie's shoulders so he can look at her. She's a tussle of hair and tears. "If you're stuck in the past, you'll miss them both. Is the bad person here right now in my apartment?"

Sophie snivels and looks at Randy George's soft eyes rimmed in eyeliner. "No."

"Then don't invite him in. Live in the now, Sophie."

THE PASSENGER

On Girard Avenue, between two commercial-style buildings, sits a wood-frame house, a holdover from an era gone bye. Inside, indie girls and boys wear black nail polish and serve coffee. Outside, on the porch, under the long-armed liquid amber, people have conversations. This is the Pannikin. The Jovi and James Franklin are sitting together in the corner under the spiky purple bougainvillea, taking in the clear and brilliant day. Eric Adams comes to pay his respects. With his long straight brown hair and his high cheekbones, he looks like an Anglo Iroquois. He is calm, almost stolid. It's the demeanor that one would associate with a bass player. The Jovi asks, "Eric, what's up? Do you know Kurt's brother, James?"

"Hey, James. I've seen you at the meetings, right?"

"Yup."

"And your brother is Kurt Franklin?"

"Guilty as charged."

"He shreds the guitar, and can really sing, too. But he's always so..."

"Yeah?" James asks.

"I said 'Hi' to him and he just stared at me. He's so… I guess the word I'm looking for is intense. He's intense."

"I think you mean insane," the Jovi says, cracks a smile, and lights a smoke.

"Hey!" James barks. "He's not insane. Eric's right, he's intense. You'd be intense too if you'd been through the shit we've been through."

"I love the guy but he's—" The Jovi stops himself and smiles at James.

"Dude," James says, "he was misdiagnosed by a hack from the County Health Department. That hack cost Kurt years of his life. He doesn't hear voices. Not anymore. Not since he quit Mellaril."

"Whoa." Eric says. "Mellaril. That shit is like Thorazine. Heavy sedative. He was on that?"

"Yeah, a prescription," James nods.

"I've heard of junkies doing Mellaril when they want to kick H, just to knock themselves out for a day or two."

"Try being knocked out for four years," James says.

"So Kurt's clean? One of us?" Eric asks. "Plug in the jug?"

"No. Kurt drinks." The Jovi says, "For him it's a God thing. He thinks the voices were demons. God rebuked 'em. Now he's cured. Demon free."

"For real?" Eric asks.

James and the Jovi nod at Eric.

"God, yeah. That's what fucked me up," Eric says. "I was your standard trash can, but freebase, shit, that was like the warm hand of God pushing softly through my frontal lobe. It scared me. That desire to be touched by God, it turned me into the devil."

"Eric," The Jovi says, "that shit is deep."

"Thanks, man."

"This guy right here *is* his brother's keeper. He got Kurt off Mellaril and helped me get clean, too." The Jovi says and grabs James's shoulder.

"You'd do it for me," says James.

"You think Kurt would want a keyboard player in the band?" asks The Jovi.

"Maybe." James says and sips his coffee.

"You mean me?" Eric asks and smiles brightly.

"Dude. I can't live at my parents' forever. Move me in. I will teach you rock."

The next day around noon, the Ford Falcon is stuffed to the gills and puttering up the hill from Windansea. The street turns from quaint to rental and then Eric's house is at the top, near the boulevard. His front yard is the size of a couch—perfect to park the Roach on. The pad is a shoebox with a door in the middle and a window on either side. Above the windows, there is a line of Spanish roof tiles that look like eyebrows. It makes the house look surprised.

Eric's girlfriend, Dane, and Larry the dog greet the Jovi at the door. The Jovi unloads his posters and art in the back-room. He takes out every white light bulb and replaces it with a blue, red, or green one. In a matter of hours, the back room, a converted garage, changes from a blank white box to the Jovi's lair.

The Jovi puts a hand on Eric's shoulder and says, "Listen, man, I'm easy. If I come home some day, and you're banging Dane in my closet, I will be totally cool with that. *Mi casa, su casa.*"

Eric laughs. "That'll never happen."

"Lesson number one: Maybe it should."

Kurt and EJ come back from L.A. and call for a band meeting at the Pannikin. Kurt says, "Look, we need two hundred bucks so we can play at the Roxy."

"Wait a second," the Jovi says, "that's not how you get a record deal."

"Well? What should we do?"

"We record a new demo—more rock, less New Romantic. We use the demo to get a manager. The manager gets us a record deal."

Kurt says, "A three-song demo is eight hundred bucks. Where do we get that? My wife fucking left me!" Kurt lifts his hands up in the air.

"I know the guy," the Jovi says. "My new roommate, Eric. He's got bank. His grandfather invented spray-on cheese. We bring him in on keys and split the demo five ways. He wants in."

"Huh?" Kurt says.

"New roommate?" EJ asks.

Kurt is silent for a full minute, then he says, "The last time I saw Echo in concert you could just feel that it was missing from their songs—all of the string parts, all of the keyboards. It was missing. If we had a keyboard player, that could be the one thing that puts us over the top, but I don't want him trying to add parts and solos and shit. We just need some synth pads behind the music, some string parts. You know what I mean. Can you buy me a burrito? Ivo took all my fucking money."

"Yeah. Sure. He'd be stoked to do whatever."

The Jovi walks into the house and finds Eric sitting on the futon watching TV. "You should get away from that," he says.

"But I trust TV. It brings me a world I can parse and understand."

"Dude. You're a full-blown Spock Rocker, aren't you? We should get you a V-necked sweater."

"Nah, man."

Someone knocks on the door.

Eric says, "It better not be those fucking Jehovah's Witnesses again—I'll give them an earful about YHWH!"

The Jovi opens the door and finds Kurt looking like a half-shorn sheep. "Franklin? What's with the hair?"

"Dude. What? It's getting long, right? I cut the sides. Let's teach this guy a song. Where's the keyboards?"

They walk into Eric's bedroom. He opens the French doors. They lead to a small square of red concrete. Kurt sits down in front of the keys. "How do you turn this thing on?"

Eric flips a switch.

"I Wanted You" materializes in a fade. Kurt is playing the keyboard part.

"Show me that again." Eric watches carefully.

"You think you could do that?" Kurt asks. "I did it on the demo. If I can do it, you can do it."

Kurt puts his Ovation acoustic in his lap. The Jovi plugs in. Eric sits at his keyboard and starts plunking, mistake after mistake after mistake until he gets it. The room fills with music. They rock back and forth in unison. "Yeah. That's it. You're getting it," Kurt says. "Let me teach you another one. This doesn't have a keyboard part yet, so maybe you can write one." Kurt begins the song.

Eric asks, "What key is it?"

"E."

He struggles as Kurt plays.

"No, man, E. E."

Eric finds E, clunks around, searching aimlessly for a hook, then it happens. Eric's eyes migrate into the back of his head.

The command between his head and hands is lost. Fingers just do their thing. A subtle vibration moves from the bottom of his throat and climbs to the base of his skull then continues down his arms to his hands where it stays.

"That's it! Right there!" Kurt strums his guitar. "Play those notes again! No, no, just the three. Yes, like that. Now again." Eric like a half-deaf circus bear, Kurt a sublime apprehension, and the Jovi the rhythm, the chunk, the attitude. It works.

When the notes are ingrained and the song is over, Eric says, "I've never done that before."

"What?"

"Created anything."

"Nah…"

"Really, man. You showed me how to get there. And I don't even know where I went…"

"It's just music…"

"No, man, that was like a trance. And you guys gave it to me like some tantric master. You busted me over the head with the clay pot of enlightenment. I stopped thinking and just let it flow through me. I never stop thinking—it's a fucking curse."

Kurt says, "You did good."

"Let's do that again."

"Later. You want to come in for a couple songs in the band?" Kurt asks.

"Hell, yeah."

"Come to practice on Monday. We're making a demo. Bring a hundred and sixty dollars. You can play on those three songs. Maybe some day you can play on more."

GIRLS JUST WANT
TO HAVE FUN

Sophie wakes up, looks out the small oval window, and sees a tiny yellow car parked on the tarmac. Two burly baggage handlers approach and greet each other with a kiss. This must be Paris, she thinks. The cab smells like something in between old cheese and horse blanket. It's hard to tell where the cabby and his seat separate. It's as if he's sprouted from the thing. At the Paris office, there is a woman, very much like Caitlin, but she speaks with an accent and very quickly. Sophie feels the critical gaze. It's not like the way men look at her. Men look at her like food. This woman looks at Sophie like a pilot looks at his plane, as if she had a clipboard in her hand. It's a walk around. Cheekbones, check. Good skin, check. Legs, check. Tits, check...

The jobs are the same, more than the same. Nobody speaks French. Everybody speaks broken English, even the Americans. It's a stone-age vernacular that everyone understands.

At night it's Les Bains Douches. The music is inescapable. It makes the room and everything in it thump and throb. Cassandra, one of the girls from the Paris model's apartment, comes back from the bar and hands Sophie a drink. "He said if we drink this within one minute, he'll give us two more for free!"

Sophie gazes over the rim of the glass into the bubbly clear liquid. She's a little tentative, as if she is looking down into a precipice. But then she says, "Okay," and throws it down. The carbonation makes her eyes water. She hands the empty glass back to Cassandra.

"Look at the floor!" Cassandra yells.

"The what?" Sophie asks.

"The floor!"

"Why?"

"This was a Turkish bath house!"

"So?"

"The floor! Look at the floor!"

Sophie looks at the floor. It's made up of little tiny square tiles. White tiles and black tiles are set together to make larger squares. "Harlequin!" She yells. "Like a jester!" She looks up from the floor and Cassandra isn't there. There's a touch on her shoulder. She turns to find a glowing face. "Sophie! Hey Sophie Clark!" He's tall with big bright eyes and a perfect chin. "Hey, I was the captain!" He yells. "I was in the paper, in Poway!" His hands shake at the end of bent arms for emphasis.

The dance that she's feeling requires Sophie to tilt her head, as if she is clearing water from her ear. He thinks it means she doesn't understand.

"We went to State! Remember?"

Sophie puts her hands over her head and dances a circle. When she returns to his eager face she gives him a smile.

Cassandra gives her a drink. It's gone again. She hands the glass back.

"I was the quarterback! In Poway!"

"What are you doing here?" Sophie asks embedded in a laugh.

"Modeling!" He yells. "What are you doing here?"

She smiles and looks into a spinning blue light.

"You go home ever?" He asks and gyrates his fists to the music. There's a line of them now, all gyrating their fists, wearing cut-up sweats and flannel shirts – male models.

"Where?" She yells.

"Home!"

She shrugs her shoulders. Cassandra is back with another drink. "I like Paris," Sophie yells to Cassandra.

"*J'aime Paris!*" Cassandra yells back. "It means I love Paris."

"I only said I like it!" Sophie yells and puts her hands over her head to continue the dance.

Somewhere in the night, a wave of happy consumes Sophie. Her tongue is the ambassador, dressed in a tux, greeting foreign dignitaries. There are staircases that descend, to harlequin floors, and great rooms filled with a waiting audience. And this time it feels good when he enters her. And she moves with all of his movements. And it lasts just long enough and ends with two sweaty beautiful people entwined in sleep. A few hours later, she wakes up and looks out the tall French door into the night sky above Paris. The moon is coming down over the silver rooftops. He grumbles and she tells him her secret, "Maybe sometimes I do miss Poway, just a little."

With a thick French accent he asks, "What is this Poway?"

YOUTHQUAKER

It's a slice of summer in January. Hot, dry Santa Ana winds and blue skies make the afternoon hours bright and warm and fleeting—the sun travels across the sky at double speed. At four, it will be cold. Eric sits on the stoop with Dane. "Something's missing," she says.

They hear the Roach coming up the hill from the sea. On the gas tank, a happy dog—on the back, riding sidesaddle, a girl smoking a cigarette.

"It's Larry," Eric says. "Larry's missing."

"Not anymore."

The Jovi kills the engine, hands him the dog, and says, "I saw the little guy cruising down by the beach, so I brought him back up. Thought you'd be stoked."

"How'd Larry get out?" Eric asks.

"You know how these dogs are, they smell a bitch in heat, and they're gone."

"Been there," Eric says. "But Larry's a girl." He looks at the back gate. It is open with the Jovi's wetsuit dripping over the side. "Can you do me a big favor?"

"Yeah, of course."

"Can you just remember to close the back gate?"

"Eric. Relax. I got you covered. Have you ever met Nänce?"

The girl on the back of the bike unfolds herself from the Jovi and puts her black boot on the curb. She runs her hand through her pixie hair then holds it out to Eric. "Yooooo must be Dirtdick's roooooommate," she says in a long, drawn-out whine.

"Nice to meet you, Nänce."

"I'm his girlfriend. Don't laugh! I know he's a whore."

The Jovi shrugs his shoulders and smiles. "Nänce knows the deal." He takes her shoulder and turns her sideways. "Dude, look. She's skinny, but how about the rack?"

Eric reluctantly eyes Nänce's breasts.

"Well?" the Jovi asks. "Do you want to grab 'em or what?"

Dane says, "You're disgusting!" and walks in the house.

Eric blushes and looks at Nänce.

"Well? You can," she says.

"They're nice, but no thanks."

"Hey, Nänce, we're gonna teach Eric about chicks. He's doing a research paper."

"Oh God, don't do that. You're awful."

"I'm not awful," the Jovi says. "I'm upfront. I watch their body language. A girl starts touching her hair or her face while she's talking to me and I know it's on. That's when I ask for it."

"Wow. And it works?" Eric asks.

"Oh, and the real trick? You want to know the real trick?"

"Yeah."

"I don't shower. When they catch the scent of another chick on you—they can't control themselves. It's like a wolf. You know a wolf will roll in a deer turd when he finds it. It covers his scent. The deer doesn't smell a wolf coming, it smells a deer."

"More like deer shit," Nänce says.

"Same difference. You know what I mean. It works. You should try it."

"So when was your last shower?" Eric asks.

"I shower every Sunday, for the Lord."

"Dude! You've had company!"

"What does that mean?" Nänce asks.

"Dude! C'mon! You make it sound gross. I've been in the ocean like every day. I got a little salt creek but…" The Jovi reaches down and rubs his weld. "But it works. I'm telling you, chicks dig it."

"What kind of chicks?" Dane is back on the porch and glaring at the Jovi.

"Wild ones." The Jovi smiles.

Dane glares at the three of them. "You are dirty. All of you." She goes back inside.

"Wow." Eric nods.

"Seriously. It works."

"He's full of shit," Nänce says. "Don't listen to anything he says. Take a shower. Why does your girlfriend hate me?"

"She just met you."

"I'm not a whore. I don't sleep with anyone but the Jovi."

"I know."

"I'm nice. Why doesn't she like me?"

HOT CHILD IN THE CITY

When Sophie returns to New York in the fall of 1984, by anybody else's standards, at sixteen, she's just a kid. In modeling, after two years in the business, she's a franchise. While in Europe she scored six covers. The checks piled up. Her mom and dad and sister, Audrey, moved into a house that didn't have wheels. Caitlin tells Sophie, "Your too big for the model's apartment. Why don't you buy a place?" Sophie takes Randy George with her apartment shopping. 1 Bond Street, she likes the name. NoHo, next to Broadway, a cast-iron building, it makes Sophie think of an ornate birdcage she saw in a Parisian shop. Two hundred and fifty thousand dollars seems like an astronomical and almost incomprehensible amount of money. The man who does her taxes tells her she can afford it. Randy George marvels at the light, holding his hand out in it, remarking on the row of windows, each with their two giant plates of glass, each with a view to the cobblestone street below.

"Let me tell you something, child."

"Yes."

"I'm so glad to have you back in town, but I will miss your phone calls. Will you promise to continue to call me at ridiculous times?"

Sophie laughs. "Of course. What's ridiculous?"

"Two, three, four a.m. When I would hear my phone ring in the middle of the night, waking me from my dreams, I somehow knew it was you, calling me after a club or after a date, calling to share with me how happy you were in that moment. I could just close my eyes and see the sun coming up over Paris, you walking down the street weaving in and out of bread vendors, carrying your high heel shoes over your shoulder."

"You could see all that?"

"Do you know what it was like?"

"A love letter?"

"No. It was like a kite. I felt like I was holding the string and watching you fly."

Sophie takes Randy George's hand and opens it palm up. She closes it. "Don't let go."

"Oh, Sophie."

"This place is big enough for both of us."

"What is this a Western?"

"Please move in with me. I won't have to call you, I'll just walk in your room and snuggle you."

Sophie's mom and dad show up in New York to sign the papers for the loft. "Have you thought about breast implants?" Jean asks over a bowl of Tom Yum Gai in a trendy Vietnamese restaurant.

Randy George spits his spring roll onto his plate and laughs at Jean. "Did you really just ask that? Of your daughter?"

Jean turns sharp to Randy George. "I don't even know who you are? As far as I'm concerned you're just some hanger-on, trying to leach off my daughter. She doesn't need you. She's got family."

Randy's lip quivers a little then turns to a smile. He nods at Sophie, stands up and walks away. Sophie slumps her shoulders, snivels, and lets out a sad moan.

Her father, Victor, intervenes. "Now Jean, that just wasn't necessary."

"I think that man is homosexual. Sophie you shouldn't be around him anyway…"

"Okay! I'll get the boobs!" Sophie yells, throws her napkin in the soup and marches for the front door.

Victor looks at Jean and asks, "Great! Now who's going to pay for dinner?"

IVO

Ivo puts tape on the reel, hangs a Persian rug behind the drum kit, and moves some boxes around until he's happy.

The band is very businesslike. EJ taps around the head of his snare drum in a circle; his ear is cocked to the sound. Each *pong pong pong* is slightly higher in pitch until *pong pong pong*, becomes *ping ping ping*. Kurt starts his vocal warm-ups from deep in his chest—*"ah, ah, ah, eh, eh, eh, oh, oh, oh."* Spewing scratches his head like a monkey.

It happens in layers. Basic tracks are first—drums, bass, guitar, and vocals. They play the three songs. Eric lays down two-finger parts on his synth. Then Kurt gets in Ivo's make-shift iso room—it's just a bunch of Persian rugs hung on drum stands. Kurt asks Ivo if he's ready. Ivo counts one, two, three. Kurt begins a cyclical, rhythmic guitar part. From the control room, the only sound is Kurt's dub guitar. It's a half-mad melody played backward. It's a riff on a hook of an unknown song. Kurt plays it through the whole song. It doesn't make any sense at all, and then Ivo hits a button on the board. The rest of the song pops up and it fits seamlessly, adding texture and depth. Then Kurt sings a vocal track, a falsetto on the tag.

Kurt walks back in the control room and finds the Jovi sitting in the captain's chair. He hops up and gives him a pop.

"Bro. That was insane. Let me throw a little something on there."

The song is cued from the beginning in the iso booth. It's "Alone, Alone." As the song gains momentum, the Jovi adds subtle notes here and there and then… guitar solo. He takes off and flutters above the band and below Kurt's impassioned plea. As Kurt's long vocal note fades away, the solo flies, full of confidence and hope and nothing but blue sky until Kurt's chaotic, backward rhythm-guitar part arrives and suddenly the triumphant notes are bittersweet, being pulled toward Earth. There's a struggle between the two, and when the Jovi's melody escapes for the final time, it's magic and everyone knows it.

The Jovi walks back in the control room. Kurt puts an arm around him, hugs him like a brother, and says, "Thank you."

KISS ME DEADLY

In the fall of 1985 Randy George rings the buzzer at 1 Bond Street. Sophie hasn't seen him in a while. She's been in Paris with a photographer. She's been in London with a gallerist. She can't decide which one she likes more. It's a nice enough day but Randy George seems cold. "What's the matter?" she asks.

In the bright light of her apartment his cheeks look hollow. Sophie hands him a cup of tea and as his hand reaches out from his sleeve into the bright beam of light it is covered with liver spots. "What's wrong with you?"

"Sweetheart, they think I'm a leper. Nobody will hire me. I haven't worked in months. I'm so afraid they're going to evict me."

"You can live here with me."

"I need to work, child."

Sophie struts in to Caitlin's office. "You need to hire my friend."

"Who?"

"Randy George. The makeup artist."

"Sophie, he's sick. Nobody wants what he's got. Nobody wants to be around it. Nobody even wants to be reminded that it's happening."

"Fine. I don't work unless he's my makeup man."

"Hah! Then you don't work."

"Did you hear me? I said I don't work if you don't hire him."

Caitlin lifts up an eight by ten glossy photo of a brunette with a mole. "Do you see this, Sophie? She's a fresh face. The next big thing. She's going to Jamaica this weekend. You missed your chance."

Sophie turns and moves towards Mr. Cassavetes office. Caitlin yells, "You can't just go in there!"

Sophie opens the door and there he is, sitting behind his desk, in his white suit, on the phone. "I'll have to call you back," he says and hangs up the receiver and smiles.

Sophie locks the door behind her. She walks deliberately over, sticks her hand between his legs, and pushes her lips onto his. He tastes a little stale, but she likes it. She rubs up and down between his legs. He yanks her panties down and lifts her onto the desk. She takes him in her hand, holds her finger over his mouth and says, "Caitlin's fired."

"What? No, I can't just fire..."

She squeezes him. "Fire her."

"Okay. Okay."

"Now."

He picks up the phone, presses the intercom button and says, "Caitlin, you're fired."

"WHAT!" They hear Caitlin scream in the other room.

"And no other girls."

"You're kidd—"

"Me only."

He looks into Sophie's eyes and nods. She's ready. "You are going to be a big star."

"The biggest." She says as she takes him in.

PLEASE LISTEN TO MY DEMO

EJ's mom's station wagon is sailing north through the last patch of green in Southern California—Camp Pendleton. The 5 freeway's four lanes of ribbed white concrete surrounded on both sides by the low hills and shrubs that used to be California. The Thunderstick three-song demo plays in the tape deck for the sixth time in a row. Kurt sits in the front. In the back, Spewing puts his leg across Ivo's lap. Ivo raps him on the shin with the skull-end of the staff of authority.

"OW! So, dudes, when we get in there, just let me do the talking," Spewing says.

Everyone laughs.

"You're a fucking used-car salesman. What do you know about publishing deals?"

"I know negotiation. That's what it's all about. Business is business."

"You don't know dick!"

"Hey, Elmer, just 'cause you went to college doesn't make you the smartest guy in the car."

"Yes, it does. And don't call me Elmer."

"You didn't graduate. Elmer."

EJ holds the wheel with one hand and reaches back and slaps Spewing with the other.

"Ow! It's true."

"Just because I had a little disagreement with the university—"

"Don't fucking worry about this college bullshit. You're going to be rock star. Let Ivo do the talking."

"He's right," Kurt says. "Ivo's gonna be the manager. He knows these things."

The station wagon shakes and rumbles as if the wheels are about to fall off. Spewing sits up, looks out the window, and yells, "Dude, I know that sound!"

"Yes. Is fucking California earthquake," Ivo says.

"Am I dragging a muffler?" EJ asks.

Outside the wagon, it's louder, sounding like Baja has broken off from the continent. Spewing spots something black and sooty and screaming approaching at a ridiculous speed. Spewing yells, "It's the Jovi. He's on the Roach."

The Jovi comes out of nowhere, pulls up a foot from the side of the station wagon, knocks on the window with his fist, and gives the thumb's up.

"Dude. See. It's the Jovi on the Roach! I told you he'd show!"

"It doesn't matter," Kurt says. "We don't need him."

"Yes," Ivo says. "We fucking do."

The band parks on Hollywood Boulevard and climbs the stairs into the gut of a small stucco office building. The Jovi's hair is windblown. He's decked in vintage leather. Outside the door, Kurt remembers the pomade in his pocket. He takes out a gob with his forefinger, rubs his hands together, and waxes back the sides of his curly hair. "You look like fucking pack of rats," Ivo says.

"You mean the Rat Pack."

"Yes. Is not what I say?"

Inside, the secretary leads the band to see Ivo's publishing connection, Mr. Grubman. The door opens and Ivo yells at a startled little man in stone-washed jeans. "Hey, you mother-fucker! I bring fucking tape."

Kurt pushes his hand through the pomade and gives Grubman a greasy handshake.

"Nice to meet you guys. I just got to say I love the fucking name of the band. Thunderprick is just right in your face—it's such a fuck you. I love it."

"Our name is Thunderstick."

"Oh. I guess that's okay. Maybe you guys should think about Thunderprick. It's got presence."

Ivo looks as if he's going to cough up his stomach.

Grubman puts the tape in his boombox and listens to half the first song, fast forwards to the second, listens to half, then fast forwards again to the next song, then hits STOP. Grubman turns to the Jovi and says, "So...who writes the songs?"

"I do," Kurt says. "I mean we all do. I bring in the skeleton."

"This rocks," Grubman says, and points at the Jovi. "This is what it's all about right now."

"Yeah. We did the tape in one day—"

"No man, this look. It's very... postapocalypse."

"What about the music?" Kurt asks.

Grubman laughs. "It sounds British. So..." Grubman turns to the Jovi. "What do you do?"

"I play guitar."

"The guitar kicks ass on this tape."

"Thanks."

"Me and him together," Kurt says, "been doing it for fifteen years. It's probably the best guitar playing you're ever gonna hear."

Grubman taps his finger on his desk. "Okay, so what can I do for you guys?"

"We want a record deal," Spewing says.

Grubman laughs. "I'm in publishing."

"We'd like to be published too," Spewing returns. "Books are cool. You get someone else to write them, right?"

EJ kicks him.

"Nah, man, this is music publishing. You know what that is, right?"

"So when we are talking 'publishing,' what exactly are we fucking saying?" Ivo winks at Grubman.

"Publishing royalties. Ownership of the songs. Payment for radio play."

"Yes, and what is that?" Ivo asks, and winks again.

FATHER FIGURE

Randy George died in the spring of 1986 at the NYU Medical Center on First Avenue. He had worked until he couldn't work any more. Sophie held his hand and met his parents who were quiet people from Missouri. They didn't really react. The father shook a little, but they were tough people accustomed to tragedy. Sophie walked down into an Irish pub and started drinking. When she came to, there was a plumber on her. She screamed for him to get off. He did. The more she drank, the more the world shed, until she reached a type of existential equilibrium. Nothing existed but now. She thought of Randy George's words to her, "Live in the now." She drank until there was nothing but now, and when she started in on the pills, even now started to slip away. Giuseppe Cassavetes hired strong young drivers to get her from place to place. They delivered the baggage that had once been Sophie Clark, to the shoots, to the plane, to the award show or benefit. And Giuseppe did not mind until one day she didn't look right. He called Jean. Jean asked Audrey, "What should we do?"

Audrey said, "Bring her home. Stick her in treatment. Dry her ass out." And they did. In December of 1987 Sophie checked in to the McDonald Center in San Diego.

WASTELAND

It is January of 1988. Thunderstick gigs in San Diego. Eric has worked his way into the whole set. The first time he plays "Rain Fall" with the band it is at Poseidon's Place, an inland bar stuck in the corner of a strip mall between a gun shop and a Noodle House. When they come out of the solo, Eric plays the three notes, his three notes, same as usual but this time Kurt continues his acoustic solo right through the chord change, right through the break. The two melodies play off each other, one simple and nostalgic, the other intricate and exuberant. The beauty of it takes Eric by surprise. Hot tears run down his face. The Jovi looks at him and smiles. "You're crying?"

"I'm not crying." Eric says and rubs his eye into his shoulder while keeping his fingers on the keyboard. "Something's in my eye."

"Why are you crying?" The Jovi laughs.

With the Jovi on guitar, Thunderstick defies classification. Kurt's deep baritone is definitely New Romantic, but the Jovi's chunky power chords belong in a rock anthem. Add a little synth pad in the background, and the whole thing is just different enough. Thunderstick opens for hair bands. Thunderstick plays Goth gigs. Thunderstick rips house parties. But we aren't getting any closer to a record deal.

Another night we are under the blacklights in Mission Valley, opening up for the Tom Zombie Orchestra. The audience is entirely Undead—white faces, black lips, black nails, black hair, black eyes. Thunderstick is set up in the middle of the dance floor, inside a chain-link fence. Space is limited. The Zombies have a lot of gear. Kurt looks out at the crowd and says, "You want dark, we go dark." He dusts off a few of the old songs about suicide and makes it hurt.

Through the whole set some dark prince in a black floor-length duster and a white frock is watching. When the stage lights come up for the Zombie's roadies, Kurt is relieved to see that the guy in the duster has an enormous foot-long wooden cross hanging around his neck. He extends a pale and frail hand from a lacey cuff and says, "I'm Vance Copeland. I want to manage you."

The giant wooden cross and Vance's calm demeanor make Kurt think Vance is some kind of holy man. "Are you from around here?" Kurt asks.

"I'm from Hollywood."

"What part?" EJ asks.

"Sherman Way."

"Sherman Way? That's the Valley," EJ says.

"It's North Hollywood," Vance answers. "I run a show, the first Monday of every month at the Lingerie on Sunset Strip. It's called 'Selling England by the Pound.' I want to manage you and showcase you and get you a record deal."

"We're not into that pay-to-play shit," the Jovi says.

"Yeah," EJ says. "I'm in finance."

"This isn't like that. You can play for free. Just let me be your manager."

"You want a contract?" EJ asks.

"No contract."

The Jovi says, "I'm down."

Kurt gets somber, eyes Vance's cross, and says, "We've been waiting for you, for someone who's right with the Lord."

"Dude," the Jovi interjects. "He's not a priest. He's a Goth."

Kurt silences the Jovi with an outstretched hand, nods at Vance, and says, "Okay. You're our manager. When's the first gig?"

NÄNCE'S PÄNTS

Dane is from a strong, nervous, Germanic line, always cleaning, never resting, often investigating. It's on one of these missions that Dane finds a pair of Nänce's jeans outside the Jovi's room. She picks them up, makes a coughing, puking gesture with her mouth, and screams. "Good Lord almighty! Eric! Get your big ol' ass in here and have a look at this."

Eric is watching a cartoon where the superheroes are half cat and half human. He is waiting for them to point their sword to the sky and say the magic words that make it pulse and swell. Dane says, "I mean it!" with a hint of fear. It gets him off the couch. He walks into the galley kitchen only to find Dane, stooped over a little pile of denim fabric, prying it open with a fly swatter.

"Look at this," she says.

Bending over, he looks into the jeans. They are yellow and green from the button fly all the way along the seam to the back of the butt.

"What is that?" He asks.

"That's kiki juice!"

"No?"

"That's juice from down there!"

"Holy shit! What's she got? That's not normal."

"*Shhh!* That's from sleeping with him. That's from sleeping with the Jovi. I told you how dirty he is," she whispers.

Eric laughs and looks at the stain again. "I gotta see this in the light." In the front room there are more windows, but it is a cloudy day, so he takes the jeans onto the brick walkway that substitutes for a front porch. He sees the swampy color in all its splendor. He is attracted and repulsed by the stain. It sets his imagination free. Warmth, activity, this is physical proof of passion. But what about the day after, or ten days after, would a dick itch relentlessly? Would it hurt to pee? Would there be a trip to the doctor? *Dane is right,* he thinks, *this is better than TV.*

"What should we do with them?" He asks.

"Put them back."

"We could wash them and leave them outside the door."

"Not with my clothes you don't!"

"We could take a sample and have it analyzed... scientifically." Dane laughs.

"Have you sniffed them?" Eric asks.

"No!"

"What'll you give me?"

"No, don't do it!"

"C'mon, just a little sniff."

"If you sniff those pants, I'm never talking to you ever again."

"Yeah, you will. You love me."

"Not anymore. Not if you sniff those pants."

Eric cautiously lifts the jeans toward his nose. Getting about six inches from the crotch, he breathes in ever so slightly. He recognizes the smell but cannot place it. He sniffs a little more. It is coming to him—something like Thanksgiving. Suddenly he feels a stinging sensation on his nose and he tastes a mouth full of denim. Dane has snuck up behind him and yanked the jeans over his head. Waving his stiff arms like some Frankenstein monster, he pulls off the jeans. And there is Dane—electric little-girl eyes. She turns and runs. With the jeans held tightly in his hand, he chases her down the street. She laughs hysterically. Her blonde hair swishes back and forth as she dodges his grasp. He tackles her on the fourth tiny yard toward the ocean and is going to rub the jeans in her face but thinks better of it. He rubs his own filthy face and hair all over her. She laughs more, grabs him by his ears, and puts her soft lips to his. "You're right. I still love you," she says.

"What are you guys doing with my jeans?"

They look up to see the silhouette of Nänce blocking out the sun. The left side of her short hair sticks up and out like a rooster's tail—classic bed head. She is wearing a tank top, nude-colored underwear, and nothing else.

"You wear underwear?" Dane asks.

"You guys are so weird!" Nänce grabs her jeans and walks back toward the house.

GIRL FROM THE NORTH COUNTRY

The Jovi, James, and Eric walk on stone steps through a garden at night to a door surrounded by anonymous smokers holding glowing orange embers. Against a wall, the open flowers of a yellow hibiscus appear suspended in midair. Inside the small wooden church, strangers assemble in a circle and talk freely about drugs and human bondage. The meeting begins. The person with the most overdoses starts the discussion with a story of impossible human redemption. Eric raises his hand, introduces himself, and tells of drinking from the bottle and running from the cops until he was outnumbered. The Jovi tells tales of coke and despair. Then she walks in. The group thinks it has seen her before, a college girl that has too much to drink, wakes up with a stranger, and does her penance here, only to laugh about it a month later over cocktails. Her glow, her smile, they tell the group: This can't be a woman who has suffered. How could they know? It's only on the inside that she is tattered.

The first time Eric sees her, nothing pops, but then he looks away and the rest of the world seems dull and gray. *Aristotle*, he thinks to himself as he looks back at her, *Aristotle would say she is a perfect form – Woman.* The Jovi notices her mouth and lips. They are so full they make one think of stone fruit after a rain, almost bursting. James catches her eyes. They are big, curious, and seductive all at the same time with that slightly sleepy look, as if it is always the end of a wonderful night. Eric is particularly enchanted with her nose. It is compact, architectural, efficient, and perfectly placed. It keeps her luscious mouth from being comic. None of them can miss her blonde hair. It has just enough curl to be angelic. Now the three of them know: This is what the winner of the genetic lottery looks like. It took the Earth in all it's horny machinations about eight to ten billion tries to create Sophie Clark.

Near the end of the hour, she raises her hand, and says, "I'm Sophie. Every time I get drunk or stoned something really bad happens."

The group laughs and nods. She appreciates it.

"I'm from here, but I've been living in New York since I was fourteen. And Paris too, I lived in Paris for a while. Oh yeah, and I lived in Milan. I don't know, my best friend died and I started partying hard, but it isn't partying when it isn't fun and you do it every day. And I like woke up and I was living with this fifty-year-old guy and he was my boss and then I found out some really weird stuff about him and my mom. It's kind of like the more I've tried to get, the less I have. And I'm always alone. I just don't want to be alone anymore. They said in treatment that I don't have to be alone anymore. I'm just really glad to be here, and I'm going to listen, thanks."

When the meeting is over, men and women converge on Sophie with numbers and names. They are hers, if she wants them. They seem to say, "You're with us. You're one of us. Be with us. Let us protect each other from the monsters in our souls." She turns away. She's headed for the door and then she stops and singles out the two– the Jovi and James. The Jovi smiles brilliant and beautiful. He says, "Let's go get some coffee and talk."

"Yeah," James adds, "let's share some feelings."

It's at the Pannikin where the two of them, James and the Jovi, vie for her attention. The Jovi is pulling ahead. "That was really deep, what you said, about the more you tried to get, the less you have."

"It's so true, right?" She asks and leans forward into the Jovi's green eyes.

"And I really could identify with what you said about your mom betraying you." James adds and nods sympathetically.

The Jovi reaches out and touches her hand. "You don't have to be alone anymore."

She's warming. It's going to happen. All is good. Until the night air is cut by a shrill woman's voice as it cries out. "Diiiirrrt dick! Theeere you are! You whore! I've been looking all over for you."

"Nänce. What's happening?" the Jovi says. "Look, Nänce, I want you to meet my friend Sophie. Sophie, this is my friend Nänce."

"Shit. I know you," Nänce says. "You're Sophie Clark. You're a supermodel. We should hang out. We have a lot in common."

TIME WAITS FOR NO ONE

When she was in rehab Giuseppe made an arrangement with Jean: Each week she would take a Polaroid of Sophie and send it via Federal Express to New York. Sophie was annoyed. "Why are you doing that?" She asked as the blue dot from the flash danced in front of her face.

"To show your father," Jean answered.

"Dad was here like two days ago. He wants me to invest in some more land with him."

"He loves these."

As Giuseppe watched the girl in the white frame turn back into Sophie Clark he readied himself for her return. He called her, asked her to come back to him. Sophie never said no. Sophie never said yes. He said, "I have something very big for you."

"All men say that." Even the receiver knew – Her smile was abundant again.

He laughed. "How would you like to be on the cover of *Sports Illustrated*?"

"Okay," She said.

Now, the day after she met the Jovi and James, she is on a plane, flying across the blue Pacific. She thinks about the two of them. She thinks she could settle down somewhere slow for a while.

CONFLICT

Vance Copeland doesn't walk, he glides, tiny steps beneath a black duster, like a geisha. He doesn't talk, he whispers. He is a professional. When Kurt calls his number, a woman answers the phone and says, "Mr. Copeland will be right with you. Vance, it's for you."

"Be right there, Mom," Vance answers in the distance.

Vance tells Kurt, "Monday, February first."

Kurt tells the Jovi. The Jovi says, "Whoa. Whoa. Whoa. I'm supposed to play with Smithy at the China Club that night. Can't do it, bro."

"Look, we're gonna get a record deal—a real record deal. This is how you said it works."

"I know, Kurt, but we went through this when I joined the band—if I have a paying gig…"

"And I told you that *that* music isn't real. This is real. You and me, we've been playing together since we were kids! Don't stop now. Not right before it happens."

"What's going to happen?"

"We're getting signed—you heard Vance."

"Dude. I will do everything I can to be there."

GIRLS ON FILM

Sophie knows the drill. She hasn't done it dry in a while, but still she remembers that even though she is only twenty, everyone on set is going to want her to be sixteen, and flirty with the straights, hopeful with the gays, and against that terrible thing that the government did with everybody else. She knows all the moves. She can skip through the air with her legs straight. She can be above you, a tower of legs and tits ready to step on your very soul. Or she can be below you, looking up, just barely covering her nipple with her perfect line of nails, as if she were shy. She's a pro. Everyone gets what they want, except for the photographer, who's a little aggressive with his hands. She shuts him down with a coy escape to her room and for Sophie that power over herself builds something beautiful on the inside. And that feels really good.

She knows that when she gets home she is going to have messages from both of them on her machine. She thinks of the Jovi like an inky black panther, his green eyes glowing in the jungle. She thinks of James, his strong features, his Buddy Holly style glasses. He's like a sexy professor in a foreign film. It's the panther, of course, who could resist? But then she remembers that girl – that Nänce girl – what she said – you whore – and Sophie thinks different.

THE FIRST LINGERIE GIG

Kurt shows up at Eric's house at noon. Kurt sits on the stoop, leaning back and knocking occasionally on the door, chain-smoking cigarettes and snuffing them out in the grass until, at one forty-five, Eric pulls up in his blue four-door BMW. Kurt barks, "We have a gig in L.A.! Where have you been?"

"University."

Kurt rocks his head from side to side and mutters in a sarcastic southern drawl, "Alright, how mellow—college kid gonna play a little rock and roll."

Eric wrinkles his brow and gets his stuff. The keyboard is gently wrapped in a towel and placed on the backseat. His amp fits in the trunk. They drive down to the beach, up the windy road to the boulevard—the two blocks to Kurt's apartment. Kurt brings an acoustic guitar, an electric guitar, and an amp down the stairs to the curb. They take out the keyboard and cram it all in. Then they place the keyboard on top of the amps. The back door won't close, so Kurt kicks it. Eric rubs the dent. They hit the road.

Down in Pacific Beach, Spewing flexes into his mirror, puts on his white blazer, slicks his hair back, and does some air guitar. He lugs his amp into the trunk of his bronze Benz. He slips his bass down the middle and heads for L.A. with a tallboy in his lap.

Downtown, EJ leaves work at five sharp, wearing a three-piece gray suit with braces. He hops in his mom's station wagon, which is already loaded with his drums, and heads north on the 5.

The Jovi wakes up at Smithy's around one, and they hop on the choppers and head over to Duke's for a late breakfast. Sitting at a table in the corner are two black-banged chicks done up in fetish leather like truck-stop hookers. Smithy tells the Jovi to do the usual. The Jovi walks over and says, "Hi, ladies. My friend Brian—you know—Smith—Smithy—would like to meet you."

The girls look over at Smithy. He shows his teeth and waves. They seem willing to party, but a little confused.

The Jovi takes the cue. "Smithy was in the Love Guns."

"Oh, of course!" the older one says. "I know Smithy. I did the wardrobe for the 'Heroin Hurts' video."

The younger one extends her hand. "I'm Mitzy. I'm a model."

"Tell it to Mr. Chubb," the Jovi says, and leads them over to Smithy's table.

The older one is Tiffany Tucker, wardrobe stylist to the stars. She spends her days shopping, returning, schmoozing, four-wheeling in the desert, getting treatments. She spends her nights dolled up in black leather and crosses. She knows everybody in L.A. She is thirty-five. The Jovi is now twenty-three.

Mitzy is twenty-six and totally over modeling. All she wants to do is act.

Smithy says, "Let's go for a ride."

They chopper up. Mitzy heads for the Jovi's Roach, but the long arm of Smithy grabs her and sticks her on the back of his hard-tail hog. Tiffany's tight leather chaps squeak as she wraps herself around the Jovi. Smithy takes them straight up the hill to his house. Mitzy calls for a cab. Tiffany wants to talk. Smithy gets bored and tells Tiffany: "I'm gonna go have a nice wank in my room. You want to watch?"

Tiffany shakes her black ponytail.

"Wanna help?"

Tiffany tilts her head to the side. "You are so cute," she says, "but no."

EJ shows up at the Lingerie at eight. Kurt walks up to him and says, "Where the hell is the Jovi?"

"Nice to see you too, Kurt."

Across town at the China Club, an announcer addresses a packed house. "Put your hands together for the Brian Smith Band."

There are hair flips, knee drops, loud sounds from amps, loud sounds from drums, loud sounds from Smithy. The drummer has a white towel wrapped around his neck as if he were a boxer. The bass player is skipping around in a little circle. The Jovi's solo is excessive. He backs into Smithy like a bear trying to scratch his back on a maple tree.

At nine Kurt goes catatonic. He's sitting on the floor below the graffiti-stained walls in the dressing room at the Lingerie. Eric approaches him. EJ says, "Don't. Leave him alone. He'll be fine."

At ten forty-one the Jovi is in a booth with Smithy, the Luig, and Tiffany Tucker at the China Club. The Luig looks at Tiffany and says, "You got any friends that want to fuck the Luig?"

"Who's the Luig?"

"Me. The drummer. Who else?"

Tiffany laughs at him.

"Hey! I may be a little guy, but God gave it to me where it counts."

"Are you some kind of tripod?"

"Hey, you laugh now, but you won't be laughing when I stick this thing in your ass!"

"Jesus Christ!" Smithy yells. "Too far, little man! Where's the civility? We are cavalier cave dwellers not French infantrymen."

"What time is it?" the Jovi asks. Tiffany tells him.

"Oh shit."

Eleven P.M. Vance puts a hand on Kurt's shoulder and says, "It's time."

Kurt looks up and sees Vance's giant cross dangling above his head. "Alright. Let's go. We start with 'Alone, Alone.'"

Kurt is up on stage. He throws his acoustic over his shoulder, hits the harmonics, and sings up high in a falsetto. EJ taps on his skins, building a crescendo for the opening. Spewing thumbs a muted bass string. Eric comes in very low with a two-note chord. A loud *screech* and *pop* break the serenity. Kurt looks over. It's the Jovi plugging in. The band takes it down a notch, lets it build again, and comes in together. The sound is steady and tranquil like a canoe breaking the sky's reflection on a placid pond.

The song builds to the Jovi's guitar solo. The band, the audience, Vance Copeland, the soundman, everyone is right there in the moment, especially Spewing. He is feeling it, jerking his head to the music so hard that the ash falls off his cigarette and down his shirt.

First song, second song, third song, fourth song, the band sounds good.

It's the fifth song, a hard-driving rocker, "My Minister." Spewing is locked in the pocket, plucking the bass strings with all he's got when his second string snaps. *No big deal,* he thinks, *I've got three strings left. I'll play this pig down to one.*

But it's different. Because the tension on the neck changes with three strings instead of four, his bass is completely out of tune. Kurt waves at him over his shoulder, motioning for him to be quiet. Spewing stares at a chick in the crowd and punches his pelvis into the back of his bass. He doesn't hear a note he is playing. Spewing pokes and pecks. Between vocal phrases, Kurt mule kicks Spewing. It catches him by surprise. Spewing dodges back and forth trying to avoid Kurt's Beatle boots while staying toward the front of the stage in the lights, where he can see the chick. Kurt is done with the verse. He turns around, chases Spewing into a dark corner, and commences to kicking, all while still strumming his Tele and not missing a note. Spewing squirts out and does a duckwalk across the stage—a bad Chuck Berry impersonation with the squat and the kick. Kurt skips up from behind and boots him hard in the ass. Spewing falls off the stage into the audience. Everyone cheers. The band keeps playing. Spewing crawls back on the stage and holds his arms up in a victory V.

WHAT'S INSIDE A GIRL?

Back in La Jolla, the phone rings at Eric's house. He picks it up.

A man with a British accent asks, "Are you in Thunderstick?"

"Yup."

"I'm a manager. I manage the Pet Shop Boys. I loved your show at the Lingerie. There was an element of danger. When's your next gig in L.A.?"

Eric walks in to the living room and tells the Jovi about the phone call.

"Element of danger? That guy hasn't seen anything yet. Did you tell him our lead singer's a human time bomb?"

"Nahh."

"Yeah, dude. If you listen carefully, you can hear him ticking. The other day he walked into the 7-Eleven and threatened to kill himself if the clerk didn't give him a pack of cigarettes."

"What'd the guy do?"

"What would you do?"

"Give him the fucking cigarettes."

"Exactly!"

"Why is Kurt like that?"

The Jovi shakes his head and says, "It's fucked up. He was a normal kid and then all this shit happened at once. He hit puberty. His dad punched his mom. Kurt fucked up his dad. They both got thrown in the can, and their mom baled."

"Baled?"

"She split, left Kurt and James with this derelict who lived next to the high school. She told Kurt that he was the same as his father. I think that's the part that really stripped the bolts in his brain. Some Ph.D. even wrote a paper on them, *Father and Son —Fucked*, I think it was called."

"What?" Eric laughs.

"But here's what's weird, after all that shit happened Kurt got really, really, really good at the guitar. He was like the rest of us, and then he wasn't."

"So?"

"It was like God blasted him with all that talent and all that turmoil and it fucking fried his hea—"

"Hey, Kurt!" Eric stares over the Jovi's shoulder.

Kurt is standing in the doorway holding his head in his right hand, looking sheepish. "What are you guys talking about?"

"It's the Franklin…How are you, bro?"

"Spewing's got to get another bass. He ruined that show. He made me kick him."

"Yeah. Totally. And maybe we should get a guitar tech—someone who could change out a set of strings and tune a guitar," the Jovi says.

"Who?"

"How about Talksley?"

"Talksley?"

"Yeah, Talksley of Loud."

"Talksley of Loud? What's with the Homeric epithet?" Eric asks. "Who is this guy?"

"Talksley's a local legend. You shoulda seen him when he was a kid. He was the baby-derel with the Mohawk who sat on top of the Pumphouse and threw rocks at tourists' cars as they drove by the beach."

Kurt adjusts his jaw, stares at the floor, and grumbles, "Everyone did that."

"Right? So Talksley wanted to see the Cramps in L.A., so he sat in front of La V on Prospect waiting for the valets to get a little lax. When some guy left his keys in his Porsche 911 and walked into the Whaling Bar, Talksley jumped in and took off. He was nearly in Hollywood when the phone rang in the car. Talksley picked up the headset and said, 'What.' The guy said, 'Hey, you little jerk, you stole my car.' Talksley said, 'Fuck, dude. This car is insane. How much did you pay for this thing? I'm going…one twenty right now. Oh my God. It doesn't even feel like it. I love this thing. How do I get one of these? Shit. I guess I already got one. Whose dick did you have to suck to get this car? Fuck. Whose dick do *I* have to suck to get this car? I love this fucking thing. The tachometer is all big and in the middle. Those fucking Germans, they don't care how…' So the guy starts screaming and actually hangs up on Talksley. Talksley parked the car on the Strip, saw the show, and after no one in the world would pick him up hitching, he took the bus home a couple days later."

"The Cramps—that's not even music," Kurt says. "Why steal a car to go see the Cramps?"

"Is this the kind of guy you want handling our gear?" Eric asks.

"He's clean now. Doesn't pull that shit."

"Will he work for free?" Kurt asks.

"I'll call him."

Ten minutes later, Talksley of Loud shows up on his Electraglide. He has long hair and a leather jacket with spikes on the shoulder. He looks like an extra in a Viking movie. The bike is a gleam machine, as thick and round as a jet engine, riding on two squishy whitewalls that look like marshmallows.

The Jovi says, "I want you to meet my roommate. Talksley, this is Eric. Eric, this is Talksley."

Talksley and Eric stare at each other as if they are looking in a mirror; they both have long brown hair to the middle of their backs with leather biker jackets.

"Nice to meet you, man," Talksley says.

"Same." Eric says and slaps the seat of the Electraglide. "The wheels on this thing could go on a Chevette."

"I could see you on one of these, Eric. You should get one," the Jovi says.

"Yeah, sit on it, bro."

Eric sits on it and says, "Let's ride over to the Pannikin."

They laugh at him. "Dude. I can't let you ride bitch. Take your car."

Kurt and Eric get in the blue BMW and follow Talksley on his Electraglide and the Jovi on the Roach. They pull into the 7-Eleven.

Eric rolls down his window and asks, "What are we doing here?"

The Jovi says, "Come in here, bro. I need some smokes and I want to show you something."

Kurt eyes the clerk and says, "I'm gonna sit in the car."

They walk straight over to the magazine rack. The Jovi looks at Eric and says, "Hey, man, remember Sophie?"

"How could I forget?"

The Jovi grabs the *Sports Illustrated* swimsuit edition from the rack, points at a goddess in a bathing suit on the cover, and says, "That's her. That's Sophie."

"Ooh. Baby likes."

"Hang on to your diaper, baby. We met her at that meeting. Remember? She's sober and she liked me, but she's fucking James."

"How does that feel?"

"I'm happy for my bro."

"Really?"

"Yeah, well quantity over quality, I guess?" The Jovi shakes his head. "Shit."

Eric takes the magazine. Sophie Clark stares at him. She's hazy-eyed, floating in the ecstatic dream of a tide pool; she is eclipsing the sun, descending from the sky to awaken Man; she is dressed in kelp as she emerges from a triumphant ocean. "I love my girlfriend." Eric whispers and repeats to himself several times over.

Talksley has his own copy. He stretches his arms out, holds up each shot, and exhales. "Hhhhholy shiiiiit! Would you look at that, man…would you fucking look…" Talksley grabs the magazine out of Eric's hand so he can hold up two of them. "Fuck. Dude. Nah. Man. Nah. That's just too much. That's just too fucking much, man. I can't…fucking no. Nah, man. It's that dick of his? It's gotta be that fucking dick of his. Does he feed that fucking thing mice, man? That's what I should ask the fucker. That's what I want to know. What do you feed that thing, man?

That's what…" Talksley keeps going. The Jovi looks wounded as the two Sophies sprawl out in front of him.

They chopper up and roll over to the Pannikin, take a booth. Spewing drops in the booth.

"Hey, how's your ass?" asks The Jovi.

"Oh, Kurt's boot? I liked it. Did you hear how loud they cheered for me? We should do that every show. What do you think, Kurt?"

"You need a second P Bass. That's what I think. It's not professional to have just one. Why do you have shitty equipment? Where's your priorities?"

"I think we should call you Hurt Me from now on." The Jovi turns to Kurt. "And you the Human Time Bomb. Hurt Me and the Human Time Bomb. That's a good name for a band. You guys need each other."

"We need a guitar tech." Kurt says, and motions with his fist in the air. "Someone who can switch out a broken string in the middle of a show. That's what we need." He turns to Talksley and yells, "WELL? ARE YOU GOING TO DO IT OR NOT?"

"Do what? Dude. This is the first I've heard of this. Shit… I mean…Yeah…you know…I don't know nothing about guitars and shit…but hell…"

"You can learn," the Jovi says. "You're rock, that's what's important. I can teach you how to change a string, set up my pedals, tune a guitar. What do you think?"

"Alright, I'm in…I'll be your guitar tech… I'm in… But, man…None of this…and, you know…I want to have…"

LOW PEOPLE IN HIGH PLACES

It's a sunny Sunday afternoon at the Pannikin. The lateral branch of the sweetgum tree is bare but speckled with bright light. The Jovi is in the corner, the seat of honor, holding court, holding coffee. Tiffany Tucker bends over, kisses him, turns, and struts to her Jeep. Her plastic pants squeak with each step. She extends herself on the running board, waves her hat in the air, and triumphantly drives off toward the 5.

"I love that look. What's she all about?" John DiBitonti asks.

"That's Tiffany Tucker. She's gonna get us a record deal." The Jovi watches her shiny black mane whip in the wind as she drives away. "Hey, man, what are you doing tonight?"

"Nah, man, tell me more…"

"She came down on Friday. Arrived at Eric's wearing jodhpurs and knee-high leather boots, like she was in a desert caravan or something. Dane, Eric's girlfriend, dug it. Eric asked Tiff what was up with the outfit. Tiff said she loved to ride. Eric said, 'Ride this' and slid her under my door. I was asleep. She's thirty-five—knows the drill—got naked. I gave her what she came for…"

"How was that?" DiBitonti asks.

"I don't know, dude. Have you ever had a chick that just, you know, really, I don't know how to say it…"

"Out with it."

"She stunk, man."

"Oh…" DiBitonti puts his hand over his mouth and chuckles.

"Should I tell her?"

"Yeah. Maybe she can do something about it."

"Anyway…so here's the part I don't know, after I give her my polluted load, she starts to put her little outfit back together. She reaches around under the sheets for her thong, it's dark, she finds some nylon and slides it on. She doesn't realize the thong ain't hers."

"Whoa, brother…"

"She says she wants some coffee, just then Kurt sticks his head in the door, fricking winces because of the funk, and says, 'Get up, bro. It's sound check.' We drive out to the La Paloma. Set up the gear. Do a song. And Tiffany is sitting there in the eighth row with Dane. The song ends. Tiff stands up in the dark and yells, 'Oh my God, you guys are good! I'm going to get you a record deal! When's the next show in L.A.?' 'March seventh,' I say. 'Consider it done,' she says. Spewing, our bass player, he lifts his hands up in the air, yells out, 'Record deal, baby!' And he leans back on the velvet curtain and disappears in a hole."

"What an asshole…"

"Yeah. Everyone laughed. Kurt finger-picked his acoustic and stomped his foot like a hillbilly and sang with a twang, 'Fifteen years old, played the Starlight Bowl. Spewing's on da stage, he fell in a ho-hole…'"

"So what about the thong?"

"After the next song, Tiff comes walking out of the bathroom, throws her chain wallet at me, and yells, 'Asshole!' I say,

'What's the matter, baby?' And she holds out a tan thong. 'This is the matter, *baby*!"'

"So whose was it?"

"Fuck if I know."

"So is she still gonna get you a record deal?"

"Yeah. Like I said, she's thirty-five, she knows the drill."

THE SECOND LINGERIE GIG

Vance Copeland has no idea that Tiffany Tucker just walked into the Lingerie with a real Hollywood manager, Adam Felder. Vance is too busy schmoozing a low-level, independent publishing person, who kind of liked the Thunderstick demo. Vance grabs a waitress by the arm, puts a five on her round plastic tray, and tells her, "Get him drunk."

"Take the five. Buy a hammer. Hit the fucker on the head," she says.

Vance pulls a ball of lint, keys, and two one-dollar bills out of his pocket, and hands her the money. She shakes her head and marches back to the bar.

Tiffany's entrance is grand. She is wearing a big-shouldered man's blazer with nothing underneath except a black lacy bra and a pair of bicycle shorts. On her arm is Adam Felder, a tall guy with frizzy hair. He wears Levi's and an expensive Japanese designer dress shirt, untucked. His hair is parted on the side; half of it combed back, the other half covering one eye. After the first song, he looks at Tiff and pushes the hanging hair behind his ear, revealing his hidden eye. He says "They're good" as if he's surprised, then the hair flops back in front of his eye.

After the show, the boys in the band approach him as he sits on a barstool with a beaming Tiffany Tucker by his side. Felder shakes each person's hand and says, "If I was going to be in a band, this is the band I would be in." He looks around the room. "I understand this guy Vance, the promoter, he thinks he's your manager."

Kurt nods and stares at the floor.

"Look, I'm not here to steal you guys away—you're gonna get a record deal—one way or the other. You're that good. You go with me, my job is to make sure it's the right record deal."

Kurt looks around as if he's ashamed of something, but then he lifts his head and nods at Felder. "I'm into it."

"Well, let's go somewhere where we can talk."

The band follows Felder's Porsche over the hill and into the Valley. They pull up at DCA world headquarters. The large and squat white building has black windows. At night it feels like an abandoned lunar outpost in a sci-fi horror film. They park illegally in front of the lobby. Felder tells the security guard he'll only be a minute.

Once inside, the band members start to realize it's just an office building.

"So…Do you work for DCA?" the Jovi asks.

"No. I used to work for Bernie Zupnik—you know Bernie Zupnik—the president of DCA Records. I used to work for Bernie's management company. Now I'm independent."

"So…Why's your office in DCA's world headquarters?"

"Me and Bernie, we go way back. Bernie let me keep my office. We sold more Brougham LTD records in the '70s than anybody. Now I manage the lead singer of Brougham LTD. Ron—you know—Headley."

Felder has platinum and gold records on the floor leaning against every wall of his office. He sits, pulls out an award, an MTV Astronaut from his desk drawer, and waves it in the air. He says, "This is for Ron Headley's video to 'Everybody Wants It.' Take a seat."

The guys survey the black leather couch. It's covered in platinum albums. EJ picks one up and looks at Felder. He says, "Just put that anywhere." EJ puts it in a black plastic trashcan.

"So who writes the songs?"

"Kurt brings in the bones. We put on the flesh," says EJ.

"Is that right?" Felder looks at Kurt.

"Yeah. I bring in the songs, then we flesh 'em out." Kurt's look goes from sheepish to fierce in a half second. He lifts his gnarled hands above his head and points at the Jovi. "Me and this guy have been playing together for fifteen FUCKING years. We played the Starlight Bowl when we were fifteen. We've been at this a while. You're just not going to find guys our age who have done that."

The Jovi takes a drag off his cigarette and says, "I do some gun-for-hire gigs on the side, but this is where my heart is."

"Oh, yeah. Tiff says you play with Smithy. Love Smithy. Smithy's great. But not like this. This is the real deal. How old are you?"

Nobody answers.

"C'mon. Each of you. I want to know." Felder points at Kurt. He answers, "Twenty-three." The Jovi: "Twenty-three. EJ: "Twenty-five." Spewing: "Twenty-two." Eric: "Twenty-three."

"You guys got a demo I can listen to?"

"Yup. Give it to him," Kurt says to EJ.

EJ hands Felder a cassette tape.

Felder puts it in his system and hits play.

After listening to it, he says, "Wow."

FATHERLY ADVICE

It's morning and Kurt's phone is ringing. He picks it up and his father, Wayne, says, "Meet me at the Pannikin."

His dad looks a little agitated, sitting in the corner beneath the spiky, flowering vines of the purple bougainvillea. He moves his head in short contained jerks and mutters and laughs to himself. Kurt sits next to him with a coffee mug and Wayne gets still. "Hey, dad."

Wayne watches four finches fly from a bush and attack a half-eaten muffin. Kurt waits for a response. None comes. "So, dad, you don't get mad any more."

"I get mad. I don't get even."

Kurt laughs a little. "I get mad then I get even."

"Causes problems."

"I know." Kurt nods.

"Meds. That's how."

"I can't."

"Kurt, some day you may do something you really didn't want to do. *They* told you to do it, but *they* don't go to jail. You do. My blood boils same as yours, uncontrollable. That's when you're ready to try the meds again."

"My wife left me when I was ON the meds."

"You're married?"

"I am."

"Where is she?"

"She lives at her mom's."

"Yup. Been there." Wayne looks around. "You walked, huh? Where's your car?"

"I don't have one."

"She took your heart and your car. Yup, been there too." Wayne gets a dark look on his face and continues in a secretive growl. "Women. They'll take everything you have."

Kurt's eyes move down to the coffee mug in his hands.

"You know, Kurt, you're her husband, you make the payments, that's your car. Take it back. Break the chain."

Kurt nods nervously. He knows Priscilla works the makeup counter at Macy's. He's never made a car payment.

Wayne wraps his hand around Kurt's clenched fist. "Kurt, let's get that car back. Let's go take back what is yours."

"How?"

"Let me see that!" Wayne leans over and grabs Kurt's keys off the table. "Look at this. What's this key to right here?"

"That's to Priscilla's car. She gave it to me when we got married. In case I needed to borrow it."

"And she never took it back?"

"No."

"Hah! There's the answer. Tonight we take back what is rightfully yours."

Night falls. Wayne and Kurt ride in the rattling diesel Rabbit out to El Cajon. Kurt gives the directions while Wayne hunches over the wheel.

"That's it right there." Kurt points to a brown Datsun B-210. Wayne stops down the block. Kurt hops out. Wayne floors it. The diesel Rabbit disappears into a cloud of its own smoke.

Kurt gets in the B-210, starts it, the little sewing machine engine hums. He's thinking about pulling away until he's stopped by a voice. For a split second he's afraid they have returned, the voices, but then he realizes it's his own voice. It is coming from the radio. Priscilla has been listening to his demo, the song he wrote for her. Something changes in his heart, and he starts to think that maybe Priscilla is the one person in the world who really loves him. He feels flush in the face. He turns off the car, walks up to the house, and rings the doorbell.

The door opens and there she is, softly backlit. Her big sad eyes tell him he has a chance. He is thinner and tanner and more man than she remembers. He puts out his hand and sings, "All of my life, I've been searching for true love…"

She hears the resonance, the undeniable truth, the ecstatic yearning, and starts to cry. That's it. They embrace. She takes her neatly packed boxes filled with plastic containers and Ziploc bags, puts what she can in the B-210, and they drive back to Kurt's apartment, man and wife.

LOADING OUT

Everyone knows that something big is about to happen. Word is out. Thunderstick has Felder. Thunderstick is getting a record deal. Thunderstick is building an army. There are many who want to fight. They show up in Eric's front yard—goat-eyed randoms standing in line to carry a guitar stand. People have seen it happening, in backyards, on the beach, in bars, at parties. It is obvious. Thunderstick is going somewhere, and for people such as Lunky the Loyal, Talksley of Loud, and Jesse the Giant, somewhere sounds pretty good.

It's a fact: There are those who want to be roadies. They are the same men who would've shown up on the dock just as a whaling boat was heading out to sea a hundred and fifty years ago. These men stand with all their worldly possessions stuffed in a burlap sack, ready to see the world and erase the past, ready to risk their lives and break their backs for adventure and nothing else. These are the men who feel the tentacles of boredom wrapping around their chests and squeezing out the very breath of their existence so tightly that they would rather enslave themselves to an exotic life than go on living the stale one they have for one minute more. These are the men who tamed the world. They are the hand in the glove. In the world of rock, they are called roadies.

No one better expresses this yearning than Lunky the Loyal. He has just gotten out of jail or the military or rehab. He shows up with the others at Eric's house. He doesn't have a car or a bike, but he's not the kind of guy who takes the bus. He stands as sturdy as a stone fence among the lesser applicants—his stark white hair sheared in a bowl cut, his muscles, his deranged cobalt-blue stare—all in all, a hell of a good-looking guy.

"I hear Thunderstick has a gig in L.A.," Lunky says in his silky birdlike voice.

"Yeah," Eric says. "It's load out."

"You guys need me up there. You need roadies."

"Thanks, but we've already got Talksley and Jesse."

Lunky looks at the ground, sad for a moment, then the lamp of genius lights up proudly above his head. "I'll be security."

Talksley of Loud was first. He's the Jovi's guitar tech. Kurt figured if the Jovi had his own roadie, he needed one too. So Kurt promised one of his oldest friends, Jesse the Giant, the position of road manager. Jesse had never managed a band, played in a band, or gone on a rock tour in his life. Still, on some primal level it makes sense that Jesse should be the Chief and everyone else the Indians. Jesse has a shirt with a collar, and the shirt is tucked into his jeans—he almost looks like he could have a job. If he walked into a motel and asked for five rooms, wearing that shirt with a collar, the clerk might give them to him. And Jesse is a natural-born alpha male. He's huge. He's athletic, the best to come out of La Jolla High for a good many years, but now, thanks to ten years on the marijuana maintenance program, he is the would-a-could-a-should-a guy. But he's good in a fight. He has hands like canned hams. He's famous for the two-hit fight: He hits them; they hit the floor. All of this together makes lesser men want to stand in line behind Jesse, but not Talksley. He's not used to taking orders. He is sitting on his Electraglide at the end of the silver metal ramp that leads into the back of a yellow box truck. Jesse the Giant stands at the side of the truck and yells, "C'mon, man! Charge it!"

Talksley of Loud revs the engine. "I don't know. bro... Not so smart, bro...My Harley in this thing? I think you should drive this fucking thing...You're the road manager...I'll ride my pig...I don't want to have to ride out backward, bro. You know what I'm saying. bro? Risk and reward, man... I don't know why it's always me...man...just because..."

"C'mon, Talksley! Start down there and just ride straight up the ramp. It's easy."

Talksley heads toward the ramp and stops.

Jesse yells, "Hey, that's a balk."

A Mercedes Benz pulls around the yellow box truck and onto the curb in front of Lunky and Eric. Spewing hops out, hair slicked back, wearing a linen pastel suit. "L.A., baby!" Spewing yells and shakes all the available hands. EJ slaps twice on the window from the backseat. Spewing opens the door and apologizes. "Sorry, dude. Child locks."

"What's up, EJ? What's with the backseat?" Eric asks.

"Spewing, the stupid fuck. He's got a surfboard in the front seat. He doesn't even surf. He's so fucking stupid. He was a half-hour late picking me up!"

"Hey, Eric bro, let me put my board in your yard. EJ told me no surfing. I'm down with that—but I wanted to check out the Bu, bro—Malibu." Spewing points to his car. "You like it? I jagged this nun!"

"Dude?"

"And I'm fucking Catholic! Put that in your rector!"

EJ marches to the back of the truck, looks in, and barks, "Hey, Jesse, where's the gear? We gotta hit the road! C'mon! Traffic!"

"It's coming. It's coming. I'm just waiting on Talksley here."

Talksley tries to untangle his long brown hair from the shoulder spikes of his leather jacket. "Bro, bro, bro, bad idea, bro, trucks are for gear, bikes are for riding, baaaaad idea, bro. Why's it always me? I don't want to drive a truck…"

Lunky lumbers over and eyes the back of the truck, then presents himself to Spewing, EJ, and Eric as they watch Talksley and Jesse from the curb. "Well? Can I go? Can I go with you? I'll do anything for you guys, security, roadie. I'll pack that truck, drive it, just name it."

"You clean?" Eric asks.

Spewing laughs.

"Since when is personal hygiene a concern around here?" EJ asks.

"Yeah," Spewing adds, "are you going to fuck him or let him carry your shit?"

"I mean drugs," Eric says. "Lunky's had a drug problem."

"I do drugs. I fall down. What's the fucking problem?" Spewing says.

EJ slaps him in the face. "That's the problem."

"I'm forty days clean today."

"We don't have a bed for you," Eric says.

"I'll sleep in the closet. It doesn't matter. You guys need me up there. You need security."

"Go ask Kurt," EJ says to Eric.

Eric finds Kurt sitting on an amp in the Jovi's bedroom, legs folded, an acoustic guitar in his lap. "You mind if Lunky is our roadie?"

Kurt shrugs his shoulders with a cigarette in his mouth and flows a flamenco version of "Iron Man." Eric takes this as a yes.

Eric walks back to Lunky, slaps his rocklike shoulder, and says, "You're in."

Lunky stares off in a dreamy way, puts his arms akimbo, and says, "I always knew it would happen."

"What happened?" Eric asks.

Lunky grins and walks into the house, lifts a hundred-pound Ampeg cabinet under one arm and a hundred-pound Ampeg bass head in the other, and marches out into the yard. At the back of the truck, Jesse the Giant and Talksley of Loud grow silent and still. It's the first time that all three roadies have been together. When Lunky's eyes meet Jesse's deep-set stare, the little beach street takes on the feel of the O.K. Corral just before a shoot-out. If there were neighborhood womenfolk, they would be closing the shutters and bolting the doors.

"What the fuck do you think you're doing? That's my job," Jesse barks at Lunky.

Lunky turns toward Jesse, the enormous weight of the gear making him move like a robot. "I'm just helping out," he says in his high-pitched voice. "I hear you're looking for someone to drive that truck."

"Yeah. Well?"

"I'm your man."

Jesse throws his head back, laughs, and barks: "Walk the ramp!"

Talksley pushes his pig backward into the street, and the metal bows under the weight as Lunky the Loyal follows orders.

EJ nods superciliously, snaps his suspenders, and says, "That's pretty good, but listen, Eric, I'm not paying that guy anything."

THE THIRD GIG

At the Lingerie, Vance Copeland can't believe the crowd that is assembling at his club. He sees A&R people by the dozen, lawyers, business managers, agents, the bearded president of Virgin Records, the tall bald president of Warner Brothers Music. All of Vance's unreturned phone calls seem to have finally paid off. His voice has been heard, and now Thunderstick is about to make him a player in Hollywood.

Vance glides his black duster and cross into the Lingerie dressing room. Tiffany Tucker and Spewing are sitting on the molting couch. Eric is nervously pacing and picking words and band names out of the graffiti-strewn walls. The Jovi and Kurt are standing together over a green rubber trashcan. Jesse is smoking a joint.

"Hey, guys! This gig is really coming together. Great crowd tonight." Vance suddenly realizes that the Jovi and Kurt are urinating in the trashcan. "Don't piss in there!"

Jesse laughs. "C'mon, Vance, lighten up. There's no bathroom in here."

"And you can't smoke that! Put that out."

Jesse smiles, extends his tongue, and puts out the joint in middle of it.

EJ storms in and grabs Vance by the shoulder and says, "We got a big problem. The soundman says he won't do our show."

"What?"

"He says he just recognized Kurt from some other show. I guess Kurt told him off. He says he won't do it."

"Won't do what?"

"The sound!"

The duster spins around and Vance glides out of the room with EJ in tow.

"I knew I knew that fucking guy." Kurt stands, slings his Telecaster behind his back, and makes for the door. "I'm gonna go show that guy a little something."

Jesse collars Kurt and pushes him down onto the sofa. "You're not going anywhere. Let us deal with this. If anybody is gonna do some ass kicking, it's gonna be me."

A minute later, Vance glides back in and says in a panic, "Who in here knows how to work a mixing board?" Vance points at Jesse. "You! Do you know how to work a mixing board?"

"That won't work," EJ says. "The guy took the cables out of the back of the board. I saw him do it."

"FUCK!"

Felder walks in, grabs Vance by the shoulder, and says, "What's this I hear about the soundman quitting?"

"Who are you?"

"Fix it!"

"I tried. I can't."

"Let me handle this." Felder walks out. EJ and Kurt exchange a look.

Eric stands up, looks in the trashcan, holds his gut and runs out of the room.

Tiff looks at Spewing and says, "Put your hair in a ponytail." Spewing nods feverishly.

Felder walks back in. "Everything's fine. You guys are gonna sound great."

"How'd you do it?" EJ asks.

"I just gave that guy a faceful of Hollywood."

"Sweet!"

"Yeah!"

"Right on!"

The band takes the stage in total darkness. Beady eyes gleam in the shadows. Everyone is here. Smithy, Dickey, Gary, attorneys, reps, agents, presidents, and pawns, and when Sophie Clark walks in the room on James Franklin's arm, blood is in the water. From the very first note of the show, every shark in town wants a bite of Thunderstick.

The show climbs from rock show to transcendence. Kurt takes off his shirt and holds his arms out wide, lifts his head to the heavens, and waits for the ascension in the middle of "Ice Blue Heart." The delicate strings of the Creator lift him. He gasps for air. EJ beats the living hell out of his drums. The Jovi chunks out thick rhythms on his guitar. Demons dance on Spewing's bass. Eric keeps his head down, long straight hair swaying back and forth like a hula skirt, playing synthesizer pads, string parts, bell sounds, and piano riffs.

AFTER THE SHOW

Felder walks up to a sweaty Kurt and says, "Who was that girl? The show was incredible. Get out of here. Let me deal with these assholes. I'll meet you guys over at the Cat & the Fiddle on Sunset."

"Cool."

The band drives over to the bar. The roadies load out the gear and join them. Lunky slaps Eric on the shoulder and says, "Good show, you got any food?"

"Let's get a couple cheeseburgers."

Lunky follows Eric to the bar. A meathead looks at Eric's long hair and says, "Hey, you look like a girl. Let's fuck."

Eric says "Bend over, bitch" under his breath and keeps walking.

The meathead has superior hearing. He grabs Eric's shoulder, pushes him, puffs out his chest, and says, "You want some of this?"

"No."

Lunky the Loyal steps out from behind Eric and says, "Yes." Lunky grabs the meathead by the collar with his left hand and hits him in the face with a jackhammering right hand. On the third punch, blood spatters all over the place. Lunky lets go and the guy falls in a lump next to a broken jukebox.

"Dude, you didn't have to do that."

"Yeah, I did. I'm not gonna let anything happen to you."

"Thanks, Lunky. You still want that cheeseburger?"

"Boy, do I."

Felder walks past the bloody blob, grabs Kurt and the Jovi, hugs them, and says, "It's on. This place is a dump. Let's go somewhere nice."

"Cool."

"On second thought, I want you guys fresh for our meetings tomorrow. Go back to the hotel. Get some sleep." Felder grabs Eric. "Make sure Kurt gets some sleep. Got it? Oh, and that keyboard intro thing was shit. That's not us. Whose idea was that?"

"Kurt's."

"Next time you're gonna do something stupid like that— don't! Got it?"

"Yeah."

"And make sure Kurt gets some sleep."

There's nothing magical about the Magic Hotel. It's a white deco apartment building built around a pool. Felder rents the band a two-bedroom suite.

"Where's the Jovi?" Eric asks.

"Fuck if I know," says EJ.

"Let's get some bitches in here," Spewing yells. "Pronto!"

EJ slaps Spewing's face. "We're going to sleep. You heard Felder."

Jesse approaches Eric. "You've got to see this."

In the bedroom, Jesse slides open the closet door and there is Lunky, propped up against the wall, sleeping chin to chest as if he were in the womb.

"Looks like a fucking baby," Jesse says. "Baby Huey maybe or that baby on Bugs Bunny who robbed banks. What a fucking crack-up. Where do you find these guys, Eric?"

"I met Lunky at a self-help group for addicts. He wanted a ride to an endless condo complex in Mira Mesa. I gave him a ride to a couch, someone he knew. I told Lunky to have hope. Lunky told me 'Nice car' and rubbed the dash with both hands."

"Yeah. Whatever."

Kurt closes the closet door and says, "I need to sleep."

Eric strips to his underwear, crawls into the single bed next to the closet and rubs the closet door with his free hand. Kurt takes the bed by the window. Jesse kicks EJ and Spewing out of the living room and takes the couch.

Eric falls asleep, his snore an unpredictable nasal gasp.

Kurt lies in bed staring at the ceiling. He gets pissed. "You're fucking snoring!"

"Sorry, sorry, I'm sorry," Eric says in a daze. Afraid to sleep, he stays awake and lays perfectly still, eyes closed to little slits as he watches Kurt.

Kurt sleeps for fifteen minutes, then gets up and smokes cigarettes and stares out the window, sleeps for a half-hour, gets up, smokes, stares out the window, sleeps for an hour, gets up, smokes, stares out the window. This time he sits longer, opening and closing the glass slats of the window, smoking and watching the houses in the Hollywood Hills as they appear and disappear.

In the morning Felder shows up with Tiff and says, "C'mon, babe. Make 'em look sharp. We got meetings and you know the rule. People hear what they see."

"Where's the Jovi?" Tiff asks.

"He's not with you?"

"*Hmmf*," she says.

Tiff works a little styling magic. Everyone in black. Spewing's hair in a ponytail. Vintage leather jackets. They look like the original bikers. Not the smelly, hippie, Henry Fonda fuckers of the seventies, but the crisply dressed assassins of the 1950s. They all have on black leather collarless jackets, with lace-up black leather vests on top of that, plus the strange and dressy addition of pleated black trousers, tight at the ankle, topped off with Beatle boots.

The four present members look perfect, still no Jovi.

Lunky walks out of the closet looking good. Tiff looks at his platinum bowl cut and mirror shades, and says, "This look is very now. He should go with the band."

"I like it. It'll confuse the hell out of the suits," says Felder.

Lunky slides a giant hunting knife into his belt and nods.

Jesse slaps his forehead, says, "What the fuck?" and leaves the room.

Kurt lifts his hands and says, "Where the fuck is the Jovi?"

Like magic, the Jovi walks in, his hand in the back pocket of a blue-eyed, dark-haired vixen. "What's up, guys? This is Alexandra. She really dug our show. She's…" He notices Tiff and her souring expression. "Hey! Tiff! What's up? Great to see you."

"Dress yourself, asshole." She dumps some clothes on the floor and starts for the door. She grabs the knob, stops herself, turns, and says, "Good luck, boys."

Felder looks at the Jovi. "You look rock. Let's go." He looks at Alexandra. "Can sweetheart find her way home?"

"Totally," she says, and tosses her hair.

Felder and the Jovi ride together in Felder's Porsche. The rest ride in Spewing's Benz.

The band arrives at Warner Bros. The whole record division is assembled on a giant redwood deck. It's a party for Depeche Mode; their latest album has just gone platinum. Industry people stand around, drink box wine, and slap one another on the back while they wait for the band to arrive. Thunderstick walks in instead. The vibe is strong. We take the place over.

Depeche Mode arrives and they look like four cancer patients from Manchester next to Thunderstick. Lunky the Loyal puts himself in a visual lockdown with their bodyguard, a short and wide tough guy with a shaved head. The two of them vibe each other until everyone in the place can feel it. The Warner security men, in their brown polyester pants and matching baseball caps, begin to circle Lunky. Lunky doesn't budge. Someone walks over to Felder and asks him why Lunky has an eight-inch knife. Felder laughs, walks over to Lunky, takes the knife, and hands it to a surprised security guard. Lunky unfolds his thick arms and puts them on his hips. The bald guy walks away. The president of Warner Bros. wants to meet the band.

Down in some A&R guy's office, a dark room crammed with rock posters, they begin the dissection of the band. "Who writes the songs?" "What producers do you like?" "Where do you play?" "How long did the demo take you?"

Virgin Records has a little airy office building all to themselves in Beverly Hills. They have a crunchy president, complete with twinkling eyes and a health-food beard. With his legs folded neatly beneath his cupped hands and his hands under his potbelly, he is like the Buddha with an attitude. He sarcastically asks the band, "So, do you ever load up the Benz and go out on the road?"

Something clicks in Kurt. He ashes on the floor, leans forward, points his cigarette at the beard, and says, "Hey, that's not my car. It's not like that for me. Don't go thinking I'm some spoon-fed just 'cause I'm from La Jolla. Nobody ever gave me anything."

Felder says, "Hey, hey, guys. It's not about the car. It's about the music."

The beard says, "Oh, I just thought, you know, maybe...So, who writes the songs?"

In the parking lot Kurt puts his arms up with his hands angled oddly out to the side and says in a fake southern accent: "Alright, look at me, how mellow, I'm a hippie, but you're fired. I'm the president of a big company, but I hate money. I hate it so much I think I'll give a bunch of it to Bob Marley's son 'cause he's got dreadlocks. Can't play a note, but he's got a cool haircut! Alright! How mellow! Look at me! Rasta-fucking-phony-ian!"

The band laughs. Felder tells Kurt, "Don't worry about it. He likes us. That's just his thing."

Spewing's Benz follows Adam's Porsche into the Valley to DCA. It's time to meet with Bernie Zupnik. Standing by the elevator at DCA, Felder looks at the band and says, "Act like we're too good for DCA. It'll drive Bernie nuts."

Bernie Zupnik is tiny and he never stops moving. His office is done up in cocaine chic—mirrored walls, white leather couches, white side tables, white carpet, and giant diffused photos of his young wife and newborn child. The band spreads out like oil on the white couch. Lunky stands by the door, meaty arms and mirror shades. He reflects a wide-angle version of this white room. Felder shakes Bernie's hand and says, "We worry about your presence in AOR."

Bernie says, "Drinks? Drinks anyone? What about Brougham LTD.? You remember them. You're not that young. We made them a supergroup. Look what we did for the LTD."

Felder says, "That was a long time ago."

"What about Lynyrd Skynyrd? We made them the biggest band in the world."

"Lynyrd Skynyrd? I got that tape," EJ says. "Half of 'Freebird' is on side A and the other half is on side B. You guys cut 'Freebird' in half trying to save a dime on tape?"

"Dude. 'Freebird'?" Spewing starts to laugh. "That's fucked up, dude."

"That was a long time ago," Bernie says. "What about Jody Watley? She's a brand-new platinum act."

"Jody Watley sucks," Eric declares.

"She doesn't suck," Felder says. "She's just not rock and roll. It's apples and oranges."

"That demo. Your demo. I'll release it as an album. What do you think of that?"

The band smiles.

Felder stops the joy. "We want to record an album."

"Okay, fine, that's what we do."

After the meeting, EJ looks at Eric by the elevator and says, "Eric, you're so stupid, what the hell? Jody Watley sucks?"

"Sorry, dude."

The elevator arrives. The band steps in. The door closes and Felder turns, smiles, and says, "Are you fucking kidding me? That little sentence just upped the deal a hundred K."

SEEING STARS

Thunderstick plays a Butterhead event. In San Diego, the Butterhead Club guys rule the night in 1988. They are a group of young men who dress like Robert Palmer and Bryan Ferry—ties and blazers with square shoulder pads. They dance like marionettes missing a string, butter their hair back like rumrunners, and make it their life's work to know every hot chick in town. The international Butterheads call people they like "motherfucker," as if it were a surname. Little nymphs and fairies pack the front of the stage and look up with adoring eyes at Kurt, who is cool and confident, playing only his happier songs. The Jovi sucks his cheeks to the bone and looks longingly up into the stage lights.

After the show, they are standing in the convention-hall kitchen when Priscilla walks in and puts her arms around Kurt. She has been back stocking the refrigerator with frozen burritos and cigarettes for a couple weeks now, and Kurt is strung together and content in a way no one has seen since he was a kid.

When James and Sophie walk into the bright fluorescent light of the kitchen holding hands, every Butterhead takes notice. "Oh my God, the show was really good," Sophie says to Kurt.

"It was like...I wanted to be up there." She laughs. "Can I play tambourine?"

"This is how it's supposed to be," James says to Kurt, Priscilla, and Sophie. "After all the shit you and me have been through, we put our lives back together." He squeezes Sophie in closer. "This is how it should be. You with your wife. Me with Sophie. Your music."

Kurt nods. "That's what fifteen fucking years sounds like!"

The Jovi walks in. Sophie throws her arms up in the air, starts to purr, and wraps herself around him, stepping up onto her toes and pressing with her chest and stomach. Then she releases the Jovi slowly, letting her hand slide down his sleeve. She is still holding his hand when she turns back to James and kisses him long and wet and openmouthed.

THE WOODEN STAKE

Kurt, the Jovi, and Eric drive up to the Valley in Eric's BMW. They discuss music and music videos. Kurt gives his video ideas for each song. "For 'Rain Fall' I think some young guy just trashes his home. Then he has to live on his own, on the street."

"That's kind of like your idea for 'Alone, Alone.'" the Jovi says.

"And 'Ice Blue Heart,'" Eric adds.

"Look, man. I want to help people who are lonely and sad and fucked over by the world. I don't want to be one of these bands that doesn't do anything good!"

"I hear you, Kurt," Eric says.

"That's really cool, Kurt."

They pull up in front of a seventies tract home and walk the flagstone like assassins. Inside, they fire Vance. He takes it well, sitting there in his bedroom, looking out at his mom's zinnias in the backyard. Kurt says, "Felder is going to help you out," and he believes every word of it. "Hey, you'll always be the guy who discovered Thunderstick."

Vance takes off his cross, cups it in his hands, and says, "It's gonna take me a second to swallow that one."

They drive over to Alexandra's apartment in the Hollywood flats. Spewing and EJ are waiting there. "What's up, dude? Has he called?"

"No."

"Where's Lunky?"

"He's cleaning my kitchen," Alexandra says.

Everyone looks at the speakerphone.

Finally it rings.

On the other end of the line, Felder asks, "Is everybody there?"

"Yes."

He whispers in a low porn-star voice. "I'm holding something in my hand, and it's making me very happy. What I'm holding. It's big. It's really big. Maybe it's too big."

The Jovi laughs and slaps Eric on the shoulder. "What the fuck is it?"

Felder snaps into his serious voice and says, "It's a deal memo. It's for seven records. It's for seven hundred and fifty grand right off the bat. It's fucking huge. It's the biggest record deal any unsigned band has ever been offered. I've outdone myself."

The band erupts. They jump up and down. They cheer. They tackle each other. Spewing and EJ run outside and roll around together in the grass. Tears well up in Kurt's eyes. Eric asks, "What's wrong, Kurt?"

"I can finally take care of my wife."

Felder yells, "Take care of yourselves. You guys call me tomorrow. I got work to do."

The band hangs up. Kurt says, "God did this. God did this whole thing. God got me off drugs. God gave me the songs. God got us the record deal."

"C'mon now, Kurt," EJ says. "Give yourself a little credit here. We've been doing this our whole lives."

"We have," the Jovi adds.

"No. Let's pray! Take a knee."

"Dude." Spewing says. "Doesn't the devil kind of control rock and roll? We don't want to piss him off, do we?"

EJ slaps Spewing. "Shut up. Kurt's right. Let's pray."

Thunderstick takes a knee and holds hands. Kurt closes his eyes and says, "Dear Lord, I told You before—You got me off drugs—now everything I do—everything we do—is going to be for You. I won't let You down. Let us bring You glory in our music and honor in our acts; let nothing take us from You. Amen."

THE TEN-YEAR DEAL

The day Thunderstick inks the deal is a perfect Southern California day, endless blue sky, a crisp sixty-eight degrees. Felder meets us in the plaza at Century City below the skyscrapers that poke at the blue before being bounced back.

"I can't go in there with you. The guy's name is Josh Stein. He's your lawyer. He's got the deal on his desk. Let's do dinner."

"Thanks, Felder." Every band member shakes his hand.

Kurt, the Jovi, EJ, Spewing, and Eric walk across the plaza on the geometrical patterns created by different hues of concrete, past the granite water fountain, and into the gut of a black-glass building. The elevator takes them up and up and up. Stein's firm has a whole floor. The receptionist smiles. "You must be Thunderstick."

Stein appears and greets them one by one with handshakes. "Come into the conference room," he says.

Mahogany doors open and from the fortieth floor you can see the whole dream and the whole mistake of L.A. Opposite the panoramic view, the conference room is lined with five Miró paintings. A few brushstrokes on white canvases—these paintings are like giant signatures, signatures that are very valuable. Twelve leather loungers surround a mahogany-and-black-marble conference table. Stein can't stop smiling as he drops piles of paper in front of the band.

"You're our lawyer. Should we sign this thing?" asks EJ.

"You guys are getting a point less than what Michael Jackson gets on his albums. For a previously unsigned band, this deal is unprecedented. It's up to you, but I say sign it."

Secretaries witness as Thunderstick puts pen to paper. EJ says, "A seven-record deal. Well, I guess this is what I'll be doing for the next ten years of my life. I'm going to be a rock star."

PART TWO

"Give the finger to the rock and roll singer as he's
dancing upon your paycheck."
—Beck

QUIT YOUR DAY JOB

Back home in La Jolla, the band waits for marching orders.

The Jovi wanders out of his room around noon. Eric pours him some coffee and says, "I am a little nervous, you know, about the studio."

"Dude. We're the Magnificent Seven. We just do our part. I throw knives and sling leads. You're like the guy who wires explosives, only you lay down the synth pads. Just assume the position. Act like you belong there. And if you can't cut it, I can cover for you. But fear not, you'll pull it off—and never bring rubbers on tour."

"I wouldn't do that. I got Dane."

"Really?"

"Yeah."

"You know, God makes something beautiful on every woman. For some it might just be their big toe or their left nipple."

"So?"

"That one thing finds me, man. The chicks are grateful for a guy who can find beauty like that. You should try it."

"So why no rubbers?" Eric whispers.

"If you bring rubbers, you'll end up fucking 'em. You don't bring rubbers, you'll just want them to blow you. Less shit to worry about if you just have them blow you."

"Yes, of course, sensei. No rubbers on tour."

"Dude. Can you do me a favor? There's this girl in my bed and I have no idea what her name is. Can you go in there and have a look? Maybe you know her."

"Totally."

Eric opens the door, puts his nose to the air, tiptoes to the bed, examines the tussle of hair at the top, and takes a step back toward the door to the galley kitchen. He grabs the door handle and starts to turn it ever so slightly when he hears a soft, sleepy voice say, "Who are you?"

"Hey, I'm the Jovi's roommate, I was just looking for somethi—"

"Come here."

Over at the bed, he extends his hand. "I'm Eric."

"You're in the band, aren't you?"

"Yeah."

"That's rad."

"Yeah."

"You want to snuggle?"

"Yeah. I mean. No. I've got a girlfriend."

She pulls the sheet back and says, "That's too bad. It was nice to meet you, Eric. Send your roommate back in here."

Eric pushes his hand under the covers until he finds warm skin—her stomach, he thinks. He tries a little Jovi magic: "You got really pretty eyelashes. Did you know that?"

She laughs.

LET'S GET PROFESSIONAL

DCA rents four furnished one-bedroom corporate con-dos at the Cokewoods in Burbank, and the band and roadies move in. The rooms are divided—the Jovi and Eric—EJ and Spewing—Kurt and Jesse—Lunky and Talksley. Talksley whines. "Fuck, dude, no. Why's it always me, man. I want to stay with the Jovi, bro. I don't want to stay with Lunky. He's a stray. I don't know where he's been, bro."

At the end of a grease-stained parking lot sits a long, flat tin-roofed industrial building. It looks like an auto shop. It's Gates rehearsal studio.

A line of choppers is parked on the left and a 1971 glossy-black Chevy Chevelle with Cragar mags is parked on the right next to Felder's Porsche. A muffled version of "Love Removal Machine" blasts from room B.

Eric nods his head to the music and says to the Jovi, "That's a pretty good cover band. They sound just like the Cult."

"That's no cover band, bro."

Felder walks out of room A. His frizzy black hair looks gun gray in the sun. "Welcome. We're in here."

They follow Felder through a large sliding industrial door into a room in which light disappears—black floor, black walls, black velvet curtains. There is a stage, bigger than any stage at any club Kurt has ever played. The gear is set up, stage lights, side monitors stacked eight feet high, the mixing board has forty-eight channels.

"Is this where we're recording the album?" Spewing asks.

"No, you dumb shit. This is a rehearsal studio," EJ yells.

"This place is so satanic. I dig it."

Felder pushes his hair behind his ear and says, "I booked this place out, booked it solid for the next two weeks. Anytime you want to jam, practice, screw chicks, whatever, this place is yours. This is Ralph, your soundman." He points at a guy with long, stringy blond hair.

We take the stage. Felder sits on the tweed couch. After the first song, Kurt walks off the stage over to the soundman and hugs him. "Thanks, bro. I've never been able to hear my vocals like that—ever—thanks."

Ten minutes in, a tall man in a three-piece suit walks in, puts his briefcase between his knees, and sits on the sofa next to Felder. Beneath his rounded snout, he is smiling broadly.

Waves of sound wash over the two of them until Felder sticks one finger in his ear and holds his other hand over his head. The band stops. Felder says, "There's someone here I want to introduce you to. He's your money."

"I'm Bill Wellington," the man in the suit says, as he stands to shake hands. "Adam tells me you guys want to hire us as your business managers."

EJ raises his hand. "Actually this is the first I've heard of this."

"Well, let me tell you what we do. We pay all of your bills. We pay your taxes. We give each one of you an American Express Gold Card and a checking account." He taps his briefcase. "You guys spend accordingly. We pay the band's big expenses that have to do with touring. We collect your royalties. You send us receipts and we take them off your taxes. Send them to us in an oily brown bag if you want, we don't care. Just send them to us. You guys are free to create. You don't have to worry about the lights going out because you forgot to pay the electric bill. You don't have to waste your time with the bean counting. We count all the beans for you."

"What's in the briefcase?" Kurt asks.

"Your contracts with us, your Gold Cards, and your checkbooks."

"I'm in," Kurt says.

"Whoa," says EJ.

"I'm in too," the Jovi says.

"Hey, bro. Can I get some paternity insurance?" Spewing asks.

"What's that?"

"David Lee Roth has it. It's in case some chick says I gave her a baby."

"I'll look into it," Wellington says.

EJ marches up to Spewing and slaps him.

Spewing cowers then crows: "Oh, don't worry about it, bro, all I really want is a Harley and a bitch to suck my dick!"

Everyone laughs.

Bill Wellington opens the briefcase. The band comes in close. Five golden American Express cards. The contracts are signed.

"The money is in. Here are your checkbooks. We put twenty-five grand in each of your personal accounts. Don't spend it all in one place."

"Yeah!"

"Right on!"

"Yes!"

"Don't do it!" EJ barks.

Kurt grabs his checks and says, "It's done. Spewing, come here. You know cars. You're driving me over to get one. Now!"

They drive down Lankershim to a boutique showroom. Kurt spots a black mint-condition 1968 Mustang Fastback.

Spewing says, "Bro, bro, bro, don't tip your hand, let me negotiate."

"That's the one. That car is mine."

Kurt drives the black Mustang Fastback off the lot. He stops at a 7-Eleven. "You guys take checks?" he asks the clerk.

"Yep."

Kurt walks through the aisles loading up on frozen burritos, Zippo lighters, smokes, peach-flavored Kearn's Nectar, chips, cookies, eye drops, nasal spray, T-shirts that say JUST DO ME, and a trucker's hat that says JUST FOR THE HALIBUT.

"That'll be eighty-six dollars."

Kurt writes the check.

Outside a bum yells, "Hey buddy! How's about a little something for a Vietnam vet?"

"You ever seen *Missing in Action 2*?"

"What the fuck is that?"

"Here, man."

"What are you doing?"

"Writing you a check."

"Make it out to my name."

"What is it?"

"Blank."

The Jovi trades the Roach and fifteen grand for a purple hard-tail, with ape hangers and a suicide shift. The bike is all chrome with steel-braided brake lines. The Jovi drives it up onto the stage.

Jesse claps his hands.

Spewing says, "Right on, bro!"

Kurt drives the '68 Mustang Fastback into the studio. Kurt is now wearing a gray turtleneck sweater with a black leather blazer even though it's the middle of summer. He points at the Jovi's chopper and yells, "Get that fucking thing off the stage! We're not fucking Van Halen!"

"What'd I say about spending it all in one place?" says Felder

"Look at my Stang."

"Yes, Kurt."

"Well?"

"It's nice," Felder says.

"Nice? It's cherry!" Jesse yells. "Elmer Junior! Where's your new ride?"

"I'm gonna hold on to my money."

"I need a fucking Harley," Jesse yells.

"Yeah, let's get Jesse a Harley," the Jovi says. "Harleys for everyone! Send DCA the bill!"

"Sounds great," Lunky says. "I would really like one too. My dad was the president of the Hell's Angels."

"The band isn't buying anyone Harleys," EJ yells. "Who's gonna make a food run?"

"So, Felder, let's talk about producers," the Jovi says. "Did you talk to Glyn Johns?"

"No. He's in Gstaad."

"What about Mutt Lange. Did you call him?"

"No. He's in Bora Bora."

"What about George Martin?" Kurt asks.

"You guys don't want George Martin. What's he done?"

"The Beatles!"

"Lately! What's he done lately?"

"So, who's going to produce our album?" Eric asks.

"You don't want some big producer to come in and ruin your songs, do you, Kurt?"

"I don't want anyone to ruin our songs. But I mean George Martin—he's a genius. Mutt Lange—that guy totally gets the rock sound. Glyn Johns—he's more of that mellow seventies rock thing, but he's done some good Stones and Zeppelin classics. I want to work with someone good."

"I've got just the right guy in mind."

"Who?"

"Me."

"What the fffff...," EJ stutters.

"I can produce you guys. You heard Bernie. He would've released the demo as an album. We can do better than that. It'll be you guys, me, and this great producer who does all of Neil Young's albums—Kostas Greco."

"I don't know, Felder. I'm not so sure this is a good idea," Kurt says.

"You guys don't need changes in arrangements, you don't need new instrumentation, you just need great takes and great sounds. Me and Kostas, we can do that."

"Look, Felder. If you're talking about Thunderstick produced by Thunderstick, I'm down with that," EJ says. "But what have you ever produced before."

"Everyone's gotta start somewhere."

"Shit…" EJ shakes his head.

"Who got you the biggest record deal any unsigned band ever got in history? Well? Who did?" Silence. "I did. The buzz, the hype, the deal—who produced all of it? Now if I can do that, I can do this."

Kurt looks as if his head were in some invisible vice. He sits down in his Mustang, looks at the steering wheel, and rubs his ears and opens his jaw. "Can you at least call George Martin?"

Felder squats next to him and puts a hand on his shoulder. "It's gonna be fine."

EJ says, "Hey, Felder, give us a little alone time here."

"Fine. Of course. You guys talk it over." Felder starts for the door. "You want to record the album in two weeks, right? You want to be on shelves by September when the kids go back to school, right? You want to keep your own sound, right? Look, it's June already. You want to keep on schedule, keep your own sound, make a great record, then it's gotta be me and Kostas and you. We'll make a great album. I guarantee it."

"Just give us a minute. Okay?"

"Yeah. I've got stuff to do anyway. Think it over. Hey, meet me at this club tonight. You're on the list." Felder scribbles on a card and hands it to the Jovi. "Talk to these guys. You'll do the right thing. I'm sure of it."

EJ closes the big sliding door behind Felder and says to the wall: "This can happen, but we've basically got to produce it ourselves. We've got to keep all our hands on the mixing board, just like at Ivo's."

The Jovi sits on his chopper and says, "Yeah, dude. A real producer would be ideal, but it's not like this is going to be our only album. If it means we could be on the road in September, that would be totally worth it."

Kurt lifts his head, holds his hands out wide, and says, "We control the album and it's going to be good. I've heard Felder play guitar—musically he doesn't know dick. I've never heard of this Kostas guy. Felder knew enough to sign us so he must know something."

Spewing and Eric sit obediently. Lunky wipes off the Jovi's chopper with a white rag.

"I can't believe DCA would go along with this," the Jovi says. "They got a lot of coin invested in this band—you'd think they'd want a surefire hitmaker on the board."

"I guess Felder's got Bernie in his back pocket," EJ says.

JAM WITH THE MAN

Broad five-way intersections, liquor stores with neon signs behind yellowed plastic windows, the remnants of railroad tracks, and smog like a yellow film—it's early summer in L.A., not really summer at all. Every day is warm at some point, cool in the evening, leather-jacket weather at night. The coast is gray all day. The San Fernando Valley is endless, utilitarian, work happening in alleys and lots and warehouses. Cars are repaired, painted, filled with fluid. Tortillas are rolled flat and round, heated, then covered with beans and rolled into cylinders. Stage lights are fastened to racks, plugged in, and switched on to illuminate glory. Clouds blow in from the beach and are stretched thin over the mountains, evaporating into wisps in the warm air.

Each day Thunderstick plays music and grinds a late lunch. Each night Thunderstick goes to clubs, then heads back out to Gates's for another jam session or they make their way to a coffee shop for a late-night breakfast.

At the International House of Pancakes on Sunset at 3 A.M. on a Wednesday, the band notices Neil Young sitting in a booth across the room. "Hey, Felder, isn't that Neil Young over there?" the Jovi asks.

Felder cranes his neck. "Yup." He is out of his seat and over with Neil, waving for the band to come join him. Neil is scruffy. Everyone in the band shakes his hand.

"Hey, man, you want to jam with us?" Kurt asks.

"Yeah. When?"

"How's about now."

"Yeah. Now is cool."

Neil drives a 1954 Cadillac Eldorado convertible. The car is cranberry red with a silver undercarriage from the door to the tail.

"This car is the tits!" Spewing yells in the parking lot at Gates, and tries to shake Neil's hand.

Felder laughs.

Neil borrows Kurt's Tele and plugs in. The jam starts. The blues. Spewing tries over and over to hand Neil a pick. Neil shakes his head no. To get him to leave Neil alone, Kurt kicks Spewing in the ass. Neil laughs. The first song lasts a little under an hour.

The second hour starts with "Vicious" by Lou Reed.

The Jovi starts in on "Cinnamon Girl." Neil does his strange hop up to the mic and sings. Neil plays a sick, one-note guitar solo—it's all tone and attitude. The song ends in a droning descent and stays there in a tribal guitar war until a riff takes over. The riff is "Gloria." Neil is doing his strange hop. Spewing is again trying to hand Neil a pick. Eric finds the key. EJ beats the hell out of his dear friends. The Jovi rocks back and forth with Neil. Kurt sings. The song ends in triumphant, melodic chaos. Everyone knows there's nowhere to go from there. Neil drops his borrowed guitar on the ground and kicks the strings rhythmically. One final *umph* and it's over.

Neil looks at the band and grabs the mic and says, "Don't let the hospital change you." Then he turns and walks out the door.

"Bros. We've fucking made it," Spewing declares.

"This is just the beginning," says the Jovi.

"I'm bringing the truck and Kostas out here tomorrow!" Felder says, and pushes his frizzy black hair back with two hands. "We've got to record this thing you're doing in here, this live thing. We've got to."

Felder can make it happen, so it does. A mobile studio sound truck backs into the parking lot between the choppers and Kurt's Fastback and Felder's Porsche. The back door opens and the awe-struck band members climb inside. Kurt finds a mixing board. EJ finds a twenty-four-track tape deck. The Jovi finds a closed-circuit TV. Spewing finds a half-empty Budweiser, and Eric finds a backstage pass to a Whitesnake concert. Three techies in black T-shirts jump out of the front of the truck and go to work. Suddenly there are thick wires running from the blackened den to the truck. EJ lifts the thick cable and points at Spewing. "You know what this means, Spewing?"

"It means us bros are gonna be famous, bro."

"No, it means that it matters. Fuck up, slide into a note, back of the pocket, front of the pocket, it all matters now. You hear me?"

The band turns when they hear the mild sound of a factory Harley, a small one, girl-size, a Sportster. There's a compact little fellow with curly black hair riding it. His little bare arms extend to the handlebars from his leather vest. He wears a string necklace with a shark's tooth in the middle.

"What is that?" Kurt asks.

"Put some Jordache jeans on him and he looks like one of the dudes in *The Warriors*," Eric says.

"It's Kostas. Your producer. Come. I'll introduce you."

Kostas has black eyes that devour light. After the introductions, Kurt says, "Have you heard the demos?"

"Yeah."

"What do you think?" EJ asks.

"You really want to know?"

"Of course." The band nods in unison.

"I like the band, but the demos are wet as shit."

"Then why are you here?" Kurt asks and points his finger.

"Whoa, whoa, whoa…," Felder interjects.

"Look, I don't mean the performances are bad, or the songs, I just mean the sound quality."

"All of our friends, all of our fans love those demos. That's our sound. That's what we're supposed to sound like," Kurt says.

"Kurt, the digital delay, the reverb, it sounds a little too British on the demos," Felder says.

"I can make you sound better and more American," Kostas says.

"The only band from the last five years that I have any respect for is Echo & the Bunnymen."

"Kurt, those guys have never sold well."

Kurt eyes Felder, then Kostas, then Felder again. "The two of you, who don't play music…" Kurt cuffs himself. "You guys are producing our album?"

"Kurt. C'mon, Kurt," Felder pleads. "Kostas used to do rough mixes for the Stones."

"So?"

"Ron and Keith always liked them better." Felder smiles as if it were secret sacred knowledge.

"What about Mick?" the Jovi asks.

"Kurt, you got so much talent and so many songs. Kostas has talent too. It's gonna be perfect. We're just here to make it happen, get it all down on tape, you guys are gonna make the album. Just play one song and come back in here and listen to the playback with a Kostas mix and you're going to flip out."

Kurt presses his forefingers into his temples. "Okay. I'll try it."

Kurt struts into the black den, plugs in, rips out the first chord to "My Minister." Kostas dives into the truck and hits the record button, maniacally fiddling with the knobs. Kurt's guitar is chunky and vicious. The band joins in.

The song ends with a long sustain.

Kurt walks out to the truck. Kostas hits playback.

"Okay," Kurt says.

MO' MONEY

The next day Priscilla drives up from San Diego. Kurt shows her his Mustang and takes her to the 7-Eleven to buy her some things. The clerk calls in his check, then turns to Kurt with a frown. "The bank says insufficient funds."

"It's okay, Kurt. It's totally cute, but I didn't really need this Care Bear."

"This isn't a problem." Kurt holds up his Gold Card.

The clerk shakes his head. "We don't take those."

Kurt walks up to a pay phone, pulls a card out of his pocket, and dials the number.

"Hey, Mr. Wellington, I need some more money. I need to buy my wife a car."

"Okay, Kurt, I need two band members to make a transfer."

Wellington calls the Jovi at the Cokewoods and asks, "Is it okay if we transfer another ten grand from the group account to the personal accounts? For Kurt?"

"Whatever."

Kurt answers the payphone at the 7-Eleven and nods. He tells Priscilla, "Forget that stuff in there. Let's go get you a new car."

Her big sad eyes get happy. "Really?"

Priscilla spots a white VW Cabriolet in a used-car lot off Lankershim. They put five grand down and sign a loan for the rest. Kurt says, "Quit your job at Macy's. I don't want you to ever have to work again." They show up at Gates in Priscilla's new car, Kurt decked out in black leather inside the white-on-white car.

"Dude," Eric says to Spewing. "He looks like James Dean in heaven."

"No. He looks like a blackhead."

"Hey! Hey!" Jesse the Giant calls out. "Looks like someone went shopping."

Kurt has a cigarette hanging from his lips. "Drives pretty good," he says to Kostas, gritting his teeth to hold the cigarette. "You want to try it?"

"Let me drive that thing," Jesse yells.

"YOU BOUGHT ANOTHER CAR?" EJ yells as he walks outside. "DID YOU TRANSFER MORE MONEY?"

"Cool down, Elmer, we're gonna make so much money none of this is going to matter."

"Kurt, you don't understand!"

"Yeah, I do."

"We need a band meeting. Just the band."

"She's my wife. She can stay."

"I'll sit outside," Priscilla says.

The band assembles in the black den. EJ lectures the other members. "We can't take more money from the band account! Kurt, you don't understand money. I understand money. It's that simple. You guys need to listen to me. Kurt thinks we're going to be rich forever just on the advance. We're not. It's for two hundred and fifty thousand dollars. Now you need to remember that Felder took seventy grand right off the top, which is unethical, but never mind that for right now—that leaves us one hundred and eighty grand at our accountant's, with another hundred grand on its way from our T-shirt deal. If you do the math, you'll realize that Felder took his chunk of the T-shirt money before it ever came to us. As I said—unethical. But listen to me, after Felder bit off his seventy grand, our lawyers took their thirty. I called them to go over the bill. It's a little trick I learned. Whenever you get your—"

"What the fuck does this have to do with anything?" Kurt yells.

"Listen to me. I never forget anything of a financial nature."

"Why are you so fucking wound up on this? It's cool. We're just spending the interest."

"Kurt, interest, even if it was at ten percent, would only amount to eighteen grand a year, or thirty-six hundred a year per guy, or three hundred dollars a month per guy. And that's if we still had the whole chunk of money. We don't. We're down to less than a hundred grand!"

"It's not going to matter. We're going to make so much money that none of this is going to matter. You're just the drummer. Get behind your fucking drumset and play a fucking song!"

EJ utters a primal scream, shakes his head, kicks over a road case, walks behind his set, and takes it out on his snare drum. The blows are so sharp that they make everyone blink in synchronicity. EJ expands the violence into an absurd drumbeat. Spewing grabs his bass, comes in locked and pumping. The Jovi chunks out thick distortions of time and space. Eric makes a chainsaw-sounding synth pad. Kurt grabs the mic, sings, yells, flops around on the stage like a bluefin tuna on a fishing boat. Coming into the final break, Spewing plays the tag a line too early. Kurt hops up, grabs Spewing by the collar, and throws him off the stage. The song ends with the crash.

Kostas runs in yelling. "What the fuck is wrong with you guys! That was the one! Never stop a song! I can fix that shit! I had the whole thing! That was going on the album! What the fuck?"

Wellington walks in behind Kostas and says, "No problem, Elmer. From now on, we'll require three band members for a transfer."

Felder walks in behind Wellington, pushes his hair behind his ear, and yells, "Hey EJ, something else, don't you ever call me unethical. You don't know unethical. You don't want me to show you unethical."

"You were listening in the truck?"

"Always."

MELE KALIKIMAKA

For James Franklin every day is Christmas. His mouth almost hurts from smiling so much. He delivers his last burrito. It has the flag of Mexico flying triumphantly in an orange wedge by its side. He tells his boss, "I've been bringing the chicken fajita burrito to tables for six years, and that's the last one." They all stand and look at it, Hans the manager, Suze the bartender, Hector the bus boy. Sophie walks in, James turns to the mariachis and says, "Hit it boys!" They start to play *"Cuando Calienta El Sol."* If he only could leap into her arms and be carried away it would be the end of the movie. But instead James kisses Sophie on the lips while the Mariachis sing: When the sun is hot here on the beach/I feel your body tremble close to me…

James, forever fighting it out just to survive, gives himself to Sophie completely. She doesn't want to be alone. He doesn't want to be away from her. He slides into her life with ease. They move into an apartment on the water at Windansea. It's first class to London, first class to Paris. He's quick with a joke and knows about Andy Warhol's Factory, and a surfer? A real surfer? How intriguing they all say.

While she does her thing, he walks the streets, takes in the sights, smells the flowers, throws francs in fountains, questions the Mona Lisa, sketches the Venus de Milo, has a perfect croissant explode in his face and sips a *café creme*. And most importantly, he's there at night, when the whole crew, the photographer, the client, when everybody assembles at a long white table, and the feast begins, and the wine pours. "We don't drink," he says when the waiter gets close.

"Just *un peu*." The waiter says.

"No, *un peu. Merci.*" James says as Sophie's eyes follow each drop of red that fills the client's glass.

KILL GILLIGAN

They grew up with the castaways. They know them from the tube. And before that, they knew them from the Jungian collective subconscious. The Skipper is the boot of authority, the brute force of it. The Skipper has appeared in many guises: the Roman centurion, the police officer, the crossing guard, the bouncer, the meter maid, the drummer. The Skipper does not question the code. He enforces it.

Gilligan is the everyman. He is trapped between two unattainable women—the girl next door and the seductress. He cannot understand the Professor or attain the wealth of Mr. and Mrs. Howell. He spends his time bumbling about, and he breaks the rules because they mean nothing to him. Swift punishment is what he knows best—the boot in the ass.

EJ is the Skipper and Spewing is Gilligan.

If the other castaways ever came to their senses, they would kill Gilligan. He's always the reason they can't get off the island. He's the one that foils every plot, ruins every plan. They could club him with a giant coconut mallet. But they never do. It never even occurs to them. There's something more to this. Maybe they need Gilligan. Maybe they love him. Perhaps something magical happens between the punisher and the punished.

At some point, everyone takes a shot at Gilligan, even Eric the Professor. Spewing back talks him once, so he shoves him to the ground. It feels good to both of them. But then Eric thinks, *Come here, little buddy.* Those words mean *I beat you because I love you.* It's the chemistry between guard and inmate, master and slave. It brings nations to their knees and in Thunderstick it brings the people to their feet.

An essential bond must exist between the drummer and the bass player. The bond can be constructed of respect and mutual admiration or, in this case, the bond is built with the kind of love that stings.

THE STARLET

These are the last days at Gates. The band will start recording the album in a week at A&M studios. The band has about fifty well-rehearsed songs. Songs from the Badd Bobby! era, songs from the Full Nelson Mandela era, early Thunderstick songs, the kicking Mellaril songs, even a happy-we're-finally-signed song. When tape is rolling, perfection eludes. But this time, instead of Spewing, it is Eric who plays the wrong chords. Kurt stops the song, walks over, and pretends to kick him like he would've kicked Spewing. Everyone laughs. Including Alexandra and her friend—she has brought around a young starlet—Mary Kathryn Elizabeth O'Donnel. She belongs to the group of eighties actresses who all have three names. She does them one better— she has four. She is adorable and innocent, cute little freckles and red hair and a little turned-up nose. Kurt's whole bad-ass thing seems to turn her on. She guffaws, slaps her jeans, and claps her hands while Kurt acts out an ultra slow-motion attack on Eric. Kurt hugs him afterward and walks off the stage. With Priscilla back in La Jolla, Kurt walks straight up to Mary Kathryn

Elizabeth O'Donnel and introduces himself. "Hey, I've seen you on that show with the space aliens that are inside everyone."

"Yeah?" She smiles.

"It's a good show." Kurt nods seriously and lights a smoke. "Good acting. I respect it."

"Thanks, I'm Mary," she says, and extends her whole body with her hand like a little girl who has just learned how to shake. He puts out his gnarled claw. She takes it and turns it to look at his wedding ring. She even touches the ring with her other hand. Kurt winces.

A smart girl, she moves on, reaches out and touches Eric's long hair. "This is so awesome."

"Thanks."

"You want to come watch me play guitar?" Kurt asks her.

She points to the stage, giggles, and asks him, "Again?"

Kurt nods.

"Yeah, sure."

It's a club on Santa Monica Boulevard. The Jovi and Kurt show up at the velvet rope with guitar cases in hand. The bouncer lifts the rope, and they all walk in together. Another bouncer stops the girls and asks for ID. Alexandra points at Mary Kathryn Elizabeth O'Donnel and says, "She's on TV."

The bouncer apologizes and lets them through.

In the blacklit disco, the walls are thumping. Retail chicks wave their hands above their heads. Muscle-bound dudes show off their fluorescent teeth. The band keeps walking—into a hall, past another velvet rope, and into another world, the back patio, a lattice of wood is strung with a thousand tiny lights, there are small shrubs and little café tables and a three-piece jazz band making real music. The guitar player adjusts his knit cap, smiles with bent teeth, and welcomes the Jovi and Kurt. They plug in and start trading licks. Mary Kathryn Elizabeth O'Donnel sits with Alexandra and Eric, and watches Kurt's thick, flat-ended fingers vibrate on his fret board.

At the break, Kurt stuffs a hundred-dollar bill in the trio's brandy glass and sits next to Mary Kathryn Elizabeth O'Donnel. "What'd you think?"

"You're really good at playing this."

"Nah. You can't really play jazz until you're forty. When I'm forty, I'm gonna play jazz. These kids who think they can play jazz, they can't. Nobody understands it until they're forty. At least forty."

"There's nothing worse than fusion," the Jovi adds. "There's nothing worse than jazzy rock. Jazz and rock are like church and state. They must always stay separate."

"Why don't you play with them?" Mary asks Eric.

"That dude is wicked-sick on the Hammond B3. Those chunky, syncopated, church-soul riffs—I can't play like that."

"I'm sure you could if you tried. I once had to make out with this really gross guy for a scene. I didn't think I could do it."

"What'd you do?"

"I ate this super gross pastrami sandwich, like covered in onions, then I stuck my tongue in his mouth. It was so totally my revenge."

Eric laughs.

Kurt asks her, "You want a drink?"

"No way. I just got out of rehab."

"One of us!" the Jovi yells, and offers her his hand.

"Yeah."

"I'm clean, too," Eric says.

"Right on. You guys are like all straight edge."

"Kinda. Yeah. But not Kurt, he likes the barley pop." Eric says. "Spewing smokes weed pretty much non-stop, and EJ can pickle himself pretty good. But me and the Jovi we're clean."

"This has totally been fun, but will you drive me home?"

Eric nods.

Outside the club, he opens the door of his blue BMW for Mary Kathryn Elizabeth O'Donnel. He walks around and gets in the car. "Oh, my God, you totally saved me," she says when he starts the car.

"How?"

"I was just like going to drink or something if I stayed in there."

"Good thing we got you out."

"Yeah. When I drink, it's not pretty."

Eric smiles. "Me neither."

"This one time I was doing a play in Chicago, that's where I'm from, and I was like so drunk I was barfing between scenes. And I was the lead."

"What play was it?"

"*Annie.*"

Eric laughs. "No way! Little orphan Annie is into the hooch."

She laughs.

"The sun will come out tomorrow…" He makes a barfing sound. "That is hilarious. How old were you?"

"Thirteen."

"Oh shit. I guess I was doing the same thing, just not on stage. Good thing you're sober."

"Yeah. My life depends on it. This is our place over here."

"Who do you live with?"

"My mom slash manager. She's probably gonna want to smell my breath when I walk in."

"We should go get you a pastrami sandwich with lots of onions."

"Yeah, I guess we should." She looks at Eric. "I guess this is goodnight." She leans over and presses her adorable Irish lips onto his mouth. He resists for a second and then slips her the tongue. She arches her back, leans into his lap, and starts lapping at his face and grabbing at the buttons on his black jeans. He reaches his arm around her waist and pries his hand into her tight Levi's. She pulls through his underwear and starts jerking up and down. His fingers are backward and squashed in her jeans. He wrenches them around, pushing into her abdomen, finding her spot. Their tongues are intertwined. She turns her head. "Holy shit, she's looking at us!"

"What?"

"My mom. She's looking at us. I have no fucking privacy!"

"Let's go back to my place."

"Oh, my God. I want to. That was so…I just lost control. Let's do that again."

"Let's do it now."

"I gotta go. Call me."

"I don't have your number."

"It's unlisted."

Eric laughs.

"Get it from Alexandra, stupid." She laughs, blows a kiss, and slams the door shut.

Eric arrives at the Cokewoods with the angry itch.

EJ is sitting in the hot tub with a Coors Light in his hand and several crumpled cans by the side of the pool. His head is bobbing a little from side to side.

"What are you doing?" Eric asks.

"Lunky and Talkssssley found sssome ssslut and they're doing a ssssex show for Spewing."

"So what are you doing out here?"

"I don't know…It's weird. I'm drunk."

"Dude. Drunk and hot tub—not good together."

"It's good for my blood pressure. Doctor said so. See you in the morning."

The Jovi is waiting for Eric in their apartment. "Did baby get some?"

"She almost did me."

"Tell me all the filthy details."

"I drove her home. She grabbed my dick. That's about it."

"What are you going to do?"

"I don't know. I feel pretty guilty—about Dane."

"You don't look like you feel guilty."

"Well, I do."

"Look, man, you just got to assume the position. You're in a band. If you don't do this now, you're going to regret it when you're an old man. You'll never be young again."

"You think I should bale on Dane?"

"Nah, man. Dane's way hotter."

"Yeah, dude. You're right. I'm a fucking idiot."

"No, you're just a filthy, filthy, filthy, dirty little horny guy. That's why I love you."

"Thanks, man. I love you, too."

"You going home to La Jolla tomorrow?"

"Yeah. You?"

"Yeah."

"Let's hang out."

"For sure."

HIGH RENT

A concrete plus sign drawn in gray, this is La Brea at Sunset. It's busy and loud. Two major thoroughfares in the L.A. grid take turns pumping cars in different directions, north toward the San Fernando Valley, east toward the mud wrestlers at the Tropicana, west toward the Pacific Ocean, and south toward the giant round Baptist Superdome for Jesus.

The storefronts have changed over the years. Fruit stands became beauty parlors, became car-stereo stores, became chicken stands, became tanning salons. The pace is jarring and inhuman. It's been that way for years. But if you stood right here in 1916 on the southeast corner, the scent of orange blossoms would've surrounded you in the first L.A. grid—the perfect green rows of an orchard with fat peaches hanging low and oranges turning from green to yellow to orange. This was the orchard that Charlie Chaplin purchased in 1917. He was sick of taking orders, so he bought the acres and paid grunting laborers to tear out the grove and build a Tudor township with a warehouse-sized soundstage.

When the camera wasn't rolling, Chaplin swam naked with hopeful girls in his pool. Every one of them surprised when he showed them the door. The little man with the Hitler mustache got old, but a soundstage in Hollywood has many lives. The TV shows *Superman* and *Perry Mason* were filmed here. In 1966 Jerry Moss and Herb Alpert purchased the lot and made it the world headquarters for A&M records. They brought in a NorCal hippie vibe with shiny stained-wood walls and hanging ferns cradled in macramé. In the years that followed, they built a state-of-the art studio where Chaplin's pool used to be.

Lunky the Loyal has been to other places like A&M, other places surrounded by high iron gates, other places with guard stations and men in uniform who ask questions, but this is different. The security is meant to keep people out, and today Lunky is free. His thick white arm hangs out of the window of the yellow box truck. His mirror shades reflect the Somali security guard's cheerful expression. "I'm with Thunderstick," he says. "Where do I unload?"

The guard looks down at the clipboard in his hand. "You are in Studio A. We call it the 'We Are the World Room.' Go thataway."

When Lunky walks into Studio A carrying Eric's keyboard cases, something about the barn-sized main room, its A-shaped ceiling, the three isolation rooms, and the wood floor is vaguely familiar. He scratches his chin and thinks to himself, *Yes, Band Aid*. This is where Boy George held hands with Tom Petty, held hands with Bruce Springsteen, held hands with Michael Jackson, and they all swayed back and forth like gospel singers for the starving in Africa. Afterward they did lines of whitey, got back on their private planes, and headed to the South of France, but some bags of rice did arrive in Kismayo a few years later. The Lunk smiles, grits his teeth, passes wind, and starts setting up the keyboards.

They are all on their way, Kurt in his Fastback, the Jovi on his chopper, EJ and Spewing in a 1975 Cadillac Eldorado convertible, and Eric in his BMW. All of them are coming from different directions, expecting different things. Kurt and the Jovi arrive at almost the same time. Felder greets them at the door. They both smile at the long hot receptionist. She smiles back. Felder looks at her, looks at the boys, and says, "Don't shit where you eat. There's plenty more where that came from."

The receptionist flicks her brown hair over her shoulder and sways from side to side. "Can I give you the tour?"

"Yeah."

The entryway is paved in hard stone. Geometric patterns backlight frosted glass walls. The receptionist is displayed inside a wall beneath a giant triangle that seems to be aimed at the chasm between her tan breasts.

Once they enter the hallway, everything is entirely different. The sounds from the busy intersection are gone. It's dark, windowless, and manly in an artless way. This is what happens when straight men are allowed to decorate. There are four studios within A&M. Studio A is the second door on the right.

They enter the studio. The vocal iso room is to their left. They walk up to a six-inch-thick mahogany door with a triple-pane window in the middle. The door is heavy, soundproof, and electronic. Felder presses the button on the right and the door sucks up into the ceiling.

They enter the control room. The console is a Neve 4792, inspired by George Martin, and it's the last one made by Rupert Neve before he left the company named after him. The board was originally installed in AIR's Montserrat studio. It is considered priceless. The black pane of glass on the right is actually another space-age door. Press the button and it disappears into the ceiling, revealing stairs. Walk up the stairs, first there is a bathroom, and then find the private lounge for Studio A. It has cable.

Go back downstairs through the control room, through the vocal iso room, and enter the main room. Fill it with water and it's like the tuna tank at Sea World. The observation glass in the center leads to the control room. On the left are the two big iso rooms, on the right the small vocal iso room. In 1988 all of this can be yours for a mere three thousand dollars a day—send DCA the bill.

The biggest little band in the world, U2, is down the hall in Studio D putting the finishing touches on *Rattle and Hum*. But Felder, Felder wants Studio A for Thunderstick. Outside of Studio D is the communal lounge. It must've been remodeled at the same time as the lobby. Triangles of frosted glass overlap each other. A saltwater fish tank is filled with neon yellow fish.

"We have caterers and runners," the receptionist says. "Just tell them what you want. The menus are in books by my desk. The coffee and fruit are replaced every six hours. Is there anything else you guys would like?"

"Your phone number?" The Jovi laughs. "Nah, I'm just kidding."

"Well you know where to find me."

Kurt, Felder, and the Jovi watch her walk away.

They stroll into Studio A.

Lunky the Loyal, Talksley of Loud, and Jesse the Giant are tangled in a mass of cords in the big room. Ernie the engineer says, "Grab me a cardioid condenser mic for the second tom and a dual for the rack."

"A what?"

Inside the control room, Kostas doesn't want to plug the Neve directly into A&M's analog machines. Instead he is trying to hook the Neve to his own tube preamp and from there to a pair of brittle-sounding Sony digital decks. The preamp is huge and old, made of baby-blue metal with dials the size of grapefruit slices and needles that look like they were stolen from a Geiger counter.

EJ, Spewing, and Eric walk in the control room. "This place is insane!" they say.

Jesse strolls in carrying a Bacchanalian three-foot-long silver fruit plate he stole from the communal lounge. "Look at this fucking thing. It's got pears and apples, and I fucking don't know what these things are. Kurt, you want some cheese?"

The receptionist glows. "If you'd like your own fruit plate, I can have it brought in once a day."

"Fuck. I like fruit." Jesse the Giant bites off half an apple. "Whuh abow oo gahs?" he says, his mouth full of white pulp.

Kostas tries to grab the reigns. "Listen, guys. I've got a ways to go with the setup here. Why don't you go out and get a drink or something and come back in a few hours."

"You guys gotta come see my new ride," Spewing yells. "My buddy jagged the hell out of this towelhead on a trade-in. It's a Cadillac convertible."

"I thought you said the guy was Iranian?" EJ asks.

"He was."

"That's not a towelhead, you idiot. That's a camel jockey."

Kurt sticks an unlit cigarette in his mouth. "Let's go for a ride."

The band piles in the Eldorado. They roll down Sunset. Eric shakes his head at the traffic and says, "In a city with the worst traffic in the world, isn't it strange that what people want to do on the weekends in their free time is sit in their cars in more traffic?"

"Loosen up, Eric. It's L.A. Look at the lights," Kurt says from the front seat.

The snaking slow road leads past the Marlboro man billboard—a cutout cowboy emerging from the trees behind the Chateau Marmont. They pass Tower Records, wind up the hill, and drift in front of the Rainbow Room. Fifteen insolent poodle-headed rockers glare at the Eldorado. "That guy just gave me stink eye," Kurt says.

"I think they all just gave us stink eye," Eric says.

"Fuckers."

The action on Sunset soon stops. Spewing needs a place to turn around. He pulls the Eldorado into a Beverly Hills neighborhood. "No respect," Kurt says. "I got a record deal, but I get no respect at the Rainbow."

"Don't worry about those guys, Kurt," the Jovi says. "Those guys can't even get into the Rainbow Room. That's why they're on the sidewalk."

"Did you see the way that guy looked at me?" Kurt says, and clinches his fist.

EJ leans forward into the front seat and says, "Pull over, Spewing. I think I just saw something."

Spewing parks the car in front of a stately Beverly Hills Spanish-style mansion. "Follow me," EJ says, "and be quiet." They hop out of the car and walk a few houses back toward Sunset. "Do you see it?" EJ asks.

"I see it," the Jovi says.

It's dark green and dotted with color, a color that seems to bring its own light. No one says a word. The five members of the band attack the orange tree, filling their hands then their shirts with baseball-sized oranges. They sprint back up to the car and pull onto Sunset Boulevard heading east. There is much less traffic in this direction, but the Rainbow Room and the poodle rockers are now on the other side of the street. Spewing pulls over.

"Alright. On the count of three," Kurt says. "One…two…three."

The volley is launched. Arching high over Sunset, the luminescent orbs land with pulpy explosions, two on the sidewalk, one on the brick wall, and one directly in the chest of a poodle rocker. He falls backward against the wall, then to the ground. He grabs his heart beneath his Dokken T-shirt and screams, "WHAT THE FUCK?" Another volley is launched, the poodle-headed rockers scramble for cover; one is hit in the neck, another in the back, and one rips off his shirt and goes into a Tai Chi posture.

"That one's mine," the Jovi says, and winds up a perfect pitch that hits the Tai Chi poodle in the center of his forehead.

Getting to his knees, the first victim points across the street and yells, "OVER THERE! GET THEM!"

The remaining rockers look across the street.

"WE'RE THUNDERSTICK! DON'T FORGET IT!" Kurt yells.

Spewing hits the gas and the Eldorado rumbles east.

"Nothing's going to happen tonight," Felder says, when the band gets back to the studio. "The digital machines won't work."

"Let's throw down a track on the analog decks," Kurt says.

"Yeah. They sound better anyway," the Jovi adds.

"That would take hours to do that. Come back tomorrow."

Kurt presses his fingers into his jaw and stares at the floor. "I really need to play right now."

THE FIGHT OF THE CENTURY

The next night is Monday, June 27, 1988. Months of hype and weeks of commercials are about to culminate in fisticuffs. Michael Spinks, 31-0, former heavyweight champion of the world, is set to fight Iron Mike Tyson, 34-0, in Atlantic City. It is widely believed that Spinks is the only man on the planet with a chance to beat Mike Tyson.

Jesse the Giant and EJ are pumped for the fight. They've had the A&M runners go out for pizza and beer and pretzels. They've set up chairs and a couch in the Studio A lounge so that everyone can have a look. Kurt, the Jovi, Spewing, and Eric want to see what should be the greatest fight since Frazier/Ali.

Two days in the studio, and Thunderstick has yet to lay down a track. Kostas is still tinkering and toiling. He is trying to make his archaic tube preamp and the futuristic digital tape deck friends.

Upstairs, the band has assembled, eaten, drank, and waited through the undercard —two hundred-and-ten-pound Latinos punched at each other in flurries like hummingbirds. All of that is done. This is it. Wearing blue and white striped tube socks pulled up to his knees, weighing in at 214 pounds, in the white shorts with black trim – Michael Spinks. In the black on black trunks, wearing no socks, only 21 years old, 4 inches shorter and 4 pounds heavier – Iron Mike Tyson. They meet in the center of the ring. Tyson scratches his head with the seam of his boxing glove and looks at the mat. Spinks stares down his long, bent face at Tyson. "Both of youz touch gloves. Good luck to both of youz," the referee says.

Kostas interrupts. "I'm ready." The little frenetic man walks in front of the TV and hops up and down. "Let's do one. Let's lay down a track."

"But the fight is just about to begin," EJ says.

Kostas turns his whole body to look at the television. "Those guys are gonna be fighting all night. Let's do one take. I can check my levels. You guys can come back up and watch the rest of the fight."

Kurt has been waiting for years to go to work. "Let's play rock, that's what we're here for. C'mon!"

Everyone leaves the room and walks downstairs.

Michael Spinks takes a knee in his corner and prays. Tyson's trainer hugs him desperately, his little white arm around an enormous black neck. Tyson pushes him away and beats his own chest. The bell rings. Tyson skips toward Spinks, starts throwing big punches. The announcer exclaims, "TYSON SHOWING NO FEAR, NO RESPECT AT ALL!"

Sixty seconds of no respect. Spinks dances. Tyson punches. Several land, one, a short right hand into the middle of Spinks's chest just below his heart, reverberates through his stomach, through his kidneys, into the bundle of nerves that make up the solar plexus. One of Spinks's legs buckles, and it seems like he's praying again but now at the feet of Tyson. Tyson cocks his right arm, looks at the crown of Spinks's head, and resists the instinct to kill. Instead, he hops excitedly back to his corner.

There's a standing eight count.

Tyson marches over from his corner, throws two punches so short and fast that they are almost invisible, and Spinks springs backward onto the mat, his tube socks above his head, his head behind the ropes. The whites of his eyes are frozen. His elbows are planted in the mat. His hands sway in a nonexistent wind.

DOWNSTAIRS

Spinks slumbers upstairs. The members of Thunderstick are quarantined downstairs. The Jovi and Eric are each in their own large glass enclosure. EJ and Spewing are together in the main room with Kurt's guitar amp. Kurt is by himself in the vocal iso booth. .

Kostas presses a button on the Neve and says, "Let's do one!" His voice sounds distant and echoey.

"What song?" Kurt's lips are inches from the mic. He sounds close, personal, inside your head. Every smacking of saliva, every breath, is audible.

Felder speaks into the Neve and says, "The money song—'I Wanted You.'"

EJ counts out four on his sticks, then four silent, then the band jumps in remarkably together for being so far apart.

After the song, Kurt asks, "How was that?"

"Not bad. Let's do it again."

They do.

"And that one?"

"Good, let's do it again."

Thunderstick plays the four-minute-and-twenty-second song three more times.

"How was that one?"

"It was like the third one. Give it the oomph of the first one with the smoothness of the fifth one," Felder says.

They play it again and again and again.

"How was that?" Kurt asks.

"Still think the third one was best," Felder says.

Kostas shakes his curly head. "No, we liked the first one."

"No. That wasn't radio-ready."

"I think Spewing is holding back—like he doesn't want to make a mistake," Kostas says.

"No, bro. I'm giving it all I got." Spewing's voice is dim. It's only being picked up by the ambient mics.

"First one," Kostas says.

"No, third one," Felder says.

"YOU DON'T KNOW WHAT YOU'RE TALKING ABOUT! I WANT TO FUCKING HEAR THESE PLAYBACKS!" Kurt yells.

"It takes a half hour to switch the digital machines to playback," Kostas says. "You still want that?"

"Yes." Kurt throws down his headphones. He stomps in and sits at the Neve like he knows what the buttons do.

Eric walks in the control room and says, "I'm hungry."

The Jovi walks in and says, "Dude. This iso-booth thing is like sex with a condom."

"Yeah. Like taking a shower with a raincoat on—not for me, bro. I want those pussy juices to run down my leg," Spewing says.

"Spewing may be right," Kostas says, scratching his chin. "Go watch the rest of the fight. Ernie the engineer will set up the playback."

"What do you mean Spewing may be right?" Felder asks.

The band walks upstairs. In the lounge, Jesse is on the couch watching MTV, smoking a joint. "What happened to the fight?" EJ asks.

"It's over," Jesse says.

"Who won?"

"Tyson. First round KO. He almost knocked Spinks's head into the third row."

"Shit."

"Yeah. Awesome."

"So," Kurt asks, "what do we do for a half hour while these guys switch out the decks?"

"Eat," Eric says. "Or sleep?"

"Smoke-out." Jesse nods.

"Get some chicks over here," the Jovi adds.

Downstairs in the control room, the Sony decks are set up for playback. Kostas hits PLAY and works the faders to get a rough mix.

"Why do my drums sound like that?" EJ asks.

"Like what?"

"Like shit. Sounds too echoey."

"That's the room."

"And it sounds kind of brittle too," the Jovi adds. "Like the high end hurts."

"That's the digital decks."

"And why are we using them?" the Jovi asks.

"With digital, I can punch in and punch out whenever you want. I can take one great bass line and duplicate it through the whole song."

"We don't need that," Kurt says. "We don't need studio tricks. This is a real band."

"It's not the digital decks," Felder says. "It's the takes. They need something."

EJ rolls his eyes, puts his hands on an imaginary statue, and says, "Yeah. It needs some tits."

"Maybe it needs a bumblebee buzzing in a jar," Felder says.

"Are you for real?" the Jovi asks.

"Just a little something to throw it off, give it mystery."

"Jesus! What are you talking about?" Kurt yells.

"I've got it," Kostas says. "I want this guy"—Kostas points at Kurt—"in front of his band. Just to get the energy back for basic tracks. Just to get the feel. We can always do overdubs later in the iso rooms."

"Look," Kurt says, "we're a professional band. We can do it any way you want. But I like to feel that energy coming off of EJ, coming off of the drums."

"Yeah?"

"Yup."

"Okay, Lunky, Jesse, Talksley, Ernie! Switch out Kurt. Set him up in the big room. The Jovi too," Kostas commands.

"What about keyboards?" Lunky asks.

"Leave 'em in the iso room. There's no time to waste. Let's get a track before sunrise!"

Ernie the engineer moves the vocal mic from the iso room to right in front of the drums and bass. Kurt plugs directly into his amp. The Jovi's amp is rolled in and mic'd up. The four of them look at one another. EJ taps out four.

They walk back into the control room. Felder asks, "Do you hear that?"

Everyone listens to the silence. "No."

"That's the sound of cash registers ringing. That's the sound of ten-thousand-seat stadiums. That's the sound of radio. See you boys tomorrow."

The Jovi and Eric walk outside into the parking lot. Eric says, "Look at that," and points at the gray rim of light along the ridge of the mountains and the tops of the buildings. "It makes the whole filthy city look like a cardboard cutout, like a movie set."

"You should write that down."

"No. I feel like I've been doing gaggers of whitey all night. I need to get back to the Cokewoods and get in bed before first light, before those damn birds start singing and ruin everything. What are you gonna do?"

The Jovi stretches his arms above his head, hops on his chopper, looks at Eric, and says, "I was made for sunrise." He kick-starts the machine to life and rides off into the silver light.

URINATING WITH THE STARS

"Dude. I just took a piss next to Bono!" Eric says as he walks into the control room.

Felder and Kostas and the Jovi laugh.

"No way!" Spewing says, and offers a handshake. "Did you look at his dick?"

"No, man. I looked straight ahead and acted like it happened every day. He said to me in that leprechaun's accent: 'Well, you seem to have turned A&M studios into a gay raj.'"

"What the fuck does that mean?" Kurt asks.

"It took me a second to realize he meant 'garage.' He thinks we've turned A&M Studios into a garage."

"What did you do?"

"I smiled, stared at the wall, and agreed with him."

Kurt leaps from his seat at the Neve and stops himself an inch from Eric's face. "YOU SHOULD'VE PUNCHED HIM! WE'RE NO FUCKING GARAGE BAND! HE INSULTS US AND YOU JUST TAKE IT!"

"It wasn't an insult, Kurt! He just means that we've got energy. He means that we're not afraid to invite our friends and relatives and have jam sessions and take photos! We're not afraid to enjoy how killer this is."

"Look. Until those guys come in here and show me a little respect—nobody talks to them. You hear me?"

"Kurt, you can't do that," the Jovi says. "Those guys sold out the Coliseum for four nights in a row. Do you have any idea how huge they are?"

"And do you know how much money they made?" Felder asks. "Two hundred and fifty grand per show per guy."

"They got other shit going on than wondering if they've made friends with Thunderstick or not," the Jovi says.

"We're gonna be bigger than that."

"Kurt, I know you like them," Eric adds. "Their music is soulful. They're Christians. That music helped me through some hard times—and I told Bono that."

"THAT'S EXACTLY IT! IF THEY CAN'T HEAR THE LORD IN OUR MUSIC AND COME OVER HERE AND ACKNOWLEDGE IT, THEN I'LL FIGHT ALL OF 'EM."

"Whoa, whoa, whoa. We're not fighting U2," Felder interjects. "I'll put together a little meeting. If they like us, it could be the best thing ever for this band. Maybe we're the first band on their next tour."

"Those guys should be opening up for us!" Kurt says, still glaring at Eric. "Don't ever do that again!"

"What? Piss next to Bono?"

"TALK TO THEM!"

In the Studio

Each night is a Thunderstick show. If Felder meets a young girl, he tells her and her friend that he's a producer now. To prove it, he brings them to watch his band record at A&M Studios. Many come and go. Two girls turn out to be pros—the Blonde and the Redhead. They watch Thunderstick lay down basic tracks—drums, vocals, guitars, bass, and keyboards. They clap and say, "Inspired!" They watch the Jovi sit by himself in the big room and rip leads. They clap and say, "Hot!" Kurt gets out his guitar and shows them what he's got. They clap and say, "Oh my God!" Felder tells the band he's gonna nail the Blonde, but it never quite happens. Like all the best party girls, these two can sense when it's about to get boring and they go down the hall and introduce themselves to U2 in Studio D. A few hours later, they appear in Studio A again. The Somali security guard and the receptionist get to know them, and they become regulars.

The band records no matter who is sitting in the control room. If the band finishes early, before 3 A.M., they go to an after-hours club. If they finish late, they go to the twenty-four-hour Jewish deli on Fairfax for breakfast.

A week goes by, and Kurt still hasn't heard a word from U2. He wonders what the hell is going on. It lingers in the back of his mind until he gets up early on Monday and washes the Mustang Fastback and parks it proudly right in front of the door, right in front of the receptionist. He tosses the keys to the valet, flashes a five, and says, "Keep her handy."

He comes back out to get a pack of smokes from the glove box and is shocked. The Mustang has been moved ten cars over and Bono's rented '57 Chevy convertible is parked in its place. It's a two-tone prop from *American Graffiti*. Kurt calls the valet over. "What happened here?"

"Yes. Is Mr. Bono's car." He smiles and nods.

"And my car?"

"Is right there." He points to the car.

"Did you know that my parents were married right there?" Kurt gestures toward the Valley. "On HOLLYWOOD FUCKING BOULEVARD."

"No. I did not know that."

"And those guys are from FUCKING IRELAND."

"Yes. I did know that."

"Okay. Don't forget it." Kurt struts back into A&M straight into the Studio A control room. The Blonde and the Redhead are sitting at the Neve, running their fingers over the controls. "Those guys in U2 are ASSHOLES!" Kurt yells. "They moved my fucking car. My parents were married on HOLLYWOOD FUCKING BOULEVARD and they moved MY car!"

The Blonde gets up from the board, walks over to Kurt, rubs his shoulders, and says softly, "You can't be serious."

"I am."

"They think you're good."

"Good?"

"Yeah, good."

"Good. That's nothing. Those guys are a joke— 'Alright, Edge, play the blues!'—that guy couldn't play the blues if his life depended on it."

"Don't be all mad." She puts her finger on Kurt's lips. "They're into you guys—what you guys have done to this place—brought in some energy. Bono told me you've turned it into a garage."

"He said that to my keyboard player too, and Eric should've fucking knocked that guy out. We've been together for FIFTEEN FUCKING YEARS. And we get no respect."

The Blonde laughs. "You're a hard guy to compliment, aren't you?"

"Yeah."

"I would introduce you to Bono, but he's having a hard time right now. He sees himself as a Vessel of God, and he has to write the lyrics before the band can write the music."

"So?"

"They're trying to finish that album, and he's got writer's block."

"And that's why he hasn't come over here?"

"Yeah."

"Oh. Okay. That's cool. Where are you going?"

"I'll be back."

Kurt paces in the control room by himself for a while. He hits a few buttons on the Sony digital decks. The tape rolls, but there is no sound. He messes with the faders. Still nothing. He walks outside into the hallway. He looks to his right and spots all four members of U2 walking in a row toward him. The drummer nods at Kurt. The others ignore him. Kurt pushes his hand through his waxed-up hair and looks over the tops of their four heads. He hears "bro, bro, bro," and turns to spot Spewing running from the communal lounge waving a paper and pen in the air.

The last member of U2 passes Kurt. The four famous dudes have conditioned themselves not to turn around when someone like Spewing starts yelling. U2 is almost at the reception area when Spewing, now in a full sprint, approaches Kurt. Kurt pulls his left hand back and unleashes a mighty slap. Spewing lands flat on his back.

Kurt walks over, leans down into Spewing's face, and says, "Thunderstick is from California. We don't beg for autographs."

"Bro. My face stings like shit. But nice left. You totally caught me, man."

That night ends at 4:00 A.M. Kostas has Ernie run a cable from the vocal iso room into the parking lot. It's attached to a mic and placed on a tripod just behind the straight pipe on the Jovi's chopper.

In the control room Kostas yells, "Okay! I'm rolling!" to Jesse in the hallway.

Jesse turns toward the parking lot. "He's rolling!"

The Jovi nods and kicks at the chopper. It comes to life with a cataclysmic growl. The Jovi revs the engine.

The needles on the Neve bounce. Kostas cheers.

The next day the Blonde and the Redhead are massaging a prostrate Kurt and feeding him grapes in the control room.

Jimmy Iovine is a big producer but a little guy. He walks in wearing his ever-present baseball cap and sunglasses. He nods at the Blonde and says, "Hey, sugar, you're wanted in Studio D. You boys don't mind if I borrow her, do ya?"

She gets up, leans Kurt's head back on the pillow, and walks for the door. The Redhead follows.

"Who the fuck was that?" Kurt asks.

"U2's producer," Felder says. "But it was good while it lasted, right? Right? That's what I say to myself when she's gone. After I've taken her out for another dinner."

"That was nothing. My neck was sore. I love my wife."

"I know. I know, Kurt."

Kurt puts his hands above his head and announces to everyone in the control room, "Don't look at me! You know those guys in U2 have wives back in Ireland!" He talks in a fake southern lilt. "Alright! How mellow! They call themselves Christians, but they can't hear the Holy Spirit in my music? Alright, God saved me, got me off drugs—God is probably telling them to say hello to me and they won't listen? Right?"

Felder chokes off a laugh, puts on a sympathetic face, and says, "All in good time."

Kurt's brother walks in the room.

Jesse yells, "James Franklin! To what do we owe the pleasure?"

"Sophie's got a job up here. Japanese commercial. I wanted to check this studio scene out. Sleep all day. Play all night. You guys are like Led Zeppelin in here, aren't you?"

"Full on, bro," Kurt says and hugs James.

"Hey, man, how is your supermodel girlfriend?"

Felder's ears perk up. "We should all be so lucky. What is it with you guys? You're just some guys from La Jolla. How do you pull this shit off? Ron Headley saw a picture of her, Sophie Clark, right? in *Elle* magazine—he calls it catalogue shopping—does it all the time. He sees one he wants, he has me track 'em down. He really wanted to meet Sophie, I mean *really*. I don't mind doing it for him, it's part of being a manager—you saw Iovine just now. So I called around, her bookers, her agents. I said to them, 'Ron Headley, you know from the '70s super-group Brougham LTD., Ron Headley winner of an MTV astronaut for his solo song "Indian Summer," Ron Headley wants to meet Sophie Clark' They all said no way, she's not interested. She turned down Headley—she must really love you."

"That is pimp shit, Felder," James says. "It's really disturbing. I don't even know where to start with that."

"Hey, Felder, bro, if I show you a picture of some whore in *Hustler*, can you track her down so I can bang her?" Spewing asks. "That's what I want, man!"

"Shut up, Spewing! You'll get laid when I say you can!"

Kostas claps his hands together and says, "C'mon, let's do one! Get in there!" Everyone looks through the glass into the tuna tank with EJ's drums set up in the middle.

"Yeah, let's do it!" they yell.

Kostas hits RECORD and the band starts "Alone, Alone."

Through the glass, Kurt can see Kostas and Felder driving the Neve. James, Jesse, and Lunky stand behind them facing the glass bobbing their heads to the music.

Outside, in the lobby, the receptionist tells Sophie Clark to wait for the red RECORDING sign to go dark. Sophie ignores her, walks up to the space-age door, hits the button, and enters the Studio A control room in long, slow strides. Felder turns around in his chair, beholds Beauty, and mumbles, "Holy shit." Kostas maintains the helm, his chin lit by the lights of the Neve. The song builds toward an impossible crescendo. The Jovi's back is hunched to the glass. He's rocking to EJ's beat. It's the hundred-meter four-by-four and the guitar lead is the baton, The Jovi is the anchor with blazing speed. He takes the handoff in stride and accelerates into the corner. He pulls and chokes on the neck of the guitar. He spins around, bends a string to perfection, and loses himself in Sophie's sleepy blue eyes. She is so close. Her hands are up against the glass. His are somewhere on his guitar. He has no idea what they're doing. He just hopes they'll keep it up. James puts his hands on Sophie's shoulder. The Jovi falls out of the lead, but the song is on to the tag anyway. The Jovi feels lightheaded. The song ends and he sits down on his amp. Sophie runs into the big room, throws her hands in the air, and calls, "Jovi!"

He gets to his feet and hugs her.

She holds his hand and pleads with him. "Come dinner with us!"

"Yeah, sure." The Jovi smiles at James.

"We have to go now. But meet us at Angeli, okay?"

"Yeah, totally. What time?"

"Nine? Ten?" she says.

"I'll be there."

James walks up to Kurt and puts out his hand. "You guys sound insane. This record is going to change everything. Rock and roll will never be the same."

"Yup." Kurt nods and lights a cigarette. "Later."

Kostas presses a button on the Neve and his voice reverberates through the studio. "You guys want to hear this one?"

During playback, no one says it, but you can hear Sophie walk in. There's no footsteps, there's no sound of the door opening. But there's a jump in the energy of the song. It suddenly becomes unpredictable and joyous and hopeful.

"Your brother's girlfriend is really something," Felder says. "Really something."

"She's a great girl," the Jovi says. "Not just the way she looks either."

"Yeah. She fucks like a banshee too," Jesse the Giant yells.

Everyone laughs except Kurt. "Watch it Jesse! That's my brother's chick."

"I'm just kidding. Kurt knows I'm kidding." He grabs Kurt by the neck and shakes him.

A soft voice interjects. "Hey guys!" It's the Blonde.

"Hey. Any message from Ireland?" Kurt asks.

"Jimmy Iovine says you guys are the future."

"What do you think?"

"I think you're right now." She smiles. Eric is lying on the couch. She walks over and plops down beside him and touches his foot.

Kurt isn't going to let this happen. He takes the Blonde by the hand and says, "I want to show you something." He presses the button on the door and leads her upstairs into the Studio A Lounge. With each step, her leggings stretch around her and become nothing more than a gauzy sheen of black on her perfect white skin. She rises away from the band, serene and ethereal, like a virgin sacrifice sent off to meet the monster monkey in the jungle.

Sitting downstairs, Felder does a head count and knows it is just the two of them up in the lounge. He gets up and hits the button on the door. It opens and everyone can hear Kurt's voice and Kurt's thick fingers pressed on his acoustic, making music that drifts down the stairs. The door closes automatically. Kostas fiddles with some knobs and starts a playback. Felder paces for a second and presses the button again. All is silent. Felder says, "Eric, go see what's going on up there."

Eric comes back a second later. "They're gone."

"They're gone?"

"They are gone."

"What happened to our Christian leader?" The Jovi laughs.

"He must be performing a baptism," Jesse says.

Felder says, "Oh fuck. I should've figured. I want Kurt to pay me back for all the raw fish I've fed that girl. I've fed her more tuna than Flipper. I'll have Bill Wellington prepare a fucking invoice."

"Oh dude. He took her to the pinball room. He's probably got her laid out on the machine right now giving her the business. Can you even imagine having sex with Kurt? Talk about an eight-second tube ride!" The Jovi shakes his head violently and lets out a primal scream. Everyone laughs.

"Don't worry, Felder," Jesse says and looks at his bare wrist. "Kurt'll give her back to you in another minute."

The Jovi musses Felder's hair.

"You guys just wait. I take the slow approach," Felder says. "I'll get her yet."

"Sloppy seconds, huh?" Jesse yells.

"Well…no…"

"Tiptoe through the tulips!" Jesse the Giant sings.

"What you think I look like, Tiny Tim?"

Everyone joins in singing in a British falsetto.

"Is that it? You fuckers."

"Where's your ukulele, Felder?" EJ asks.

"You guys don't even know the words to that song."

"Fuck, nobody does," Jesse yells.

"That's enough," Kostas says, "stop the singing."

The door sucks into the ceiling. Kurt enters, scanning the floor. He has the look of a tomcat recovering from general anesthesia. Every guy suffers through a postglurp cascade of shame, but for Kurt it seems much worse. The Blonde comes down, cheery, kisses Kurt on the cheek in front of everyone, waves, and walks away.

After the space-age door closes and seals behind her, Felder says, "You sly devil."

Kurt looks around, quite somber, and says, "Look, man, nothing happened. I love my wife. I don't know what you guys are talking about."

"Fair nuff, let's do a song" Kostas says.

"Alone, Alone."

Again.

During the middle of a lifeless guitar solo, Kurt fiddles with the little headphone mixing board in front of him. He reaches down and turns a knob in between strumming his guitar. He pulls off his headphones, grates the pick violently on a guitar string, and stomps on the headphones until they break into four pieces.

The song ends.

Felder speaks into the mic in the mixing board and says, "Alright boys, that'll be all for tonight."

The next day Kurt calls a band meeting, roadies included. "No more chicks in the studio," he says. "I love my wife. I called her last night, and she's going to come up here and stay with me as long as she can."

"Great, Kurt, where am I supposed to stay?" Jesse says sarcastically.

"You can stay on the couch."

"Fuck that. I'm too big for a couch. Maybe you guys don't need me up here anyway. I'm the road manager. We're not on the road."

"Look, man, I need you up here. You're helping out. We just need to deal with this chick thing."

"I'll sleep on the couch," Lunky says. "You can have my bed."

"Fuck, I don't want to stay with the roadies," Jesse the Giant says.

"What the fuck, bro?" Talksley says. "Like what's wrong with us, man? Why would you talk such crazy talk? What'd I ever do to you, bro? Dude."

"You know, Jesse, in some ways you are a roadie," Lunky says.

Kurt stops him and declares in the voice of a barbarian king: "I am a sinner. I know that. But some of you are bringing sin into this band and you don't even know it."

Beneath Kurt's stare, everyone is penitent.

"I hear ya, bro. Me and God, we got a special agreement on that stuff," the Jovi says. "I'll try and reel it in a little."

Lunky bows his head and says, "Sorry, Kurt…"

"Yeah, and I tangled with that little actress chick," Eric adds.

"Look, Kurt," EJ says, and stares over Kurt's shoulder. "We all respect you and you're the leader of the band, but frankly, you're also the only guy who's banged a chick in the studio. Why don't you just bring Priscilla up here, and don't worry about the rest of us."

"Nothing happened! Besides, it doesn't work like that. This is a real band. It's like a country. You can't have slavery in half the country and half the country free. Either we walk with God, or we don't, all of us."

"Fuck," the Jovi says. "That's deep."

DEAD WEIGHT

Spewing's dad shows up at A&M, carrying a video camera all the way from the parking lot to the control room. He walks up to Kurt and says in a droll German accent, "This is very professional. I am very impressed. Kurt, I know that you made this happen. I am giving you Patrick. Think of him as your son now."

Kurt nods and shakes the father's hand. It is like an Old World apprenticeship without the buggery.

Eric is not a great musician, but he's a steadying force and unlike Spewing, he doesn't blow takes. He's been bulking up, ordering lasagna and everything else that can't get away until someone calls him lardo and tells him to "sneak up on a few salads." It's okay. In rock, fat passes for formidable. Plus, Eric believes in the band. While Kurt is in the tuna tank, Felder whispers doubt. "It still needs something. Maybe it's the song. Maybe the song is the problem."

Eric lifts his arms in Kurt fashion and asks aloud, "The songs? The songs? The songs were plucked from the Ganges River, dyed blue with their own divinity. The problem is not the songs."

"I see why they call you Spock," Felder says. "Maybe it needs a bumblebee buzzing in a jar."

"Dude," EJ barks, "is that all you got? A bumblebee buzzing in a jar?"

Many a night in the tuna tank is spent searching for the perfect take. Kostas has his first and only good idea. "Hey, enough of repeating the same song over and over again. Why don't you guys just play the set like it's a live show, like we're back at Gates? Everyone together in the same room."

It works.

"That's something I can sell," Felder says. "We're gonna do guitars now, we'll call you when we need you." He shoos Eric and Spewing towards the door. "Making an album is a weird combination of teamwork and fuck-the-teamwork," Felder says. "But Eric, before you go, there's something I need to talk to you about. You see the band's entourage is sucking the band dry. We've gone over budget. DCA is pissed. We have to get rid of the dead weight. We need to fire Lunky and Talksley."

Eric looks at Lunky through the glass. He is breaking down the keyboard rig. "What about Jesse?"

"Kurt says he stays. Besides, he helps keep Kurt under control. We can hire Lunky and Talksley when we get a tour. It shouldn't be too long from now. The Jovi said he'd tell Talksley. Do you want to tell Lunky?"

"You remember the night you told us about the record deal?"

"Yeah?"

"We went out dancing to celebrate. We danced to the Brothers Johnson's 'I'll Be Good to You.' Everyone danced."

"So?"

"Kurt danced like a lead singer, waving his arms without sense or rhythm. Jesse danced wooden like a football player. The

Jovi danced smiling like a rock star. And Lunky danced with this crazy, unexpected snaky rhythm and these rolling hips like he was taking off his clothes for a crowd of sex-crazed secretaries."

Felder laughs. "Am I missing the point here?"

"I just don't feel good cutting him loose. Who knows where he'll end up?"

"You're hilarious. You think he'll end up dancing on top of some bar on Santa Monica Boulevard for a bunch of screaming homos, don't you?"

"Kinda."

"I'll get L.A.'s biggest drum tech, Raymo, to hire him. Would that make you feel better?"

"Fully."

Eric solemnly walks out through the tuna tank into the glass iso booth. "Lunky, I got some bad news. The band is broke."

Lunky is rolling cords, tying them, and putting them in Eric's gig bag. He doesn't look at the lavish recording studio. He doesn't look at all the expensive equipment. He just looks at Eric. "I don't care. I don't need money. If you just feed me, I'll be fine."

"I can't do that. You need somewhere to live. You need money."

"No, I don't."

"Felder lined up a job for you with one of the top drum techs in L.A. This guy Raymo, he's gonna train you. When we go on tour, you'll be there. You'll be EJ's drum tech and my keyboard tech."

Lunky's heavy round head tilts toward the floor. "If that's the way you want it."

The Jovi and Kostas ride their Harleys up to Neil Young's ranch. Along the way, the Jovi pulls into the median, parks the chopper, pulls down his leather pants, and shits on the tarmac. Kostas pulls over. "What are you doing?"

"What does it look like I'm doing?"

"You couldn't wait?"

"Sometimes a hard-tail will just jar the shit right out of you. It's fucking great!" The Jovi stands up, appreciates his work, pulls up his pants, gets back on his chopper, and launches into the fast lane.

A few hours later the Jovi calls Talksley. "Guess where I am, bro."

"Where?"

"I am at Neil Young's ranch in NorCal. And guess what else."

"What?"

"I got you a job. You're going on tour with Neil and the Bluenotes. You're gonna cut your teeth with a legend. You'll be Neil Young's second guitar tech."

"Lunky ain't going? 'Cause if he is…fuck, bro… no way, bro."

"No, man."

"Does this mean I'm done with Thunderstick?"

"Of course not. When we get a tour, you'll be there."

UPGRADE

Late at night, almost into morning, EJ is hanging with Sven Davidson in a bar in Silverlake. "How did that slasher film work out for Nicky?" EJ asks.

"Dude. It's a fucking franchise. Unfortunately, she got gutted in the first one. We're hoping she can come back in a dream or as a dead chick or something."

"What about Panthers and Pathogens? Are you guys still big in Japan? How's the wandering minstrel thing working out?"

"Fuck. Dude. The lute is a bitch. I miss my Fender P Bass. I miss rock and roll."

"Why don't you come play with us?"

"You guys got Spewing. The guy's a mess, but he can play bass."

"He's cost us a lot of coin in the studio. Kurt's sick of it."

Out in his 1967 convertible LeSabre, Sven listens to the Thunderstick demo and says, "Sure. I'd do that gig."

"Come meet us at A&M Studios tomorrow afternoon."

Around noon the next day, Sven opens his closet, takes out three or four tunics and tosses them into the trash. He pulls out his old black leather motorcycle jacket, some black jeans, and an ashy black T-shirt with the sleeves cut off. He puts them on and drives over to A&M. The receptionist leads him through the hall into the control room. He's in shock. "You guys are recording your *first* album in here? They gave you how much money? Panthers and Pathogens' advance was ten grand—total. You've been recording for a month? Holy shit!"

Kurt, the Jovi, and EJ say, "The job is yours if you want it."

"Yes, I want it."

Sven goes home, calls the lead singer of Panthers and Pathogens, and says, "Not into it anymore."

The lead singer says, "Me neither, but I'm no quitter."

I WANT CANDY

Sophie knows it's always there, but she also knows it's always different, a true shape-shifter. It's a glass of wine poured from a crystal decanter, a pill that helps you relax, a pill that helps you rally, a line of powder on a mirror, smoke from nature, smoke from science. It's grown by benevolent bushes or made by men in labcoats. The coast is clear and there it is staring up at you, asking you, "How's your day?" It's always wrapped differently, multi-colored circles on a garish purple, bears blowing whistles and holding hands, trees with stars and bulbs, six-pointed stars and spinning tops, or just brown paper tied up with string.

There was a pretty good reason for popping the pill that the other girl had, but it's already left Sophie. There was something wrong with how she felt, or how she thought, or there was nothing wrong at all and she just realized that she was cured of whatever that terrible sickness was that had her. It was circumstance. Things had happened. Bad breaks. Misunderstandings. Life is out of our control, even the gurus will tell you that. It's just that sometimes it's too much so. What's done is done. She feels fine, better than fine. And tonight she will tell James that she has changed her mind. Or she will tell him that the client wants to see her alone. Or she will tell him that he just can't come.

When she comes back to the hotel room late that night he smells it on her. It saddens him deeply but he's decides he's going to cup her gently in his hands until she comes to her senses, until she realizes the error of her ways. Right now, she wants to be on top. He looks up at her. She is backlit by the blue light of the clock radio. Her arms move in a Hindu dance. Her eyes glow inside the silhouette.

Landing back in San Diego she looks out the window at the planes and wonders what was that girl's name? Nänce. She looked like she knew where we could score. She looked like she understood.

WHEAT FROM CHAFF

Lunky the Loyal arrives on Eric's street, right where it all began, driving the yellow box truck filled with Thunderstick's gear.

"Hey, Lunky! How are you, man?"

"Hey, Eric," Lunky says in his high-pitched voice. "Not good."

"Huh?"

"Raymo's fucking me."

"What?"

"Nothing about drums, nothing about tuning. He just tells me to take this shit over here and move it·over there. Then he tells me to go get that shit and put it with this shit. It's nothing but moving shit and stacking shit."

"Isn't that what you did with us?"

"I can't believe you'd say that."

"Well, no, you did a lot more."

"I was security. I really worry about you guys without me. You're gonna need me."

"Hey, Lunky, you'll be back. I'll make sure of it."

"I miss you guys. I miss Thunderstick."

"Me too, Lunky."

Eric's phone rings. It's Spewing. "Bro. Did you do your overdubs?"

"Yeah."

"Bro. I never did mine, bro. I've called EJ and Kurt a hundred fucking times and they won't call me back."

"Dude. Overdubs are stupid and useless anyway. The live tracks sound better."

"Are you guys fucking me?"

"No. I guess your tracks were good enough. The gear's all back here in the dog room. We're out of the studio. We're over budget and out of time. They probably wanted to save money and cut out bass overdubs. Kurt's doing vocals and that's it."

"Really, man? Are you lying to me?"

"No, man. I wouldn't do that."

Eric hangs up.

"Who was that?" Lunky asks.

"Spewing."

"You guys fired him, right? That's what Raymo told me."

ƆVEN LAYƆ IT DOWN

Sven sits in the control room in an office chair placed next to the Neve and Kostas. A thin black cord goes from Sven's Fender P Bass to the big room, where his Ampeg sits all alone with a mic in front of it. He punches in a bass line on "Ice Blue Heart." Kostas says, "Perfect. On to the next."

Sven punches in a bass line on "Wanted Love."

EJ laughs and says, "That was easy."

Sven punches in a bass line on "World War IV."

Kurt says, "Next!"

Sven punches in a bass line on "Rain Fall."

The Jovi says, "I don't want to jinx you, bro, but I think you're gonna single-take the entire album."

"That's a real musician," Kostas says. "This is something I can work with—a real bass player."

"It's gonna be like he never existed," Felder says. "There won't be a note of his on the album. His name won't appear anywhere. We're going to erase Patrick Spewing like he was never born."

Eric calls the studio. The receptionist answers. "Hey, it's Eric from Thunderstick, can you ring the studio?"

The Jovi answers. "What's up, bro?"

"That's what I was going to ask you."

"Just hanging out with Sven, doing some bass lines."

"Did we fire Spewing?"

"Yeah. He's history."

"Nobody told me."

The Jovi cups the phone and calls out to the others: "Hey, you guys! No one told Eric we fired Spewing."

"We did," EJ yells. "But we didn't tell Spewing yet. We were gonna tell Spewing first."

The Jovi speaks into the phone. "Dude. They were gonna tell you after they told Spewing. Come up here and meet Sven. You're going to dig him. He's super cool." The other line on the phone rings. "Gotta go, dude. Call you later."

The Jovi punches the other line. "Hay-low!"

"Jovi. It's Patrick. What's going on? Is that bass I hear?"

The Jovi cups the phone and says, "Dudes. It's Spewing."

EJ grabs the phone. "Spewing, you're fired."

"What'd I do?"

"It just wasn't working out. We tried, but you couldn't pull it off. Go get your shit from Eric."

"You can't just fire me."

"Yeah, we can."

"No, you can't."

"Yes, we can."

"No, you can't."

"Yes, we can."

EJ hangs up the phone.

"Dude. Where should we go to celebrate?" the Jovi asks.

"There's this place on Wilshire that serves martinis and meatloaf until two in the morning?" Sven says.

"Perfect."

The new band has a steak dinner in Beverly Hills. The room is stark, white, and minimalist. The booth is leather. The band sits beneath the restaurant's only decoration, a giant mural of the Hagler-Hearns fight.

Eric arrives in a sweat and the five bandmates lift a glass to the new bass player, to the album, to the tour, and eat their meat rare.

August is for mixing. Kostas and Felder are clueless. EJ and Kurt don't leave the room until a suit from DCA shows up and kicks them out. The band returns to La Jolla to wait for an album release and a tour—all of which should be happening in September. Sven takes a room in his grandmother's thatched-roof house overlooking the ocean. The Jovi moves back into the pool house at his parents'.

A HOUSE OF GUITARS

"We're a signed band. Can someone tell me why we're playing at a guitar shop in Clairemont? In the middle of the day?" the Jovi asks during soundcheck.

"We need to play in front of as many people as possible right now," Kurt says.

"C'mon, Kurt. Until we get a tour, we should just relax. It's like baseball. When the season's over, we shake hands, go our separate ways, and meet up again at spring training."

"Not in this band. I have a physical need to play—respect that. If someone asks us to play, we're there."

"Dude. There's a monstrous storm off the coast of New Zealand. That means a major south swell is on tap. Let's go down to Tarantula Bay in Mexico. Camp. Surf. Kick it."

"We're playing this gig."

"Hey," the soundman yells. "I can't run this PA you rented *and* the A/C. They suck too much juice. It's one or the other. Pick your poison."

"It's a hundred degrees out there," Eric says.

"A hundred and three, actually. It's September, and surprise, surprise, the Santa Anas are blowing," the soundman says.

"Turn off the A/C. We need the PA. People need to hear this voice." Kurt points at the guitars hanging on the walls surrounding the tiny stage. "And what are you going to do with all these guitars?"

"Leave 'em."

"Look, man, we're a professional band, with the biggest record deal in the history of this town. We can't be playing up here with all these guitars."

"How am I going to sell guitars if nobody can see 'em?"

"You know, Kurt, you're the one who wanted to play in a guitar store in the first place," EJ says from behind his drum kit.

Kurt looks back at the soundman. "Can you just take some of 'em down?"

The soundman walks over to where Kurt is standing, takes one guitar off the wall, and asks, "Happy?"

The band walks next door and changes in the bathroom of a travel agency. Sven eyes his glistening panther done in fresh ink on his skinny arm. The Jovi gets dolled up in a pirate blouse with leather pants and motorcycle boots. Kurt looks in the mirror and adjusts his dog collar. They take the stage. The audience sits on the floor of the guitar shop in the hundred-degree heat. Most of them are surfers from Windansea. They want to see this band that just recorded a huge album with U2. It's sunny and hot, so they are dressed in slaps, board shorts, and tank tops. Looking out at the audience, everyone in the band except for Kurt begins to realize something important is missing—booze. And it dawns on them that this is a really bad idea. Then Nänce walks in through the crowd up to the stage and tugs on the Jovi's pant leg. "Heeeyyy, Diiiirtdick. I need to talk to you."

The Jovi looks over at Kurt. Kurt shakes his head no. The Jovi says to Nänce, "Wait a second."

The wheel of Kurt's arm grinds over the strings of his Telecaster. The train starts to move, builds momentum. It's strong. Then it gets weird. In the middle of "Alone, Alone," Kurt yells at Eric. "You're fucking out of tune! What's fucking wrong with you?"

Eric looks down at his synthesizer. "Kurt, it can't be out of tune."

"Just stop playing! Stop fucking playing! You're ruining the song!"

Eric stops, stands in the tiny space behind his keyboards, and dodges the head of Sven's bass. When the song ends, he walks off and sits with the surfers and Nänce on the floor.

"What happened?" Nänce yells in his ear.

"It's so hot that none of the guitars can stay in tune. They all keep going flat, but sometimes they all go flat together. That's why Kurt thought it was me. Kurt's singing off key to stay with the band."

After a couple more songs, Kurt gives up singing and the gig degenerates into a forty-minute free-form jam that thins the crowd down to almost nothing. Kurt turns up his amp. It is an assault on the senses, so loud that it makes the body secrete oil and sweat, ears make wax, eyes tear up. All feel ill. Nänce sits curled in a ball with her fingers stuck in her ears.

The storeowner eventually walks up to Kurt and says, "That's enough."

Kurt, dripping with sweat, nods his head.

The Jovi walks off the stage in mild disgust. Nänce runs after him. "Hey Dirrtdick!"

"What's up, Nänce?"

"I've got some good news."

"What?"

She takes his hand and pulls him into the stockroom. She kisses him awkwardly and grabs at the buttons on his sweaty leather. "Guess what?"

"What?"

"Guess."

"You want a pounding."

"Yeah… and what else…?" She yanks his pants down his moist thighs.

"Hey, you're not going to be able to talk with my cock in your mouth."

She takes it out and strokes it. "C'mon, guess."

The Jovi sighs and leans back against the wall. "Umm, you… I don't know…"

She slaps him on the ass. "You give up?"

"Yeah. I give up." The Jovi's eyelids are drooping. He runs his fingers through her short dark hair.

"Sophie wants to have a three-way. You, me, and her."

"She what?"

Nänce stuffs him back in her mouth. The Jovi pulls her up. "She what?"

"You heard me. She wants to do both of us."

"No. Not Sophie. She's not like that."

Nänce giggles and tries to drop back down. He holds her up. "Tell me you're shitting me?"

"No. She's bi. She wants me, but she really wants you. Says she's gonna fuck your lights out."

SHE SELLS SANCTUARY

Sophie has become good friends with a B-rated model named Summer. Like most of the B models, Summer is very good-looking, tall and blonde, but kind of insecty—too many vertebrae, really long from the hip to the shoulder, and no curves. Summer's mother is a psychic named Phoenix who owns a little curio shop on the strip up near Fourteenth Street in Del Mar. They sell crystal medallions and crystal balls and crystal rocks and candles and dream catchers and books on the black arts. Like most parents, Phoenix looks at Sophie and looks at Summer, and can't understand how one girl makes millions of dollars and the other makes thirty-six thousand—if she is willing to live in a shoebox apartment in Tokyo for half the year. Phoenix thinks that Sophie can help Summer get better modeling jobs and bigger contracts. Phoenix offers Sophie a few free readings. Sophie shows up for the first one. Phoenix lights up a joint, and the two pass it back and forth until it's a tiny, soggy triangle. Phoenix snuffs it out and the session begins.

"What do you want to know?" Phoenix asks and holds both of Sophie's hands across a small table covered in a red silk embroidered cloth.

"I want to know why it's gone. When I was a little girl it was everywhere, surrounding me, if I turned fast enough I could see them hiding and giggling and somehow I knew they were looking out for me. But they weren't. They weren't there when I needed them."

"So you want to find out…"

"Where did the magic go?"

"This is very common. I treat this all the time. There are evil elements that try to wall you off from your magic. It's the challenge of rebirth – you will face the same problems in every one of your lives until you overcome."

"You mean I've been here before?"

"It's so obvious to me. Let me call upon the spirit world for confirmation."

An eerie quiet comes over the room. Phoenix has frozen, still looking at Sophie, but departed. She has gone to the other realm. Like a good shrink, Phoenix lets that silence become a participant. Phoenix re-enters Phoenix, and her eyes and face become animated once again. "Oh, Sophie. What I have just seen… I was right. You've lived this life before."

"What life is that?"

"The life of an immortal beauty."

"What did you see?"

"I saw you on a barge in the Nile with Marc Anthony. I saw you beheaded in the market square in France."

Sophie chuckles. "I'm sorry, but that's a bit much."

"And I saw him. He's worried about you."

"Who?"

"He's an artist…"

"Hmm?"

"He paints women's faces."

"Randy George."

Instantly Sophie is flush and moved. Tears stream down her face.

"Sophie, we can overcome all of this. You just need to come and see me every day when you're in town. I'm going to teach you some spells. You're going to win this time around."

Sophie wipes her cheeks and asks, "Do you have another joint? One for the road?"

"Sure." Phoenix says. "Do you just want to buy a dime bag?"

"Okay. One more thing. Can you ask Randy George? The man that I'm with, he's super nice but there's this other one that I think maybe I'm supposed to be with. What does he think?"

Phoenix closes her eyes, shudders, then spits into Sophie's upturned palm. She rubs the spit in circles, searching deep into its glimmer. "The one you are with, he is a warrior. You are a butterfly."

"That is like so…" Sophie holds her hands over her heart and shakes her head.

"I have something for you." Phoenix hands Sophie a book with a pastel drawing of a woman in a negligee sitting on a crescent moon that hangs within a Roman arch above a small stream. "You don't have to be powerless anymore."

Sophie opens the book and it falls to a chapter entitled *Spells of Love*. "Thanks, I guess."

"Be careful. Powerful stuff in there. Don't try any until we go over them first. You don't know what dark forces may rise up."

"Mmmm, okay."

"And something else…"

"Yes?"

"Do you think that Summer would work more if she had larger breasts?"

"Uh, yeah. She's flat-chested, isn't she?"

Phoenix nods sadly and pats her own chest. "It's my fault."

HOW SOON IS NOW

Sophie takes out her sacred book. On the endpaper she puts a line through the name JAMES FRANKLIN and writes underneath it: BOBBY DUGAN, BOBBY DUGAN, BOBBY DUGAN.

She hears a knock on her door.

When she opens it, she is mildly surprised. It works. Her powers are strong. He's standing right there.

"Hey, Sophie, how's it going? Is James here?" The Jovi smiles.

For a second she's sad and lost and then he touches her hand and she has hope. "I…" She holds her breath, searches his eyes. "You're not here for James." She exhales and moves closer.

"No."

She pulls him in and bolts the door.

"I'm here for you."

Blood flushes, air stills, he pushes the flowing material from her body and plunges every ounce of his strength into her softness again and again until he isn't hard and she isn't soft. Until, they are one.

CHANGES

"Can you believe she asked me to move out?" James says to the Jovi, Eric, and Kurt at Chuck's Steak House. "It's gotta have something to do with the psychic. She just started seeing this bitch, Phoenix, and then she changed."

"Really?" the Jovi asks and feels a twisting in his gut. "Where are you staying?"

"In Kurt's living room. On the floor. At least until we work this shit out."

"A psychic?" Eric asks. "Like what? Tarot cards? Palm reading?"

"Yeah, all that. And past life shit, too," James says.

"Spiritual warfare," Kurt says and nods in a powerful, knowing manner. "I should've expected this. We need somebody heavy in the spirit to straighten her out. We should call in Pastor Ron."

"Who's Pastor Ron?" Eric asks.

"Pastor Ron pulled me out of Juvi. He brought us to the Lord." Kurt says and holds his hands out towards James and the Jovi.

"Have you made up your minds?" a perky waitress asks.

"Four New York Strips. Rare." Kurt hands her the menus.

"Okay. Help yourself to our salad bar."

The meat arrives on the table, and Kurt bows his head and is about to say a prayer.

James interrupts him. "When Sophie comes back to me, I want you guys to be my groomsmen."

Eric smiles brightly. "Thanks, James, I mean it's an hon—"

"Sorry, Eric. I meant Kurt and the Jovi. I want Pastor Ron to marry… us… like… did Kurt and Priscilla… Yeah Pastor Ron, I need to…" James stops himself. Then starts on his steak with a sharp knife then stops again. "Not… hungry." Behind his Buddy Holly–style glasses, his eyes are red. "I had… dream…" Then he sobs a little.

Kurt puts his arm on James's shoulder and says. "Everything will be okay. We've walked through trials greater than this. Let's pray."

JEALOUS GUY

It is October, and the album has been mastered. A release date is set—January 21, 1989. The band is just waiting for the album, the tour, and the publishing deal.

The Jovi rides his chopper up to L.A. to the Chateau Marmont. At the desk they hand him a key. He sprints to the room. She is naked and waiting.

The Jovi's insides are knotted, every muscle in his body is twitching as he hovers above her. "This is going to cause a lot of problems," he says.

"For who? Not for you." She takes him and guides him in. Her eyes flutter and she moans.

Afterward the Jovi strokes her hair and says, "It's just going to take a little while."

"I don't belong to James. I never did." She reaches over to the bedstand and takes out a joint. "I don't see what you're so worried about." She strikes a match and breathes in deeply.

The Jovi is a little startled. "You're getting high?"

"As long as I don't drink. It's fine."

The Jovi nods his head slowly at the ceiling. "Yeah."

Sophie throws her long leg over the back of the purple chopper and they ride. She holds him tight as they sip the cold moist air in Topanga Canyon. She arches her back in a bend of freedom as they breathe in the warm dry air at the top of Mulholland. The sky is no longer blue but azure, the L.A. smog no longer gray but brilliant yellow.

The Jovi rides back from L.A. just in time for band practice. Thunderstick rehearses at an industrial site out in Mira Mesa. The lease had a NO ROCK BANDS clause, but they signed it anyway. Bill Wellington sends the check. The whole complex is brand-new and almost vacant. Somebody complained about the volume, so now the band doesn't practice until after midnight. James shows up and asks the Jovi, "Where've you been?"

"L.A."

"Who were you with?"

"Alexandra."

"I thought you guys broke up."

"Not totally. You know the drill."

Kurt grips his head and says in a fake southern accent, "Alright, how mellow, nobody has any idea how much pain I'm in. My TMJ is killing me and nobody cares. My music makes the pain go away. Alright, best singer in the world has no one to play with. Alright. How mellow. No respect."

"We're here now," the Jovi says, and chunks out a guitar chord that makes the walls shake.

Two days later James knocks on Sophie's door and says, "I know you're fucking him."

"James," she says with a laugh, "it's my body. You're out of line."

"You can have anyone you want. Why'd it have to be the Jovi?"

"He's my soul mate."

"Did Phoenix tell you that?"

"I would've figured it out on my own eventually."

James stomps over to Kurt's apartment. "Look, man, I just want you to know that the Jovi is fucking my girlfriend!"

"No," says Kurt. "He knows what that would do."

"That fucking psychic told her that he's her soul mate! Such fucking bullshit!"

"Call him," Kurt says sternly. "Band meeting."

The Jovi walks over to Kurt's apartment and hits the buzzer. He climbs the stairs and lets himself in. Before he is two feet in the room, James slugs him in the eye. The Jovi falls to the ground. James dives on top of him and hammer punches his ribs. The Jovi doesn't fight back until he hears a crack and feels a sharp pain. He pulls James's arm under him and rolls on top. In a crushing blow, Kurt drives his own shoulder into the Jovi's ribs and screams, "Get off him!"

James gets to his feet. Kurt sits on the Jovi's chest. Both of them look down at him. "Well, is it true? Did you fuck James's chick?"

The Jovi nods and holds his hands over his face. Kurt lifts his fist, then stops, looks around, and shakes his head.

"Tell him you're sorry. Tell him!"

"I'm sorry. I'm sorry. I'm sorry."

"You have everything, why do you have to take from me?" James picks up his glasses but doesn't put them on. His eyes look out of place.

"This is the Garden of Eden. She's the forbidden fruit. You can have any chick—just not her. Do you hear me? You can't have her!" Kurt says.

"Yeah, yeah."

"He can't take it." Kurt thrusts his finger at James then thumps his own hollow chest. "I can't take it. You know our mother left our father. It's different for us. You don't understand. You'll never understand."

The Jovi starts to say something but stops.

"I know what it's like to sin. I know. God knows I'm a sinner. Okay? Just ask for forgiveness and don't do it again."

"She's yours. Your chick. I shouldn't have…"

"Tell James you'll never do it again."

"I'll never touch her again."

"Swear it!"

"I swear."

Kurt gets off the Jovi. He stands up, looking crooked and broken in the middle. They shake hands.

"We just need to work through this," James says.

The Jovi smiles. "Yeah, we go way back. We can't let a chick…"

"No. Me and Sophie. We can get through this. You can't just turn it off—what we had."

"Yeah. I know. You can't just turn it off."

DON'T WORRY BE HAPPY

Sophie, Felder, and the Jovi have lunch in L.A. at the Ivy on Robertson. Above the white tablecloth, below the green trellis, Felder studies Sophie. He's waiting for a moment he remembers when he thought he saw her eyes flash. It happens. She looks up from the endive, pear, and goat cheese salad. "Is everything okay, Adam?" Her eyes go dark, like a jewel's facet turning in the sun. Beauty disappears then reappears with shocking color and light.

"Don't worry about a thing," he says, "it's good for the band."

The Jovi smiles, exhales.

"The fact that you're dating a supermodel—it's what we want. We'll get some press. People will get your vibe. Kurt'll get over it. C'mon! What's the big deal? No worries."

"Adam, is that all I am to you?" Sophie laughs. "A supermodel?"

"No, no, I didn't mean it like... I meant..." Felder puts his finger on the Jovi's swollen eye and says, "James fucks with you again, and I'll give him a faceful of Hollywood."

The Jovi laughs and hugs Sophie.

"Don't you love this?" Sophie holds her arm out in a beam of light.

"What?" the Jovi asks.

"The golden sunshine of fall."

Soon it is December, dark at five, then a damp beach chill. Two months, and still James won't let it go, still sad, and restless on the floor in the living room. Priscilla had to ask for her old job back. She sleeps in the bedroom by herself until Kurt comes home in the early morning hours, smelling faintly of perfume and motor oil. James is awake, lying on a lumpy futon, staring at the popcorn ceiling. "You know, his dad's a doctor. Our dad's nuts. The Dugans have never had any respect for us."

Kurt looks around with nervous eyes, goes into the bedroom just as Priscilla is coming out in her work clothes. He kisses her on the cheek and gets into bed. Priscilla makes James a cup of coffee, and the two of them sit silently.

Then she says, "Have a good day."

The Jovi rides out to Mira Mesa for practice. Everyone else is already there. Kurt has his guitar on and is picking bluegrass-style and staring at the wall. The Jovi opens his guitar case, looks sick and hot in the head. He turns to Kurt and asks, "Did you do this to my guitar?"

Kurt drops his Telecaster on the floor. "What do you fucking expect of me? You're fucking my brother's girl." He walks out.

EJ and Eric look at the Jovi, then at the guitar. They turn away in disgust. The Mustang's engine roars and its tires screech.

The Jovi's sunburst Les Paul has been disemboweled. The strings have been pulled off and the pick-ups are hanging from the guitar on stringy red wires like two eyeballs popped from their sockets. On the other side, the word "BACKSTABR" is crudely carved into the pristine finish. Clearly, Kurt ran out of space for the second "B" and the "E."

"Gibson gave me this guitar. Do you fucking hear me?" the Jovi yells at EJ, Sven, and Eric. "You know what I'm going to do? I'm going to fix this guitar, and I'm going to play it. And Kurt's going to look over at me, and he's going to see it, see me playing it. That's what I'm going to do."

NIGHTCLUBBING

Kurt and Eric are on the 805 freeway. It's five lanes of economy cars and the dim light they cast on the world, but it leads to Club Metro. Kurt lights a smoke and says, "No more masturbation."

1988 is almost over.

"Masturbation leaves you weak and alone. I used to masturbate a lot when I was on the drugs. No woman wants you if you masturbate. I don't know how they know, but they do."

"Yeah?" Eric asks.

"Yeah. But here's the hard part. When you stop masturbating, it gives you what you need, that little something that makes you get with a chick. And that's a sin. But I don't know which one's worse—the sin of masturbating or the sin of cheating on your wife."

"Cheating, right?"

"Maybe. But being alone is the biggest sin there is against God. And masturbating really makes you alone. It's like you never really live your life. It's like you're watching your life on TV. Life is a gift from God—to waste it, that's worse."

"When I got with that little actress, part of me felt really guilty and the other part felt really alive. Something in my head said, 'You'll only be young once. Go for it.'"

"I know both of those voices. One is from the devil. Try it for a few days."

"Try what?"

"Don't masturbate."

Kurt and Eric enter Club Metro. They walk the gauntlet of eyes through the poolroom. A chesty brunette leans out across the green felt. Her tits roll forward and stop at the top of her U-shaped spandex neckline. She looks up at Kurt and winks. Kurt and Eric escape into the blacklights. Another girl bumps into Kurt, puts her hands on his chest, and giggles. Eric thinks to himself, *It's natural selection like the apes. One male gets a whole harem, the other males are sent off into the woods alone.*

"Isn't that Nänce over there?" Eric asks Kurt.

"Yeah."

They walk over. "Hey, Nänce. What's up?"

"Yoooou teeell meee."

"Is the Jovi here?" Eric asks.

"Dirtdick?" Her blue eyes are surrounded by delicate, discolored skin. Nänce looks very sick and very beautiful at the same time. "I don't know."

"Is he with my brother's chick?"

"Don't know." Nänce sips a red drink through a straw. "Hey, have you met Phoenix? She's been saying some trippy shit about you."

"I don't know anyone named Phoenix."

"That's funny. She knows you." Nänce smiles.

"Who the fuck is Phoenix?"

"She's Sophie's psychic. She says you and James are warriors—Sophie is a butterfly."

"I'm a Christian. I know where that information comes from—it comes from demons."

"Tell James you can't grab a butterfly by the wings. You know what happens, right? The wings come off in your fingers; they fucking disintegrate. And you look at your fucking fingers and it looks like a smudge of color, like makeup."

"Fuck Phoenix. Tell her to leave my band alone."

"You know what else she says about you?"

"SHUT THE FUCK UP!"

Nänce quivers, then smiles. "Fucking forget it. You'll find out soon enough." Nänce disappears into the sea of bodies on the dance floor.

Kurt marches into the poolroom, slugs down a beer and asks the Lycra-topped girl, "What's up?"

The club is a labyrinth. Eric is lost in dancers, then on a couch under some stairs, then by the bar three people deep. Everyone looks really beautiful, then beauty goes home and what's left looks desperate. Eric searches for Kurt Franklin. He is nowhere to be found. Outside, Eric calls a cab.

Kurt opens his front door very slowly. He can see a lump of bedding in the middle of the living-room floor. "Was she there?"

"Who?"

"Sophie. Was she?"

"No, man. Where?"

"Club Metro. How about the Jovi, did you see him?"

"No."

"He's fucking her. I know it. They're probably in L.A., probably fucking right now."

"No, man."

"It's like when we were kids. He has everything. We have nothing."

"Nah."

"Yeah. You started this band and you're broke. You write all the songs."

"It's a band. We share."

"You're the only one sharing. What do those guys share with you?"

"What are you guys doing up?" Priscilla asks from the door to the bedroom.

"I'm always up. I just fucking lie here at night and stare at the ceiling."

"Hey, Scilla, I'm sorry," Kurt says.

"It's okay. I have to get up anyway. What time is it?"

"I don't know. I'm gonna take a shower and get some sleep." Kurt kisses Priscilla on the forehead and walks past her into the bathroom.

"What's that smell?" Priscilla asks, and wrinkles her nose.

"Smoke? Beer?"

"No. I know it. It's a really cheap lotion that all the strippers buy. Did you go to a strip bar?"

"No, babe. Some girl spilled a thing on me."

"A what?" She laughs.

"A coconut drink."

"Oh, okay."

THE HAMMER OF WITCHES

The next day Kurt drives out to Pastor Ron's Vine Church. It's a brand-new metal-roofed rectangular auditorium in Sorrento Valley. There are rows and rows of folding chairs facing a small blue-carpeted stage beneath a giant crucifix.

Pastor Ron has a close-cropped orange mustache and an earnest expression. He smiles when he sees Kurt. "My rock star." They hug and walk into Pastor Ron's office. It's a white drywall box. Pastor Ron sits back in his folding chair and takes off his round wire rims and rubs them on the tail of his denim shirt. "What's going on, Kurt?"

"It's about a psychic."

Pastor Ron squints at Kurt. He's very concerned. "Witchcraft! What's happened?"

"Sophie, my brother's chick, she's consulted a psychic, and the—"

"The witch."

"Yeah, the witch told my brother's chick to leave him."

"Kurt that may be a good thing, if this poor girl is under satanic influences, you don't want her in your fam—"

"No! It's bad, because now she's with the Jovi, you know, Bobby Dugan."

"Oh. You're worried about Bobby…"

"No. I'm worried about the band. I don't think I can play with the Jovi if he's with my brother's chick."

"It's a plot, Kurt—You sing for the Lord—The devil is trying to break up your band."

Kurt nods while a determination builds inside. "First the devil tries to make me think I'm crazy, now he's trying to wreck my band." Kurt lifts his palms up to the acoustic tile above them in a grand query. "Trial after trial."

Pastor Ron steers his VW van. Kurt smokes and hangs his heavy hand out the window. The wind sends sparks from his cigarette across his knuckles.

"What are we going to tell her?" Kurt asks.

"I don't know," says Pastor Ron. "To stop?"

They park before a tony strip of shops in Del Mar. Between a hair salon and an upscale Irish pub sits Phoenix's curio shop.

They enter and Pastor Ron approaches the register. Kurt picks up a dreamcatcher. "Don't touch anything in here," says Pastor Ron.

Kurt lets it fall from his hand.

A woman closes the cash drawer and looks up at Pastor Ron. She has a grizzled shrunken face like a carved apple beneath frizzy curls. "Listen, Phoenix," says Pastor Ron in a terse tone. "I need you to stop attacking this man with your witch—"

"I'm not Phoenix. Stay right here." The woman walks away.

Kurt and Pastor Ron wait. Surrounded by crystals, pointy hats, and didgeridoos, the eyes of a hundred wolfs seem to bear down on them from framed posters on the walls.

"Oh my…" Pastor Ron mutters as an iron-haired beauty glides towards him in a white robe.

"Whoa…" Kurt says when he locks eyes with a tall blonde girl, Summer, in the back of the shop.

When the iron-haired beauty gets close, Kurt looks at Pastor Ron and sees that his mentor is enchanted. Pastor Ron cannot speak under this woman's gaze. To him her eyes are like spinning plates. Black then green then black again.

Back in the VW van Pastor Ron asks, "Kurt, have you been unfaithful to Priscilla?"

Kurt looks down, very dejected. "Yes."

Pastor Ron nods. "Those who are given to lust, the devil has power over them."

"That's what I said to the band!"

"The devil works with illusion. Illusion is just perception. My wife is beautiful on the inside."

"I thought she has indigestion?"

"You're a good person, Kurt. You're heart is good. The devil will never have any power over your soul. He'll just make you think things are a lot worse than they are."

"That didn't go so well in there," says Kurt. "If she gets her info from the devil, why did we get our palms read?"

"Know your… enemy…"

"And what did she mean when she said I have a murderer's thumb?"

Pastor Ron glances down at Kurt's thumb. It looks like it's been sawed off, like the nail goes the wrong way. "Stay away from the harlots. Love God. Love Priscilla. Love your neighbor as yourself. When you can't walk anymore, He'll carry you."

"Maybe we should just douse her with some Holy Water next time."

HOW DCA SAYS MERRY CHRISTMAS

On December 15, Felder calls the Jovi and starts yelling. "We're fucked. We're so fucked. I can't believe how fucked we are!"

"What's up?"

"It's Bernie. It's fucking *Rolling Stone* magazine. DCA fired Bernie! The whole fucking music division! They were all getting ready to take their Christmas break and DCA says, 'Merry fucking Christmas, you're fucking fired!' Pink slips on every desk."

"Whoa, no way. No one can fire Bernie."

"Okay, they didn't *fire* him. They actually promoted him to the board of directors. But he's banished from the music division. He's not allowed to have anything to do with the music division until they clean this up. They're bringing in a new team from Capitol. We're fucked."

"What happened?"

"Go buy this month's *Rolling Stone*. They're calling Bernie the King of Payola!"

"Well, is he?"

"Of course. I can't believe it. Those brazen fuckwads at *Rolling Stone,* they bite the nipple that feeds them. How do they have the sack to act surprised? It's common fucking knowledge!"

"What is?"

"The radio business—the whole thing comes down to hookers and blow. When you hear some crap song on the radio—you don't like it and no one you've ever met likes it—even the DJ can't convince you he likes it—I'll tell you who likes it—the label and that's it. Every major label—and some of the minors—hire independent promoters, IPs, to get spins—radio play. It's regional. There may be an IP for Southern California, or Chicago, or the Bay Area. The record company pays the IP to promote an artist, the IP gets to the program directors—the people who make the playlists, the people who pick the music that gets on air—and bribes them with whatever it is they like: tickets to the big game, young hookers, old hookers, little boy hookers, coke, crank, cash, whatever. The record company gets to control what's on the radio, the program directors get laid, and we get rich! That's how it works."

"The people who listen to the radio get shit?"

"Fuck 'em! They should buy albums. This is standard operating procedure. No big deal. The IPs get a little dirty, but the record company stays clean—that's how it has always worked until Jerry Finklestein. I want to kill that fucking Finklestein."

"Who's Finklestein?"

"A Portland-based IP, got popped for possession and rolled on Bernie to avoid a mandatory sentence. They expected to reel in some sort of Colombian drug lord. They didn't expect to get Bernie Zupnik, the president of DCA Records, served on a silver platter. That's why we're fucked!"

The news puts Thunderstick in a fog. Kurt calls a meeting of the band. We all show up at his apartment. Kurt says, "It doesn't matter. We just recorded one of the best albums in the history of rock. The new people are going to hear it and know the truth. You can't keep the truth down."

EJ stares over the Jovi's shoulder at the fake wood paneling and says, "It would only be logical for the new people to consider the substantial investment DCA has in our band and our album. It only makes sense for them to try and promote our band to recoup said expenditures."

The Jovi says, "Bernie's still on the board. He's still Bernie Zupnik! And Felder is still Adam Felder. They're still on our side. They'll fuck whoever it takes to get our album out."

"This probably means our album isn't coming out in January," Eric says.

"Shut up, Eric! You don't know that!" Kurt presses his index fingers into his temple, locks and unlocks his jaw, and turns his head to the wall. "We have to stay ready. It's always darkest before the dawn. This only means something good is about to happen."

James walks in, takes one look at the Jovi, and says, "Well? Are you still fucking my chick? How's that going for you?"

"We're just friends."

"Nänce says you're fucking her."

"You can't believe Nänce."

"Look, James, we're having a band meeting here, can you give us a minute, this is important," EJ says.

James turns around, walks out, and slams the door.

"Sophie's not your friend. Just know that," Kurt says sternly, looking at the Jovi. "We're your friends. We've been playing together for fifteen fucking years. Nobody our age has that."

"I know—"

"She'd fuck me." Kurt looks around to make sure that Priscilla isn't there. "You know that, right? She'd probably fuck me too."

"No, she's not like—"

"She would. I'm probably next in line."

"You're the one that would fuck anything."

Kurt turns to the Jovi, the veins in his neck filling with blood and his eyes sinking to blackness. "Do you have any idea what's going on here?"

"Hold on there, guys, cool down," EJ says.

"There are other realms at work here. The devil is fucking with our band. My brother's chick. DCA. The witch. My jaw. None of you could even deal with this kind of pain. I have the worst TMJ that anybody has ever had. The pain starts in my fucking head and shoots down my arm until I can barely move." Kurt slugs himself in the jaw. Bone on bone, the sound reverberates. He looks around the room, unfazed. "I'd do anything just to make the pain go away. I am a sinner. How many fucking times do I have to tell you that? I have sinned on my wife."

"Look, we're all sinners, Kurt," EJ says. "It doesn't matter. What matters here is this business. Our band is a business."

"EJ's right," Sven says. "We've got to treat it like—"

"Look," Kurt points at the Jovi. "You invited evil into this band! Pastor Ron knows. Everybody knows but you. That psychic is behind this whole thing. I wish we could drown her like in the old days."

"Kurt, actually, only the ones that weren't witches drowned. That was kind of the problem—congratulations your daughter wasn't a witch, oh but she's dead—"

"SHUT UP, ERIC!"

NEW YEAR'S EVE

In a few hours it will be a new day, a new year, one year from a new decade—1989. It's New Year's Eve and Thunderstick is playing at a Persian disco called Maxime's in downtown La Jolla. Unlike the House of Guitars gig, unlike so many of the other gigs that Kurt has forced Thunderstick to do, this gig looks like it will be fun. He tells the band over and over, "We need to play in front of as many people as possible right now."

Before the gig, Eric tells Kurt, "Dude. I've done it."

"Done what?"

"I haven't beaten my heater in like weeks. I'm about to explode."

Kurt laughs.

"I can feel it—some male fluffing force building in my loins. It's working. The chicks can feel my fluff."

"Where's Dane?"

"L.A."

"It's New Year's Eve and your chick isn't with you?"

"Some job for Tiffany Tucker—I don't know."

"You got to straighten that out. Dane's a great girl, but you're the man."

"I know, man. I wish I could freeze her and thaw her out when all this horniness goes away."

"You can't."

"That little actress in L.A.? All I can think about is that second I stuck my hand down her pants. I don't know how to stop it."

"Pray about it."

"I don't want to. I love Dane—true love. But I just want to throw true love in the fire and pull it out while it's still smoking."

"Dude, what's come over you? This whole band. It's like you guys are under some dark force."

"You think?"

Thunderstik rocks, forty-five minutes worth. Then it's house music all night long.

Carrie Gomez is a beautiful Mexican girl with dark skin and coarse straight black hair. Her mouth is wide and turned up at the corners. Her strong hands grip Eric's shoulders and rub. He wants to get her out of the bar before she spots the Jovi, James, or Kurt and leaves with one of them.

"I saw you at the beach," she says, after they get in his blue BMW.

"Really? When?"

"A long time ago."

"You remember?"

"Yeah. I don't forget hair like this. I liked you from the first second I saw you. Do you like me?" She puts her strong dark hands in her lap.

Eric notices the nurse vibe—white hose, short orange six-ties-style dress. "Oh yeah. You look like a popsicle. I love that."

"What do you do to a popsicle?"

"What do you do? *Hmmm*. You lick it, right?"

"Yes."

He gets her back into his bedroom in the converted garage. Carrie is tender and talkative from the start. Eric feels eyes upon him. He looks around the room, sees little demons perched in the corners of the ceiling. He thinks they must belong to the Jovi—this is his old room. He turns his face from the nape of Carrie's neck and sees the suffering Christ. He starts to think that whatever Kurt has is contagious.

The next morning there is a persistent knocking on Eric's front door. He drags himself out of bed, opens it, and finds two high school jocks standing there in baseball caps and sleeveless sweatshirts. One of them says, "Are you Eric Adams of Thunderstick?"

"Yes."

The other one hands Eric a brown envelope and says, "You've been served." They turn and run as if they think Eric is going to chase them.

Eric closes the door, sits on his black leather couch, opens the envelope, and finds that the envelope does not contain fan mail or a promotional copy of the album. It's a lawsuit. Spewing is suing Eric and everyone else in the band for four million dollars. Wrongful termination. His attorney is straight out of some North County strip mall. He has a photo of himself in the top left corner of his stationery like he's a goddamned Realtor.

Oh, shit, Eric says to himself. He calls Kurt and says, "Don't answer your door."

"Too late."

"Come over and we'll call Felder."

Kurt walks the two blocks. They call Felder. Felder says, "We're gonna cram that guy's head so far up his ass he's gonna have to unzip his pants to pick his fucking teeth."

"How's that?" Kurt asks.

"This is fucking easy. I've seen these guys do it a million times. We come at him with two smoking barrels. We hit him with so much paperwork and delays that it runs up his legal bills and he just folds."

"So you're going to call Stein and get him on this?" Eric asks.

"No, man. Stein's a deal guy. He doesn't do this kinda thing. We call in the litigators."

"Stein took thirty grand and that's it—now he's done?"

"Yeah. Basically."

"How much are these guys gonna be?"

"More," Felder says. "It'll come out of the T-shirt money."

"I need that money to fix the TMJ in my jaw," Kurt says.

"Don't worry, Kurt. I'll tell Wellington to get you a loan. How's about that?"

Kurt presses his index fingers into his jaw and stares at the floor. "Fucking Spewing."

"Dude," Eric says to Kurt, "I saw the devil. He's fucking with me."

Kurt presses his finger on the receiver, looks Eric in the eye and says, "Have you seen any talking animals?"

THE PEN AND THE SWORD

Felder calls the litigators and asks, "What do you need for a retainer?"

"How many albums have they sold?"

"Zero."

"Eighty grand."

Felder calls Stein. "Execute the Summerland deal."

"The merchandizing deal?"

"Yup."

"When?"

"Now."

Felder calls Bill Wellington and says, "When the Summerland money comes in, send eighty grand to the litigators."

"These guys are going broke."

"Don't worry. I'm working on a publishing deal that could be worth five hundred grand."

"Nice."

UNCONTROLLABLE URGE

Kurt is a generous guy. No one would ever doubt that. Up in L.A. he gave away the last of his money to bums on the street. Now he still wants to reach out to those guys, the guys he understands. Kurt and Eric are on their way out to dinner in La Jolla before a gig at Club Metro. Eric asks Kurt, "What are the other signs of witchcraft?"

"I told you about talking animals, right?" asks Kurt.

"I'm good on that."

"Being unable to find your cock."

"What?"

"Yeah, Pastor Ron told me a witch can steal your stuff. You have to go and make the witch give it back to you. It's in his book."

"What book is that?"

"*Malleus Malificarum.* It's five hundred years old and full-on."

"Whoa." Eric reaches between his legs. "This is getting weird."

"The devil really doesn't want our album to come out."

On the sidewalk a young bum, midtwenties and clearly crazy, is hanging out in front of Le Grande Gamin. He has a scruffy beard, a red homeless-man tan, shell-shocked eyes, and a tightly wound little bundle of clothes and bedding under his arm. Kurt walks up, looks him in the eye, and says, "Hey, man, are you hungry?" The guy nods and Kurt says, "Do you want to have dinner with us?"

Inside the fancy restaurant, the three of them sit down among the tourists, golfers, and retirees—Kurt and Eric in their black leather gig gear, the vagrant in torn flannel. Kurt and Eric sit with menus in their laps. The homeless man sits looking at the walls and ceiling as if they are a new and troublesome technology. When the waitress comes over, she tries to take the bundle of clothes and bedding off the table and put it on the floor. The vagrant squeaks. She acquiesces. Kurt orders surf 'n' turf for three. They sit silently. Kurt looks at the vagrant, ready to say something, but somehow holds his tongue until finally, after the salad, he starts: "I know what it's like. Living on the street. Abandoned by everyone who said they loved you. People call you crazy, but you're not. Don't listen to them—the voices—they're not real."

That line catches the vagrant's attention. He looks at Kurt with eyes like painted Ping-Pong balls. Kurt continues: "You just have to ask God to make the voices go away. You have to tell the voices to go away in the name of God, in the name of Jesus, and they'll go. It really works."

The steak comes and the vagrant digs in. He eats every single thing on the plate, the beets, the parsley, the lemon wedge, everything except the lobster shell. He mops up the melted butter with a loaf of bread. The check comes quickly. Eric pays it. On the sidewalk, Kurt asks Eric for twenty bucks. He gives it to him. Kurt gives it to the vagrant. They get in the black '68 Mustang and drive to Club Metro. James greets them at the door.

The Jovi shows up, spots James, plugs in, plays one set, unplugs, and leaves.

"What the fuck was that?" Kurt asks.

The place is packed. The club kids like club music. It doesn't matter.

EJ says to Eric, "It's totally without merit. I expect a judge to throw it out of court."

Eric says, "It's still gonna cost us a lot of money just to get that far. Where's that gonna come from?"

"Well." EJ looks around the place, keen and detached, as if he were an Eskimo scanning a gray hunk of tundra. "What we really gotta do is get Kurt to split the publishing. It's not fair if he takes fifty percent for the words and another twenty-five percent for the melody."

"Fifty percent for words?"

"Yeah. We should split it even. It's what the guys in U2 do. It says all songs written by U2."

"Where *is* Kurt?"

"Over there."

"Should we ask him about the publishing now?"

"No way, dude. He's got another Betty cornered."

In the corner, carnal thoughts fill Kurt's head. She's talking. He can't hear what she says, but he can feel her breath on his neck. He shouldn't. He loves his wife. But he can feel the heat from her skin. He shouldn't. She might be a witch. How can he tell? He reaches out and takes her hand. She is soft. "Come with me."

He watches her response. It's hard to say "Where?" without smiling. She opens her mouth. He places his mouth on hers. Tongue to tongue, it's like two fish fighting.

"I don't care where," she whispers in his ear.

He pulls her through the blacklights, through the pool-room, past the smiling spandex-top girl, past the bouncer, to the door of the black '68 Mustang Fastback in the parking lot. She grabs and pulls at every part of him. He lifts her onto the hood, devours her neck, and mounts her.

"Oh..." It comes from her center. "Your... Oh... You're..."

Kurt's hands grip her cold flesh. His hips drive into her. She folds around him. Her unsteady breath excites his heart like a drum roll. Her sighs have a sharp sound at the end. "Your band is really ggggooooood, oh." He pumps harder. "I like your vvvvvvoice, oh." He finishes in a quivering animal death jolt and pushes her into the car. He rolls over her into the driver's seat and collapses. She leans on her side and runs her hand up and down his chest. "It's ok," She says. Kurt looks over. "You're the biggest." Her skirt is up high underneath her breasts that lie below her open blouse, overlapping each other like two U's. Her skin folds in tiny lateral creases down her belly into the fold of her legs. The darkness isn't enough. Kurt can't stand her immodesty. He tugs her skirt down to her hips and says, "You just sleep with guys like this?"

"No. I like you."

"My wife would never do something like this."

She laughs. "I don't want to marry you."

"That's not what I mean."

She runs her finger up her thigh and lifts her skirt. "You're moody."

Kurt stares out the window at the swirls in the dark gray stucco on the side of the club. "I'm the best singer in the world."

She laughs.

"I'm for real."

"Okay."

Kurt sees James walk out the front door of Club Metro and turn toward the parking lot. James casts an enormous black shadow on the stucco wall.

"Duck down!"

Kurt starts the car, drops it in gear, and the tires spin and smoke as he speeds into the back alley.

"Where are we going?"

James hears the chirping tires, looks up, and spots Kurt's Mustang sliding into the alley. He shakes his head and walks back into the club. "Did you come here with Kurt?" he asks Eric. Eric is standing in a corner grinning.

"Yeah."

"He just took off."

"Shit. That's the second time he's done that to me."

"Yeah. You want a ride?"

"You don't have a car."

"I know. I met this chick. She can drive us."

James and Eric squeeze into the back of a Karmann Ghia.

James says, "Nicky, this is Eric, my brother's keyboard player."

From the passenger's seat, Nicky says, "Oh my God! Your band is awesome."

Eric shakes her hand then reaches his hand out the short distance to the driver. "Hi, I'm Eric." The driver doesn't turn around. "Hi, I'm Eric. I'm the keyboard player," Eric says a little louder. The driver doesn't flinch. He sits back in his seat.

"Oh my God! I forgot to tell you. Sandy's deaf!" Nicky pats the driver on the shoulder and points at Eric in the backseat.

"Nahlow," Sandy moans.

"I'm hungry. You girls hungry? HEY, SANDY! DO YOU LIKE THE MUSIC IN THE CLUB? YOU KNOW LIKE YOU CAN FEEL THE VIBRATION 'CAUSE IT'S SO LOUD, RIGHT?" Eric asks.

"Yelling won't help her hear." Nicky flaps out Eric's question to Sandy on her hands.

"Ngyah." Sandy nods and smiles at Eric.

They end up at a twenty-four-hour diner off the freeway in Pacific Beach. Dust covered plastic plants surround the bright white booth. It is trimmed with red piping. The girls get up to go to the bathroom together. Eric gathers his courage and asks James, "How did Kurt get so…?"

"Yeah?"

"—Kurt."

"I don't know. It just kind of happened. He was pretty normal and then our lives got destroyed."

"Do you think he's like Van Gogh? So creative 'cause he's—?"

"He's not crazy. I can tell you why I think he got so good, but you should ask him yourself."

Eric nods, "That could be dangerous." Eric smiles. "Tell me what you think, I'm curious."

James takes a sip of water and looks around the restaurant. "Okay. This one night when we were kids, before they split, our dad opened up for B.B. King at Croce's. 'Cause it was a bar and we were kids they wouldn't let us in the audience. We had to sit on the side of the stage. Our mom sat right in front. We watched her. She was kind of blue from the stage lights. By herself watching dad on his stool. He started playing this insane Asturian flamenco thing on his acoustic. It was fucking intricate and beautiful, faster and faster as he played building to this insane climax. The people in the bar were laughing and smoking and talking and fucking around. You could here them the whole time. It was pearls before swine for sure. When it was over my dad walked off the stage and handed his acoustic guitar to Kurt. He said, 'Watch this guy. He's not bad.' Kurt sat there, side-stage, and played every note that B.B. King did. It was like an echo."

"Whoa."

"The people in the audience couldn't see Kurt. They were too busy going apeshit."

"What is it with white people and the blues?"

"Yeah, I know. So, B.B. King got annoyed with the kid copying his licks. He had the bouncers throw us out."

"So how did that make Kurt so good?"

"Kurt told me afterwards, after our mom left us, that *that* night was the only time he ever saw mom look at dad like she loved him, when he was up there on the stage."

"Ouch."

"Kurt told me when dad spoke through his guitar, mom understood."

"Fuck."

"He's been playing for four hours a day ever since. You'd probably be pretty good too if you played that much."

"I'll never be like Kurt, the Jovi, EJ, or even Sven."

"You can hang."

Eric shakes his head at the sugar. "So that deaf girl? She's kind of sexy. What do you think it would sound like if she had an orgasm?"

"Eric—"

"It could be uncouth like a foghorn or it could be like Lorelei on the banks of the river Rhine – the most beautiful thing you've ever heard."

"You don't have to do that wingman shit with me, I'm not the Jovi."

"I want to hear it. Really."

"You're..."

The girls are back. They sit in the booth.

Sandy slaps the tabletop and motions at Nicky. Nicky says, "Sandy has something she wants me to tell you."

Sandy uses her hands. Nicky translates. "Sandy says, she can read lips, even from a distance, and understand us, so she wants to teach Eric some sign language so he can understand her."

"Oh, cool." Eric says. He hunches his shoulders towards the deaf girl and tries to look suave and attentive.

She holds out two fists. Then, slowly, she lifts both of her middle fingers. "FUGME? FUGOO!"

Kurt drives alone across town. The car rattles. He wants to know why the car rattles. The day he bought the car it was perfect. It didn't rattle. That same afternoon he broke the sliding louver above the gear shifter. It wouldn't go down; he couldn't get his smokes. He forced it. It came off in his hand. Six months later, a lot of the car has come off in his hand. And now it rattles. Kurt decides that he's going to turn the tide tonight, change all that. Tonight he is going to stop every rattle. There's only one way to do this: drive, listen, stop, fix it. He drives, hears something in the right rear tire. He stops, takes off the hubcap, tightens the lug nuts, looks in the hubcap, nothing, puts the hubcap back on, drives. He still hears it. There it is again. He stops at a gas station. He stuffs blue paper towels in his pocket, looks around, drives away. There it is again. He stops, takes off the hubcap, crunches the blue paper towels in his hands, stuffs them in the hubcap, drives on. Yes. Silence. But what's that? The muffler. It must be the muffler. He drives, looking for bumps in the road. Yes, something is loose, something in the exhaust. He's smart. He parks the car halfway on a curb, two wheels up. He gets out, slides under the car. It's dark. He flicks his Zippo. He sees a hole but no bolt. He takes off his belt, wraps it around the muffler. It's hot. The belt is too big, too long. He needs to punch another hole in the belt. He needs something sharp, something like an ice pick. In shop class they called it something like an awe—an awl, that's what he needs. Idea. Wrap it twice. Once. Twice. It's done. Drive. What's that? Something in the trunk. Some noise in the trunk…

Hours later Kurt opens the door to his apartment very slowly and steps into the darkness.

"Big night?" the lump of bedding on the floor asks.

"Hey."

"Was she there?"

"Who?"

"You know who."

"No. No, she wasn't."

"You fucked her, didn't you?"

"No, man."

"I know you did."

"What are you talking about?"

"She told me."

"Who?"

"I can hear her."

"How?"

"I can hear her fingernails scratching on the hood."

257

"Who are you?"

"You know me—I'm the one who knows you…"

Kurt recognizes the voice. "I rebuke you in the name of Jesus!" Kurt walks over and stands above the lump with his fist cocked. "What you got now, fucker?" There is no response. "WHAT YOU GOT NOW, FUCKER?" He kicks the blanket into the air, grabs it, whips it from side to side like a dog with a chew toy. A beam of bedroom light falls across Kurt's feet.

"Honey? Are you okay?"

Kurt turns to find Priscilla standing in the doorway, outlined in radiant yellow light. He drops the blanket, goes to her, kneels at her feet, holds her robe, and cries. She runs her fingers through his hair.

WHEN THE WHIP COMES DOWN

Thunderstick shows up at the studio for Monday practice and there is no power. It's been shut off. The next day we have a band meeting at Eric's house and call Bill Wellington. He says, "The rent and utilities are paid in full. I'll call the landlord."

Five minutes later Wellington calls back. "Which one of you geniuses signed a lease for the band with a no bands clause in it?"

"We thought if we played after ten, no one would care. They did, so, ten became twelve, twelve became two, two became three, how can those fuckers complain now? We play in the middle of the night."

"They're done complaining—they're evicting."

"This is a good opportunity to take some time off," the Jovi says. "Without a tour date, there really isn't any reason to practice five nights a week anyway. We should move our stuff out and take a hiatus."

"Cool."

"Yeah."

"Okay."

"No fucking way," Kurt says.

"What are we going to do without power?" Eric asks.

"It's the only thing that takes away the pain in my jaw. I have a physical need to play. Respect that!"

"I do. But we can't really practice without electricity."

"Let me deal with that."

The next day Kurt calls everyone and says, "Be there at three A.M."

"Did you get the power back on?"

"I rented a generator."

"No fucking way."

When he tells EJ, EJ says, "Kurt, that's ridiculous. I'm not paying for a generator, and I am not playing at three in the morning."

Kurt says, "Alright, how mellow, I write all the songs, but somehow I'm the brokest guy in the band. No one listens to me, alright, how mellow. I guess I'll just take my fifty percent of the publishing for the lyrics—my two hundred and fifty grand."

"Fine, we'll be there."

Every member of the band shows up at three A.M. Eric is sick, sneezing, coughing, and whimpering about razor blades in his throat. The Jovi is there in body. His mind is on a beach in Barbados with Sophie spreading for the lens. Sven is sleepy-eyed and slow. Jesse the Giant is stoned and contemplating the thick extension cord that runs between his legs, under the garage door, and out to the VW-sized generator. Nobody has remembered to bring a plug-in lamp so we practice in darkness.

When we show up the next night, the locks have been changed. It's a relief to everyone except Kurt.

We go to Eric's house and call Bill Wellington. He tells us: "Financially speaking, we are pissing blood. We can't afford that studio anyway."

Wellington calls the landlord and threatens a lawsuit. Thunderstick gets their stuff and moves it into the Vine Church. Pastor Ron says, "You are welcome to practice at night after services."

Thunderstick loads in and sets up on the blue-carpeted stage in the giant auditorium between two hundred empty chairs and Jesus hanging on the cross.

BRASS IN POCKET

Kurt's physical need to play is like a tether. For Eric, Sven, and EJ, it keeps them from sleep, interrupts dinner plans, and keeps their ears ringing throughout the week. They don't care. For the Jovi, Kurt's physical need to play is keeping him from the love of his life. He takes her to the airport, watches her fly away, waits for her call, drives by her new house up on Gravila. He wonders with whom she's talking. Who's she looking at now? When she calls it's like a thunderbolt of joy.

He picks her up in front of the terminal. "Could you do me a big favor?" She asks. "My script is up and it's too late to call my doctor."

He finds himself in the places he had tried to forget, making the connect, at 40th and El Cajon. Standing in front of a rancid wooden shack, he thinks to himself, I don't ever want Sophie to come to these places, but there she is, sitting in the Jeep. Back at her place, he stares at the pills for a long time. He wants to make sure they're legit. He wonders if he should try one for her.

She comes over and takes them out of his hand, looks at them closely and tosses two down with a glass of water. "It's just for my nerves," she says.

"I know, baby."

THE NEW DCA

The word comes down from the top. And the new top is Jaime Seller from Capitol Records. He hires someone to hire all the other little someones. The little someones are upgraded assistants, sons of singers, daughters of friends, someone from radio, someone from Harvard with an MBA and a coke habit. They all know one another from summer camp or Hebrew school or rehab. They all listen to music and use the word "genius" until it means "stolen." They're all really fucking nice when they talk to you. The chicks look at you with big doe eyes and slip off their wedding rings. The guys have hockey hair and silk social-club jackets like union workers wear. Nobody understands Jeff Beck, New Order, and Lords of the New Church but them. Nobody develops artists anymore but them. Nobody cares about music but them. They might like you. They might hate you. You'll never know. They're planning your release and then the word comes down from the top and the word is: Stop working on Thunderstick.

Felder can sense it, smell it, see it in the evasive eyes of the DCA employees. He calls Jaime Seller, leaves a message, and doesn't get a call back. He lets a week pass. He calls again.

"What can I do for you, Adam?"

"What's going on with Thunderstick?"

"You tell me."

"We delivered a great album. We want a release date, some spins, some promo, and a tour."

Seller laughs. "That's what everyone wants."

"Well, that means we're everyone. It's not a lot. We make the music—you guys promote the music—that's what record companies do."

"Really?"

"C'mon, Jaime. These guys are really good. Have you listened to the album?"

"Sure."

"Well?"

"Adam, it doesn't fit."

"What do you mean—doesn't fit?"

"It's not AOR, it's not New Wave, it's not really New Romantic. I don't know who would play it."

"Look, Jaime, you're the president of DCA. You don't ask people to play it. You tell people to play it."

"Adam, have you heard my new band—Bang Tango? These guys are really something special. They're like the Cult and Poison combined."

"Let these guys play for you. It's a whole 'nother animal live."

"Adam. I'm a very busy man."

"Alright, Jaime. I read you loud and clear."

Felder presses the button on the receiver, dials Bernie's number. "Seller's fucking us. Can you call him?"

The next day Felder gets a message from Seller: "Thunderstick showcase February 2—somewhere close—forty-five-minute set—seven o'clock."

PLANET OF THE APES

It is band meeting time again. It is one of those days—crisp, onshore wind—the sky is filled with hang gliders. Eric finds Kurt standing at the edge of the cliff with his arms over a wooden railing staring down at Black's Beach. "Hey, Kurt, listen to this: I caught Spewing walking around my house with a tape measure and a skinny German dude." The human kites circle high above the ocean in garish Sunday-school colors.

Kurt distorts his face at Eric. "What the hell?"

"That's what I said to Spewing. He looks at me and says, 'Hey, Eric, this is Gerhard. He's my architect. We're figuring out how we're going to remodel your shitty house after I take it from you in court.'"

"I hope you punched him," Kurt says.

"No. I told him he was trespassing. He looked at me with a straight face and said, 'Not for long.' Can you believe that shit? Is he gonna win?"

Kurt squints into the sky. A purple triangle, a hang glider, blocks out the sun for a second. "I've always wanted to do that, kinda."

"I guess it might be okay." Eric looks at Kurt. "I'm stressed, man. The devil. The lawsuit. DCA."

Kurt wrinkles his brow, befuddled. Eric waves his hands in the air and says, "Where the fuck is the Jovi?"

"He'll be here." Kurt brings the Zippo flame to his smoke. "Ease up. That's Black's Beach down there, Planet of the fucking Apes." He smiles and laughs and glows for a second. "Seen some days down there."

"It is Planet of the Apes. All you need is the Statue of Liberty sticking her head out of the sand and a beautiful mute girl riding bitch on your steed. Carrie Gomez would do." Eric imitates Charlton Heston: "Get your hands off me, you damn dirty ape."

"What are you talking about?" Kurt exhales a small cloud of gray smoke from the sides of his mouth.

"Nothing. How's the jaw?"

"Good. I got an appointment in L.A. with the top doctor in the world. You think you can drive me? Mustang's down."

"Yeah. Sure. Anytime."

The Jovi shows. Nobody apologizes. Nobody has to. Sven says, "We're pirates set to plunder."

"We're a business," says EJ.

"Just wait a couple months for my brother to mellow out. You can make her your chick in a couple months. Would you do that for me?" Kurt asks the Jovi.

"Yeah. Of course." The Jovi pushes his hand through his hair and looks down at Black's Beach. "You think there's any waves?"

"A little something. So, Felder says we've got to showcase for DCA."

"Like we're not even fucking signed," Eric says in disgust.

"Shut the fuck up! We are signed. We play for them. They cop our vibe. It's on. They'll promote us. They aren't stupid." Kurt presses his finger into his temple, opens his jaw. "We're still going to be the biggest band in the world. Keep your head in this fucking thing, Eric."

"Yeah, I just meant it kinda…"

"It doesn't fucking matter. If we stick together, everything is going to be fine."

"Kurt's right," the Jovi says.

"Kurt's fucking right," EJ says.

"He's right," Sven says.

The Jovi takes Eric aside and throws him an injured look. "You're hanging out with James."

"Yeah."

"I didn't know you guys were close."

"He's a good guy."

"That's… Yeah. Maybe you can redirect some of this shit off of Kurt."

"What do you mean?"

"Don't let James wreck this whole thing."

"Hold on, it wasn't James who fucked his best friend's chick."

"It's not like that. It's pure love. The real thing. Love isn't like you think. Love isn't like cute little puppies and everyone's happy. Love comes and fucking torches everything else in your life. That's what it's supposed to do."

"How do you know it's love?"

"She's cured my whoring. I don't even look at other chicks."

"You said you'd wait."

"Chicks like Sophie don't wait. And believe me, Kurt doesn't really care. He just wants to be famous."

For the showcase Felder rents the biggest room at the most expensive rehearsal studio in the Valley and sends the bill to DCA. The Jacksons are using the same room to prep for Michael's "my-brothers-are-broke" tour. They have choreographed dance routines, a horn section. Thunderstick doesn't dance. The only thing theatrical in the Thunderstick show is Kurt Franklin's self-exorcism, but Felder has strictly prohibited that. At Felder's urging, Kurt brings Priscilla and some of the others from the Vine Church.

EJ and Eric pull into the parking lot. As the headlights turn across the gravel, they illuminate a hulking figure listing from side to side, pissing, holding his dick like a garden hose. It's Jesse the Giant. He squints into the headlights and flips them the bird.

"Holy shit, look at that thing," says EJ.

"What?"

"His dick! I got more than a gerbil, but I ain't got that. His poor girlfriend, no wonder she's a little cross-eyed."

Eric laughs. "So, if you have more than a gerbil does that mean you have a hamster?"

"Fuck you, Eric! I got a fucking Guinea Pig."

"Shit, a Guinea Pig, that's pretty good, those things are like two handfuls, I don't think I got that. But don't they shrink when they get wet like a poodle so maybe—"

"I'm not short! It's just my neck, you know. If my neck was a normal length, I'd be six feet, just like the rest of you." EJ stares off into space. "I'm serious. Look at it."

"Yup. You're right. Your head is pretty much mounted on your shoulders."

Jesse stumbles over to the car window, breathes some beer in Eric's face, sticks his big mitt inside, and shakes Eric's hand.

From the stage, the sound is pretty close to flawless, not a single note out of key, not a single transition stumbled over. Thunderstick is driving it home, but the new people stand huddled down in front, curious but unmoved, like dogs watching a butcher take apart a pig through a plate-glass window. One guy bobs his curls in the back—the only human movement in the crowd.

After the last song, the silent crowd parts as Bernie pushes his way up onto the stage, grabs a sweaty, shirtless Kurt by the dog collar, grabs one of EJ's broken drumsticks from the ground, huddles up the band, and says, "Three hundred dates! I don't want to see you again 'til you've done three hundred dates!"

"You liked it?" Felder asks.

"Did I like it? These boys are going to conquer America—that's how much I liked it! I want you to meet my wife." Kurt is smiling his genuine smile as Bernie grabs him by the dog collar and leads him away from the rest of the band. A sweaty EJ slaps Eric on the back. "We did it!"

When the place has cleared out, when there is nothing but gear and roadies, Eric spots Felder sitting on a black-carpeted speaker and staring off into space.

"What's up, Adam?"

"I fucking knew DCA was wrong. Why didn't I trust my instincts on this one?"

"I thought Bernie loved it."

"Bernie's our guy, but he's as good as gone. Seller, that cocksucker, he had the nerve to say to me: 'The band is good. I look forward to working with you.'"

Eric laughs. "That sounds alright."

"Eric, in Hollywood that's like saying 'I don't see it.' In this business, if you like something, you say you love it; if you hate it, you say you like it; if you love it, you say you'd kill your firstborn for it, especially when it's on your calendar. We're on his fucking calendar. I could see it in his eyes. He's gonna string us out until Bernie's gone, and then he's gonna—"

"What's up?" Kurt walks up with Priscilla under his arm.

"Great show, Kurt. Great show. We're okay. Everything's okay. They dug it."

On Monday Felder is sitting in his office when his assistant, Carol, says, "Adam, I've got Mr. Seller's office on line one."

Adam picks up the phone. "Jaime. I was hoping you'd call."

"Mr. Felder? This is Sheryl, Mr. Seller's assistant."

"Okay. You got me. Put him on."

"Mr. Seller is busy right now. He asked me to pass a message along to you."

"Are you fucking kidding me?"

"No, Mr. Felder, I'm not kidding you. His message is this: After hearing Thunderstick live, he believes the album needs to be remastered and at least a few songs rerecorded."

Adam is speechless.

"Hello? Mr. Felder?"

"I'm here."

"Mr. Seller also asked me to tell you that he would like the album to sound more like Bad Company."

"Bad Company? Bad-Company-from-1974 Bad Company? Bad Company with the song "Bad Company" off the album *Bad Company*?"

"No, Mr. Felder. Mr. Seller likes the 1988 release *Dangerous Age*."

"Are you fucking kidding me?"

"No, Mr. Felder, I'm not kidding you."

"Those guys are fucking forty! Forty? They're fucking fifty! That's not Bad Company—that's reconstituted Bad Company. That's a sad, middle-aged, comeback album. Kids don't listen to that shit."

"Mr. Felder?"

"Yes?"

"That's all."

Felder slams down the phone and seethes. "Carol, if you ever tell me that Mr. Seller is on the phone and he's not, our love affair is over. You hear me?"

"Sorry."

"Get me someone from the band on the phone."

Kurt doesn't answer his phone.

Eric does. Felder explains.

"Are you kidding?"

"No. That's what everybody wants right now—Bad Company. Look, we have to do something. As of right now, we're off the calendar."

"They bumped the release?"

"We need to change the album, make it more rock, less alternative, more AOR, or they're never going to even release it."

"Who's gonna tell Kurt?"

"You."

There is silence.

"Just fucking around. I'll tell him."

Felder calls Kurt.

"I got some new songs," Kurt volunteers.

"We're on a shoestring here. We've got one day, Kurt. One day in the studio. No fucking around like before. One day. Got it?"

"Yup."

The opulence of A&M studios is all behind Thunderstick now. We go into a tiny studio in the heart of the Valley, no runners, no catering, no valet parking, no hippie icons, no U2, no excess. We need to rip out four tracks in one day. Kurt doesn't even let the Jovi try a single guitar lead. He takes Eric's thirty-watt mini-Marshall, puts every button on ten, plugs in his Strat, and just kills it. If the little amp had a uvula, it would be shaking wildly in the back of its throat. Kurt has unleashed the Kraken, and the thing comes out of the water with its giant lizard head, mouth agape. It is one of those control-room moments when the hair on your arm stands up and everybody watching gets real still. After the lead is done, Kostas hits a button and the playback stops.

"How was that?" Kurt asks humbly.

Kostas leans into the mic on the mixing board, presses another button, and says, "I think you got it." Then he releases the button and laughs.

It's clear the Jovi is being stepped on, but he nods and tries to be good-natured about it. "That's pretty good. Kurt should play lead on a couple songs. I'm cool with that." His eyes have a watery gloss to them.

Kurt and Eric spend the night at Dane's roach-infested apartment off Orange, and the next day Eric takes him to see the TMJ specialist. The office is in Brentwood on a eucalyptus-lined side street. Kurt is in with the doctor. Eric sits in the waiting room, waiting, reading, checking out the white hose on the nurses. After Kurt has been in there for a while, the tall and pasty doctor comes out and asks to see Eric.

"You want to examine me?"

"No, I'd like to talk to you."

Eric follows the doctor down the hall into the examination room. He sits on a white sheet of paper in his black jeans.

"Are you Mr. Franklin's caregiver?"

"I'm his keyboard player."   ·

"Can I ask you a question or two?"

"Shoot."

"I see from his records that he has been on psychiatric disability from the state for six years."

Eric laughs. "Oh, not anymore. He called those people and told them that he got the biggest record deal in the history of rock. He told them he didn't need those checks anymore."

"Yes, I see that here too. So that really happened?"

"Yeah."

"That's interesting."

"Why?"

"His social worker thought he was delusional. She noted it as cause for concern."

Eric laughs again. "He bought himself another ten years of checks, huh?"

"You think this is funny?"

"No. Of course not. Just the thought of, you know…How's his jaw? He said he might need braces or a retainer or something."

"I've looked at his jaw, x-rays, bite. I don't see anything. It seems perfectly normal." He looks down at his clipboard. "Is he still on Mellaril?"

"No. Kurt kicked drugs. He's a new man."

"Kicked?"

"Cold turkey."

"Not on a doctor's recommendation, I imagine."

"No. His brother, God, that's it."

"God?"

"You think there's any way that demon's are causing the pain in his jaw? That's what Kurt keeps saying."

The doctor looks at Eric for a long second then says, "Well, I think Kurt may want to reconsider psychiatric medication. It would probably do his jaw more good than braces. Has he tried lithium?"

On the 5, Kurt sits in the passenger seat, looking a little caged. He pushes in a cassette. "Ocean Rain" by Echo & the Bunnymen. He blasts the music and sings along. Eric thinks to himself, *That doctor has no clue at all; it's impossible; there must be something wrong with his jaw.*

While singing loudly to "Villiers Terrace," Kurt snaps. He ejects the tape, throws it out the window, turns the radio to static, and screams at the top of his lungs. Then he starts kicking the dashboard until it bends into a crease.

"Cut it out, Kurt! Stop it!"

He continues kicking until the bent plastic breaks off. Eric slams on the brakes and pulls onto the side of the road somewhere near Oceanside.

"Nobody has any respect for what I do! I'm the best fucking singer in the whole world and nobody fucking cares. I have to redo the best album that has come out in ten years, and I get no respect!"

"I know. I know. I'm on your side. Don't fucking take it out on my car!"

"Then why don't you do something? Help out! What? I can't do everything myself! Just fucking leave me alone." Kurt gets out of the car, slams the door so hard the glass shatters, and stomps off into the dry brush.

THE HAPPY PILL

Priscilla is standing in the bright light in her Minnie Mouse heels with a basket of sample packets in one hand and a spray bottle of perfume in the other. Near a kiosk of sunglasses, Eric watches her greet strangers. Most shun her, walk away. She doesn't care. She just smiles for the next one. He walks over tentatively.

"Hey, Priscilla, how's it going?"

"Oh! Eric! Oh my goodness! What are you doing here?"

"Nothing. Just shopping, I guess."

"Really?"

"No. Not really. I wanted to talk to you. It's about Kurt's doctor in L.A."

She tries to smile. "I told Kurt not to stick you with the bill."

"It's not that."

"Um…okay. Let me take my break."

They sit in the atrium beneath an escalator and a palm tree. Priscilla puts her hands on her lap, leans forward, and says, "Do you think that specialist can fix Kurt's jaw?"

"Well…I don't…What I came here to tell you is that the doc in L.A., he said nothing was wrong with Kurt's jaw. He said

276

whatever is causing all that pain is not something he can physically see."

"Oh." Priscilla puts her hand over her mouth and looks off toward the Burrito Barn.

"Kurt needs to go on lithium or something like that—that's what the doc thinks would fix it."

Fear chases hopelessness across Priscilla's face and down her neck. She swallows them down and says in a slow, drawn-out voice, "I think you're right."

Kurt's father, Wayne, is alone in the desert, doing wind sprints on his banjo. He fingerpicks ferociously fast then stops cold, waits two seconds, plays ferociously fast, then stops cold, waits two seconds, plays ferociously fast. His phone rings. Outside his window is a brown dry riverbed. His phone rings again. He stops picking, grabs the receiver, and yells, "Who is it?"

"Mr. Franklin? It's Priscilla Franklin. Your daughter-in-law."

Wayne surveys the room with the corners of his eyes. "I didn't do it."

"Do what?"

"Whatever you said I did."

"I didn't say you did anything."

"As long as we've got that straight."

"What?"

"I didn't do anything."

"I know, Mr. Franklin. I was hoping you could talk to Kurt for me."

"Kurt?"

"Your son."

"Uh-huh."

"It's about psychiatric medication. I think Kurt needs to go back on medication. Maybe lithium. Could you talk to him?"

"Of course he does. Gotta take your meds. I take mine."

"Could you talk to him?"

"He doesn't listen to me."

"Yes, he does."

"Okay, put him on."

"He's not here right now. Can you call back later?"

"I didn't tell Kurt to steal your car. It was his idea."

"Mr. Franklin? Do you mind talking to him?"

"No problem."

Wayne doesn't call. A couple days later Priscilla calls Felder and asks, "Could you tell Kurt to try the meds?"

"Sure."

When he hasn't called in a few days, Priscilla gives up on Felder. She asks him herself. "Kurt, would you just try lithium, it's a salt, it's not a drug."

"Okay."

It takes a couple of weeks for his levels to stabilize, and then there are fewer rants, fewer gigs, not too much practicing—the physical need to play is under control. Felder says it is good for the band. Kurt is still himself, but now he's an edited version, sort of like a movie you might see on an airplane. You get the general story, but there's no bare breasts, no foul idioms, no bodily fluids. The spark that made Kurt incendiary is now a twenty-five-watt bulb. There is something gentle about him, almost vulnerable, almost mortal.

Kurt walks over to Eric's house. "I've got a new song."

"Great."

Kurt sits on the couch and starts strumming and singing. The song is a benign three-chord dud. When it is over, Kurt looks at Eric and asks, "What do you think?"

"That's good."

"Really?"

"Yeah. Really good."

"What do you think of that change?"

"Kurt, you're the best songwriter alive. I've never written a song in my life. It sounds really good to me."

"I don't know. These songs I've been writing, they sound really good the day I write 'em. Then the next day, I just don't know. I wonder if I'll like this one tomorrow?"

"That's just part of the process, right?"

"Never used to be."

"It's normal."

"Normal? Normal—stable?" Kurt chuckles to himself. "They told me I would still be able to write music on the meds."

"You can! You just did!"

"Yeah, I can, but is this song as good as the ones on the album?"

"Um…maybe."

"This stuff I'm taking—it isn't like Mellaril. It's just a salt. I'm just a little bipolar—nothing else. I'm not crazy."

"I know you're not. Are you happy? You seem happy."

Kurt shrugs his shoulders, strums a different chord. "What do you think of that? Maybe that's better. Does that sound better?"

"Yeah, that's better."

He plays the other change. "No, I think I like the first one."

"The first one. The first one, for sure."

He strums the two chords back and forth with increasing speed. "At least I can sleep now."

"Where's the Jovi? You should play it for the Jovi. Write songs together, you know."

"The Jovi? My brother hates that guy. I don't want to ask him. I hope he's not with that chick. He isn't around here. That's all I know."

MARCH

Felder tells Carol to call Jaime Seller's office and get Seller on the phone. Carol dials the number. Sheryl answers the phone. "Mr. Felder would like to speak to Mr. Seller. Is he available?"

"Please hold. I'll check."

Carol holds.

"Yes, Mr. Seller is available. Is Mr. Felder on the line?"

"Please hold for Mr. Felder." Carol puts the phone on hold. "Hey, Adam. He'll talk to you."

"I know he'll talk to me, but is he on the line? I'm not gonna get on the fucking line and wait for him again—that's fucking bullshit. The last time I called, he had me sit there on hold for a full fucking minute. That was fucking humiliating. I'm not going through that again. Get him on the phone."

Carol presses the hold button. "Hi, Sheryl, this is Carol, I have Mr. Felder ready for Mr. Seller. Is he on the line?"

"Is Mr. Felder on the line?"

"He's ready for Mr. Seller. Is Mr. Seller on the line?"

"Mr. Seller will get on the line after Mr. Felder is on the line."

"Please hold." Carol punches the hold button. "Seller won't get on the phone until he knows you're waiting."

"That fucking, cock-sucking motherfucker. You tell Sheryl to put that bag of shit on the fucking phone right now."

Carol presses a button on the phone. "Hello, Sheryl? Mr. Felder says to put that bag of shit on the phone right now."

Felder lunges for the phone and grabs the receiver. "Hello? Hello?"

Carol presses a button and says, "Hi, Sheryl, Mr. Felder is on the line for Mr. Seller."

"Thanks, Carol, I'll have him on in a second."

"You tricked me, you fucking—"

"Hello? Adam? Are you there?"

"Jaime. It's me, Adam. How are you?"

"Good. Good."

"So what do you think of the new songs?"

"New songs?"

"Yeah. Thunderstick? My band? You asked us to give you some new songs. More hard rock, you said—like Bad Company you said. Songs—"

"Sure. Those songs. They're fine."

"So are we back on the calendar?"

"Sure. How's April twenty-sixth sound?"

Felder smiles. "Sounds great."

ELƩEWHERE IN THE WORLD

Seller knows that New Romantic is dying out, and from its ashes the weed of Glam-tainted Metal is rising. This is in no small part thanks to the monstrous success of Led 'n' Lilacs. When they opened up for the Cult at SDSU in 1988, the front man, Otto, was wearing pink spandex pants tucked into white knee-high boots, and a row of feathers adorned the mic stand. The drummer was pretty solid, but nobody was buying it—just another screeching hair band from L.A., everyone thought. A year later, after some Tiffany Tucker type told them to toss the spandex in favor of ripped jeans, and after Arty Azimoff twisted the arm of every program director in the country, they are a phenomenon—selling out Wembley Stadium, opening up for the Stones.

Kurt hates them, but Kurt hates everyone. Kurt hates them so much that he is willing to play hard rock just to prove he can do it better than Led 'n' Lilacs.

For Thunderstick, a release date is good news. Felder restarts negotiations over the publishing deal.

APRIL

April 25, 1989, the band gets dolled up in their gig gear and drives to L.A. We walk into Felder's office. Felder is surprised. "What the fuck are you guys doing here?"

"We're here for our album release party—like that thing they were doing for Depeche Mode over at Warner Bros., right?" Kurt says. "You know, where you get to meet all the people that work for you."

"Release party? There's no fucking album!"

"What?"

"DCA hasn't asked for the artwork. The designer has been waiting for the go-ahead. Nothing. From the time the artwork is in, it's a four-week turnaround. We're probably looking at June. June at best."

"No fucking way!" Kurt puts his hands above his head. "I'm not going to make it to June."

"Kurt, you gotta. You know who Bang Tango is?"

"No."

"They're his band. Seller signed 'em in January. Their album-release party is tomorrow, April twenty-sixth, our release date.

Coincidence? No. Everyone at DCA is mobilized on this thing. They got Bang Tango T-shirts and hats on every suck-ass in town. You know what Seller is saying?"

"What?"

"He's saying fuck you, Bernie! Fuck you, Felder! Fuck you, Thunderstick! DCA is mine! You want your album released? Fine, come in here, lick my balls, suck my dick, and I'll think about it! That's what he's fucking saying."

"Then go in there and lick his balls!" EJ yells. "C'mon, Adam, do—"

"So he can humiliate me again? Have me wait in his office? Put me on hold? No. His bands are already signed, recorded, mixed, mastered, and released. He ate 'em, and he's already shitting 'em out. I don't eat other people's shit. I'm gonna get us a new record deal."

WORKING THE
PHONES FOR GOD

Kurt drives home in a rage, but he knows how to handle this. He knows how to get a little respect. He gets home, plays a song, puts down the guitar, lights a smoke, and calls information. "Give me the number for DCA."

"We have several listings. Would you like DCA Worldwide Studio Tours?"

"No. The record company."

She gives him the number. He holds the smoke in his mouth. The pen in his hand has no ink. He presses really hard so the numbers are indented in the back of the phone book.

"DCA Global, how may I direct your call?"

"This is Kurt Franklin of Thunderstick and you need to release my album. You said you would release it on April twenty-sixth, and I want you to live up to your word."

"Please hold."

There's music. It's Bang Tango.

"Hello, DCA Records, how may I direct your call?"

"Yeah. This is Kurt Franklin of Thunderstick. You need to release my album like you said you would. It used to be that somebody's word meant—"

"Please hold."

Different music—Jody Watley.

"Hello? DCA Records."

"This is Kurt Franklin, I'm the lead singer of Thunderstick, who is this?"

"Please hold."

Is that Debbie Cherry? Kurt thinks.

"Hello? DCA Records."

"Debbie Cherry? Bang Tango? Jody Watley? Why don't you play some Thunderstick on your phone thing? People would like to be put on hold if they could listen to the pretty singing."

"Sir? Hello? DCA Records, how may I help you?"

"THIS IS KURT FRANKLIN. GIVE ME JAIME SELLER!"

"Mr. Seller is in a meeting. May I take a message?"

"YOU TELL HIM THIS IS KURT FRANKLIN OF THUNDERSTICK. MY BAND MADE THE BEST ALBUM ANYBODY HAS MADE IN TWENTY YEARS, AND HE NEEDS TO BE A MAN, A REAL MAN, AND RELEASE IT LIKE HE SAID HE WOULD! ON THE DAY HE SAID HE WOULD!"

"I will give him your message, Mr. Franklin."

"Good. Thanks. Thanks."

Kurt hangs up and calls Eric. "Hey, man, I just wanted to let you know, everything's cool with DCA. I just had to straighten some people out."

"Full on."

"Yeah. I know how this business thing works."

MAN VERSUS MACHINE

It's May and still no release date. But Kurt still needs to play. So the blue folding chairs at the Vine Church are treated to a world-class concert two nights a week.

After three hours of practice, EJ says, "Kurt, I think that's enough."

Kurt puts down his guitar and holds his hands like a praying mantis. "He who works his lands will have abundant food, but he who chases fantasies will have his fill of poverty."

"Fuck. That's heavy," the Jovi says, and drops a lit cigarette on the concrete floor. He presses the toe of his black boot into the ember.

"You want poverty?" Kurt asks the band.

"I want to go to a titty bar," EJ says. "We've practiced enough. C'mon, Kurt, you know you want to go too."

"That's exactly why I won't go. Those who are given to lust, the devil has power over them."

The Jovi nods and turns away. "What about you, Eric, are you down with it?"

"What are those places like?"

"Eric's never been to a strip club?" The Jovi smiles.

"Jesus Christ!" Jesse yells under the giant crucifix. "C'mon, Eric, I'll introduce you. Those chicks fucking love me. They fucking call me Kid Salami! Look at this." He grabs his inner thigh through his leather chaps.

"He's not kidding," the Jovi says. "He's got a fucking kielbasa in there."

"I'll go."

"Look, man, I don't like where this band is headed. The Lord said: 'My son give me your heart and let your eyes keep to my ways, for a prostitute is a deep pit and a wayward wife is a narrow well. Like a bandit she lies in wait, and multiplies the unfaithful among men.'"

"Whoa. That's deep. You're just full of the Holy Spirit tonight, aren't you?" the Jovi says.

"Yeah. Somebody has to be."

"So we'll see you on the rack at Dirty's?" Jesse laughs.

"I'm married."

In his BMW with the missing window, Eric follows Jesse and the Jovi down Mira Mesa Boulevard. EJ follows close behind in his mom's station wagon. The Jovi's hard-tail purple chopper with ape-hangers rumbles and growls. Jesse's factory Sportster hums. The two bikes are side by side. The two red taillights become the enchanting and evil glowing eyes of a harlot. *Yes,* Eric thinks, *a red-eyed, nylon-clad stripper slithering across a dance floor, writhing on her belly.* He grins, remembers the road before him, looks up, and watches the Jovi hit a significant pothole at about sixty miles per hour. Because his bike is a hard-tail—no shocks in the back—the back of the bike bounces the Jovi perpendicular. He's still holding the handlebars, his feet pointing to the sky like he's doing a handstand. It would be a magnificent circus trick if it wasn't for the fact that the tail of the bike is three feet in the air. The Jovi only stays on his hands for half a second. The wind and momentum push his body back toward the ground. He curls his legs and reaches for the footpegs. He finds them. The pieces come down together. For a split second it looks like the Jovi is going to pull it off. Then his bike goes sideways in a rapid, fishtailing action that flings him out of the saddle above the handlebars. When he comes down this time, there is nothing beneath him but blacktop. He lets go of the bike, extends his left leg, and skids on his side, his head up and alert. The bike, the beautiful bike, tumbles and spits sparks. The Jovi turns his body, gloves down, head up. Eric slams on the brakes only to be jolted forward then backward as EJ crashes into his back bumper. The Jovi spins on the blacktop then hops up, running in giant, elongated lunar strides. *He's running with a broken leg*, Eric thinks to himself. The chopper is still spinning and shooting golden sparks in the night. The years of work, the chrome, the handlebars, it is all being compressed into a tube of scrap metal. As the chopper tumbles and slows, Jesse stays by its side. As the chopper moves toward the shoulder, Jesse moves with it. He is constantly looking at the riderless machine until his own bike smacks into the back of a parked Ford. Jesse travels headfirst over two cars and disappears into the darkness. EJ and Eric stop, certain that Jesse is dead. The Jovi is standing on the other side of the boulevard. He seems to be okay.

"Fuck it, Eric. You fucked up my car. Oh shit, is Jesse dead? I'll bolt to Burrito Barn and call an ambulance."

"What should I do?"

"I don't know." EJ runs toward the restaurant.

Eric kneels by Jesse's massive body. Jesse is facedown in an expanding pool of blood, unconscious, one arm up, one arm at his side, the heels of his cowboy boots turned outward.

Eric thinks to himself, *Don't move the body.* What is left of the Jovi's chopper is now colorless and leaking fluids. Jesse's bike is crushed, sticking out of the ass of the black Ford. Eric listens in the stillness and hopes for a distant siren.

Instead he hears a gurgling groan and looks down. Jesse the Giant has brought his hands to his head and is trying to push himself off the tarmac. Eric grabs his shoulder and says, "Don't move."

Jesse slowly turns to Eric, his powerful forehead caked in blood and hair. "How's my bike? Where's my weed?"

Eric mumbles something about incomprehensible miracles. Jesse grunts and drags himself over to a sapling planted by the sidewalk.

"Jesse, man, are you okay?" the Jovi yells, as he runs across the boulevard.

"Smoke." Jesse groans.

The Jovi fumbles with a pack of cigarettes, takes two, lights them, and hands one to Jesse. Jesse's shoulders are now propped up against the little tree. He takes the cigarette with a trembling hand and breathes in the smoke.

The sirens get closer, then arrive.

The paramedics ask a lot of questions. They wrap Jesse's head in white gauze and help him to his feet. Jesse towers over the paramedic who holds his forearm. If the paramedic was wearing a crinoline dress, it would look like prom night in Calcutta. Jesse's cigarette dangles from his mouth. "Sir, you can't smoke that in the ambulance. Sir. Sir, you can't…" Jesse throws the smoke on the ground and puts both hands on the chrome railings, stepping into the back of the ambulance himself to join the Jovi. EJ and Eric can see the two of them through the back window, lit in an eerie fluorescent glow. The ambulance pulls away and Jesse the Giant and the Jovi ride off together into the night.

PART THREE

"Why should the Devil have all the good tunes?"
—Rowland Hill

WHITE LIGHT WHITE HEAT

The Jovi and Sophie are out to dinner at Chuck's Steak House on Prospect. Sophie tips the goblet and the last few drops of red slide into her luscious mouth. Her teeth outlined in crimson, she smiles at the Jovi like a happy vampire. The bill comes. The Jovi throws down his Gold Card.

It comes back, but there's no receipt and no Gold Card.

"Hey, I think you forgot something."

"Oh really?" the waiter says.

"Yeah. Where's my plastic?"

"Sorry, sir, you must pay cash."

"Wait a second, bro, bring back the plastic, and we'll talk this over."

"I can't do that."

"Why not?"

"There was a reward."

"I've got it." Sophie pulls a hundred-dollar bill out of her wallet.

"Sorry, babe." The Jovi wipes his forehead with his sleeve. "So I dropped off what was left of the purple chopper with this tweaker I know down in Point Loma. He's gonna work on it when he can't sleep. So, until it's done or until the publishing money comes in, can I borrow your Jeep to drive to practice?"

"I would love to watch you guys."

"Okay, okay, that's cool."

"Let's go pick up Summer. Make it a party."

They stop in front of an adobe house in Del Mar. Sophie sounds the horn. Summer skips out and hops in the yellow Jeep.

"Hey!" the Jovi says. "There's a new bounce in your shirt. Those are nice!"

"Sophie got them for me for my birthday!"

"You can't see them like that!" Sophie reaches over and lifts up Summer's shirt. Summer giggles, pushes Sophie's hand away, and then lifts up her shirt herself.

"Wow! I must say they look pretty natural," the Jovi says. "You didn't go overboard. Just a nice C cup or so. And nice nipples too, small, pink. The boys are gonna love those."

They walk into the Vine Church and every head is bowed. Pastor Ron holds the microphone with two hands as if it were precious. Sophie points at Pastor Ron and whispers, "He looks like he's about to take that thing to the tonsils."

The Jovi laughs.

Pastor Ron looks up, spots Sophie, and starts speaking in tongues.

The three of them walk into the daycare room. Eric takes one look at Summer and says, "They're gonna be praying for a while, and Kurt's not here. Let's go get some pie!"

They drive over to Aunt Polly's Pie Place off the freeway. Eric tries every trick in his very short book. "Hey, you know, Warhol hung out with models because he said they were like living works of art. You girls are like art. You know what I mean... You should be in a museum, like standing on a white box, you know, naked!"

The girls laugh.

"You first," says Summer.

"Actually I want to be an actress," Sophie says.

Summer holds her blonde hair in one hand, leans across the table, and licks the dollop of whipped cream off the top of Eric's pumpkin pie. Eric gets up and comes back with a whipped-cream dispenser. He shoots up his whole plate with it, a ring around the outside, two eyes, a smiley face. Summer licks the whole thing clean. Sophie grabs the dispenser and shoots some in the Jovi's mouth then kisses it out.

"Let's bring some pie back for Kurt and the guys," Sophie suggests.

"That's my girl. What a sweetheart."

Back at the Vine Church, Sophie stands in front of Kurt, her outstretched arms holding a pie.

"I brought these for you. I thought you might be hungry."

Kurt hesitates, then takes the pie.

"Thanks." He stares at Summer as he relentlessly shovels pie in his mouth.

"Do you like my pie?" Summer asks.

"Yeah."

"I baked it just for you."

"Don't worry, Kurt, hair pie has no calories," EJ barks out.

"Dude. You gotta look at her tits," the Jovi says to Kurt. "They're perfect!" Right then a dark cloud passes over the room. They turn around and Pastor Ron is standing in front of the jungle mural. He's about the size of the giraffe.

"Whoa. Just kidding," the Jovi says.

"A pie party? And I wasn't invited?"

"Just some good clean fun. Pastor Ron is always invited. You want some pie?" the Jovi asks.

"No. No, thank you. I don't believe we've met." Pastor Ron holds his hand out to Sophie. She takes it. He won't let go. He stares into her slightly sleepy eyes, unaffected by her lush lips. She's getting uncomfortable. Slowly, he twists her wrist, squints and asks, "Sophie Clark. You think the devil loves you?"

She pulls her hand away and says, "Of course he does. I'll prove it." She turns her enchanting gaze to the Jovi. She holds both his hands. "Well? Do you love me? Confess it! Confess your love for me."

"I…" The Jovi pauses, looks over at Kurt, then Pastor Ron, then back to Sophie. "I love you, but I'm not the devil."

Pastor Ron laughs. "God loves you, Sophie."

Sophie's cheeks get flush and her eyes tear up just a little. "Bobby isn't the devil. His light is white. He's my angel."

"If you like angels, we have them flying all over." Pastor Ron lifts his arms to show the majesty of the mini-industrial building. "You should come to church some time."

"I'm here." She stops. "No, totally."

After Pastor Ron walks out of the room, Sophie turns to the band and says, "I want to watch you make a song."

"I don't know about that." Kurt gets real quiet and his eyes shift around the room.

"Please, just one. You guys are going to be the most famous band of all time. I just want to… I don't know, like, be a part of history."

Kurt is bashful. He takes out his acoustic and strums a song. He plays a couple bars, starts to sing the verse, and then stops.

"No, no, let me try this one." Then he starts playing another song. "No, I don't like that one anymore." He starts another one, all of them new. Then he starts singing "I Wanted You," a song from the album. His voice is on. EJ hums the harmonies during the quiet part.

"I love that song! But it's, like, on your album, right? I want to hear a new song, watch you guys create."

The girls stay through the whole practice. When it is done, Kurt looks at Summer and says, "Hey, let's go grab a drink."

"Let's drink and dance," Sophie says with an eager expression.

Eric picks up some of the pie mess, and Sophie says, "Don't bother with that, the roadies will get it."

Eric laughs. "What roadies?"

They go to Maxime's, but it is a Tuesday night and pretty dead. They dance to a couple songs, just the five of them under the spinning lights, the Jovi, Summer, Sophie, Kurt, and Eric. Then they sit in the back in a black leather booth. Sophie reaches over and grabs Kurt's hand. "Let me see." She flips it palm up. Kurt hesitates for a second then gives in. She looks in his palm. "Do you see this? This is your fame line. You're going to be very famous. Here, look at mine, it's the same."

Kurt pulls the candle over and looks into her hand.

"See. It's totally true."

"Yeah, I know we're gonna be famous, no matter what my hand says."

"It's going to be hard on you."

His eyes soften.

"I can help you navigate it. I'm already helping the Jovi."

"Yeah, dude. She's totally straightened my head out about this whole fame thing. We just need to make insane music. That's all we need to worry about. Everything else is going to be fine—she told me."

Kurt looks into Sophie's curious, sleepy eyes and asks, "What about my thumb? Phoenix said it's a murderer's thumb. Am I going to kill someone?"

Sophie pouts. Then she leans down and kisses Kurt's strange thumb.

The Jovi winces.

"I've been around people like you, Kurt. You don't fit in with the rest of the world. You aren't like them. You're the stuff of legends. You're from another realm," says Sophie.

Kurt's head turns. "What do you know about the other world?"

"Things," she laughs. "I'm learning. I've caught glimpses my whole life."

"So here's the deal. The meds are like a wall. The wall keeps the voices, the demons, all that shit, over there. But it's like the songs are over there too, and I can't get to them."

"Ahh. That's why you couldn't write a song in the church."

"What do you mean?"

"Your demons bring you your songs. That's what Phoenix said."

"Fuck Phoenix! God gave me those songs."

"For me it's the opposite." She leans over and whispers in Kurt's ear, "The drugs for me are the door, the door in the wall."

Kurt's hand slips under the table. Sophie pulls it back up above the table, gives Kurt a knowing glance, and hops out of the booth. She grabs Summer and leads her out onto the dance floor. Sophie holds Summer's hips and slowly, rhythmically grinds to the music.

Kurt swallows real hard. "I just realized something. My job is to write music—not to be stable. I'm writing songs for the ages. That's all that matters—the music. Those pills, that's not the way God made me. That's some science thing."

"You seem happier on the pills," Eric says.

"Happy doesn't matter." Kurt gets back his hard look, finishes his beer. "I gotta get home, my wife and James are gonna wonder where I am."

As he walks out, Summer grabs her ankles and Sophie drives into her hips from behind in big, elongated strokes.

LATER

Kurt opens the door and steps into his dark apartment. The lump of bedding on the floor says, "Hey."

"Hey."

"How was practice?"

"Good."

"You guys playing any time soon?"

"Yeah. You getting any sleep?"

"No. Have you looked at the fucking magazine rack at the 7-Eleven? It's all her. She's on, like, four covers right now."

"Yeah. Well, what can you do?"

"I can even smell her right now. Like she just walked in the room. Fucking weird, huh?"

"I guess. Good night."

"Good night."

In his bedroom, Kurt can see the outline of Priscilla turned on her side beneath the white comforter. He reaches beneath the cover and holds the sole of her foot against the palm of his hand. "You loved me when no one else did," he whispers. She grumbles and rolls onto her stomach.

Kurt closes the bathroom door and turns on the light. On the counter, his brush, his towel, his hairwax, Priscilla's makeup—all of it is in disarray and it doesn't bother him. In the mirror he sees that his hair is a jumble of lines and curls, none of the hairs doing what they should, and it doesn't bother him. He pours himself a glass of water, opens his bottle of lithium, and empties out a pill in his hand. He tosses it in his mouth. He sticks out his tongue, the white pill cradled in the center.

This keeps you in there, he thinks, looking at the guy in the mirror.

This makes everything okay.

It steals the gift.

He takes a gulp of water, tosses his head back, then looks in the mirror very sternly.

Are you tonguing your meds?

The man in the mirror opens his mouth, lifts his tongue, and reveals the white pill underneath.

You don't want to make the doctor angry now do you?

He takes another gulp of water.

Well? Show me. Did you?

He opens his mouth, lifts his tongue, no pill.

What about the sides?

He smiles. He sticks his finger in his mouth and pulls his lip to the side. The pill is in the back, wedged between a molar and the gum.

This is your last chance. Do it again, and we're going to start giving you the needle.

Kurt takes a slug of water, swishes it around in his mouth, then shoots it out in a stream at the mirror.

I don't have to listen to you.

Kurt spits the pill into the toilet.

You can't do that.

Just did. This is for the music.

Kurt takes the bottle of pills and pours it in the toilet. He flushes. The pills spin and bob and lose their command.

BACKYARD PARTIES

It's the beginning of June. Thunderstick has a gig at EJ's mom's house in Birdrock; it is EJ's little brother's birthday party. The gear is set up in the backyard beneath a mature, blooming, lemon-scented magnolia tree wrapped with white Christmas lights. The younger kids in La Jolla really look up to Thunderstick, and there is a keg—hence the big crowd.

Eric is with EJ in his filthy room, looking around for a clean place to sit. Someone knocks. EJ lifts the bottom of the Madonna poster that hangs over the giant hole in his door, and they can see Sven. He sticks his head in the hole. "This is nice. I like what you've done with the place."

"In the old days you could punch a door and nothing would happen. Shitty construction these days."

Eric picks up one of the old green bottles of beer, holds it to the light, and notices it is cultivating inch-thick white mold above last remaining swallow. "Dude. You done with this?" He brings it towards his lips.

"Shut up, Eric!" EJ says.

Kurt kicks the door open, walks in clutching his skull, and yells, "I just heard from Felder. The album isn't coming out for another two months."

"Fuck," Eric says.

"Fuck is right," Sven says.

They sit silently for a second. The walking bass line of a rap song drones from the yard through the wall. Kurt presses his fingers into his jaw, and slowly opens and closes his mouth.

"Kurt, are you still taking the happy pills?" Eric asks.

Kurt glares at him. "I wish people would stop FUCKING ASKING ME THAT!"

"Sorry, dude."

Kurt opens his mouth and twists his head until his chin touches his neck. "I feel better than ever."

"What's up, guys?" The Jovi stands in the door with a big smile on his face. "You guys! Good news. One of my swimmers found his way home."

"What?"

"Dude. Of all the little guys that I have spilled in my hand, in my car, in my shower, in smiling mouths, in little dummies and hoors, only one swimmer has ever been able to make it to the Promised Land."

He looks at the band.

They look back at him.

"Sophie's pregnant! We're getting married."

"You're getting married to Sophie?" Kurt looks concerned.

"Yeah, that's what I said. She's pregnant! We're getting married."

We all stand there for a second; the dull sound of teenage laughter from the yard fills the silence.

"What, nobody's going to congratulate me?"

Thunderstick takes the stage and begins the set with "Alone, Alone." The song starts mellow and builds momentum—a solid opener. It sounds good, and the kids seem to like it. There are three cute girls dancing together at the front of the crowd. Then, somewhere toward the back, two teenage boys start wrestling with each other, pulling hair and clothes, throwing punches. Kurt sees this from behind the mic, stops singing in the middle of the chorus, drops his guitar, runs off the stage, grabs one of the kids, and works him over. The other kid doesn't know what to do. He steps away. The other members of the band look at one another and then look out into the crowd as Kurt is finishing up the kid with a barrage of uppercuts. The band slows the song down to a sad halt, and Kurt pushes the slumping kid into a planter box, looks around at the shocked faces, and yells, "DON'T *EVER* FIGHT WHEN WE'RE PLAYING MUSIC!" Then he walks off toward the cars on the street with the crowd parting before him like he is the pontiff or a man on death row.

SWEAR TO TELL THE WHOLE TRUTH

Thunderstick is ordered back to L.A. for depositions in the *Spewing v. Thunderstick* four-million-dollar lawsuit. Spewing's lawyer claims that his client was kicked and slapped repeatedly while on the job. Thunderstick claims that Spewing was woefully inadequate, cost the band one hundred thousand dollars in lost recording time, and had a confirmed drug habit that he tried to push on every other member of the band. Everyone is right. Why can't we just shake hands and go home? Or settle it like men with some senseless violence followed by a group hug. Instead, Kurt and EJ sit at a conference table being deposed by Spewing's shopping-mall attorney, the leather-faced law books looking down at them while the clock runs and the bands' dollars disappear.

The band drives over to Felder's office afterward. Felder says, "I've got some good news and some bad news and some more good news. First the bad news, apparently the name Thunderstick is already taken—not in the U.S. but in the UK. The drummer from the band Samson did a solo project and called it *Thunderstick*." Felder pulls out the actual album and shows it to the band. The dark eyes of a tortured soul stare from inside a black leather mask embedded with a thousand shiny metal studs.

"Whoa," Eric says. "That guy looks like I feel."

"That takes creepy to a whole new level." The Jovi adds.

"Yeah and he's wearing a fucking rubber suit and an asphyxiation collar," Sven says. "I want to party with this guy."

"Lucky for us he never got the trademark in America," Felder says, "but it screws us for our foreign sales. We've got to change the name of the band."

Kurt looks at the black eyes on the cover. His expression changes from dismay to fear to anger. He puts his hands above his head and screams, "NO FUCKING WAY! THIS IS CLEARLY THE DEVIL FUCKING WITH US! IT CAN'T BE REAL!"

Sven taps the album with his finger, turns to Kurt, and says, "It's real."

There is a moment of silence, everyone looking from the album cover to Kurt as he sinks down into a leather chair, his head in hands.

"So what's the good news?" the Jovi asks.

"We've got a release date. This time it's happening. Our album's coming out in August!"

"Sweet!"

"Insane!"

"Rad!"

"Look, man, we're Thunderstick! Do you get it? That guy is not Thunderstick!" Kurt says, as if he didn't hear the good news.

Felder nods at Kurt. "I know. I know. Look, the best thing to do is come up with a completely new name."

"NO! HELL NO! I WANT EVERYONE TO KNOW WE MADE IT!"

"Cool down, Kurt. I talked to the lawyers. The other option is to make a minor change, like call the band Thunderstix, T-Stick, or spell it funny, like with no C."

Felder takes out a piece of paper and writes THUNDERSTIK. "See, like that."

Kurt sticks his finger into his jaw socket, tilts his head, and says to the floor, "Okay. Thunderstik. No C. That's what it has to be."

"You said you had more good news?" the Jovi asks.

"We're doing a photo shoot."

"Alright, boys," the Jovi says, and looks at the band on the leather couch. "This one's for history."

The photographer takes the band to an abandoned factory yard filled with rusting iron, trash, and dirt. He guides Kurt inside a tin-roofed shack, places him strategically in a beam of sunlight, and tells him to hold a steel wagon wheel to his chest and scream.

"I'll open my mouth, but I won't scream. That's stupid."

"I need it. For the shot."

"No."

"Listen, we've coordinated this whole thing with the art director. She told me what she needs, now it's my job to get it."

"I scream if I'm scared or if I'm pissed. I'm not going to sit in here and scream for no reason at all. I'm not going to do that. Don't ask me again."

Felder walks up to the photographer, gives him a knowing nod, and says, "Try a couple with the open mouth, no scream."

The rest of the band waits outside the shack. After about ten minutes, Felder brings out Kurt and brings in the Jovi. The catering arrives—Indian food. Kurt opens one container and says, "People eat this? It looks like glue."

Eric finds some roasted chicken and hands it to Kurt.

"Why's it red?" Kurt asks.

"Dunno. Let Felder eat the glue. Is there another chicken in there somewhere?" Eric discovers more red bird. They sit outside the shack on giant splintery railroad ties with their Styrofoam plates in their laps. Then it starts. The Jovi is screaming his lungs out as if some grizzly bear were sucking out his intestines like they were spaghetti. The photographer loves it.

"Yes! Yes! That's it, like that. Hot! Hot! Fierce! Fierce!"

The Jovi responds with a scream.

EJ, Sven, Kurt, and Eric look at one another. Kurt smirks, then chuckles, and the rest of them burst out in laughter.

A half hour of screaming passes before the Jovi comes out, puts an eyeball on the Indian food, and says in a hoarse voice, "What were you guys laughing about?"

The band returns to La Jolla, and the gift returns to Kurt with a vengeance. "I've got a new song," he says. It's a love song, but it has nothing to do with Eros, nothing to do with carnal desire. This is a song a mother might sing to her child. This is a song that God might sing to Adam and Eve before the Fall. This is a song about love as completion, love as redemption, love as connection to the Infinite—and it's not in the words, it's in the melody, the phrasing, the hook, the intonation. Kurt sings and plays the tag a few times, stops, and says coldly, "It's something like that."

"Holy shit," Eric says, "that's a fucking hit if I've ever heard one."

"He's right, Kurt," EJ says. "That's the best song I've heard you write since the parking garage, since you quit Mellaril and didn't sleep for three weeks."

"I guess we got our lead-off single on our second album," Sven says.

"I wrote it to my wife. She's everything I want. That's the name of the song. She's no illusion. She's real. Can you hear it in the song?" Kurt looks over at the Jovi.

"That song's cool."

A week later they drive back to L.A. to meet with the art director in a breezy studio in Los Feliz that looks like a tree house for adults. The art director lifts a slip of wax paper and reveals a mock-up of the album cover.

Felder says, "That's very NOW!"

"That's cool," Sven says. EJ and Eric agree. The whole concept is integrated perfectly. It's a distorted photo in sepia tones. A human figure is lost somewhere, lost in a scream, but somehow the overall feel is soothing. It's sort of like the song "Alone, Alone." The subject matter is disturbing, but the execution is sublime.

Kurt takes the mock-up in his hand, squints, brings his face in close, puts it down, walks straight over to Felder, and says, "That's him!" He points at the Jovi. "I know it is. You can't fool me. No fucking way! I am not having *him* on the cover of *my* album."

Felder looks over at the Jovi. The Jovi shakes his head.

"Look, Kurt, no one can tell," Felder says.

"I can tell."

"Kurt, they're actually going to release the album in one month. It's for real this time. We don't want to do anything to fuck that up."

"You already fucked it up. You should've known."

"Look, Kurt, there's no time for another shoot, she's put hours and hours into this."

"Change it. That's all I'm saying." Kurt storms out.

CAſTINϛ CALL

Sophie is in L.A. for the weekend; the band has another meeting at DCA on Monday. Sven, the Jovi, and Eric are hanging around town, so it's time for martinis and meatloaf on Wilshire.

Eric arrives first with Dane. Sven walks in a few minutes later with Nicky. He's been with her for years—Nicky Strand, not exactly a household name, but she played the sleazy daughter in a classic film adapted from a classic novel, and she was the lead in the fourth of eleven summer-camp slasher flicks. She has been a pregnant nun in Iran, a kidnapped, quilt-making corn farmer in Indiana, a chemically castrated choirboy in Kansas City. She has lived all of these lives before your very eyes on the tube. She is what they call a "working actress."

The Jovi pulls the handle on the tall glass door, and the crowd parts for Sophie Clark. In a matter of seconds, a hush comes over the room, heads turn. She holds them all in the palm of her hand. She strides past the host to the booth, the Jovi trailing behind. There's a barrage of kisses and hugs from a procession of bootlickers who want to remind Sophie that they met her here or there. Sophie greets each one with a big smile and a small kiss. One particularly rodent-faced exec comes up giggling. "Sophie Clark, oh my, do you remember me? I'm just, oh no, you don't. Oh my, what have I done? I never met you! I thought I said hello but I never did." Then he turns around and walks away. Sophie squeezes Eric's thigh beneath the table as she holds in a laugh. *Her hand is big*, Eric thinks, *but not horsy big, elegant big*. It wraps around and makes him feel like a little schoolboy on his way out for ice cream. He looks over at her profile and thinks that she belongs on a French coin, one lifted arm holding a rifle, one breast exposed.

Sven lifts his glass and says, "Nicky and I have some big news. First, Nicky got another film!"

Everybody claps.

"What is it?" Eric asks.

"I'm a hooker! Again! That's why I went to Yale. Sven, really, don't be so rude. We must congratulate Sophie and the Jovi. Alright, let's see the rock!"

Sophie holds out her hand. On her ring finger is a fractional stone on a gold band. "It's just for now. We're going to get ring tattoos on our honeymoon in Fiji."

"May your years be long and your days be joyous, or is it the other way around—long days and joyous years? I don't know!" Nicky pauses with a comic expression. "Oh well! A good wife doth a good husband make—that's what I'm counting on." She pulls Sven by the neck and kisses his forehead. "We're getting married too!"

There is a strange exchange of glances among the women at the table. It's the secret language of women that men will never understand.

Dane breaks the silence. "Eric is afraid of commitment."

"No. I'm just immature."

The table falls back into awkward silence. Darren Getty, an aging gigolo and the star of such movies as *Blow-Dry* and *The Real Jesse James*, walks up. He says, "Sophie! Darling! How are you?" His eyes twinkle and his teeth shine.

Sophie leans up and presses her breasts into his chest in a big smoochy Hollywood hug. "Hey, Darren! This is my fiancé Bobby and Eric and Sven and Dane and Nicky."

"Of course, hello, Darren, it's been a while," Nicky says.

"Do we know each other?"

"Yes, of course, don't you remember—*Lie to Me Once More*? You were having a tryst with my stepmother and then you ran for governor? We had four shooting days together."

"I won that race, didn't I?"

"Just look at you—the other fellow didn't stand a chance!"

"Great. You're still in the biz, right?" He puts his hands on his hips and nods at her for second. Something sharp is coming together in the back of Nicky's mouth.

"Well, anyway, here's my assistant's number, Sophie. Call me! The screen tests with you-know-who were dreadful, and I'm still casting the part of Spicy Trufant in *Muggsy Malone*."

"Oh, really?" Nicky asks. "From the comic strip? They're letting you direct? And you're not going to cast your rock star girlfriend? Tsk tsk, rather daring of you. What will her publicist say?"

"She'll say the same thing she always says."

"What's that?"

"Mr. Getty and Ms. Cucinotta are the best of friends. Besides, we're looking for a face people can't forget—a face like this." He reaches over and holds Sophie's chin in his hand.

Sophie takes his hand in hers and says, "Ooh, what a bummer. I think I'm out—I'm pregnant!"

He guffaws. "You're kidding, right?"

"No."

"Well forget it, then."

"Hey, I'm Bobby. Maybe Sophie can be in your next movie."
The Jovi holds out his hand.

Darren Getty waves to somebody across the room. "It's been
great, gotta run, call my assistant."

"So you're getting into acting?" Nicky asks, then calls out
across the room. "Waiter! Pour yourself a tequila shot and hand
me the fucking bottle!"

"She's just kidding!" Sven says.

"Quiet, darling. I'm ruminating."

ALBUM ORIENTED

Felder wants the band to meet the radio people at DCA, so on Monday, we show up at world headquarters. When we walk in, a guy with a soccer-rocker haircut and a high school letterman's jacket with DCA written across the back runs up and says, "I've been listening to your album, and the damn thing's got balls!" He pumps his fist in front of his chest like a little kid trying to get a trucker to honk his horn.

Kurt nods approval.

"This is no finesse move. This is a strong move to the hoop for a slam-dunk! I am going to have you guys on every AOR station in the country. Fifty adds a week until you're number one. C'mon, high fives all the way around." Palms slap together.

Kurt says, "You know, me and him,"—he points to the Jovi—"we've been doing this for fifteen fucking years. We've been waiting for someone like you—someone who sees what's really there with his own eyes." Kurt extends an arm and gives the guy a rough, manly hug.

"You guys are the tits! Look, I'm late for my two o'clock. We'll be seeing you guys—on the radio!"

The members of Thunderstik are quickly ushered out of the building. Standing in the parking lot beneath a clear blue sky, Kurt lifts his hands and says, "Do you believe me now? I told you DCA was into it. That guy knows what's up. I don't want to hear any more doubt. Why is it I have to be the hopeful one for the whole band? Well? We're gonna be huge. We're the best fucking band in rock—fifteen fucking years!"

"You were right Kurt," Eric says, smiling. "You were right."

EJ says, "You heard the man! Slam-dunk! Jaime Seller might hate Felder, but he's not stupid. He knows our album's good."

"No. More. Doubt." Then Kurt gets in his black '68 Mustang Fastback, starts the engine, revs it, jerks out into Lankershim Boulevard, and a little Japanese econo car plows into him on the driver's-side door. The little car backs up, and a chubby bald guy walks around to look at his broken headlight. Kurt fumbles with the handle on the Mustang. It won't work, so he crawls out the window. He looks at the dent, looks at the bald man, and starts furiously kicking his own car and screaming, "GOD DAMN DEVIL! EVERY FUCKING TIME! GOD DAMN DEVIL! THINGS START GOING GOOD, AND THE DEVIL HAS TO FUCK IT UP! WHY DO YOU DO THIS TO ME?"

The little man gets back in his car and speeds off without asking for insurance or a license. Kurt gets in his car, does furious push-ups on the steering wheel, and peels out into traffic, narrowly averting a landscaping truck on his way to the 101 freeway. EJ, Sven, the Jovi, and Eric look at one another with blank expressions.

"You guys want to go get some lunch at Ben Frank's?" the Jovi asks.

"Yeah."

"Sure."

"Sounds good."

FELDER GETS DOPE

During this summer, the summer of waiting, Thunderstik is in the starting gate, but the world of music is changing. Just ask a guy named Tone-Lōc. The way that it happens in music is that one song can change the entire musical landscape. In 1989 that song is "Wild Thing" by Tone-Lōc. He samples the turnaround drum fill and guitar hook from "Jamie's Cryin'," pays the guys in Van Halen a stipend, loops it over a dance beat, slaps on a rhyme about fornication, and makes all the guys at Delicious Vinyl millionaires. No one can deny that rap music has an energy that Richard Marx, Skid Row, the Smithereens, and all that other crap on AOR radio doesn't have. Chuck D is going to change the world while Skid Row ushers in the nipple ring. There's really no comparison. It is a short ride for Tone-Lōc—here today, gone later today. Months after his hit, people are already calling him Tone-Broke and Tone-Joke, but the urban invasion is on. Felder sees the whole thing coming. He takes on three white rappers, formerly from Brooklyn but now thoroughly entrenched in the L.A. scene: the Ill-Bred Boyz. Their first album had a song that became a teenage-rebellion anthem, but they were in a huge legal fight with the producer and the record company that released it. The four of them are like piss in a pan together. Felder no longer wants to don a vintage biker jacket and stand with his Tele between Kurt and the Jovi. He now wants to wear shorts to his ankles, a sideways baseball cap, and scream out "Whasup, boy-eee?" He's not alone. White people all over the world are throwing away their eyeliner, hairspray, and black leather jackets to don puffy satin suits and do the Roger Rabbit. Time is running out. Maybe Felder knows this. Maybe not. Kurt calls Felder and asks, "What's going on with the album?"

"Don't sweat it, Homes. Seller is dissing us, but we're gonna drop some science on his ass with my mad skills. This publishing deal is going to pop his lid."

"What the fuck are you talking about?"

"Seller is disrespecting us," Felder says in his normal voice.

"Is that a word?"

"I think so."

"So what's going to happen?"

"I'm going to get you guys a huge publishing deal. DCA is going to release the album. It's all good."

"Cool. People need to hear the Truth."

"So get your asses up here. Let's do this thing."

"Okay."

"One more thing. Can you rap at all? Maybe just in the middle of the song. Deborah Harry did it, maybe you could too?"

"Fuck no."

"Okay."

It is the middle of July. The band walks into Felder's office at DCA World Headquarters. Felder is giddy. His frizzy black hair gyrates on top of his head. "I can't believe I fucking did it! I amaze myself. I fucking amaze myself. I salvaged the publishing deal. I don't know how I talked these guys into it. I just… Sometimes I amaze myself. Carol? Carol! Bring in the deal memo."

Carol brings in a document about a quarter-inch thick. Felder ceremoniously slaps it on the table and says, "Let's sign this puppy and pick up the kayeesh, boyeez!"

"Whoa, whoa, whoa, has Stein seen this thing?" EJ asks.

Kurt presses his index fingers into his temples and cocks his head toward the wall.

"Of course. It came from Stein's office."

"Shouldn't we have him explain the deal to us before we sign it?"

"Look, EJ, you do what you want, but this thing needs to happen immediately. Call Stein, drive over there, just do it right now. Until this is inked, these guys can back out at any time."

"Why would they back out? They've heard the album. They know how good it is," Kurt says.

"Look, Kurt, it is, but remember this, we have no fucking idea what DCA's gonna do with the album. Do you get that?"

"What does that have to do with publishing?" EJ asks.

"Well, let's see, where do I start. Number one, you're fucking broke. Wellington said there's almost nothing left in the band account.

"Number two, we owe people money. That fucking T-shirt money, the hundred K is recoupable *and* refundable.

"Number three, publishing companies have their own promotion people just like DCA does. These guys know that if you don't get radio play, their ownership of your publishing rights is worthless. Are you following me? If DCA doesn't do shit with AOR—"

"But that guy, he said it was a no-finesse move, the slam-dunk guy," Kurt says.

"Kurt, let's get real here. Can you deal with that?"

"Yeah." Kurt is starting to brood. "I know the business."

"I don't know that guy. He probably does that same spiel with every band that walks in there."

"WHAT THE FUCK ARE YOU SAYING?"

"Cool down, Kurt. Don't start that shit with me, I'm on your side. And quit fucking calling DCA and yelling at secretaries because they didn't release your album! I heard about your phone calls. You do that again and I'll fucking drive down to La Jolla and rip your fucking phone out of the wall, you hear me?"

"All I said was they should release the album like they said they would!"

"Kurt, I don't care what you said. Don't do it again!"

"I wasn't even yelling that loud."

"How much will you make off this publishing deal?" EJ asks.

Felder smiles and looks away. "What's fucking with you guys? You bite the hand that feeds you?"

"WHO'S FEEDING WHO? WE'RE GONNA BE THE BIGGEST—"

"Yeah, yeah, yeah, I know, Kurt, I know. But what you don't seem to get is that the music is only part of it. Your music is good—really good—I've never doubted that. But, really, music is not a very big part of this business. That sucks. But it's true."

"Look, since we're all getting real here," says EJ, "how do we know you're not just looking to make another quick pop with another hundred K?"

"EJ, you're too fucking smart for your own good. In this fucking business, if someone comes to you and says, 'I brought you five hundred grand, but I'm going to take a hundred—just twenty percent,' you say, 'Thanks for my four hundred K, where do I sign?' You guys want a hundred percent of nothing? Keep your hundred percent of nothing. You want eighty percent of something? Quit fucking around and sign this fucking thing."

"Good enough for me," the Jovi says, reaching for a pen.

Kurt puts out his hand and pushes the Jovi back in his seat. "Who will own the songs?" Kurt asks, and begins pacing between the window and Felder's desk.

"You will, and they will. There's a part of publishing that you can't sell—that's the law—you'll always own that. The other part? They are buying that from you."

"I heard that the Beatles did this, and now they can't get their songs back. Fucking Michael Jackson owns their songs and puts them in commercials!"

"Kurt, that's the Beatles."

"I don't want anyone to own my songs. I don't want to be watching TV and see... hear my song on some sinful commercial for sex or drugs."

"Kurt, you're broke. You owe Bill Wellington twenty grand. One album! You have hundreds of songs. You've played them for me. They're good songs, too."

Kurt stops pacing, sits on the arm of the leather sofa, and presses his fingers into his jaw.

"Your wife, Kurt, she's back at the mall, working. Your car barely runs—you can buy another one! Your jaw—what about your jaw?" Felder asks.

Kurt lifts his head. "Those are some of my best songs."

"Kurt." Felder pauses and tries to look sensitive. "Are you feeling okay?"

Kurt rubs his temples and stares at the floor. "Why do people keep asking me that? I'm fine."

"Are you taking your meds?"

Kurt looks up and the veins bulge in his neck. "I'm off the meds for the band—for the fans—I'm doing it because I'm the best fucking singer, the best fucking songwriter, in the whole fucking world. This is REAL!"

"Kurt, I'm just trying to help—"

"You're not my fucking father! You can't tell me to—"

"Kurt, if not for yourself, do it for your wife." Felder holds out a pen to Kurt.

"That's it! God gave me those songs. I can't sell them. I'm not doing it."

"Jovi? Sven? Eric? Why are you guys so fucking quiet over there? Talk some sense into this guy."

"I am only on for one song," Eric says. "My vote doesn't count for much on this."

"Same," Sven adds.

"I'd sign the fucking thing, but Kurt is always saying they're his songs. I guess that's the way he wants it," the Jovi says.

"Kurt, don't do this to me, don't do this to yourself. We need a little help right now. This could be it."

"No. They're our songs." Kurt lifts his arms toward the rest of the band in a strange air hug. "This is the Beatles, right here."

Felder shakes his head. "What can I do with you guys? What can I fucking do?" Felder stands up, turns toward the window in disgust, and yanks at his hair.

The intercom beeps. "Adam, it's Abe, Gabe, and Dave from the Ill-Bred Boyz on line one. They say it's urgent."

Felder wheels around and throws a brown envelope into Kurt's lap. "Pick your fucking album cover. I don't fucking care—tell Carol which one you like." Then Felder puts on his headset and motions for Thunderstik to leave his office. "What's up boy-eeez?"

The band walks out of his office, leaving him in there with his MTV Astronaut and his platinum records and the Ill-Bred Boyz. We stand in front of Carol's desk. Kurt opens the envelope and pulls out two mock-ups of the album. One has a screaming ghostly negative of someone who looks very much like Kurt, a hideous face of rage taking over the entire canvas. The other is an all-white album with the word "Thunderstik" in a brown Western font in the middle, then an illustration of a lever-action Winchester 1873 below that.

"Dude. This is so cool," Eric says, and holds up the white album. Everyone else agrees.

"I like this one." Kurt holds up the screaming specter.

"Dude, that one's kind of depressing," Sven says.

"Look, man—this one looks like our music—that one, I don't even know what that's all about."

"Thunderstik—that's the name of the band. You made it up. That's what the Indians called the rifle, a thunderstick, because it was a stick that made a sound like thunder," Eric says.

Kurt looks a little confused.

"You didn't know that?" Sven asks.

"I knew it. But I just liked the name. Our band has nothing to do with guns or the Old West. It's this one." Kurt hands the screaming ghost to Carol and walks away. Then he turns at the door. "THE ILL-BRED BOYZ? THAT'S NOT EVEN REAL MUSIC. THEY'RE GONNA BE HERMAN'S HERMITS. WE ARE GONNA BE THE BEATLES. PEOPLE ARE GOING TO FORGET THOSE GUYS EVER EXISTED!"

Carol is a little puzzled. Kurt tries to slam the door, but it is an office door with a regulator box on the top that makes it open or close very slowly. He struggles with it for a second, then stomps down the hall.

MORE THAN THIS

Up from the beach, about a half mile from Windansea on Gravila Street, there is a small house with a Spanish tile roof and stucco walls, hardwood floors, and a large, round, sunken tub. The front yard has soft sporadic grass beneath a broad shade tree. In the backyard, which gets more sun, a thicker green grows. Next to the main house, there is a little casita that once was a garage. Inside is a small mixing board, five electric guitars, a Marshall head, a Hi-Watt cabinet, and the Jovi, who is crouching down over a microphone, singing in his quiet, raspy voice with an acoustic guitar in his lap. Tape moves slowly from one turning wheel to the next. A red light blinks.

In the yard, the sound of wind, then wind chimes, then Sophie, her voice sparkling with happiness. "Bobby? Bobby? Are you out there?" The Jovi hears nothing. His eyes are closed. He's trying to hit the high notes in a song about feelings. Sophie walks in, her legs long and toned. She pushes a blonde curl behind her ear. "There you are."

He stops singing, takes off his headphones, pushes the stop button and smiles at her. She folds the cloth of her nightgown in her hands; the material slides along her brown skin from her knees to her thighs past a small patch of blonde hair to her navel. She looks down. "Kiss her."

"Yes!" The Jovi puts down his acoustic. He brushes his lips against her skin, rising to her breasts, to her neck, to her jaw, to her lips, then sinking back down.

"No, silly! Our daughter. Kiss our daughter."

"Right. Right." He moves his lips to the center of Sophie's stomach. He looks up at Sophie rimmed in blue. "See how much happier you are when you don't drink – don't do any pills."

"Belly to belly," she says, pulling the nightgown up to her clavicle. He yanks his white tank top up and off. His torso is wiry and tan. Sophie gets up on her toes and presses herself into him.

"It's better, right?"

"Look what I made you." She reaches for a drawing.

He takes it in his hand. "'Little Wing.' I love that song. It's your song."

The piece of notebook paper is decorated with water-colors—red hearts and musical notes that seem to flutter about the page. The moisture has changed the paper, creating valleys and sunken hearts. A hypnotic scroll starts in the middle and leads in a circuitous path to the distant lyrics of the Jimi Hendrix song.

"That's the coolest thing anyone's ever given me."

"Can you play it for me?"

"Yeah, I think I know that song."

The Jovi starts strumming his acoustic, whispering the lyrics, his voice on pitch with only occasional cracks. She puts her hands in his lap and kneels by his side. His voice becomes more confident, bolder; he's singing about butterflies and zebras and moonbeams, and then he stops as if something has shifted.

"Did you hear that?"

"Don't stop. Keep going."

"I think I heard Kurt or somebody."

He puts down the guitar, walks out of the casita, and hears nothing but the wind chimes.

"Finish the song." Sophie has followed him, holding the acoustic, strumming the only chord she knows, an E.

He runs over to the gate, swings it open, and finds Kurt standing there in his black gig gear, poking his fingers into his jaw and staring at the ground. He looks up at the Jovi and nods.

"How long have you been standing there?"

"Hey. Just a second."

"Where's the 'Stang?"

"I walked."

"Fuck, dude, I wish you'd knock or yell or something."

"Yeah, I was about to."

Sophie stretches out onto her tiptoes and wraps her arms around Kurt. She lets him go, holds his arms, and looks in his evasive eyes. "Come in. Can I make you some tea or something?"

"Yeah. Yeah. Sure."

Kurt sits at a bar stool at the kitchen counter. The Jovi pulls his long gray tweed coat off a hook and puts it on Sophie's shoulders. She laughs and flips the weight of it off her back. It slides to the ground. The Jovi looks at her nipples, her navel, and her everything through the sheer fabric, and he quickly looks over at Kurt. Kurt's head is cocked toward the window. He's staring at a bird in the backyard. "This place is really nice."

"Good energy, right?" Sophie pours some coffee in a cup and slides it to Kurt.

He looks down into the black brew and pulls at the curls in his hair. "I'm having a really hard time right now."

"What's going on?" the Jovi says.

"My jaw. Nobody could deal with this kind of pain. None of you even know what it's like."

Sophie walks behind Kurt, reaches over his shoulders, and rubs his jaw with both hands.

He exhales and sinks into his shoulders. "I've sinned on my wife."

The sun's rays beat down through the kitchen window, reflect off the water in a ceramic bowl in the sink, and dance in octagons on the ceiling like turtles crawling over each other's backs. Sophie moves her hands to his shoulders, leans in to his ear, and whispers, "How have you sinned?"

Kurt turns his head and looks into her slightly sleepy eyes. "I've cheated on her with women, other women."

Sophie leans in and presses her soft full red lips on his mouth.

"Whoa, whoa, whoa," The Jovi yells.

"Now," Sophie whispers to Kurt, "Did that mean anything?"

Kurt is puzzled. He looks at the Jovi and back at Sophie. "No?" He asks.

"No. Of course not," she says and turns to kiss the Jovi. "This is the man I love."

"I get the point," the Jovi says, "but I don't like the teaching method."

"It's only your heart that can be true or untrue. Your body is totally different." Sophie looks for a reaction from the Jovi. He's starting to perspire. "The spirit…"

"The spirit is willing," Kurt says, "but the flesh is weak."

"Dude. Can we all just keep our flesh to ourselves here, okay?" The Jovi asks.

"You know she left me first. She left me when I had nothing. I was on drugs. I was alone. James saved me—"

Sophie turns sharply at the sound of James's name. "You saved yourself."

Kurt looks down at his hands above the blue tiles on the kitchen counter.

Sophie walks over and stands before the Jovi. She reaches back behind her, runs her hands down his hips and tugs him tight to her backside. The Jovi's hands meet around her waist. "Leave her," Sophie says.

"I would, but Pastor Ron says divorce is a sin. He married us."

"Were you married when she left you?"

"Yeah."

"It didn't stop her. Why should it stop you?" Sophie takes the Jovi's hands away from her waist.

"I guess."

"So do it. Life is short. Live in the now." She steps into the sunlight. Her arms are folded, her feet are set wide apart, she is an illuminated A with two sets of lush curves, one at her breasts and one at her hips "When you're an old man, you're going to look back and think of this moment and all the things you could've had but didn't get because you didn't have the courage to take them for your own. Everything that's coming to you—and it's going to be a lot, you have no idea how much your life is going to change when this album comes out—everything that's coming to you, you earned, you deserve, it's yours. It's right there in front of you. All you have to do is take it."

Kurt looks up into the shining vision of a woman and nods his head.

THE ALBUM-RELEASE PARTY

DCA releases the album *Thunderstik* by the band Thunderstik on Friday, August 18, 1989. DCA plans an album-release party for the band at the Hard Rock Café in La Jolla. Thunderstik shows up around seven P.M. It is still sunny, and there is a beta-cam crew from a local television station waiting for them outside. The reporter says something about local boys made good. The band members smile and stand around for the camera.

They walk inside and the hostess asks, "Do you have a reservation?"

"We're Thunderstik," says EJ.

The hostess smiles. "That's nice, do you have a reservation?"

"We're supposed to have the whole place! Isn't there anybody here from DCA? You know, DCA, the record company."

She smiles and shakes her head.

"They didn't call you? They were supposed to send someone from PR and a big box of albums too. None of us have seen it. We were supposed to sign albums and give 'em away. They're here to film the whole thing from Channel 8."

The hostess cranes her neck to look outside at the betacam man. "Oh, I think I did know about this. Let me go get the manager. But do you mind if I seat these people first?" She takes a mother and two boys past the band, holding menus to her chest.

Kurt presses his index fingers into his temples, cocks his head down at the floor, and looks away from the film crew. "What's going on here?" he says under his breath, forcing a laugh.

The hostess comes back with the manager. He says, "Thunderstik!" and grins into the lens with lots of gum and tiny teeth. "We're all ready for you, come right this way."

Kurt turns to the film crew and nods as if everything is cleared up. The manager leads them, film crew in tow, through the busy restaurant past the kids' birthday parties with balloons, past the line of people trying to buy T-shirts, past the happy-hour crowd at the bar to a large wooden booth at the back of the room beneath a neon-splashed triangular guitar in a glass case signed by Eddie Van Halen. "Here we are. All set. Oh, yes, there's a package for you." The manager holds out an oversized brown envelope. EJ takes it.

"Well, open it," the Jovi says, smiling at the camera.

EJ pulls it open and slides out one single copy of the album. On the cover is the screaming ghost. On the back is a black-and-white photo of the five band members guarding an outdoor staircase in a desolate industrial rust garden. In the foreground a large Kurt is staring away, then a medium-sized Jovi, then Sven, EJ, and Eric up the metal steps getting smaller and fuzzier.

Kurt laughs. "Just try walking up that staircase. Look at that. You'll never make it."

"Great! So that's the album," the Jovi says.

EJ turns the envelope upside down, as if he were expecting ten more albums to fall out. Nothing does.

"Did they make more than one?" Sven asks.

And with that, the camera crew kills the light. Now the band members' eyes are readjusting to the dim but pleasant light in the restaurant. The cameraman eases the betacam off his shoulder and says, "Thanks, guys."

Eric walks out to his car, gets a cassette of Thunderstik songs, hands it to the hostess, and mercifully she plays it on the house speaks. The band sits in the booth and eats barbequed chicken. Sven, EJ, and Kurt drink a lot of beer. The Jovi and Eric drink Cokes. When the check comes, Kurt turns to Eric. "Can you float me?"

"Sure." Eric pulls out two twenties.

That night, after the leads, after sports, after the weather, at precisely 11:29 and 46 seconds, the anchorman says, "And we leave you tonight with this. What happens when local rock band Thunderstik hits it big? They celebrate the release of their first album at the Hard Rock Café. Thanks for watching. Goodnight and God bless." On the left side of the screen, the band stands in front of the restaurant, and on the right side the credits whiz by, white Chiron type on a black screen.

The next day Eric drives Kurt down to the Tower Records in Point Loma to buy the album, CD, and cassette. In between Throbbing Gristle and Tina Turner there is a plastic placard with THUNDERSTIK at the top, but there are no albums, no CDs, no cassettes. "Look at this," Kurt says. "Tower is sold out. I told you it's going to happen."

EJ, Kurt, and Eric sit in Eric's living room, listening to the radio and take turns calling the request line. They call and call until the girl on the other end seems to know their voices. "So are you *in* the band?" she asks sarcastically.

"No. I just dig those guys," Eric says. "They're sold out, you know. Can't find that album anywhere."

It finally happens. They play "Kick It Clean" on 95X. Thunderstik rides the airwaves, Thunderstik rocks the auto shops, rocks the house painters, rocks the carpenters. EJ, Kurt, and Eric hear it and think, *Yes. We are going to be rock stars.* The music is the truth, and you can't keep the truth down. It will happen.

AISLE. ALTER. HIM

It is August 26, 1989. The Dugans' backyard is filled with flowers and family. Candles float in the pool. The bride arrives at sunset, tan and dressed in white. She walks the aisle to meet a waiting and smiling Jovi.

In the morning they fly first class to Fiji. They stay in a private resort. They fuck like rabbits and get tribal Fijian tattoos.

THREE MINUTES AND FORTY SECONDS

In the contract, DCA has allotted eighty thousand dollars to make a music video. Felder shows the band some really cool reels and then tells them: "We can't afford any of those guys. My buddy said he'll do it."

"What's your buddy done?" EJ asks.

"You'll love him. He did the Debbie Cherry video."

"Oh shit, that video has hip-hopping hoboes," Eric says. "What does this guy know about rock and roll?"

"This guy lives rock and roll."

The people at DCA submit a script that they think will go with the song "Kick It Clean," a song about Kurt kicking Mellaril. The script goes as follows: Kurt is in a hotel room with a really beautiful girl in her underwear. The scene is postcoital, moody. The blinds create bars across their bodies, and a slow fan oscillates shadows in the heat. He sings the song. Then he goes out of the hotel room and there is the band playing their instruments in the hall, or down by the pool, or maybe not playing their instruments at all. But one guy has drumsticks, and he's rat-a-tat-tat-ing on the banister.

Felder reads the script, scoffs at it, and tells DCA: "Look, I'm the one with the MTV Astronaut; I know how to make art."

Then he hires the guy from the Debbie Cherry video.

It is a low-concept performance video. The band will play on a soundstage in front of no one, with a fire in a junked car burning nearby and sparks spitting from the lighting rigging. The director tells Felder he is going to make Kurt and the Jovi look like stars. If he could do it for Debbie Cherry, he can do it for them.

Eric has one minor problem. He doesn't have much of a part on that song. There is a hit that sounds like gunfire in the distance, and he whacks that five times in real fast succession after Kurt sings the big line on the chorus, but he really doesn't have anything to do. Eric asks Felder, "Should I sit this one out?"

"No, it's our first video. They gotta see all five guys. Make something up."

The Jovi laughs. "If I were you, I'd do something like this." He starts rhythmically rapping out the beat to the song between his left and right hands on the keyboard, as if he were playing the bongos.

"Yeah, that's cool. I'll do that."

Tiffany Tucker shows up wearing airtight shiny leather pants, a wife-beater with a crucifix, and collagen-injected lips. A pretty woman, she never really had lips. Now she has these motionless, gigantic pink lips stuck on her face. Her doctor has pumped them up until they have turned inside out, and a little clear saliva lingers on her now-visible gum line. She gives everyone in the band big air kisses and tells them, "Oh God, I've missed you boys! It's so nice to be working with you." She lights a cigarette and puts it between her gummy lips. After she found Thunderstik and brought the band to Felder, who made a boatload of money, her big reward is a job, a regular paying job, on a video for a rock band. Dane is still her assistant.

Dane is constantly being sent to get this, steam that, go back and get those. Dane has a constipated look on her pretty little face, and she acts as if she is always looking for something on the floor. To Eric, beneath her cut-off black trousers, her bare calves look shiny and sexy. Near the wardrobe rack, he puts his hands on her hips. Her mop of blonde hair swings about and she looks at him with cold and distant eyes, like she is some beautiful bird of prey. "You've changed," she says.

"I'm a rocker now. That's good, right?"

"No." She says and squints at Eric like he's bright. "We're done."

"No. You love me. You've always loved me," Eric says and smiles and tears up a little.

She dips down into a bag and brings up something, a black velvet mat with ten silver rings—skulls and goats' heads and sharp, pointy things. "Tiff says put these on."

"You're giving me rings? Satanic looking rings? Really?" Eric asks.

"Put them on."

"You don't love me?"

"Hi, Honey." Tiff arrives in a flurry. "With your long fingers on the keyboard, you'll look fierce. Trust me."

She puts Kurt in a leather blazer, the Jovi in leather pants and a T-shirt with cutoff sleeves.

The director shows up and disappears into the bathroom with Felder. A half-hour later, the two of them shuffle out and sit Indian-style in front of the band like two gurus, one with long, straight brown hair, one with a frizzy black Brillo pad on his head. The techs set up the real gear, cords and all—the director is into authenticity. They have a PA system, and on the PA system they play the album version of "Kick It Clean."

"What do we do?" Kurt asks.

"Pretend like you're playing the song," Felder says.

The techs cue up "Kick It Clean," hit PLAY, and everyone in the band hops around pretending to play their instruments as if we are in a junior high air-guitar contest. Felder and his buddy don't move. The DP changes camera angles, directs the band, and asks for solos.

Between takes, with his ears ringing, Eric yells to the Jovi, "Dude, Dane dumped me!"

"Nah! She loves you!"

A week later they send EJ the video. Everyone meets at EJ's mom's house to watch it. We all agree that it has begun—We got radio play, we have a video.

"We're the best fucking band in rock," Kurt announces.

"Damn straight," the Jovi says.

Afterward Kurt and Eric drive down to Tower Records. The placard is there, but still no CDs. They ask for the manager. He is a white guy with dreadlocks down to his ass and a hoop in his nose. Kurt shakes his hand and says, "Have you guys ever seen anything sell like this? I keep coming in to buy Thunderstik, but it's always gone—sold out."

The manager chuckles, punches the computer keyboard, and says, "We sold five."

"Huh?"

"Yeah, dude. Well, fifteen actually. Five CDs. Five cassettes. Five LPs. It's all we ordered. Sold them all the first day. We ordered five more. Of each. Shoulda been in on Monday. Try again Friday."

"Dude. Can you order more?" Eric asks.

"Yeah. Let me get the form." The manager puts a piece of paper on the counter. "Here. Put your name here. Address here. How do you want to pay for it?"

"No, man. You guys should order a bunch. We're from here. We're from San Diego," Kurt says, clutching his head.

"Yeah, we don't get many tourists in…"

"He means the band." Eric says.

"No way!"

"Yeah."

"Oh. Cool. Okay. I'm on it, dude. I had no idea."

EJ, Kurt, and Eric listen to the radio and watch MTV at the same time. They watch the "AltRock Hour," the "Fresh Rock Hour." One guy at the beach says he has seen the Thunderstik video, but he's a guy who lives in his car—it doesn't seem possible.

Eric calls Felder. "Hey, Adam, what's up with the video?"

"I'll get back to you. I'm real busy right now."

The next week Eric calls Felder again. Carol says, "Adam's busy. Can he get back to you?" Another week passes, September is ending in a flurry of hot Santa Ana days. Football is on TV. The club scene is quiet Sunday to Wednesday. Eric calls Felder at home and finally catches him. "What's up, Adam?

"Hey."

"So, dude, what's up with MTV?"

"Oh! Hey, babe, put that down. You heard me, put that down."

"Adam?"

"Yeah. You remember Celine from the studio? Right?"

"The blonde?"

"Yeah. Very funny! Very funny, girl."

"So, Adam, what's up with MTV? Is your buddy gonna play the video or not?"

"My buddy? Oh yeah, my buddy, yeah…He said DCA sent the video in a brown envelope with no letter, no promo, so it went straight to the vault."

"So is he gonna play it?"

"Said he can't. Very funny. Where did you find that? Put it down, you could poke an eye out with that!"

"Why not?"

"Huh?"

"Why can't he play it?"

"No spins. No push from DCA."

"No hookers? No blow? No nothing?"

"You know the game. Why can't Kurt be more like you? Don't tell him, okay?"

"What are we gonna do?"

"Gotta go. It's been great. We should hang sometime. Give my best to Sophie, okay?"

"It's Eric here."

"Right."

The receiver clicks several times before Felder gets the phone to stay in the cradle.

Eric drives down to Tower Records. The dreadlocked dude has finally scored some copies of the album, CD, and cassette.

He waves his hands over the CDs like he's doing some kind of magic trick. "It's not that bad, dude."

"Thanks."

"What do you play?"

"Keyboards."

"There's keyboards on this thing? Whoa, I had no idea."

"They're in there—you just gotta turn it up really loud."

"Right on. Right on. You guys make a video?"

"Yup."

"Where is it?"

"I don't know."

"On MTV?"

"Look at all these rows and rows of rock records. There's only twenty-four hours in a day and after commercials and Milli Vanilli, what's left? It's hard to get on MTV."

"That's a fact, man." He gives Eric a soul shake.

"Thanks, bro. Can you play it once in a while? In the store?"

"For reals," he says, sliding the credit card slip under Eric's hand.

THE THRILL OF IT ALL

Felder books Thunderstik a gig at the China Club in L.A. When Sophie and Summer show up, Kurt is already wearing his dog collar and black gig gear. Sophie looks at him, puts her finger through the collar, and lets out a little bark. Felder loves it. He has a photographer snap black-and-white photos of the band backstage with Sophie.

Sophie says, "I totally get this thing—it's like Lou Reed in the *Transformer* stage—like that, and the cover of *Rock 'n' Roll Animal*. Right?"

"Well, it's my own thing, you know, but kinda…"

"Let me do your makeup."

Kurt turns pink with joy. Summer and Sophie bring Kurt under the light of a ventilation hood. They turn the corners of his eyes up with eyeliner and mascara, a little rim of red around the lips, and then they white-out the rest. Kurt looks in the mirror. A rock 'n' roll dope fiend stares back at him. Sophie stares over Kurt's shoulder, pushes her hair back with both hands, and stretches out like a cat in the sun. "Hold on, something's not right." She digs her nails into the shoulders of Kurt's black T-shirt and rips the sleeves off.

"Are you getting this? Are you fucking getting this?" Felder screams at the photographer. "Listen, the guys from Polygram are here. Slay these fuckers! Don't break anything! Just make music! Show them the pretty singing, right, Kurt? We may need a new label."

"Are you sure we want to change horses in midstream?" EJ asks.

"Don't break anything."

Kurt nods. "Let's do it like Elvis."

The rest of the band takes the stage in complete darkness. Count it out. Come in together. "Do It Tonight." It's a tough-sounding, hard-driving rock anthem. When Kurt walks out on stage four bars in, the crowd screeches in approval.

We finish with "Rock 'n' Roll" by Lou Reed.

Afterward, Sophie wipes off the Jovi with some paper towels in the back room. Kurt's makeup has run down his face and he is staring at the half grapefruits in Summer's dress like he is gonna juice 'em.

Felder motions to the Jovi, Kurt, and Sophie. "Come with me. There's somebody I want you to meet."

They follow him down the hall into a catering prep room. There are broad metal trays covered with asparagus sprouts wrapped in ham. Sophie grabs one and pushes it in the Jovi's mouth, then grabs another and puts it in Kurt's mouth. A little bald guy in a leather jacket shakes the Jovi's hand, shakes Kurt's, and hugs Sophie.

"This is Joshua Weiner from Polygram," Felder says.

"I always wanted to sign you guys. Maybe in our next lifetime."

"Really?" Sophie says. "Maybe you wanted to sign us in your last life too, and you just can't get your shit together?" They all laugh.

Felder says, "Well, Josh, you never know, do you?"

"You guys are on DCA for what? Seven albums. I hope they don't screw you the way they screw everyone else. Seven albums on DCA, that could be a death sentence for this much talent."

"Well, we'll see. We'll see."

Sophie grabs another piece of asparagus and crams it in Weiner's mouth. Weiner is left chewing and laughing and wanting.

They walk back to the changing room and Kurt vanishes.

Felder takes the Jovi and Sophie to a swank underground after-hours party off of Vine. A guy waits by a little basement door with a walkie-talkie. He brings the three of them into a little black antechamber. A hostess in a Lycra dress brings them to a booth. Otto Led, the lead singer of Led 'n' Lilacs, is sitting in a booth on the other side of the room with a bandana on his head. He stares and bares his little gray teeth at Sophie. Sophie is pregnant and not drinking and ready to go home after a while.

While they are driving home, Sophie says, "We should move to L.A."

"Why?"

"After our little girl is born, I don't want to be traveling so much. If we live in L.A., I could go on movie auditions, and you could record your music. My mom said she would move up and help me."

"Hey, my mom can help us down in La Jolla."

"Yeah, but it's, like, boring."

"It's not New York, but I don't know...boring?"

"And Darren thinks it would be better for my career if I could go on auditions and be around—"

"Darren Getty? That guy's still calling you?"

"You know, he told me that if I weren't pregnant, he would've given me that role in *Muggsy Malone*. He told me to get an abortion—he said that's what a real actress would do."

"Are you fucking kidding me? If I ever see that guy, I'm gonna fucking punch him in his little twinkly eyes."

"He's just trying to help."

"He cast his girlfriend! You know that?"

"Yeah. She's not pregnant!"

"That's the way that whole thing works. The casting couch."

"Not for me, maybe if you're a nobody."

"Don't…"

"I've got a name."

"I know."

"A career."

"I know, baby. You'd never do that."

"It's my body. I can do what I want."

"What? You mean like sleep with some fucking—"

"No! I just mean nobody can tell me what to do with my body. It's mine."

"Oh. I gotcha, but really, right now, you're sharing it with our baby." He rubs her belly. "Is it nice?"

She smiles and holds his hand on top of her stomach. "Yeah. But I could use a drink."

"No. You're kidding right?"

After a few miles, Sophie curls up and dozes off. When she wakes, they are pulling off the freeway. "Oh, this little baby makes me sleepy."

DISAPPEARING ACT

Even while she's kissing Kurt and running her hands up and down his sides, Summer is different. Kurt doesn't know this yet. He thinks it's the usual race to completion as he presses her against the Fastback, bites her neck, and paws at her skirt. But then she stops rubbing him, stops kissing him, puts her hands above his pounding heart, and pushes him away.

"No!"

Kurt wipes his mouth with his hand and leans toward her, bent and panting in the moonlight.

"You're like a wolf. Why don't you try talking to me first?"

"Okay. What do you want to talk about?"

"The weather."

Kurt looks over his shoulder at the gray L.A. night sky. "There's nothing up there."

"That's not true, there's a moon and satellites and space trash spinning around the planet. Try it. Tell me something about the weather."

"Okay. It's sixty-seven degrees and dark."

"That's not romantic. Try something like: Isn't this an enchanting night? But I fear one kiss from you, my love, and the heavenly firmament may fall."

"That's lame."

"I've heard you sing things like that—not exactly, but close."

"I know, but that's different."

"How?"

"It just is. Let's get out of here."

"Wow. You're such a Romeo. Let's get out of here—that probably works every time."

"Forget it."

"Okay. Bye." Summer walks back toward the entrance to the China Club.

"Okay. Okay. Pardon me, dear beauty, would you like to go for a ride in my chariot?"

"You're right. That's lame. Oh, well? Aren't you going to open the door?"

He does. She slides in, folds and unfolds her legs, and bats her eyelashes.

The 5 freeway is a river that flows in both directions. Like the Seine, like the Thames, like the Hudson, it brings commerce and filth to its banks. In the day it is covered with silver-backed cars and belching trucks. It is bright in the night with glad-eyed Hondas and Subarus.

Kurt sails south on this river of lights with Summer by his side. The Mustang is not what she once was, five out of eight cylinders fire in an uneven cadence tonight. The car whinnies and neighs and shakes her head, backfires, and slogs on. When she can feel the moist air of San Diego seeping through the holes in the car, Summer grabs Kurt's thigh and squeezes. Kurt reaches over into Summer's lap and wedges his fingers between her clenched thighs.

"Two hands on the wheel." She lifts his hand away.

She unbuckles her seatbelt, gets up on her knees, and puts her face down in Kurt's lap. She unzips him, reaches in. She drops her head down and licks from the base to the tip. She drops her lips down around the head and Kurt feels lightheaded. The road blurs. He lifts his foot off the accelerator and pulls the car toward the shoulder. Summer feels the uneven engine slow. "No! Keep driving." Her long fingers move to his right knee and push it down, speeding up the car. She bobs up and down, her lips popping each time they pass the ridge. Kurt lets out a moan and she stops, lifts her skirt, and faces the passenger-side window on her knees. One hand on the wheel, one hand inside her, he slips his fingers in and out, sliding in the wet warmth with the movement of her hips and the uneven sound of the engine. She breathes in exaggerated gulps, as if she has just come up from the depths of the sea. Then she stops, pulls down her skirt, flops down in her seat. "That's all."

"No? Why?"

"You're married for one."

"I don't know if that's going to last."

She laughs. "Sure. That's very funny. Two, you're driving."

"You can't just do that to me."

"Look, Kurt, I really like you. But I'm not the kind of girl who fools around with married men."

"But I like you too."

"Well, you know where to find me."

Kurt drops Summer off at Phoenix's house. There are wind chimes and sticks woven into symbolic geometric shapes in the yard.

"Is your mom a witch?"

"My mom is weird."

"If I leave my wife, would you become a Christian for me?"
She smiles and slams the door.

Kurt steps into his dark apartment. The lump on the floor
says, "Hey. How was the gig?"

"Good."

"Was she there?"

"Yeah."

"Fuck. You let her come to your gigs?"

"Yeah."

"You don't care anymore, do you?"

A woman's voice near the lump asks, "Who are you talking
to?"

"That's my brother. This is his apartment."

"Right on."

Kurt steps into his bedroom and closes the door. He drops
his clothes on the floor and slips beneath the sheets. Priscilla is
sleeping on her stomach. He runs his hand up her leg, feeling
the tiny hairs bristle at his touch until his hand stops between
her legs. Right now it's just skin and hair, a flap of skin that he
rubs, hoping for transformation. He breathes her in, puts his dry
lips on her back. The skin loosens up and separates with moisture. He is hard. He finds the moisture and pushes. It resists. He
pushes a little harder.

"Oh my God. Oh, it's you. Thank God. What are you doing?"

"Nothing."

"I was dreaming that the devil was trying to have sex with
me."

"Well he's not. It's your husband."

"Oh, stop. Please stop."

"Okay. Okay."

"Leave me alone for a second, would you?"

"What the hell is going on here?" Kurt jumps out of bed and throws his hands up in the air. "My own wife won't have sex with me." He kicks one leg in his pants, then the other, zips up, and walks past the lump and down the stairs.

THE BOOK

In the morning, Kurt calls Eric. "Get your ass over here. Now!"

The door is open, the shades are drawn, and Pastor Ron and a group from the Vine Church are sitting on the dumpy sofa in front of a massage table. Kurt is standing in the doorway to the bedroom, wearing nothing but a towel.

"What's up, dude?"

"These guys figured out what's wrong with my jaw."

"What?"

"Show him." Kurt motions to Pastor Ron. Pastor Ron holds a bundled blanket in his arms. He sets it down on the coffee table and ceremoniously unwraps it. Inside is a book, not an old leather-bound book with a giant lock, just a regular brand-new book with a pastel drawing of a woman in a negligee sitting on a crescent moon.

"So?" Eric says.

Pastor Ron shakes his head in disgust. "It's a book of spells. Doesn't it bother you?"

"Why should it?"

"Look." He uses the corner of the blanket to open the cover. Written on the inside is:

~~James Franklin~~
Bobby Dugan
Bobby Dugan
Bobby Dugan
Kurt Franklin
Elmer Watts Junior
Sven Davidson
Eric Adams
Adam Felder
Darren Getty

The names have Wiccan symbols beside them. Eric reaches for the book.

"No! Don't touch it! That's why it's in the blanket. It's evil."

Kurt looks Eric up and down. "That's why the devil attacked my jaw. 'Cuz I'm in her book. Do you still have your…" Kurt looks over at Pastor Ron. Pastor Ron nods at Kurt. Kurt continues. "Penis?"

Eric laughs. "Kinda."

"It's not a joke, Eric." Pastor Ron says. "Check."

Eric pulls on his jeans and looks down. "It's there."

"Clearly, she's put a curse on the band, we don't know what's next," Pastor Ron says.

"Who?" Eric asks.

"Sophie Clark!"

"How'd you guys get this book?" Eric asks. Nobody answers. They look at him with hollow eyes. "Who are these people?" Eric points at two dudes and an old lady sitting in the corner.

"They're heavy with the Spirit. They are going to break the power of the curse and fix my jaw."

"This is nuts."

"No, Eric, it's not," Priscilla says from the bedroom. She walks out, big sad eyes, business suit, black tights. "That's what I thought, but now I know it's true. Eric, you have to believe them." She kisses Kurt on the cheek and says, "Bye, everyone," as she walks out the door.

Pastor Ron's mustache moves above his trembling lips. "Eric, you're in the book too. Kurt tells me your back hurts. Coincidence? No. Klaus can fix it." Pastor Ron points at a compact Austrian with a strawberry-blond 'fro who steps forward and cracks his knuckles. "First let us pray. Everyone take a knee, put your hands on each other's shoulders. Good. Good. Dear Lord, we ask that you protect Kurt and Eric. They have wandered into the devil's den, done battle with evil, and suffered the lacerations. Kurt, Eric, repeat after me, to the demons that attack Kurt's jaw, to the demons that attack my wife with indigestion, to the demons that attack this band—we banish thee in the name of Christ."

Then Pastor Ron's head nods off to the side, and he whispers in an unknown dialect for quite some time. Pastor Ron comes to and speaks in a strong voice. "I watched Satan fall from heaven like a flash of lightning. See, I have given you authority to tread on snakes and scorpions, and over all the power of the enemy, and nothing will hurt you."

"Yes, Father," Kurt says.

"Eric? Don't you have something to confess?" Pastor Ron asks from within his trance.

"No. I'm cool."

"I can feel something."

"I'm not exactly a good person, if that's what you mean."

"Tell me."

"God loves the cripples; I can barely deal with a smelly grandparent."

"That's just the beginning. There's something more, some kind of demon upon you. I can feel it. It's in this room. You've seen this demon too, haven't you?"

"Yeah, once I kind of did. I think it was Kurt's demon. I think what he has is contagious. The thing jumped on me for a while."

"Where did you see it?"

"In my bedroom."

"What were you doing?"

"I was doing Carrie Gomez."

"Fornication! I knew it."

"Look, I believe in God. God got me off drugs. It's all this devil stuff I'm not sure I believe in."

"Eric, if you believe in one thing, you must believe in its opposite. How can you believe in the goodness of God and not believe in the evil of the dark one?"

"Dunno."

"This band has fallen under a heavy satanic influence, and it must be purged before Kurt's jaw can heal, before the band can be successful."

"Look, I'm not the only fornicator in the band."

"Eric, woe to you who are rich, for you have received your consolation on earth. Klaus! Hold him." The compact Austrian man grabs Eric and wraps his arms around Eric's shoulders and neck. "Ask for forgiveness, Eric!"

"Forgive me, Father, for my fortune in cheese!"

"Demon, I rebuke you in the name of Jesus." Pastor Ron reaches back and slaps Eric in the face with everything he's got.

He collapses on the floor. "Fffuck."

Pastor Ron nods and solemnly declares, "Okay, it's time to get to work." They put Kurt on the massage table, and Klaus starts manipulating his arms and legs and neck and back. The others lay hands on him. Pastor Ron starts with the tongues again. Eric opens his eyes to a side view of the world fringed in brown shag. The smell of old carpet fills his nostrils. Time fades in and out, and then Eric is facedown on Klaus's table. Klaus rubs. Eric moans with pleasure. "Strong hands." Klaus flips him over, bends Eric's knee to his chin, and cracks his back like a lobster shell. Eric sees stars and feels a little nauseated. Klaus looks down. "Dahn't vorry." Eric feels Klaus's flaccid dick poking into his elbow. Eric moves the elbow. The penis, sheathed only in silky short shorts follows Eric's elbow wherever it goes. Klaus makes a loud groaning sound while he rubs Eric's calf and pushes his cock and balls into the sole of Eric's foot. Klaus walks around the table to the top; he grabs Eric's shoulders and lifts him in the air, setting him down in a seated position on the side of the table.

"Thanks," Eric says.

"You know, Klaus is very poor. Can you make a donation?" Pastor Ron asks.

Eric opens his wallet. There is a twenty. He hands it to Klaus.

"I don't know about you," Kurt says, "but I feel a lot better."

BETWEEN THE BARS

Felder books Thunderstik a gig at the Lingerie in Hollywood, so they can play for Ron Headley's touring agent and Josh Weiner from Polygram. The dressing room at the Lingerie is layered with even more graffiti and band stickers and filth. EJ and Eric are the first to arrive. Waiting for them in the horrible dressing room is Bill Wellington in a gray three-piece suit. "Hi, fellas. Would one of you mind signing for this?" He motions toward a brown cardboard box.

"Sure, what is it?" EJ asks.

"It's all your financial records, checks for the guys who have something left in their accounts, bills for the others. We are terminating our relationship with the band."

Kurt walks in with Priscilla under his arm. "What's going on?"

"Our accountants are firing us," EJ says.

"Hello, Kurt, we were hoping you could write us a check tonight for the loan."

"I don't have anything at all. I don't have a car. My wife drove me up here. I don't have money for smokes."

"This is an urgent matter that requires your immediate attention."

"I'll send you a check when I get home. What do we owe you?" Priscilla says.

"We need the entire loan amount, plus interest. It comes to twenty-one thousand seven hundred forty-three dollars and seventy-six cents."

Priscilla turns to Kurt. "You borrowed twenty-one thousand dollars without asking me?"

"I bought you that car!"

"I didn't need that car. I don't know how we are ever going to…" She puts her face in her hands and runs out of the room.

Kurt yells at her as she runs away. "We're going to make so much money this isn't going to matter!" Then he turns to Wellington. "You're going to be sorry you fired us!"

"I'm willing to take that chance. Good-bye, gentlemen."

Twenty minutes later Kurt is sitting, stewing by himself, when Sophie and Summer walk in wearing matching, formfitting, short Azzedine Alaïa dresses—the dress that Sophie is making famous. She has a closet full of them. These dresses are tight Lycra socks that stretch from a woman's breasts to the very top of her thigh. There is so much leg and so much tit and and so much hair that Sophie and Summer look like they just walked straight out of a giant ball of flame in a rock video—except for the bulge in Sophie's belly. Kurt does a double take. He hops up and runs over to Summer, holds her hand, and asks gently, "What are you doing here?"

Summer and Sophie put their hands on his shoulders and push him down.

"Sit in the chair."

"We're here to do your makeup."

He fights off a smile. "Look Sophie…Summer…I don't think…"

Sophie leans in and whispers in his ear. "Sshhh."

Kurt sits calmly, obediently. He even looks up when Sophie tells him to. She takes out a long black mascara pen, brings it slowly to his eye, and presses on the flesh, moving the black line halfway across the bottom of his eye.

"WHAT THE HELL ARE YOU DOING TO MY HUSBAND!" screams Priscilla. "YOU GOT YOUR OWN HUSBAND. LEAVE MINE ALONE!"

"What is your problem? I'm just doing his makeup."

"This is my problem—right here!" Priscilla dumps the book of incantations out of the blanket onto the floor. The thing flops open, its spine bent back revealing the names written inside the cover.

"Where did you get that?"

"Take my husband out of your book!"

"Did you go in my house?"

"Take him out!"

"This is personal. This is none of your business." Sophie picks up the book and holds it as if it were a child. She runs her finger across the woman on the cover. "You have no right—"

"The first name in there is James," Priscilla says. "Do you even remember him? You used to fuck him? He was the Jovi's best friend. He sleeps in my living room now. Does that ring a bell? He's heartbroken! He loved you! Do you even remember him?"

"I never hurt him! I loved—"

"Don't you do that to my husband! Take him out! You slut!"

Sophie's face creases up like burning paper. She sits back on the hideous couch. Summer drops down next to her and pulls her in to her chest. "It's for his own good," Sophie says with a quivering voice. "It's not black magic. It's white. I don't want your husband—"

"I DON'T CARE."

The Jovi steps in between the girls. "Look, Priscilla, everything's okay. There's no need for this. We've all been through a lot…"

Kurt walks over and stands right in the Jovi's face. "Don't tell my wife what to do."

"Dude. I'm not telling her what to do."

"Yeah, you are. Don't ever tell my wife what to do."

"Well, don't tell my wife what to do."

"I wasn't."

"Well, *she* was. She was telling my wife what to do. So I told her not to do it."

"Don't tell my wife what to do. I'll tell my wife what to do," Kurt says. "Not you."

"Nobody tells me what to do," Priscilla says.

"Me neither," Sophie says, sniveling on the couch.

"Fine. Then nobody tells anybody what to do," the Jovi declares.

"Well, you can't tell me what to do. If I stop telling people what to do, it's 'cuz I want to. Not 'cuz you told me to. I'm the lead singer of this band. It's my job to tell people what to do."

"Just don't do it." The Jovi grits his teeth.

"I won't. Because I don't want to."

The Jovi shakes his head, turns around, and kisses Sophie on the forehead. She stands up, grabs Summer by the hand, and pulls her out the door.

Priscilla does Kurt's makeup—over does it, it isn't cool. Thunderstik plays. Kurt sings. He looks like a big bad-ass drag queen. Priscilla stands in the crowd, looking up at Kurt like a conscience. Kurt stares straight ahead, not looking at his wife. He's hoping to see Summer or Sophie or Felder or Weiner or Headley's touring agent. All he sees is a bright white spotlight shining in his face.

Afterward, the Jovi pulls Eric aside. "Dude. Breaking news. Summer says she wants to fuck you."

"No fucking way."

"No, dude, for real. And let me tell you something else, this buddy of mine is a gynecologist, and he told me if you ever wonder if a woman keeps it nice and clean and orderly down there, just look at her toes. Look at Summer's toes."

"What about 'em?"

"They're fucking perfect, nice polish, no corns, no calluses. My buddy says when some girl comes into the exam room with chewed-up feet, he knows he's gonna to need pruning shears and a gas mask when he goes down there to have a look."

"The wisdom of the Jovi. It never ends, does it?"

"Never, bro. Stick around, you can learn a lot from me."

"So how do we proceed here?"

"Divide and conquer. Wait for Kurt to leave with Priscilla. When he leaves, we meet the girls over at this club off Vine. Take her by the hand and bring her out into the middle of the dance floor."

"Kurt and Priscilla already split."

"Good. It will be loud and dark on the dance floor, and you're a filthy little guy—let nature take its place."

Driving with the Jovi over to the club, Eric feels happy and high. The doorman knows the Jovi. The girls meet them inside. Eric's eyes move straight down Summer's body to her toes poking out through her high-heeled sandals. The Jovi is right. She has really clean-looking feet with fresh, clear nail polish. Eric looks up and she is smiling at him. He leans over to the Jovi. "Dude. She's a eucalyptus tree and I'm a koala bear."

"Baby needs to keep his diapers on for another minute."

Sophie says, "Eric, you guys were really good tonight. I've never heard that piano part before."

"Me neither! There's piano on those songs?"

Sophie laughs.

"You girls were at the show? I thought you left."

"Totally! We wouldn't miss it."

"Sorry about Priscilla."

"Huh?" Sophie cups her ear with her hand.

"Never mind. Hey, Summer, you look hot. Get it? It's a play on words."

"Dude. Shut up or you'll kill it," the Jovi says. "The less talking the better. Go dance with her."

Eric holds out his hand. Summer takes it. They join the throbbing throng, rubbing bellies, gyrating. She backs up against Eric and starts rubbing up and down until he grabs her and says, "Little baby's gonna burst!"

She laughs and pulls his hand underneath her dress. "Surprise! No panties!"

"Is it too early to say I love you?"

She reaches back and unbuttons his black bluejeans. "Yes."

Eric feels the room shift, lifts his hands to her breasts, runs his fingers around the rim of her nipples, tugs at them from outside the dress, breathes in at her neck. "I want you to know, so far, this is the best night of my life."

She flips around and bites him on the neck. He runs his hand up her leg, gently grazing the little hairs on the back of her thigh. "I feel like someone's watching us," she whispers in his ear, and stuffs him back in his jeans.

"Isn't that the point?" He moves in for her lips.

She holds him a few inches away. "Did Kurt go home with his wife?"

"Yeah."

"She's a real bitch."

He kisses her clavicle. "Let's get out of here."

"What fun is that?"

"I'll show you."

"What. Are you going to take me to your car?"

"No. I'm gonna take you to the hood of my car."

She laughs. "You guys in Thunderstik are all the same. It's all about the touchdown, the home run, the knockout punch; you guys just want to get to the top of the mountain, stick your flag in the ground, and go home."

"And sleep. So?"

"So then you're done."

"I like to climb the mountain again in the morning."

"What's her name?"

"Who?"

"Kurt's wife."

"Priscilla. What are you gonna ask for a lock of her hair?"

"No. That's Sophie and my mom. I'm a realist."

"Me too. We're perfect for each other." Eric moves in.

She softly touches her lips to his. "I'm perfect for you. I don't know if you're perfect for me."

"God damn it. I did it again."

"Did what?"

"Talked myself right out of getting laid, didn't I?"

"You're a nice guy."

"Ouch."

ſOUTHBOUND

"Who's that girl?" Priscilla asks Kurt while they are heading down the 5 freeway to San Diego.

"What girl?"

"That blonde girl."

"Sophie?"

"No, the other girl."

"I don't know. Never seen her before in my life."

"You had sex with her, didn't you?"

"No, baby. I don't even know who she is."

Kurt watches as Priscilla's big sad eyes well up with tears. He presses his index fingers into his temples, opens his jaw, and stares at the floor.

"I know you know who she is. Why do you lie to me?"

"Who is she? I told you, I've never seen—"

"SHE'S THE WITCH'S DAUGHTER! DON'T LIE TO ME! IT'S AN INSULT!" Her hands tremble on the wheel. "SHE'S NOT THE FIRST EITHER, IS SHE?"

"You have no idea what you're talking about."

"I DON'T?" Her chest heaves. "YOU COME HOME AT FOUR, FIVE, SIX IN THE MORNING WITH WOMEN'S PERFUME ALL OVER YOU. I KNOW WHAT'S GOING ON."

"NOTHING'S GOING ON!" Kurt takes a deep drag off his smoke. "I DO THIS FOR YOU!" He holds the cigarette in the air, sinks the ember into the flesh of his hand. It smolders. Sparks fall. He screams, pounds the same fist on the dashboard, and shakes his head violently.

They sit in silence.

"Kurt? Are you taking your medication?"

"LOOK AT ME! I'M DOING THIS FOR YOU! FOR US! FOR THE MUSIC! I CAN'T DO ANY OF THIS ON MEDICATION."

Priscilla sees a sign for a rest stop. She swerves into the exit lane and slows the car to a halt between two giant big rigs. "Look at me. I have to be at work in six hours. I have to be cheerful for customers in six hours. The least you can do for me is tell me the truth. I want to hear the truth come out of your mouth. Have you been faithful to me?"

Kurt looks down, a putty-colored pustule the size and shape of a pencil eraser has sprouted from his hand. He pulls it off. It bleeds. He looks up into Priscilla's eyes, "I did this for you."

"It's over, Kurt. Get out of my car."

PRE/IDIO PARK

Sophie leans back on the table. A tube exhales clear fluid onto her belly. A white plastic wand makes slow sensuous circles. Everyone in the room stares at a black-and-white screen. The technician grins and says, "It's a boy!"

"No, it's a girl," Sophie says.

The Jovi points at the monitor and says, "Look at that, he's right. We're having a little dude." He leans in to kiss her tummy, and she pushes him back.

"Phoenix told me it's a girl. I know it's a girl."

"Boy, girl, it doesn't matter."

"Yes, it does. I don't want to have a boy."

"Yeah, you do."

Sophie sits for a minute. She stares intensely at her stomach. "I gave up so much. We're having a girl. I am going to make sure of it."

Sophie goes to see Phoenix, taking a lock of the Jovi's niece's hair.

Under a full moon that illuminates the burial mounds at Presidio Park, while the highways hiss in the distance, Summer, Phoenix, and Sophie dance around a fire, say words backwards and eat soft-boiled quail eggs—spells specifically designed by Phoenix to turn the baby boy into a baby girl.

Afterwards, Sophie and Summer drop Phoenix off at her house in Del Mar. Summer comes out of the house with a rectangular bag with four wheels and a leash. She loads it in the back of the Jeep.

"Thanks for taking me to the airport."

"Oh it's nothing. I know what that flight to Japan is like, and you've got to fly to LAX first."

As the Jeep starts to move down the quiet street, Summer asks Sophie, "Why do we like them?"

"Guys in bands?" Sophie asks.

"Yeah." Summer laughs.

"'Cuz they're up there. And they're trying to do something beautiful. It's like they're in touch with their feminine side."

"Kurt was certainly trying to touch my feminine side, too."

Sophie giggles. "You like him, don't you."

"Nah. It's just for fun."

"You should watch out. He's got the murderer's thumb, your mom told me."

"He's not going to kill anyone."

"Really? Your mom said it. The White Witch of Del Mar. She's been right about everything else. She talks to the dead."

Summer grimaces. "That's kind of what I need to tell you. You're super nice. I love hanging out with you. And you bought me these and they are awesome, but I just think there's something you should know..."

Sophie's slightly sleepy eyes get angry. "What? You're kind of freaking me out."

"I don't want you to put too much faith in my mom or that book."

"Is that it? Is that what you wanted to tell me?"

"She asked me about your life, she asked me about you, before your first consultation."

"So?"

"I told her about your friend. The makeup artist…"

Sophie pulls the Jeep over, in front of the freeway. "Oh my God— Why would you do that?"

"I didn't know how far it would go—"

"But it worked! I did the spell and the Jovi was right there." Sophie grips the wheel of her Jeep, and her face is instantly hot and wet. Her nose runs. "He's my soul mate."

"Yeah, he is. Sophie, I just want you to know that you don't need that book to get what you want."

"I thought I had powers."

"Sophie, you do. Your life is charmed, but you did that."

"No, it's not charmed. You don't know."

"You don't need my mom or any—"

"I know that!"

"Then what is it?"

"I thought I had an angel. I thought Randy George came back for me…"

Summer looks out the opaque plastic window. "If he could, he would, Sophie. Love is real."

WELCOME TO THE CLUB

Thunderstik is out at the Vine Church. Eric stands in the urinal next to Sven and lets out a loud groan. Sven laughs.

"Dude, don't laugh, it hurts when I pee."

Sven claps his hands. "Clap on! Clap off! Clap on, clap off!"

"Only sailors get the clap."

"Sailors and pirates. You best be seeing a doctor, matey."

The two of them walk back into the daycare room with green elephants and purple giraffes painted on the walls. Kurt is sitting in a miniature plastic chair. "When are these people going to stop praying! I have a physical need to play some music!"

"Do they have any more of those chips?" EJ asks.

Eric opens the cupboard and throws him a can of Pringles.

The Jovi walks in, late as always. "I just talked to Felder. We're off DCA. Stein did it yesterday. He called and asked. They said fine, sent him a fax."

The can exhales as EJ pops the top.

"It's over," Eric says.

"It's not over," Sven says, "the disappointment will last for years."

"NOTHING'S OVER!" Kurt yells. "IT'S ALWAYS DARKEST BEFORE THE DAWN!"

"I just meant the DCA thing. It's on to the next deal, right? Felder knows what he's doing. He wouldn't fuck us just to fuck us," Eric says.

"IT JUST MEANS WE NEED TO PRACTICE EVERY NIGHT UNTIL WE'RE SIGNED AGAIN! I WISH THEY'D STOP FUCKING PRAYING IN THERE. IT DOESN'T WORK! PRAYING DOESN'T WORK! GOD DIDN'T FIX MY JAW!" Kurt presses his fingers into his jaw, arches his back, and howls at the acoustic tiles in the ceiling. "THE ONLY THING THAT MAKES THE PAIN GO AWAY IS MY MUSIC! I HAVE A PHYSICAL NEED TO PLAY! RESPECT THAT!"

Thunderstik waits silently for the last stragglers to stop praying and leave the warehouse. As Thunderstik assembles on the stage, Sven says, "Hey. You guys, Eric's got the clap."

"I do not."

"Yes!" The Jovi walks over, shakes Eric's hand, and hugs him. "Yes, my brother, now my work is complete. The student is now the master."

"It's not the clap. It's probably like a urinary-tract thing or something. What do I do?"

Kurt slings his Telecaster over his shoulder and picks some chords. "I just tell the doctor I got a cold and need some antibiotics. That works."

"I drink cranberry juice—prevents that shit from even starting," Sven adds.

"I just call my brothers," the Jovi says. "They have some pill that's like a tactical nuke. You pop one, it goes down in your

GI tract and greases the whole fucking village, burns it to the ground."

The four look over at EJ. "What do you do?"

"He just watches the Playboy Channel and spanks his own shit," Sven says.

"Shut up, Sven! I get more pussy than you even know."

"But who, my dear, gave you the fucking clap?" the Jovi asks. "Not Summer. Not with toes like that. Where else you been putting that thing?"

"You fucked Summer?" The veins in Kurt's neck start to fill with blood.

"No, dude. I'm just fucking around. He didn't fuck Summer."

"You fucked Summer?" Kurt sets his guitar down. He squares his shoulders.

Eric moves behind a road case.

"Well? Did ya?" Kurt's eyes sink to blackness.

"Nah, man," Eric answers sheepishly. Kurt nods and turns away. "We just fooled around."

Kurt spins around, grabs Eric's leather jacket, and heaves him off the blue-carpeted stage down into the folding chairs. He lands with a squirming crash. Kurt jumps into the chairs, picks one up by the legs, lifts it above Eric's head. Eric assumes this is his end. But EJ, the Jovi, and Sven all fall on Kurt at the same time. Kurt leaps up from the pile onto the stage, shaking himself like a wet dog. "You have a chick you don't even deserve—and you go after Summer? What the fuck is going on in this band? Everybody's fucking everybody else's chick. This shit's got to end. I'm fucking serious. This is the whole reason why the devil is fucking with my jaw and the band—because we let him." He points his finger at Eric. "You fucking stay away from her."

"I don't see what difference it is to you—you're married."

"MY WIFE LEFT ME! I TRIED TO BE A GOOD HUSBAND AND NOW SHE'S GONE!"

"God. I'm sorry," the Jovi says.

"Your wife left you?" EJ asks. "Again?"

"Yeah. Again."

"Don't worry, Kurt," EJ says. "She'll come back."

"Of course she'll come back, BUT WHAT AM I SUPPOSED TO DO UNTIL SHE DOES?"

"Play music."

"Good. Let's get serious about music. We need a record deal here." Kurt plugs his guitar in, chunks out a vicious power chord, and yells at the crucifix hanging above the stage. "LISTEN TO ME!"

THE IN-LAWS

When the Jovi gets home, there is a brand-new Ford F-150 pickup sitting in the driveway.

Sophie is sitting with her father at the kitchen table with a stack of official-looking documents in front of her. Her checkbook is in her hand. Sophie looks at the Jovi with cold disdain.

"Ooooh! Look what the cat dragged in!" Jean screeches.

"Hi, Mom." The Jovi hugs her.

"Where in the world have you been? It's almost midnight."

"Practicing."

"You've got a little baby on the way. You can't be coming home at midnight when you're a papa. Right, Victor?"

"Right, honey."

"What's going on here?" the Jovi asks.

"Just a little visit," Jean says.

"What's all that?" He points at Sophie, who is reading with her head down, her elbows on the table, and a handful of hair in her hand.

"We're in business together. You've heard of father-and-son businesses. This is a father-and-daughter business," Victor says. "We're developers."

"Right."

"We've been talking," Jean adds. "And, really, this little hiatus is fine, but Sophie's got to get back to work. You don't have a problem with that, do you? You're not one of *those* husbands? The barefoot-and-pregnant kind? Are you?"

"Yeah, of course. She should do whatever she wants. I got no problem with that."

"And what about you? Where do you see this rock–and-roll thing going?" Jean asks.

The Jovi laughs. "Funny you should ask. We just heard tonight that we're off DCA."

Sophie looks up from her checkbook. "You're what?"

"Felder asked if we could get out of our contract. They said fine. It's done."

"I guess I do need to work."

"It's only temporary. He's gonna get us a deal with Polygram any day now. Remember that guy—Weiner?"

"Well, that settles it," Jean says. "You'll be a stay-at-home dad. Sophie will be the breadwinner."

"Whoa, whoa, whoa. What about my band?"

"You can play with your friends whenever you want. Sophie's only modeling another two or three years, and then it's on to bigger and better things—she's going to be an actress. She's friends with Darren Getty."

"I mean, we can both do what we want, you know."

"Let's get real here, shall we?" Jean pinches the Jovi's cheek. "How much money has this band made you?"

"I don't know. The lawsuit and managers take their chunk, and we haven't toured yet, it was just an advance…"

"Don't be shy. It's all family here. How much?"

"I made forty-three thousand dollars last year."

"Sophie can make that in three days during the shows or for three hours in an ad campaign. Do you see my point?"

"What do you want to do, Sophie?"

"I just want to go to sleep. I'm really tired. Dad, I signed all of these. Can I please go to bed now?"

"Of course, sweet Sophie." Victor picks up the papers and kisses her forehead, then he holds up the check. "Don't worry, sweet Sophie, this will be the last one."

Jean hugs the Jovi and kisses him on the cheek. "You need to be supportive of your wife right now. This is a hard time for her. She's been working nonstop since she was fourteen. I don't think she knows what to do with herself."

"I know."

"Think about what I said. You're such a sweet boy. You'll do the right thing."

Sophie and the Jovi get in bed. He starts kissing her neck. He runs his hand up her leg.

"I'm not in the mood."

"You want me to rub your feet?

"No."

"Your back?"

"No."

"Can I ask you something?"

"No."

"C'mon, babe. I just… Why is Darren Getty in your book?"

She shakes her head at the Jovi. "Forget that stupid book. It doesn't work. I'm the only thing that works around here. And you made me pregnant."

"No we all… We all do the best—"

"Not my dad! He's so stupid. He's been building houses in the desert, and no one wants to buy them." She tries to laugh. "I don't know why. They're perfectly good houses—nicer than where I grew up. But no one wants them. I told him he must be doing something wrong, and he said no, that it was just a buyer's market right now and sure to turn around, and something about the fourth quarter and basketball…"

The Jovi hugs her. "Baby, baby, you're so sweet. Don't worry about Victor. He's a big, tough guy. He'll be just fine.

"I'm not worried about him!"

"Then what's wrong?"

"It's my money. He's lost all of my money."

"No, baby, we got this house and I can play music and you can work. We're going to be fine."

She pushes him away. "Why's it always me? Everyone wants something from me. I'm sick of it."

"I don't want anything from you."

"You just want everything."

They hear a knock at the door. They look at each other. Then Sophie says, "It must be my dad. He must want another check."

The Jovi gets up and walks over to the door. He looks through the glass and sees Kurt standing on the porch, staring at the floor, pushing his fingers into his temples, locking and unlocking his jaw. He looks up at the Jovi with a dark stare, the whites in his eyes illuminated by the moon. The Jovi cracks the door open. "Hey, dude, what's up?"

"Hey, man, can't sleep."

"Sorry, bro, bummer."

"Can I talk to Sophie?"

The Jovi looks over his shoulder. He sees her down the hall, sitting up in bed. She shakes her head and lifts the sheet to her neck.

"No, man, she's asleep."

"Look, it's really important. My wife—she's gone—I did like Sophie said. I want to talk to her about fame, fame and the demons that give me songs." Kurt rubs his face as if it were a big piece of putty.

"Sorry, dude. Call us tomorrow. Sophie's tired."

"You have no idea what I'm going through, man, the pain, no one believes me anymore. I need to talk to her about that book and…"

"Kurt. Look. No. Nothing. Go to sleep. Call us in the morning."

"I can't, man. There's this thing in my living room and—"

"Kurt. Stop. She's pregnant and asleep."

"Look, man, if it wasn't for me, you wouldn't even have her. It's 'cuz she sees you up on stage playing my music—that's why she loves you—that's how fucking powerful this music is. And when that music is just in my head, all that power goes around and attacks all the good things in my head too—and I think she needs to fucking respect that and get out of bed and help me out with this fucking thing. It's important."

"Good night, Kurt."

"She told me to leave my wife. I need to know what she meant by that."

"She just meant that if you're happy, stay. If you're unhappy, leave."

"Look, man, that's not good enough, I need to ask her myself. Why won't she do that for me?" The veins in his neck start to bulge. "I mean, after all this, and she goes off with fucking Eric?"

"Who went off with Eric?"

"Summer did."

"Is that what this is all about?"

"Where is she?"

"She went to Japan to model."

"Is she really in Japan?"

"Yeah, man, she is."

"Look, man, it's about time people in this band started to respect me. None of this would have ever happened if it wasn't for me. I made the whole thing happen. I quit the drugs, man. I didn't do it for me. I did it for the people who are going to hear our music and be saved. Can you even understand that?"

"Good night, Kurt. Let's talk in the morning."

The Jovi closes the door on him. Kurt doesn't move from the porch. The Jovi walks back into the bedroom and lies down next to Sophie.

"That's it. We need to move to L.A.," she says.

"No, baby, Kurt's just having a tough night, and he really likes you. But, you know, if we need to, I'm cool and all…"

"My mom was right."

"Okay, babe, I'll watch our little one."

"That's not what I'm talking about. I'm talking about people who steal—and don't even know they're doing it. A poor man will take everything you have and not even realize he's stealing from you—that's what my mom said. She was right."

"That's bullshit. Rich or poor I would never steal from you."

"Let's just go to sleep. I'm tired."

GOLDEN-EARED ARTY

At the end of his hand Felder's chrome-plated MTV Astronaut turns from side to side and moves backwards – a moonwalk of sorts. "I'm Adam F and I'm here to say/I'm a bad mother fucker from around the way…"

"Adam! Adam! Pick up the phone, Adam!" Carol says through the speakerphone.

"Okay. Okay." He fumbles with the receiver. "Hello?"

"Adam, it's Arty Azimoff here."

"Arty! Golden-Eared Arty. How the hell are ya?"

"Good. Adam, listen to me, I'm sure you've heard, DG is giving me my own label. I'm looking for bands. I've heard the Thunderstik album. That song "Bleed Me"—that's a signature song right there—that should be on every AOR station in the country."

"Oh, yeah, fucking yeah, good song." Felder rubs his face. "I agree."

"So I heard you're off DCA, is this true?"

"Yeah."

"But I heard you're talking to Josh Weiner at Polygram. You know I don't get in the middle of these things."

"Weiner? Fuck Weiner. You're Golden-Eared Arty! You want Thunderstik. I'll get you Thunderstik."

"I want to see them play."

"You got it."

/PLIT PER/ONALITY

Priscilla's things are gone. Kurt surveys his bedroom in disgust. He hears the lump on the floor in the other room. "Where's your wife, Kurt?"

"Leave me alone."

"She's probably at her mom's. Did she take the car? That car belongs to you. You bought that car. We told you to steal it when you could."

"Shut up."

"You can't live half-in and half-out, Kurt."

"I'm all good."

"Half of you belongs to us."

"I rebuke you in the name of Jesus Christ." Kurt slams the door.

There's a big thick magic marker in Kurt's hand. He draws a line down the middle of the wall, down the middle of the bed. He takes everything that is evil and puts it on the left side: pornography, cigarettes, the lyrics to a pop song, a picture of Sophie torn from a magazine. And he puts everything good on the other side: a wrinkled picture of Priscilla, a can of peach-flavored Kearn's

Nectar, a microwave burrito that Priscilla had left in the freezer. He places his guitar in its rack in the center of the black line, and he lies down in the middle of the bed. He takes the black magic marker and presses it against his crotch, dragging it up his torso through the middle of his chest and up his neck all the way to his forehead. He lies on his back and makes the sign of the cross.

The phone rings. It's on the evil side. It rings and it rings. Kurt reaches over with his evil hand and puts the evil phone to his evil ear. "What."

"Kurt. What's going on down there?" Felder asks.

"My wife left me. I'm trying to purify."

"Look, man. Pull yourself together. I've got some good news."

"What?"

"Golden-Eared Arty wants to hear the band."

"Good."

"So I booked us some time at a rehearsal studio up here in the Valley."

"No, man. I can't rehearse anymore."

"What the fuck are you talking about?"

"When we play, and there's no one there, I can't deal with it."

"Why?"

"You see, this band puts off so much energy that if there isn't a crowd of people there to soak it up, the energy goes to the back of the club or church and bounces off the wall and comes back and attacks the band."

"Kurt. Are you taking your meds?"

"I'm writing songs. Songs that will last forever."

"Okay. I'll find somewhere to play where there are people."

"Mexico, man. They're Catholic down there. They still believe in God down there. I need people who believe in God in the audience."

"Kurt. I need you to pull it…what's that? Fuck, I gotta go…"
Felder hangs up.

Kurt hears a knocking on the door. He opens the bedroom
door tentatively. The lump isn't there. The knocking persists. He
opens the door. Two jocks stare at a naked Kurt with a black line
running down his body.

"Are you Kurt Franklin of Thunderstik?"

"Yes."

"You've been served."

Kurt casually reaches for the brown-paper envelope but
grabs the jock's arm instead. He pulls the guy in and slams him
in the eye with a solid short left. The guy stammers. The other
jock kicks Kurt in the shin and pushes him to the ground. The
jocks hold hands and jump down big sections of the stairs then
take off running down La Jolla Boulevard.

Kurt opens the envelope. It's the accountants. They're suing
Kurt for the loan money.

IN THE MORNING

The Jovi finds Sophie in the bright morning light, in the kitchen filling a cardboard box with mismatched dishes and books. He runs his hands from the back of her waist around to the middle of her belly. The little mound fits perfectly. He waits for a kick.

"What are you doing?" He asks quietly.

"This is the first step."

"What is?"

"These are giveaways. It's the first step before you move."

"Nah." The Jovi looks out into the yard. The low December sun has a spotlight effect on the glistening dew-covered grass. "It's so nice here."

"It *was* nice here." She lifts up the book that Phoenix gave her. She puts it in the box.

"I'm glad to see that thing go." The Jovi says.

"Oh are you? Maybe I should keep it." She smiles.

"I wonder if Pastor Ron knows that he's the last one who believes in witchcraft?"

"Kurt too, kinda." The phone rings. Sophie reaches for it and puts it to her ear. She turns away and huddles with the phone held in close.

The Jovi pours himself some coffee and says, "We should keep this place. It's nice."

The Jovi hears Sophie say, "Oh… Okay… That's great…" She turns back to him. Her sleepy eyes are glossy and distant. She puts the phone back on the receiver.

"What's wrong?"

"It was Giuseppe. *GQ* wants to shoot me for the cover. Pregnant and everything." She starts crying.

"Why are you crying? That's good news."

"I'm fat."

"You're pregnant." The Jovi reaches out to hug her.

Sophie pushes him back. "You know what I mean. I'm fat."

"Baby, you're fat in all the right places."

FiFTEEN FUCKING YEARS

Eric answers his phone. It's EJ. "I just got off the phone with Felder. Arty Azimoff wants to sign the band. He wants us to showcase this Saturday night in Mexico. We're going to open up for one of Golden-Eared Arty's bands."

"Which one?"

"Sally's Strung Out."

"That's awesome. What about Weiner at Polygram?"

"Felder said fuck him. This is Golden-Eared Arty. He found the Crüe. Get ready for a real record deal. That's what Felder said. None of this DCA bullshit."

"Sweet."

"Hold on, it's the other line." Eric waits. EJ clicks, comes back. "This is bad. Come over here right now. We're having a band meeting."

"At your mom's?"

"Where else?"

EJ's mom is an interior designer. Colonial reproduction furniture is strategically arranged around a formal sitting room. If they had white wigs on, EJ, Sven, and Kurt would look like they are about to sign the Declaration of Independence.

"What's up?" Eric asks.

"It's the Jovi," Kurt says.

"Is he okay?"

"No."

"What happened?"

"He's an asshole. That's what happened. Sit down and shut up."

Eric sits in a Queen Anne settee. The grandfather clock tocks but doesn't tick.

"It's just like when we were kids," Kurt says. "I should've known he'd let me down."

The Jovi drives up in Sophie's Jeep and parks it outside. He walks down the fuchsia-lined slate walkway in a pair of tight ripped jeans, comes in, and sits in a leather wingback chair. "What's up, guys?"

"You heard about the show Saturday?" EJ asks.

"Yeah, man. That's just not going to work for me."

"What the fuck do you mean by that?" Kurt asks.

"I mean I can't do it. We need to reschedule."

"You think you decide? You don't decide! I decide!"

"I can't change this. Herb Ritz is going to shoot Sophie pregnant and naked for *GQ*—it's a big deal. Let's play for this guy Arty some other time."

"This is the most important thing in my life—this band," Kurt says. "We need to play for this guy and get another record deal. You can go with that chick some other time."

"That chick is my wife."

"So?"

"My family."

Kurt nods. "This is so fucking typical. You know, you're always going to have a perfect life."

"Dude. What the fuck do you mean by that?" The Jovi eyes Kurt.

"I see where this is going." Eric interrupts. "Can I say something?"

"No," Kurt responds.

"Let him talk," Sven says. "Go ahead, Eric."

"I know I'm the least worthy of the knights. I know I can't contribute much to this band musically, but I also know you guys belong together."

"How do you know that?" The Jovi asks.

"Remember my first gig at Poseidon's Place? Remember when we came out of the solo on "Rain Fall"? I played my three notes. Kurt kept playing his acoustic solo on the through the break. And I started crying."

"Yeah. I remember," The Jovi says, "you cried 'cause he was stepping all over your part. That's what he does. He did it to me in the studio. What's that got to do with anything?"

"No. That's not why I cried. I cried because it was the first time I've ever been part of something really good. This band is really good. Don't throw it away."

"Every band I play in is really good," Kurt says.

"Me too," the Jovi adds.

Sven and EJ shrug their shoulders and nod in agreement. Eric shrinks back into the corner of the settee.

"Like I said, it's just like it's always been." Kurt says to the Jovi. "Your family is perfect and mine's all fucked up. Yeah, I can come over when it's convenient. Well, sometimes you have to do things that aren't convenient—do you even get that?"

"How long did you stand out there last night?"

Kurt seems puzzled. "Life isn't just a bunch of...I mean... Your dad's a fucking doctor." Kurt stands up and lifts his hands in the air. "My dad's nuts! Is that what you want me to say? Do you feel better now? You got a real tough life, huh?"

"Kurt, I'll ask you once, and I won't ask you again, leave my family out of this—don't ever fucking mention them again. Don't ever fucking come to my house again."

"What about *my* family? What about James? You fuck my brother's chick like it doesn't mean a thing. I'm just supposed to take it? If it's your family, it's sacred—if it's mine, it's shit."

"Dude. That's enough. I quit. I'm out."

"Are you gonna play the gig or not?"

"No. Didn't you hear me? I quit."

"Then that's it—fifteen fucking years—and that's it?"

The two of them stare at each other; the grandfather clock strikes noon with a reticent chime.

"Don't do this," Eric says.

"It's done," Kurt says.

The Jovi walks to the door and looks at the band. "I'll be seeing you guys around, I suppose."

Kurt asks the Jovi, "Do me one favor?"

"What?"

"Don't tell Felder a fucking thing. Don't tell him you quit."

"Okay."

THE RETURN OF
LUNKY THE LOYAL

In the fifteen months since he left Thunderstik, Lunky the Loyal has seen the world. After Raymo was done with him, Lunky went on tour with a heavy-metal band. He was the builder of the beast. He set up and broke down a gigantic, mechanical, fire-breathing, satanic Cyclops. There was glory in this position; Lunky met tender Japanese girls and girls with rough calluses who could milk cows by hand; but it wasn't Thunderstik. Lunky would often sit in the back of the beast during a show and watch the enchanted faces of the audience. Life was pretty good until the beast got to him. Lunky blew a fuse on crystal meth, pulled off a few of his own fingernails with some needle-nose pliers, and the circus dropped him off in Sioux Falls, South Dakota.

Lunky has run out of money and meth. Sober by default, he finds himself standing at a bus stop, staring off at a frozen cornfield. The bus stops. Lunky has no ticket. The bus leaves. Lunky walks into town and calls Eric collect from a pay phone. "Eric, it's Lunky," he says in his bird-like voice. "I want to get clean. I need help. Can you get me a bus ticket?"

IDLE HANDS

The remaining four members of Thunderstik assemble on the blue-carpeted stage beneath the crucifix. Kurt stares at the back wall. He grinds out a chord, waits a second, and shudders. "I can't do this. I know all the songs. I wrote all the songs. That's just going to have to be good enough."

"What's wrong?"

"Without an audience to soak it up, the energy bounces off the wall and attacks me. We'll just have to wing it in Mexico."

"Kurt, if we can't practice," EJ says, "maybe we should just put this gig off for a few weeks. Maybe you can stabilize on your meds and the Jovi can come back to the band."

"We don't need him."

"What about the meds, Kurt? I've never, ever heard you say you can't play music before."

"I can play—better than I've ever played in my life. It's just that I might attack one of you or myself."

Eric slides his keyboards to the back corner of the stage. "Dude. If he says he can't play, he can't play."

NEVER BEEN TO SPAIN

Lunky gets off the bus in downtown San Diego. He has no bags, no magazines to read. He sniffs the air, looks down, and spots a smoldering cigar on the ground. He picks it up and takes a puff. He places his massive frame in front of a bulletin board. In the center is a flyer.

Saturday, December 10th. One night only!

At the Lazy Lizard in Ensenada, Baja California, Mexico

SALLY'S STRUNG OUT

with special guests: Thunderstik.

"What day is it?" Lunky asks a man in a blue sweater.

"It's Saturday."

"The tenth of December?"

"Yup."

Lunky spots a red San Diego trolley rumbling south. He thunders after it, grabs a rail, and hops onto the back hitch. The wind blows through his white hair. His bright blue eyes smile. He grits his teeth.

WELCOME TO MEXICO

The Seine ends in confrontation, in the English Channel, staring off at the enemy on the other side. The River Thames opens to the North Sea from whence the Vikings came. The river 5 ends at a concrete archway, painted orange and green, manned by stone-faced military mustaches with machine guns – Welcome to Mexico!

From La Jolla, Tijuana is a half-hour, Ensenada another half-hour from there. It's close, but cross the border and instantly the world smells like burning plastic. No trees, the land is lumpy and brown like a burlap sack. The people are real – Mama's love their babies. Babies grow up to love their mothers. Men have hands of stone. They will use them to knock you down or hand you a *cervesa*. Tougher and rougher than Americans, the French kneel to the British, the British to the Terrible Norsemen, and some day we too may kneel to our more brutish cousins from the south.

The Sally's Strung Out tour bus passes under the orange-and-green concrete archway and Gary Faker, the insect like lead singer, chirps out, "Hey, is this where Mexican Brown comes from?"

A white-haired hag yells: "Yeah, you dumbshit."

"I fucking love it already! Let's score some dope that hasn't crossed the border up someone's asshole!"

Sally's Strung Out is from the Silverlake area of Los Angeles. While Sven's old band veered from Glam to Wandering Minstrel, Sally's Strung Out kept the androgyny and show of Glam, but added heroin chic, Latin American mysticism, and Dionysian sexual carnival. A combination that proved commercially irresistible.

The metal bands of the early eighties reveled in the delectability of sin, but there was the attitude somewhere within the music that they knew what they were doing was wrong and that someday they would straighten out and go home and behave. Sally's Strung Out believes they are already home. There is nothing wrong with shooting junk, shoplifting, group sex. It's rock and roll. They also believe that these acts can be made sacred through ritual. Their last album, *Nothing's Wrong*, went double platinum.

Gary Faker is a performance artist and stripper from New York who learned to surf and play guitar at eighteen, and his alt-rock kids have descended on Ensenada to attend a rock show where they can actually drink alcohol. They arrive like locusts, eating ecstasy and drinking *jamaica* until their laughing mouths are stained red.

Kurt and Eric drive beneath the concrete archway and wave at the guards. Eric begins to worry. "Dude. Should I get Mexican insurance?"

Kurt looks at the clock on the dash. "No."

Kurt knows the way to Ensenada. He knows the loops. He knows how to get on the Tijuana-Ensenada Cuota. The city falls away. The shoreline emerges on the right. "Fuck," Kurt says, "I think there's waves."

Civilization reappears in an oasis of filthy hand-painted signs and half-finished concrete construction. In the center of this, a lime-green stucco monstrosity tilts in a dirt parking lot, rebar sticking out of the top like hairs on the scalp of a giant mis-shapen head. "This must be the Lizard," Kurt says.

The parking lot is filled with teenagers—dyed black hair, black nailpolish, metal rings in lips and brows, guys dressed in gauze, girls dressed like truckers. "Fuck," Eric says. "This doesn't exactly look like our crowd."

"These kids are gonna flip when they hear us."

RETURN TO GLORY

The Jovi and Sophie board a propeller plane in San Diego that rattles and shakes and let's them know that they are leaving a place for primitives and heading to L.A., where the real world begins in the first class lounge.

Then the flight, it's twelve hours of reclining and movies and "May I get you…?" and you're there. Paris is a city of circles, of riverbanks, of high doors and high fashion. And Sophie knows that the Jovi will be lost here. He won't understand them—the men who take the shots, the women who call them, the men in their black turtlenecks, the women in half the skin they were born with. He won't understand, but he'll be kind and effervescent. He'll shake hands with Giuseppe as if he were her father, as if *he* was the one who made her. But Sophie knows that *she* made herself. And she's about to do it again.

"Here, take this," Sophie tells the Jovi. It's the day of the shoot. The day she will stand naked before a crowd of onlookers and one lens that connects to millions of eyes. A lens that she will crawl through and be born again, bigger and better and richer than she's ever been.

"What is it?"

"It's a few thousand dollars in francs. Go entertain yourself. Mommy has to work."

BATTLE OF THE BANDS

Backstage is a yellow concrete room. A concrete divider separates the room from a stainless-steel prison toilet. Sally's Strung Out prefers to hang in their tour bus, so the whole room belongs to Thunderstik.

Felder walks in with a short, heavy-set guy with reddish hair stuffed in a beret. "Guys, come over here. I want you to meet Arty Azimoff."

"Hey," Kurt mumbles, and shakes his hand.

"Golden-Eared Arty," EJ says, and offers his hand. Sven and Eric follow.

"I've heard your album," Arty says. "I gotta tell you, DCA really dropped the ball. You guys should be as big as my other band, Led 'n' Lilacs. You should be that big right now! That song, 'Bleed Me,' is a signature song. It should be blasting on every AOR radio in this country. Hey! There's four of you? I thought there were five."

"Yeah, where's the Jovi?" Felder asks.

"He's always late," Kurt says. "He'll be here."

"What, you go on in a half-hour, right?"

Kurt nods and sneers into the flame as he lights a smoke.

"Alright. We're gonna go say hi to Gary Faker and get a nice cold beer."

Kurt extends his craggy hand a second time to Arty. "Thanks, man. Thanks a lot."

Arty and Felder walk out the back door.

EJ screams, "WHAT THE FUCK ARE WE DOING! KURT, YOU CAN'T JUST LIE TO FELDER LIKE THAT! WE HAVEN'T PRACTICED—"

"Keep your voice down. He lies to us all the time. I know all the guitar parts—I fucking wrote them. We're the best band in California whether we have five guys or four guys or three."

"I know, Kurt, but this just seems idiotic."

Eric nods. "Those kids out there are fucking weird. And there's a lot of them. And this is Mexico."

Sven shrugs his shoulders and bobs his head in agreement. "There's only four of us."

The band members are silent, and in the distance they can hear a three-part chant droning against the concrete walls. "HAIR-OH-WIN! HAIR-OH-WIN! HAIR-OH-WIN! HAIR-OH-WIN!"

"Jesus Christ, they sound like zombies!" EJ says.

"What the fuck are they saying?" Kurt asks.

"No, man, I know these guys from Silverlake." Sven shakes his head. "Gary Faker shoots up on stage. It's like the full-on apex of the show."

"Fuck," EJ says, and drops his head.

"Fuck is right." Sven stares at the same spot on the floor.

"We're gonna gèt killed out there," Eric says. "The Jovi's probably getting sucked off right now by his supermodel wife in a fucking four-star hotel, and we're about to blow our shot at a record deal and get eaten alive by a bunch of teenage zombies!"

"AND SOME DAY THE JOVI WILL KNOW THAT HIS BEAUTIFUL WIFE AND HIS SATIN SHEETS ARE A CURSE!"

They look up at Kurt. "What?"

"We're going to rock this place tonight. You hear me?"

"Fuck," Eric says glumly, "I should've stayed in college."

"What's wrong with you? That's over for you. You're not some spoon-fed schoolboy anymore! You're a rocker! You belong in this band!"

"You think?" Eric smiles and puffs out his chest just a little.

"We're going to take this stage tonight. This is the only stage in the whole fucking world I'm interested in. And tonight is the only night that matters. You want to walk the commencement stage? Is that what you want? And have some bald man hand you a diploma? Is that what you fucking want, Eric?"

"FUCK NO! Anyone can graduate from college—dolphins, chimps, collies, they all got degrees."

"Goddamn right! It takes something real to seize a stage in Mexico, make an unruly crowd submit, and then take them to the edge of insanity. No man knows his worth surfing two-foot waves! A man only knows what he's made of when he paddles out into fifteen-foot sets at Black's Beach! In the rain! That's what we're going to do tonight—AND THE BROS AT THE BEACH ARE NEVER GOING TO FORGET IT!"

"GODDAMN RIGHT!" Sven yells.

"You should be glad there's only three of you. The fewer men the greater share of royalties. I want you to know that every man who takes the stage tonight with me gets an equal cut when this thing is over and we get a new record deal. I'M SPLITTING

THE PUBLISHING FOUR WAYS—YOU HEAR ME? FOUR WAYS!"

EJ smiles. "That's mighty white of you, Kurt. Let's pray!"

Thunderstik takes the stage. Kurt looks out at the crowd. A fetid stench lingers at the edge of the platform like brimstone. Kurt turns to EJ. "No happy songs tonight." EJ nods.

Thunderstik starts with the hard-rocking ballad "Bleed Me." The guitar solo starts slow and sweet, but builds until Kurt's fingers move in a blur as if they were a swarm of bees stinging every note except the one he wants. It is a solo built on inference. The metaphor is the genius—it's like the outstretched hand of Adam reaching for the outstretched hand of God. Kurt has come in contact with the moment before they touch.

EJ is a one-man Zulu nation. He pounds out rhythms. They become urgent, then lie back, then become urgent again. Sven is playing things in between the driving bass lines. Up high, down low, he is everywhere. Eric's little melodies complement the sound as he fills some of the space the Jovi left behind.

Thunderstik finishes with "Mind Mesmerize," an apocalyptic song that ends in an intense growing din of chaos. The sound is so thick it surrounds everything. It marches off the stage and leaves the audience spellbound.

The music is over. Kurt is exhausted and sweating. Teenage zombies pledge their allegiance to the band. "You ARE punk rock!" they yell.

The band meets Felder and Arty near the stage while the roadies for Sally's Strung Out set up.

"So," Kurt asks. "What did you think?"

"It was excellent, but where's your guitar player? This fellow, the Jovi, I've heard so much about?" Arty asks.

"He quit four days ago."

Arty laughs. "It's always a movie, isn't it? Just trying to keep the great bands together. Talent hates talent. Gift hates gift."

"We don't need him," Kurt says. "You heard it tonight."

"Felder tells me you and the Jovi have been playing together since you were little kids."

"We have."

"You don't just find that kind of chemistry. Put the band back together—the one that made that album—and we got a deal."

"Sweet!" EJ belts out.

Eric high-fives Sven.

"I'll call him tomorrow – get his ass back in the fold!" Felder smiles. "YES!" He tries to high-five Kurt, but Kurt leaves him hanging.

The lights dim. The house announcer says, "Please put your hands together for Sally's Strung Out!" The music starts with a chaotic drumroll and a birdlike screech.

"LOOK, MAN. I APPRECIATE THE OFFER," Kurt yells over the music. "BUT THIS RIGHT HERE IS THE BAND. YOU EITHER TAKE US OR YOU LEAVE US. YOU HEARD IT TONIGHT. YOU KNOW THE TRUTH."

"NO, NO, NO." Felder is beside himself. "He doesn't have to decide between Jagger or Richards!"

Golden-Eared Arty scratches his red beard and looks at Kurt. Kurt's tan, slick chest is heaving. Gary Faker has dropped down on his knees in front of a little sacrificial shrine center stage. The crowd is once again chanting "HAIR-OH-WIN! HAIR-OH-WIN!"

"WELL?"

"NO. I PASS!" Arty turns and walks away.

Felder grips his frizzy hair on the top of his skull and screams, "YOU FUCKTARD!"

Kurt turns to see Gary Faker sit down a young girl on a crude wooden stool before him. Gary Faker drips the wax from a black candle across her arm and across a skull carved out of volcanic rock. The white-haired hag ties off the girls arm then moves behind to hold the girl up.

"STOP THAT!" Kurt yells.

Gary stands and tilts his head at the mic. "A virgin."

The crowd cheers.

He lowers a bent spoon over the candle, sticks a needle in the spoon, pulls blood from a vein in her arm, pushes the plunger down, and she nods off.

"NO!" Kurt yells.

The white-haired hag eases her to the floor. Quickly, like he wants in on the fun, Gary Faker loads the dart and has it in his arm. As the plunger drops, he too collapses on the stage.

"What the fuck is that?" Kurt asks EJ.

"It's Santeria."

"What's that?"

"Mexican magic."

"Goddamned devil won't leave me alone." Kurt walks right out into the middle of the stage. The band is playing a frenetic pseudotribal beat. The white-haired hag is stroking the girl's hair. Gary Faker is rolling on the floor in a trance, taking his clothes off. Kurt grabs the microphone. "THIS GODDAMN DEVIL BULLSHIT IS WRONG! GOD GOT ME *OFF* DRUGS! THIS IS BULLSHIT! DRUGS ARE BAD!" He kicks the shrine over; the candle rolls to the edge of the stage. The skull drops heavily at his feet.

The crowd boos and throws beer at Kurt. The band stops playing. A Samoan bouncer and a black bouncer eye Kurt from below, not sure if this is part of the show. Kurt says into the microphone, "Hey, Golden-Eared Arty!"

Arty turns.

"I got another song to play for you. Gimme that!" He grabs a guitar and starts strumming. He motions to EJ, Sven, and Eric. "You guys get out here, one more song. C'mon, Arty, don't leave!"

EJ looks at Sven and Eric, and says, "Let's rock."

Sven grabs the bass. EJ pushes the drummer off his stool. Eric muscles out the bongo player. We begin "Alone, Alone," building it softly on a muted bass string. Kurt lifts his arms in the sign of the cross, closes his eyes, and sings up high in a choirboy falsetto. Gary Faker rises up behind Kurt in nothing but a red thong. He lifts a Telecaster with his feeble white arms and whacks Kurt in the back of the head. The kids cheer. Kurt shakes it off, wheels around, grabs Faker's neck, drops to a knee, and smacks Gary's head on the stage. Blood flows from the singer's hairline. Kurt continues singing about loneliness. Someone in the audience yells "Louder!"

The security guards look at each other and shrug their shoulders. Gary Faker motions to them and points with a long ladylike finger at Kurt. The security guards take Kurt's still outstretched arms and twist them behind his back. Kurt yells, "LISTEN TO THE PRETTY SINGING!" Eric stops playing the bongos, picks up Gary Faker's Telecaster, and takes a big swing into the back of the knees of the Samoan bouncer. He doesn't budge. Sven runs over and bites the black guy in the calf. The black guy kicks Sven off the stage into the mosh pit. The teenage vampires attack him in a mob, pulling hair, slapping, kicking, stomping. Eric karate chops the Samoan's neck. He turns around and growls. Eric dives off the stage after Sven. The mosh pit swallows him in a single gulp. EJ leaves the drum kit. "LET MY SINGER GO!"

Like overfed serpents, the Samoan bouncer's arms swim through Kurt's elbows and meet behind his neck. The black bouncer tackles EJ and pins him to the ground. Gary Faker motions for his drummer to play a beat. The beat starts. It's a sort of jazz march. Gary Faker tap-dances on the stage like a giant cricket. He rubs the blood from his forehead up and down his chest, and holds the heavy stone skull in the palm of his hand. The white-haired hag grabs Gary's hand, and begins an open waltz. She holds knitting needles in her free hand. They kiss the bloody skull and dance over to where Kurt struggles. They look at each other, look at the audience, count to three, and kick him in the stomach to the beat of the drums.

Someone in the audience screams, "BEST SALLY'S SHOW EVER!"

"KILL THEM ALL!"

In the darkness at the bottom of the mosh pile, Eric exhales what he thinks is his last breath. He cries out, "Don't let me die in this unholy place!" And his prayer is answered instantly. The weight of the young vampires is lessened one by one. There is light. Eric looks up and sees Lunky the Loyal's glowing halo of platinum hair surrounding his smiling face. Lunky tosses the last few teenagers like salad.

Sven and Eric get to their feet. Lunky jumps up on the stage, kicks the black bouncer in the gut, throws a monstrous uppercut that catches the Samoan in the throat. Kurt straightens up, gasping for air. The white-haired hag twirls over and stabs Kurt in the shoulder with a knitting needle. Kurt pulls it out, leaps in her direction, grabs her by her mane, and flings her backward onto the ground. Her head hits the floor with a loud crack. Kurt grabs Gary Faker by the hair and forces him onto his knees. Kurt pries the stone skull from Gary's hand and cocks his arm. There's a drumroll. Gary looks up at Kurt, nods his head, and says, "Rad."

Kurt looks at the audience and yells, "IS THIS WHAT YOU WANT?"

Some cheer, some gasp. Behind Kurt, the white-haired hag crawls to Gary's rescue. The young girl is know curled over and weeping.

Kurt looks down. The back of the hag's head is split open, and dark black blood runs down her white hair. Kurt stands above the two of them and lifts the skull in the air. Then he hears a woman's sobs. Something changes. He is sick of it all. He says, "I'm not my dad." Then he swings the skull across his own jaw, shattering the part of his mouth that makes all the music. The part that is divine. The skull makes a dull thud on the stage. Kurt drops to his knees, holds his flabby jaw gently in his hands, and weeps.

Suddenly there is a vast emptiness, a void that is soon filled with the sound of Federales clubbing the audience. The teenagers run for the exits with their hands over their heads. The members of Sally's Strung Out run for the safety of their tour bus.

Lunky looks down and spots a row of canisters with stringy wires attached to them at the edge of the stage—pyrotechnics. He grabs a whole row of them, puts them under his arm, and says, "Follow me!" He turns and runs full blast through the fake wall at the back of the stage.

"Wow!" Sven says. Eric and EJ grab Kurt, and the whole band follows Lunky out the hole in the wall.

THE CAVALRY GETS LOST

After escaping the melee at the Lazy Lizard, Lunky and the band wander the streets of Ensenada. Lunky still has the pyrotechnics under his arm. Sven asks, "Should we go back and get our stuff?"

"It's not worth going to jail," Eric says.

"Let's call Pastor Ron. He'll pick us up." EJ says.

The band wanders to the beach. In the last minutes before sunrise, Lunky sets off the fireworks for some children on their way to school. Lunky holds the canister under his arm as the sparks fall around him. The little faces light up with joy.

Pastor Ron and Wayne Franklin park the VW van in front of a small café. They walk in and find the band seated at a wooden table.

Wayne says, "Kurt, it's time for you to go where you can get some help."

Pastor Ron stands silently by Wayne's side with his arms folded.

Kurt looks at his father and then at Pastor Ron. "Oo I af oo oose?"

"What?" Wayne pushes a fly off his cheek.

Pastor Ron wiggles his mustache.

Eric walks over to Kurt's side and says, "He's asking you if he has to choose. Choose between science and religion, between God and meds. Are you"—Eric points at Pastor Ron—"going to tell him he needs to pray, and are you"—Eric points at Wayne—" going to tell him he needs meds?"

Pastor Ron softly shakes his head. "Gosh, no. I was gonna tell Kurt he should seek psychiatric help too."

Kurt stares at the floor and twists his head.

The seven of them get into Pastor Ron's VW van and head north. Kurt sits Indian style between Pastor Ron and Wayne. He holds his swollen and useless jaw as he slowly rocks back and forth. They are stopped by traffic eight hundred yards from the American border. Pastor Ron pushes a button on the dash and the radio crackles to life. Wayne fumbles with the dial.

"OP!" Kurt yells.

"I don't understand."

Kurt points his thumb to the left. Wayne turns the knob slowly.

"OP! ISSEN!" Kurt holds his hand at his ear.

"That's us!" Eric yells.

Pastor Ron turns the volume up. It's "Rain Fall" by Thunderstik. It's Kurt's acoustic guitar solo. Wayne turns it up until the speaker distorts. Wayne smiles and nods to the beat. He reaches back and puts his hand on Kurt's knee. "You did it, son. You really did it."

Kurt nods his head. "I OWE."

THE FAMILY MAN
CLEANS HIS GUN

It is more like an operation than a birth. Sophie is awake but not all there. Harley comes straight up out of her belly.

The doctor says, "Congratulations! It's a boy." And he holds the little gray guy in his hands so they can see him.

Sophie looks over at the Jovi in quiet defeat. "Fucking Phoenix." She shakes her head.

The Jovi kisses her. "I'm so proud of you."

She tries to smile through her oxygen mask. A nurse pulls down Sophie's gown and puts Harley on her breast. Sophie stares off into space with a blank expression. The Jovi searches her sleepy eyes. "It's the miracle of childbirth." He kneels at her side.

They've been at their new home, in L.A., in Laurel Canyon, with Harley for five nights when Sophie opens a bottle of wine with dinner.

"Drinking? Already?"

"I'm not pregnant anymore. I can do what I want."

She drinks the whole bottle by herself. Suddenly she is happy and flirty. She runs her foot up the Jovi's leg at dinner. He kisses her and puts his hand down there.

"You're disgusting. Not yet."

There is a bottle of wine at every dinner until one night Sophie gets dressed up and says, "I'm going out."

"You look incredible. You look like you never even had a baby." The Jovi says with Harley cradled in his arms.

"You think?" Sophie swishes her hips back and forth in the mirror.

"Absolutely."

The Jovi falls asleep with Harley on his chest. When he wakes up, his son is gone and it's three in the morning. The Jovi finds Harley sleeping in his crib in the nursery. The Cambodian night nanny is asleep in the rocking chair next to him. The Jovi walks into their bedroom and the bed is still made-up. He walks around the house and out onto the porch. The house is perched on the side of a ravine like a crow's nest. Aside from a coyote's occasional cry or the hoot of an owl, the canyon is quiet at night. The Jovi notices the pattern, the Morse code of the owl. Sophie comes in around four.

"Where've you been?"

"It uz a biz-ness dinner. I can cuntrol it."

In bed he spoons up next to her and kisses her ear and runs his finger down her back. She rolls away. "Stop. I'm tired."

"Could you just call me when you're going to be out super late?"

"Of course. Of course, sorry. I should've called."

There are other nights just like that one. The Jovi wakes up and it's three in the morning and his wife isn't in bed next to him. He imagines her dead by the side of the road. He pictures her being raped and robbed. He thinks of her smiling at some guy's line of crap. He looks at the ceiling. He looks at the clock. It's been twenty minutes. The sheets feel itchy and hot. When she finally comes in, he wants to scream. But he doesn't. She gets in bed. It's four thirty-three, and she's asleep. The Jovi lies awake. When he hears her slight snore, he says, "I love you."

The Jovi wakes up in the morning and she isn't in bed. He walks in the kitchen and she is dressed up and standing next to five suitcases. The Jamaican day nanny has on a fancy church hat and a dark blue suit. She has Harley in her arms.

"What's going on?"

"We're going to Paris for a week to work."

"You're what?"

"We're going to Paris for—"

"I heard you the first time. 'We' means 'not me'?"

"We're going to Paris for a week to work." She sounds like a stage actress who is trying too hard to enunciate her lines.

"And you're taking our son? He's too young to fly! I say no way!"

"They want him in the shoot. That's the whole thing. Don't you get it? Babies are hot."

"He's not hot. He's my son. You're not taking him. You can't do that."

"Look babies are really in right now—"

"Yeah, I get it, babies—the hottest accessory for fall. Why can't you use a doll or something? He's a person."

"You don't get it! It's not up to you. I'll be back in a week. We'll talk about it in a week."

"What is this?"

"I need some time. Why can't you understand? You said you'd always support me—anything I wanted to do."

"Okay. Okay." She feels like a stranger. "Let me help you with the bags."

After yet another night of staring off into the canyon and then lying in bed, the Jovi thinks to himself, *I should spank it. If I spank it, I can fall asleep.* He jiggles himself around. Nothing is happening. He gets up, walks to the bathroom, looks at himself naked, and notices the dirty clothes hamper. He digs through it, finds Sophie's nightgown. He brings it to his face and breathes it in, the sweet smell. He takes the nightgown to bed.

The sun comes up and he drives down to a coffee shop. Unable to eat, unable to sleep, but still good for a cappuccino. He turns to find Tiffany Tucker, dressed in a black leather trench coat, standing in line. "Tiff! Tiffany Tucker!"

Tiffany gives him a big air kiss. "The Jovi! Darling!" She reaches out and holds his wrist, as if feeling for a pulse. "How are you holding up?"

"Okay. Can't complain. How's my Tiff?"

"Really, darling, we're old friends, no reason for the stiff upper lip with Tiff."

"No. Really things are fine. I'm fine."

"Well, if you insist, good for you. A little intestinal fortitude is so rare these days."

"Yeah. Thunderstik, my bros. Fuck, it's a bummer." The Jovi looks her up and down for a second. "But you know—"

"Thunderstik? Oh, that's old news. I was thinking of your more immediate problems."

"What are you talking about, Tiff?"

"Oh, come now, you don't know?"

"Know what?"

"Well then, I absolutely wish you my best." She turns her shoulder. The leather makes a broad sweep across his leg. She begins to walk away. He grabs her by the latte and turns her back around.

"What is it? What are you talking about?"

She looks at him as if she is trying to figure out the best place to put the knife. "Your wife. Darren Getty. The two of them. You didn't know?"

"Know what?"

"They're an item. It's all over town—they're all over town. Just about killed his ex. He brought your wife on set with your son. What's his name?"

"Harley. No way, Tiff. She's in Paris."

"Oh? Oh no. I just saw them at a party, what? Two days ago. I guess we're always the last to know. Well, must run, would love to catch up some more, but I've got a call time in twenty…"

The Jovi goes back to the house and calls Jean. "Where the fuck is my son? You call your daughter and tell her she's got thirty minutes to get my son back to my house, or I'm calling the cops and charging her with kidnapping."

The Jovi hangs up, paces the floor, and throws coffee mugs at the eucalyptus trees near the deck. The phone rings. It is Sophie. "Thirty minutes or I'm calling the cops."

He paces more, punches the floor. When he looks up, she is standing in the doorway holding Harley in her arms, smiling at the Jovi like maybe she loves him just a little.

The Jovi runs over and takes Harley from her arms. He kisses the child and holds him up against his tears. He feels her hand on his neck. He spins around. "GET OFF ME!"

Harley starts to cry. The Jovi lays him on his back on the sofa. The Jovi turns to Sophie. "So you're fucking Darren Getty?"

"What?" She lets out a little laugh.

"Is that your next career move?"

"No."

"Is that what your mother told you to do? Like she told you to fuck Giuseppe? Find an actor who directs? Is this another career move?"

Sophie's face contorts. "We were in Paris."

"You can't stop lying, can you?"

Her sleepy eyes get angry. "Okay. Fine. He's nice. He's successful. This is the best thing for me."

"Sophie, you're not a commodity. Stop selling yourself."

She blinks and a tear runs down her cheek into her ample mouth. She smiles a crooked smile at the Jovi's green eyes. "I can't."

EPILOGUE

"Without love, men cannot endure to be together."
—Thomas Carlyle

IT'S ONLY ROCK 'N ROLL (BUT I LIKE IT)

In February, I answer my phone.

"Eric, it's EJ. Did you get a new keyboard?"

"Yeah."

"Wheels?"

"Yeah. A Bronco."

"Sweet! Friday night we're opening up for A Flock of Seagulls at FM Station in the Valley. This gig is going to be huge. It could be the break we need."

"Right on! Is Kurt's jaw better?"

"No. It's still wired shut, but he says he can sing fine."

"Umm… Okay."

"And Josh Weiner from Polygram is coming to the gig. Kurt talked to his secretary."

At soundcheck Thunderstik sits and watches A Flock of Seagulls set up. It doesn't look like the band from the video. The keyboard player has dark curly hair, a thick beard, and weighs four hundred pounds. The drummer is black and looks about fifteen years old. But when they start with "Space Age Love Song" it sounds just right. The song has several bars before the vocal starts. I search the stage for the lead singer and his distinctive awesome hair. A hunched-over middle-aged man with thin, long, stringy blonde hair starting about half way back his skull turns to the microphone and sings. "I saw your eyes…"

"Is that the same guy?" I ask Sven.

"Yup." Sven says nodding and continuing to nod. When he stops he says, "Dude, you have to check out their tour bus."

After the song ends, we walk outside and around to the back of the club. There sits a rusting Winnebago with threadbare, smoke-stained curtains. Even from a distance it smells like wet dog. "If this doesn't pan out tonight," Sven says, "I'm moving on."

"What are you going to do?"

"The Jovi says he can get me an audition for the Cult. They're going on tour."

"Nice. When did you see the Jovi?"

"I bumped into him in a bar in Silverlake. He was playing an acoustic set with his baby strapped to his back. One of our songs, 'Rain Fall,' I think. He said Sophie ran off with that old gigolo-actor, Darren Getty. Can you believe that shit?"

"Wow. That bitch is like the sun: One man's dark night is the next man's bright day."

"We drove over to Felder's together, took turns pissing through his mail slot."

"Even the baby?"

"No. He just watched. What about you? Are you going to stay in Thunderstik?" Sven asks.

"I'll never be in another band as good as this one."

"So?"

"I'm gonna ride it out for as long as I can."

As we take the stage, Thunderstik still expects throngs of people to mob the entrance, and record execs too. Unfortunately the '80s are over. The stage lights are low and bright, but it appears that only eight people are sitting out there. None of them is Josh Weiner. Kurt belts out our best songs with his jaw wired shut. As the last one dies down, Summer emerges from the light and steps onto the stage. She's beaming. Kurt pulls her under his arm and turns to me, "I CALL OOO EN EE AVE A IG IORIN," he says.

"You'll call me when we have a gig of importance?" I translate.

Kurt nods.

"I'm out?"

"ORRY." Kurt kisses Summer on the forehead.

"All you ever wanted was him," I say, more impressed than betrayed. "And now he's yours." She slips her hand in Kurt's back pocket, shrugs her shoulders, and smiles a devilish smile.

I roll my cords and stuff them in a bag, put the keyboard under my arm, and move toward the door. A soft hand taps me on the shoulder. I turn and Dane is staring up at me. "That was a really good show," she says.

"Thanks, I thought we sounded pretty good. I can't believe you came."

"I always liked the music. Why wasn't the Jovi on stage?"

"He baled. Look—I've been meaning to call you. I've been a real shit—"

"Eric—"

"This whole thing went to my head. I'm no rock star. It's fucking obvious to everyone but me."

"You can play—"

"Not like those guys."

"Yeah, but you enjoy it."

I reach for her hand. "We used to laugh..."

She pulls her hand away and points to the stage. "Eric, that is what you always wanted most."

"Yeah. It was. But some big label is never going to send the jet for me, it's just not going to happen and... that's okay. But when I see you I remember—"

"I came here with my boyfriend. He went to the bathroom. He's going to be back in a second. He just wanted to see the show."

"Boyfriend?"

"Boyfriend."

"He'd heard of Thunderstik?"

"No." A man's voice answers. "I'm here to see A Flock of Seagulls." He has long mutton-chop sideburns and a button-down sweater.

I glare at him.

"Eric, this is Dodd," Dane says. The lights go dim.

"Hey, they're about to start." Dodd says and lifts a Super 8 camera to his eye.

"You're a fan?" I ask.

"No, I'm a filmmaker. I want to do a documentary on them. I think it's funny as shit – what they've become." Dodd says as he stares through the glass rectangle.

"Don't laugh at them." I say and point my finger at his sideburns.

"Man. It's the 90's. You should move to Seattle."

"Space Age Love Song" begins with its straightforward drumbeat and echoing digitally delayed guitar riff. It sounds just right. The singer is on pitch, on time. I believe him when he sings. "I was falling in love..."

Dodd chuckles and pans from the four hundred pound keyboard player to the balding lead singer.

Dane reaches up puts a hand on Dodd's shoulder, and smiles at me.

Outside the air feels thick and cold in my lungs. The parking lot is big, empty, and glistening from a light rain that has just stopped. The whir of distant cars on the freeway sounds like an unrelenting ocean. To the west there is a jagged rim of light along the ridgetop.

I get in my Bronco. When it starts, "Alone, Alone" is in my cassette player, the tape we made at Ivo's. I hear all our parts, some big, some small, and they fit together flawlessly. The song soars. I am warm and light. The rest will fade away, but not this. I will always be haunted by the hope I feel when I hear our music.

10628591R00261

Made in the USA
San Bernardino, CA
20 April 2014